DARKBLOOD

DARKLIGHT 4

BELLA FORREST

CHAPTER ONE

W e could say what we wanted about the Immortal Plane, but this place had a devastating beauty.

I hated it for its strange splendor.

When I first laid eyes on the cityscape in my sleep-addled state, I thought for half a second that somehow the harvester had suckered us, rowing us to San Francisco instead. The Immortals had built dwellings and streets on sharp hills that nearly reached our height on the cliff. The streets, which appeared as streams of light, swooped down through buildings that rimmed the seaside. A gigantic, glittering bridge connected to an island half a mile or so out to sea.

Yesterday, we had all watched in horror as Kono, a vampire I'd met at the Hive, was caught by hunters, a group of sadistic Immortal rulers. It also meant the safehouse we'd intended to use as a base during our mission had either been raided already, or likely would be soon after Kono was tortured for information. Even more frustrating was that we'd been unable to leave the cliff for the rest of the day and the following night due to rolling patrols of hunters moving around the edge of the city, likely looking for any more vampire incursions.

After an unwilling but sorely needed rest, we were finally ready to plot our invasion strategy from our vantage point. We stood together, a misfit band of humans and vampires about to infiltrate the most dangerous city in any dimension.

"The island is where the ruling caste lives," Kane told us with muted disdain. He and Dorian had spent several hours questioning scouts in the Hive about the city, while Sike and I looked for information about the curse. "They siphon their luxury off the hard work of others. It's where we'll find the Immortal Council—the rulers of the rulers—sitting around talking about whatever monsters discuss." He sneered in the island's direction.

I marveled at the city. The buildings in the distance loomed large and strange in shape, with overwrought architecture of various designs. I was no connoisseur, but the rulers seemed to like stitching together as many competing architectural styles as possible. Greek columns sat next to gilded wrought-iron fences while Gothic spires mingled with art deco windows. Clearly, they'd had access to some human inspiration when building the city, but they'd put their own twist on it.

I frowned through the scope of my rifle as my gaze landed on a creepy black building closer to us. It was simply one large sphere, eerily perfect in shape and texture. Next to it, a cottage had been assembled from a dull white material. I squinted, and my stomach lurched as I realized the building was made of bones. I skipped over the rest of the houses, deciding to spare my senses until it was absolutely necessary to face those horrors.

The shadows of the buildings and trees stretched deeper and darker than they should have. They flickered in one moment and solidified the next. What was somehow even more jarring, however, was the sheer quantity of soul-lights trapped in golden lanterns or gathered on strings. They decorated the tops of most buildings and wrapped around poles lining the streets. Every available rooftop and corner appeared to be covered with them. In the Hive, there had been a sense of respect in the way the souls were used as illumination. Only as many as necessary were used; they weren't used like bunting on parade day. Here, the whole city was aglow with souls, a beacon in the surrounding dim light of the

Immortal Plane. It created its own version of daylight, but it was a light that felt false. I twisted my mouth uneasily. Everything was too weird and bright in Itzarriol.

In the air above the city, I spotted glittering things. It was hard to describe what kind or size they were, as the lights flitted over the buildings. The glowing objects darted around in patterns, dancing this way and that.

"Gaudy," Kane said scornfully. He was right. The Immortals' city perfectly exemplified them. Everything was garish, colorful, and too much. It was hard to put my finger on it, but the entire city felt off balance. Like admiring a painting with its frame an inch askew.

"This place gives me the creeps," Roxy said and cracked her knuckles. "I guess we'll have to get used to it."

Somewhere inside that bright island, a seedy darkness pulsed like a heartbeat. If the city was a monster, we needed to find the brain, where the Immortal Council made decisions and planned their diabolical strategies. Where they would have planned their union with the Bureau and begun the extermination of vampires. If the Immortal rulers continued to operate unchecked, the darkness in this plane would continue to grow and spread until it consumed the Mortal Plane as well. I refused to allow that to happen. Our friends back home counted on us to do our best here. The future stood before us, perilous and fragile.

Below the cliff, the waterfall plunged into an aqua pool. It was hard to tell through the spraying water, but it looked like there was a garden at the end. I made out greenery, but you never knew what something *really* was in the Immortal Plane.

"What a lovely sight," Kane muttered.

We trekked down a small, nearly-invisible trail running down the mountain to the garden, where we crouched behind a thicket of tall scarlet trees with thick, seaweed-like vines hanging from their branches. A sickeningly sweet odor, like synthetic jasmine, enveloped me. I wrinkled my nose. It was nothing like the jasmine fragrance my mother preferred to spritz on her wrists.

It was best to keep inside the greenery, despite the smell. We didn't want to end up like poor Kono. Despite the hours that had passed since his capture, we continued to see the occasional hunters combing the edges of the city, both on the ground and in the air. The patrols had finally thinned enough that we had a window of opportunity to enter the city.

I marveled at the pool of aquamarine water collecting at the end of the waterfall. High above us, the cliff spewed blue water downward in a powerful rush. Fractals of gold and amber glinted in the water. It was all too bright and too colorful to be authentically charming.

Beneath the spray of the waterfall, a massive statue rose from the center of the pool. The blue water spilled over the towering figure of an Immortal ruler who glared into the distance for eternity, decreeing everything inferior with his frozen stare. He had a sharp nose with a straight bridge and a broad, handsome face, but his eyes were narrowed to slits like a serpent lying in wait for its next meal. The tilt of his chin was cruel. The sculptors had taken great care to trace the perfect tendrils of long hair coming from his head. An elaborate crown of jewels sat atop his glorious tresses.

"He'd be pretty if it weren't for the ominous aura of pure evil," Roxy whispered. She flicked a hanging vine out of her face to get a better look. The plant hissed and curled upward.

"You've got that right," I admitted and followed her gaze. Something unsettled me about the statue, beyond its imposing presence, that made me want to crawl out of my own skin. I felt intensely observed.

Laini glowered at the construction. "Fitting that he made them build it so enormous that people would be forced to look up at him forever," she said, her voice as rigid as the statue. Her usual calm was nowhere to be found. Perhaps she had left her peace permanently on the harvester's boat, lost in the tormenting mists of the Gray Ravine.

"Who is this ugly mug?" Roxy asked, glancing around at the vampires. "I like to know when there's someone worth hating."

"Oh, he's worth hating," Kane said flatly, crossing his arms. "This monstrosity represents Irrikus. He currently heads the Immortal Council."

"He's in charge?" I asked, searching the statue's face with new eyes. For a moment, I half-saw Alan's face on that final day in the boardroom. "Leadership must favor the cruel in these parts."

"For over a thousand years, he's personally headed the charge against vampires," Dorian said, his voice as dark as the bursts of shadow swirling beneath his skin. "His campaign stretches back into our grandparents' time."

My heart burned slightly, though he stood on the farthest side of our hiding spot, but that pain couldn't compare to the anger I felt when I looked up at the cold face of Irrikus's statue. A thousand years. This struggle was on a scale I couldn't begin to comprehend. I shut my eyes for a moment. This Immortal had taken so much from my friends. This was the face of the being that had ordered the brutal destruction of Vanim. Skeletons still lay where they fell in the streets—unburied, unmourned—because of him.

I balled my hands into fists, pressing my fingernails hard into the soft flesh of my palms. If I ever got the chance to meet this Irrikus, I hoped it came with the opportunity to put a bullet through the middle of his smirking, arrogant face.

"Utterly lacking in coherent design," Laini muttered, staring at the glittering cityscape below us. Her comment reminded me that before Vanim fell, Laini had been training to become an architect. "Pathetic and obscene. Itzarriol." She shuddered, violet eyes flashing black for a moment as her anger surged.

"It's sort of pretty from afar. Like the Las Vegas strip took a hit of acid," Roxy supplied, unfazed. Laini grimaced, and Roxy corrected herself. "Sorry. I meant it's *terrible.*"

"It's fine," Kane said, though his voice was tight. "It's just that Itzarriol represents everything wrong about the Immortal rulers. You'll see. It might look like a magical world, but it's closer to cursed."

A vine crept into my vision, and I batted it softly away from my face, earning both a wave of jasmine smell that burned my nostrils and a little hiss from the plant. We needed to discover the source of the conspiracy between the Immortal Council—who had kept their solid boots on the necks of vampires for hundreds of years and chased them out of their own cities—and the members of the Occult Bureau's former board led by my uncle in the Mortal Plane. Whoever we'd thwarted by taking down Alan and his corrupt board in the Bureau was probably furious at what we'd done, and we needed to find out what their next moves would be. I just hoped we weren't too late.

Dorian's eyes briefly flashed my way, and I brushed a stray lock of my hair behind my ear, trying to catch his gaze for a moment to get a sense of his emotional state, but his glance deliberately didn't linger. Our mission was of vital importance—if we were to manage the curse, then we had to be vigilant about not causing each other pain.

I fought the butterflies rising in my stomach. The stakes were now higher than ever, and thanks to the development of our curse, our next task would be harder than anything that came before. Since coming to the Immortal Plane, Dorian had started feeling the pain that had plagued me from the beginning. The last time we'd gotten too close—on the shore of Lake Siron after barely fighting off the hunter Inkarri—we had both passed out. Dorian had woken up hours later, but I had been unconscious for three days. We couldn't afford to repeat the mistake, especially not here, deep in enemy territory. For a while, I hadn't even been sure it was safe for me to join the team for this final stage of the mission. I'd worried I would be more of a liability than a help. But Dorian insisted that he needed me, both for the qualities that made me such a good soldier as well as the personal support we brought each other. All Dorian and I had to do was keep a distance of fifteen feet between us to manage the pain, and it was working so far.

Whatever the outcome of our mission, my mind rested more easily knowing the rest of our vampire and human companions were safe in Scotland, trying to learn what they could about the Bureau-Immortals conspiracy in the Mortal Plane. Of course, the shooting at a press conference in Edinburgh a few days ago meant that Major Morag Bryce, Bravi, my brother, and the others might be grappling with much bigger issues right now. But who knew how long it had been since we'd left the Mortal Plane? I wished I'd thought to bring some kind of calendar, but there was no point. The days passed strangely here, and I was only just beginning to get used to the patterns of when the soul-lights were bright and when the winds blew the glowing amber lights away, creating almost complete darkness. Had it been a week? We'd spent several days at the Hive—one of the final secret hideouts for vampires in the Immortal Plane—and left behind a severely wounded Sike and Bryce with the stoic Arlonne as their guardian.

The Hive vampires were a blessing in many ways, but they were not the battle-ready allies Dorian had hoped to find. When we began our journey, I'd also desperately wished for more recruits to add to our ranks, both here and in the Mortal Plane. Seeing the chaos of the Immortal Plane had changed my mind. Maybe it was a good thing that the Hive was focused on preserving what they had, hoping to survive without direct conflict for as long as they could. They refused to approach Itzarriol except for the occasional feeding, using their safehouse in the city to hide from the rulers. But now even that safety had been stripped away from them.

"This mission is deathly important," Laini said. She spoke so softly that it drifted over us like a melodic but ominous whisper. "And we have very little time before the hunters find the safehouse… if they haven't already."

"Then we should begin," Dorian said, a weight in his words that acknowledged the heaviness of this moment. Our next step would take us well past the point of no return.

Kane cocked a finger gun at the statue. "After we succeed, I propose we use the human guns to destroy that monstrosity."

Dorian took one last look past me to regard Irrikus. His glacial eyes were brighter than they should have been in the shadow of the greenery. He scowled, then gave a slow, controlled exhale.

"Maybe on our way back out we can take it down," he said. "It would be an honor to see to the destruction of this beast's monument, after he laid waste to Vanim."

On our way back out.

We would have to succeed first.

His determined promise wrapped around us, shifting the mood to one of action. I rubbed my hands together and mentally catalogued every weapon on my person. A handgun in a shoulder holster under my jacket, a disassembled rifle with a scope in my pack, two knives tucked into the boots I wore, and my own two hands. The small pack on my back had been provided by the Hive vampires to carry the bare essentials for my survival: dry food rations, water, medical kit, fire-starting supplies, light-weight rope, notepad and pencil, rifle, and ammo from my original pack. The rest of my gear was in my Bureau pack back at the Hive. I tested the straps of the light canvas pack, grateful for the reduced weight.

Dorian looked confidently over the landscape with a determined set to his jaw. "Those buildings are nearly in the tree line. We should be able to climb to them," he said and gestured for us to move. We followed his lead in silence, the five of us traveling as one efficient organism.

He led us through the tall, rough brush that started a few dozen feet from the quieter outskirts of Itzarriol. The vines tangled into bunches on the ground and hissed as I trampled them under my boots. Roxy relished stabbing at their little tendrils with her knife. I followed behind her, taking up the rear. The heartburn in my chest was enough to make me struggle slightly for breath, but wasn't impossible to deal with. It was like running with a weighted vest on, something I had done regularly to maintain my fitness for the Bureau. Except now I was doing it in another plane of existence, under threat of discovery by hunters at the safehouse we were supposed to use as shelter. I took a deep breath and kept going. Forward was the only way to go. Forward to help the Hive vampires who might still be hiding in the safehouse, wondering what had happened to Kono, with no idea that hunters would soon be on their way. Forward so we could make it back to our wounded friends left under the protection of the Hive and return to our friends back home in the Mortal Plane.

Dorian's broad shoulders stayed hunched below the tall tangle of grasses and vines as he moved assuredly toward the trees lining the back of a towering, curved structure. Was it a building? It was hard to tell—it twisted so organically that it didn't seem possible that it was a deliberate construction.

Laini carefully scanned the area, her violet eyes quick to take in every-thing. "There's no darkness close by from the living," she reported quietly. "Only from the souls in the ground."

I wondered if it was tough for vampires to differentiate between the kinds of darkness, depending on whether they came from a living being or from a loose soul. Inkarri had been confused when she'd interrogated me during our battle by the lake, as if she wasn't sure what to make of my energy. I'd wanted to scream at her cruel face that it was live human light energy she sensed.

"Keep an eye out for skimmer patrols," Kane whispered hoarsely. "The Hive said there are always a few flying over the city, even if they weren't stirred up by Kono." He bent to avoid a bunch of fruit hanging from the oily, seaweed-like vines on the tree.

I'd become familiar with skimmer patrols over the past day of hiding, though I had yet to see the flying vessels up close. I kept my eyes on the sky, looking for the flashes of white edged with soft light moving deliber-ately among the aimless souls, warning of the incoming craft.

A small rustle sounded up ahead. Dorian put his finger to his lips and motioned us forward. For a long moment, nothing moved except for us. Dorian took a step forward, and something small darted away through the grass.

Up ahead, the vines and grass and algae-covered trees gave way to a clearing in a park area. Shivering lavender grass covered the small hill. Leading up the hillside, the trees Dorian directed us toward swayed slightly. They were like the palm trees I had seen on rare childhood vaca-tions, a far cry from the hardier trees of Chicago. Their leaves appeared rigid and tough. When they brushed against one another, they let out tiny metallic scrapes. Roxy glanced over her shoulder and sent me a furtive glance. What sort of bizarre nature grew razor-sharp palm leaves?

As we trudged toward a city bathed in the light of innumerable souls, I shivered, unable to help myself. Dorian's cloak flapped ahead in the slight breeze, the same wind brushing the groaning leaves together and ferrying the souls above us. In this place, he was the leader we needed, just like when we were on the run from the Bureau and I had taken up the primary leadership position on the human side. Admiration felt warm when it spread through my body, and it melted away some of my unease. This was the person I had chosen to follow for now, and I had chosen him for a reason. There were feelings so deep inside me that they frightened me. Maybe one day I would put a name to them...

Dorian darted around a patch of tall flowers—the stems black and the flowers white—weaving effortlessly across the grass. He radiated confidence despite our intense circumstances.

My stomach sank for a moment as a thought teased across my mind like a spider's ghostly legs tiptoeing down my neck. *He charges ahead too often. He's right to take point on this, but we can't afford for his confidence to become recklessness.*

I hopped over a puddle of aquamarine water. It reflected the clouds of amber souls drifting in the gloomy sky above us. For a moment, I saw a flash of my own face. My skin had paled from our time on the run. I ached for real sunshine.

Keeping to the shadows, staying low and fast, we stealthily hurried to the structure. As we drew closer, it finally began to resemble a building. It was hard to tell with the structures inside Itzarriol. The buildings stretched and bent strangely, sometimes seeming to change shapes as I squinted at them. Would I ever get used to the Immortal Plane?

I caught the profile of Dorian's handsome face.

Maybe I would find a reason to want to.

CHAPTER TWO

The ghost of tension that hung over us had only grown stronger by the time we gathered at the base of the trees. Laini looked around, listening intently for something. Maybe the call of a hunter's horn, or the sound of velek hooves thundering toward us. Kane rubbed his chin, staring at my backpack.

"You little turtles will never make it up there quietly," Kane said sourly.

I shifted the bag. "It's not that heavy."

Dorian reached out a tentative hand, feeling the bark. "The bark isn't going to be easy for the humans."

I stepped up to another tree, dragging a finger down it. He was right. The bark looked rippled from afar, but up close, it was much smoother. There was a slight grain and lumps here and there, but not enough to get a good grip, even if we wrapped our rope around it and counterbalanced ourselves as we walked up the trunk. It would take too long, leaving us vulnerable to being spotted.

Laini began to stretch. "We need strength and speed here."

Dorian caught Laini's movement, and a lopsided smirk crossed his face. "I'll get up there and drop a rope down. You two will carry the humans on your backs for this one. It'll be faster and easier." His eyes darted briefly toward me. "Laini can carry Lyra."

"What is that?" Roxy muttered, eyeing the height. "A two-story-high tree?"

"It's not *that* bad," Kane said and shook his head in Dorian's direction. "Thanks for volunteering us as babysitters, brave leader."

"Like we want to be vampire backpacks," Roxy shot back. They dissolved into good-natured whispered bickering, both of them grinning as they prepared to climb. It was best for them to get it out of their system now, since they wouldn't have a chance in the city. Laini rolled her eyes and crouched, patting her back.

"Get on, Lyra. Let's leave the two whiners to climb together." She winked at me, but there was something sharp in her eyes that I wasn't used to seeing. It was as if the Immortal Plane had shifted her sweet nature into something rawer.

I climbed onto Laini's back, which was surprisingly sturdy beneath my weight. Dorian was already halfway up a tree, his strong fingers finding ridges and knots to grip until he reached the more robust branches. Then he clambered from one to another quickly and easily.

"You'll choke me if you hold on like that," Kane hissed quietly.

"You're trying to throw me like a sack of potatoes," Roxy protested. "And I only choke people if they ask me very nicely, so feel flattered."

Up above, I could see Dorian had already made it to the treetops. He carefully held back the leaves, which were apparently as sharp as they looked, as he dropped a rope down for our less dexterous pairs, tying it around the thick branch he was balanced on as Laini, and then Kane, practically ran up the sleek tree trunk with the extra aid. We made it to the treetops and stooped in the branches, keeping clear of the razor leaves. Laini gently eased me off her back but kept me close as we tried to get our bearings. The smooth bark felt slippery beneath me, which was alarming at this height, but the tree itself was as solid as stone, not swaying even a little in the breeze. Looking out at Itzarriol from the trees was almost mesmerizing, if I forgot about the pack of power-hungry homicidal rulers inside the city limits.

Once everyone was gathered and steady, we followed Dorian as he stepped lightly onto the nearest rooftop. We were forced to reduce the fifteen-foot limit, and the burning heat flared in my chest. I fought the pain, knowing that the stealth aspect of our mission required that we keep close.

The rooftops on the nearby buildings—consisting primarily of tiles in jarringly different colors of blue and neon pink with splashes of dirt brown—overlapped a little with shadows from the bordering trees, but it wasn't much. I frowned as I crouched, carefully placing my feet on the bright stone to make sure I didn't send a tile sliding down the angled roof. Dorian placed himself at the very opposite edge of the roof. Still, a bead of sweat dripped down my forehead.

Kane and Roxy scrambled to join us.

"You're being very inconsiderate," Roxy muttered, swiping at a cut on her cheek where Kane had evidently run her into a leaf by accident.

Kane snorted, but there was a punch of amusement in it. "My apologies, Your Royal Human Weakness."

Dorian gestured for us to follow. It was a small movement of his hand, but the kind that came from someone wholly immersed in their leadership role, completely focused on getting us safely across these rooftops. It was *very* attractive.

I massaged the tiny knot in my chest, knowing that any increase in feelings could pose a risk to our mission. The mission. The Immortal rulers. The compromised safehouse. Serious risk of capture and torture. God, I needed to get my head on straight and focus.

Reaching into the front pocket of my pack that held the scope from my disassembled rifle, I surveyed the dazzling cityscape of Itzarriol through its magnifying lens, searching for any sign that hunters were on the move in the direction we were heading. The dim sky was often hazy with soul-light during the brighter times, but the illumination here was a maelstrom of chaos. Lights flashed across the sky just above the city, strobing to the dull amber-edged clouds. Souls pirouetted inside the clouds, sometimes escaping to float up or down, only to land in another cloud. The sleek white form of a skimmer momentarily cut through the colored clouds, thankfully too far away for its pilot to spot us.

It was nauseating and beautiful, but I didn't see any commotion that suggested hunters were on the move.

I put my scope away as Laini gently nudged my hand. We were moving. We leapt from one roof to the next, leaving the shadows behind with the treetops. Fortunately, the tops of the bizarre buildings—made of a disconcerting mix of materials and textures—often held elaborate chimneys, statues, or metallic frescoes that provided us with cover.

I let Roxy overtake me again to put more distance between Dorian and me. We crept along as carefully as we could, using the occasional clouds of colored smoke rising from the chimneys to hide our movement, the scaled leather of the Hive-made boots helpfully quiet on the polished brass of the roof. Figures wearing ornate robes began to dot the streets, and I kept my eyes peeled for any individuals wearing the garb of hunters. The knives hidden within my boots provided a familiar sense of comfort.

Just a young woman, her closest supernatural friends, a compromised safe-house, and a perilous mission. Typical Tuesday. Not that I'm even sure it's a Tuesday.

From beyond the rooftops, I could hear the rising mirth of a city that reveled in its power. Laughter rose in the air alongside the silvery tinkling of bells. Kane swore as we all ducked behind a series of golden statues depicting various horrific-looking creatures that I had no names for. Dorian turned to glare at him, but the loud music easily covered our movements.

Was Itzarriol always so violently vibrant? Was this place like the stories I had read about ancient kingdoms celebrating large feasts every night? Irrikus's stony face drifted back into my mind. I wagered the Immortal rulers celebrated themselves and nothing more. What a fitting people to potentially reach out to Alan and the old board, who did the same.

Dorian led us quickly and made sure to point covertly when we passed certain buildings. He told us the night before that there would be landmarks that the Hive used to reach their safehouse. It was located in a quiet section near an extensive collection of gardens in one of the suburbs.

We had more than the intel from the Hive vampires on our side, though. The vampires' innate ability to sense darkness meant it would be difficult for an Immortal to sneak up on us. And a living human soul hid well among this jumble of frequencies. Or auras. Or whatever. But I remembered Dorian mentioning that vampire senses became less reliable with multiple presences. Would they get confused by the buffet of darkness teeming on the ground?

The buildings began dropping in height. Voices around the sides of the buildings were louder, closer. My pulse staggered as someone ran right by the alley next to us. Sound still had a strange way of traveling even in the confines of the Immortal capital. Kane turned to the side slightly, showing off his strong nose and the hint of a fang.

Definitely darkness around us.

I ducked behind a diamond-studded chimney as tall as four men and peeked around the edge for a moment. I could now make out the tops of heads as they walked past, footsteps clacking across tiles and stones. Towering hairstyles with green, pearl-studded combs sat atop the fussy heads of two Immortal rulers, defying the laws of gravity. Perhaps they were *literally* defying the laws of gravity somehow. Laini prodded my side, urging me to continue. She growled under her breath. Her fangs were fully extended, black-ringed violet eyes blazing with hunger, reminding me of her moment on the harvester's boat. I nodded and focused on where I was putting my feet as I caught up to the others. The vampires were on high alert, but my wandering eye kept returning to catch glimpses of life in the Immortal city.

If Las Vegas paid homage to gaudiness, Itzarriol had transformed it into an organized religion. Dazzling silver, gold, and evergreen ribbons were tied in bunches from impossibly ornate lampposts that held jars stuffed to bursting with souls. I spotted flashes of scarlet robes that swept through the spaces between buildings. A few groups appeared to be sashaying down the main street. A house shaped like a gingerbread cottage began to crumble on the other side of the street. Nobody stopped to pay it any mind. The house melted then sprang back up into a castle made entirely of bubbles. The next moment, all the bubbles popped simultaneously, exploding into glitter that spelled out "Zedera's Magic Mansions". Apparently, it was an ad… for a magical architect.

Next to it, a hot pink temple built in Greco-Roman style trembled as thunderous drum music played within its walls. The temple was built on a higher platform, and a group of tall, beautiful Immortal rulers dressed in shimmering robes of gold gathered around the fountain. With a jolt of alarm, I realized they would be able to see us from their vantage point if they looked up even a little.

Dorian clicked his tongue, and Laini and I ducked behind one of twelve spindly black chimneys all twisting together out of the roof. The others, who were farther ahead, took refuge on the next roof behind the large towering bust of a woman. Laini glared at the merry group of partiers. We would have to wait for them to slip inside.

One of the Immortal rulers, the tallest with long braids of pastel pink hair, abruptly held up an elegant finger. She plucked something from her bag dramatically while her friends tapped their feet, clad in heels that must have put another ten or more inches on their already willowy height.

At least we can be sure they aren't hunters.

The pink-haired Immortal fished a silver tin out of her clutch and undid the top. She dipped a finger into a glittering yellow substance. I squinted, and Laini cursed quietly. The Immortal smeared the substance over her lips. It glistened with a familiar amber glow. Nausea and rage surged up my throat. She had applied *dark energy* to her lips! My eyes flicked to the others. The same shade was liberally spread on her companions' eyelids. Their cheeks were dotted with it. One wore an amulet with a soul squirming inside. She placed a loving hand on it as if to remind the pink-haired one that she wouldn't be outdone by soul lip gloss.

They had completely separated the cold reality of death from their extravagance. They used souls like water.

"Ruling class," Laini whispered over the cover of the music. The women disappeared inside in a fit of laughter, despite nobody having made a joke. "Vapid and evil. Powerful and cruel."

I dropped my gaze to the streets below. Immortal wildlings, stone and shaggy grass ones like I had seen before, walked through the street. An Immortal ruler with shorter hair, dressed a fraction less nicely than the women had been, carelessly dragged a fine linen sack behind him along the golden cobbles. Something in the sack kicked wildly. He ignored it.

We hurried ahead again, stopping to rest across from a bakery, based on the scents swirling around us. I leaned forward a fraction, hidden as I was under a statue of a bulbous shrieking decay, to watch a small boy with long hair trot happily out of the entrance. He paid our group no mind, too short to see us. For a moment, he waved his treat around with delight. I caught a glimpse of glowing red eyes and fangs painted on with frosting. It was a vampire cookie. He bit into its head, severing it at the neck.

We moved on.

Up ahead, I occasionally caught sight of Dorian looking out to survey the scene. His extended fangs glinted as the smoke continued to change in brightness and color above us, a kind of laser show against the soul-light of the sky.

The building beneath me trembled slightly. I stopped to stabilize myself and spotted a type of Immortal Plane creature that I'd never seen before moving down the road. His skin was metallic, resembling the palm leaves from earlier, but the color was like brass. More oddly, he had two sets of arms, one pair strong and muscled, and another pair that looked almost vestigial folded across his chest.

As we continued along—the vampires keeping a sharp focus on any approaching auras that could be hunters—I tried to piece together a little of what I'd seen. The ruling class favored long hair and gaudy outfits, the ends of which could survive trailing only on these impossibly clean golden streets. But how did they get this obscene amount of wealth? Maybe it came from the dark energy taken from souls by harvesters. It was depressing to think humans contained enough evil to fuel these extravagant displays across a whole city.

The stench of smoke hit my nostrils at the same time I heard Dorian hiss.

Laini jerked her head up. I froze. Roxy had leapt to the next roof and stopped, dropping into a wary crouch. Something droned in the distance above us.

"Incoming patrols!" Laini said. "They're close."

A whooshing noise closed in on our group. We hurtled to the next roof and into the shadows created by four pairs of bulky gargoyle statues. Their uncanny gem eyes sparkled, as if they were amused to hide trouble-makers. I ducked beneath one of their huge paws, and Roxy did the same. Dorian took the very last gargoyle, keeping his distance from me as best he could. My chest still burned, but there was no helping it.

Kane sucked in a sharp breath as the whooshing sound grew closer. I scanned the sky, trying to look past the dazzling neon glow of the city. Blurry white shapes, like giant paper airplanes, whizzed over our heads. They were as big as redbills but moved with an audible mechanical whir. Their frames were lined with tiny yellow lights, glowing balls that danced and bobbed. The white plane dipped down, circling closer to our area. Finally seeing them up close, it wasn't difficult to guess that these were skimmers.

Laini shot me a grim look. Roxy watched with hard eyes, her hand moving toward her holster. Every nerve in my body burned fiercely from both Dorian's proximity and the tension.

The skimmers hovered above the roofs of the building two doors down. My nervous breath caught in my throat. The skimmers' wings folded inward as they sank to the street and completely disappeared from view. I exhaled with relief.

"Maybe we'll be safe for a while longer," I whispered hopefully to Laini.

Her wide eyes and furrowed brow told a different story. Dorian whispered something I couldn't hear. Kane swore.

"What is it?" I asked. Roxy leaned in beside me, closer to Laini than Kane or Dorian.

Laini's face paled considerably. "If Dorian's directions are right, the skimmers just touched down where the safehouse should be."

My hope and burning heart sank. We were too late.

CHAPTER THREE

Using the cover provided by the gargoyles, Dorian cautiously gestured for us to keep moving. The commotion on the streets continued, but we would have to get closer if we wanted to see what was happening. I stayed close to Roxy as we leapt to the next rooftop. I nearly slid in a puddle of water on the pockmarked roof, distracted by the burning that burst into my chest, but Laini helped me right myself. Dorian was too close; there was little room to escape in the shroud of shadows that covered us. We had landed on a strange roof, which bent and buckled in various places, making it difficult to cross. Keeping our steps silent and crouching low, we hid behind black stone parapets and watched through the diamond-shaped openings in the stout wall.

Below us lay a riot of gardens packed with flowers, bushes, and trees in an overwhelming combination of colors and textures. At the edge of the park area nearest us stood a four-story building with powder-blue stucco walls. The structure was protected by a thick wall of trees with glowing purple flowers, which had no gap for entrance that I could see. The trees moved and shifted, their flowers stinking of decaying earth. The breeze carried the scent into our faces in our shadowy hiding place.

My shoulders sagged as we studied the scene. It was definitely the safehouse, and we were definitely too late.

In the streets surrounding the tall building, a commotion erupted on the gold pavement. The skimmers had folded themselves up, and a group of ruler-caste hunters, decked out in armor similar to that of Inkarri and her companion from the lake, milled among them. A crowd of rulers had gathered in the street, hanging back at a respectful distance to watch them work.

I immediately recognized two of the hunters hacking at one of the trees with long, curved swords. One, a male, had hundreds of red-and-black braids falling to his knees, most tipped with wicked barbed hooks. He had been the one to capture Kono as he tried to flee Itzarriol the day before. The other, the female, was the porcelain-white Immortal ruler who'd accompanied him, her armor glittering silver. Her arms, bare but for a set of rose gold bracers studded with gems, rippled with muscle as she smashed her sword through the wall of trees. Violet flowers shook violently and let out a weeping sound as they dropped like snowflakes. The petals sizzled against the gold pavement. Chips of wood followed, and more branches leaned down to cover the resulting gap.

Other hunters moved forward to join her charge. The tallest, a man dressed in a pine-green outfit to match his long hair, smashed through the splintering bark.

There was a crackle and flash of light as one of the hunters let off a blast from a gem-powered gauntlet like the one Inkarri wore, destroying a portion of the wall large enough for several hunters to charge inside. They'd finally created more damage than the trees could repair.

"We know you're here!" the male with long braids bellowed.

Through the wreckage, I saw branches strewn across a courtyard inside the garden wall. As the hunters raced through the hole, sounds of struggle leaked from inside.

"All of you leeches, out," the green-haired hunter snapped as he emerged from the hole, his weapon bloody. "Try anything else and I'll stomp on your head until your fangs crack."

A parade of crestfallen creatures began to emerge. First came a pair of wildlings partially covered in rock, but with patches of algae on their heads and scales skirting their necks like collars. They looked similar to the aquatic wildlings who had taken us to the Gray Ravine. One clutched at his neck, stemming a trail of black blood. He wheezed, and his female companion tried to support him. The green-haired hunter smacked her away. She recoiled and growled, showing a row of tiny pebble-like teeth, before trying to bite the hunter, but he was far too quick. He smashed the pommel of his sword down on her head, making her let out a piercing scream.

Watching such brutality while helpless to intervene was becoming a distressing norm for us these past few days. My throat tightened with disgust that quickly turned to white-hot rage. Laini squeezed my arm, pulling it away from my holster, her eyes trained forward.

Behind them, one of the four-armed metal beings came forward, but she looked up carefully at her captors beneath her lashes. For half a second, she dodged to the side, as if to try to escape. Faster than my eye could track, the white hunter brutally kicked one of her legs out from under her. The blow shouldn't have been enough to damage metal, but it seemed she wasn't made of metal after all. There came a definitive *crack*, a scream, and the creature fell to the ground, her leg hanging at a sickening angle as she struggled to stand. She failed, collapsing onto her front. On instinct, my hand flew to my gun, and I had to force myself not to draw it. The poor creature groaned as she dragged herself forward using her arms, to avoid another kick. Someone in the crowd cackled, a terrible, dark sound that echoed over and over in my mind.

A woman dressed in a stuffy high-collared robe released a melodramatic gasp as the next shapes emerged from the house. The four-armed woman's attempt to escape had inspired others. Two cloaked figures darted forward.

"Fangs! I see fangs!"

Indeed, the telltale snarl of a vampire sensing darkness rang out. I gripped Laini's hand as we watched, helpless to aid the two vampires. The hunters descended upon them with fierce blows. A hand reached out from the struggle, more human-looking than the rulers. The white hunter snatched the hand up and twisted it violently, earning a pained cry.

"No," someone else in the crowd cried. "What are those *insects* doing here?"

From my position I could only just see through the gap the hunters had hacked into the wall of trees, but I could see well enough to watch the hunter drag two vampires to their feet. One of the vampires clutched his wounded hand, another his leg.

The green-haired hunter growled and shoved them along. "Try to fight, and we can give you a pleasant blast of magic straight to the face."

Kane hissed under his breath, the sound a tiny pressure release for his rage, as the vampire in the back smashed into his companion. They looked like brothers. If I'd seen them in Chicago, I would have pegged them as fresh college graduates, young and clean cut. One brother had shadows dancing beneath his tan skin, but the other—the one who had been pushed—only had trickles of shadow on his face. Only the first had managed to feed recently.

If only we had come earlier… would it have made a difference? Kono's capture flashed through my mind, and my brain offered up a string of things we could have done differently. It had been too dangerous for us to move after his capture, stuck up on the cliff watching patrols of hunters and diving skimmers scour the edges of the city. The dark fury of my frustration weighed my entire body down. If we'd arrived even minutes earlier maybe we could have warned them… but we hadn't. We failed to get here in time, and our allies would pay the price for it.

My stomach clenched as a familiar voice cut across the scene, accompanied by the harsh sound of solid wheels clattering on gold.

"Good find," Inkarri said, clearly relishing the situation. Her velek with its trademark gemstone followed obediently. She grinned and grabbed the chin of the weaker vampire, forcing him to look at her. "I take it their friend broke quickly after being taken to the sanitarium?"

The female hunter nodded, her hair glittering like it was coated with flecks of ice. "Zeele is good at his job. The leech only gave us scraps of information, but that was all we needed."

I noted the names and other hints the rulers were giving away. We might not be able to save Kono, but I already had a name and a location that could be worth investigating if we got the chance. *Zeele. The sanitarium.*

"What are the official orders?" the male hunter with the red-and-black braids asked. He ripped the cloak off one of the vampires with a sharp yank, using it to wipe his armor and sword clean of bark and sap from his tree rampage.

Inkarri waved a hand. "Collar them."

Obediently, the green-haired ruler and his companions stepped toward the captives. They each removed something from their side satchels, and though I couldn't see the source from my angle, I saw a bright green spark leap into the air. The hunter snapped a crackling circle of magic around the stronger vampire's neck.

"Two on him," Inkarri said, running a finger across the shadows on his skin. "He's found himself a recent meal. He did what leeches do best… feed off those stronger than him."

Kane jerked forward as if to jump off the roof. Dorian snatched him back, shaking his head fiercely.

Nobody spoke, but I could feel the anger coming off Kane in waves.

Laini hadn't let go of my arm. She squeezed it again and shot me a pained look, gesturing her head to the scuffle.

We were all thinking the same thing. Could we interfere? We hadn't been able to help Kono because he'd been too far away, but we would have the element of surprise in this situation. With the other two vampires and their allies, our odds against the rulers were much better than they had been the night before. Roxy exhaled heavily through her nostrils, her shoulders shaking from frustration as we watched.

Dorian made fierce, quelling eye contact with all of us. He made the hard decision, shaking his head and mouthing, "Too dangerous."

We might have reinforcements if the captives helped us, but our allies were already injured. The hunters would call more of their troops.

I cursed every part of this impossible situation and made a mental promise that these captives would see justice. Somehow, some way, we would save them—but not right now.

The vampire's fangs extended slightly at the hunter's comment, but Inkarri only chuckled as her comrade placed another green collar around his throat. The vampire's chest rose and fell sharply, but he gave no other sign of pain, glaring at Inkarri with obvious hatred. His brother crumpled to his knees, clawing at the collar.

Two giant, black equine creatures with manes of blue flame dragged a copper-plated carriage toward the ruined safehouse. It had two double doors in the back and a small barred window on the side. A gurgling laugh came from a tiny imp who sat on a cushion on the front of the cart. It leered at the group of prisoners as it slowed the carriage to a halt, the wheels squeaking against the gold surface. The sound sent goosebumps over my skin.

"Disgusting," a woman from the crowd said, her chignon hairstyle glittering with diamonds. She covered her mouth with a gold-trimmed handkerchief as if breathing the air near the captives might kill her, and her voice was edged with fear.

My eyes were trained on Inkarri and her hard smirk, remembering her cruelty at the battle at Lake Siron. When I recalled her terrible voice, I could almost *feel* the sway of it still pulling me. It coaxed me into submission, made me want to please her. If her gem gauntlet hadn't malfunctioned in the nick of time... I forced my fingernails into my thighs, wishing I could pull my handgun and drop her where she stood. This hunter was responsible for the broken bodies of Bryce and Sike. She had snapped Sike's arm without a thought and gleefully shot down their redbill.

More carriages stopped to watch the show, blocking those behind them. A herd of velek pulled a smaller ornately decorated carriage, with curlicue patterns of gold and purple and a glittering roof of gemstones. It halted, and the velek twitched their heads from side to side, stamping their feet lightly. Reinforcements, or more citizens being inconvenienced by a sudden roadblock? Two riders sat in the front of the carriage on a glittering bench. One was another of the strange metallic creatures, who used one of his four hands to scratch beneath his chin. He furrowed his brow as he stared at the racket. The other rider—an Immortal ruler with long silver hair and slate-gray skin—made a quick gesture of annoyance.

Okay, so not everyone is impressed by this spectacle. I scanned the faces in the crowd. Most of the nearby wildlings seemed focused on their own kin who had been captured, while the rulers leered and stared unabashedly at the vampires.

The parapets we hid behind vibrated slightly as Inkarri's booming voice washed over the area.

"Do not fear," she called out, her voice feigning charm. "We've merely caught some vermin. Load them up."

The unfed vampire looked up at the sky in futile supplication, mouth slightly open, panting. His gaze crossed mine, and he swallowed, his expression sharpening at the sight of strange vampires on the rooftop. But he didn't give us away, and the rulers were too focused on the spectacle in front of them to look up. Tears stung my eyes.

"I'm sorry," I mouthed.

CHAPTER FOUR

The double doors of the prisoner cart flew open without being touched, and Inkarri's lackeys forced the captives into the back. I caught the barest glimpse of battered wooden benches built into the metal walls of the carriage. The wildlings went in first, the sparks from the green collars around their stout necks looking absurdly like costume jewelry. The metallic woman followed, dragging her broken leg. The cart's floor bowed under her weight as she lumbered inside.

Inkarri appeared to take great pleasure in watching the two vampire men stumble into the back. She snapped her fingers, and the green-haired hunter slammed the door shut. The imp cracked his whip and said something in a harsh tone. The horses took off, but the cart left much more slowly than it had arrived. The bitter taste of hatred filled my mouth. Somewhere in the crowd, a female ruler gave a wild wail and fainted. The annoyed rider from earlier applauded sarcastically. Inkarri glared, and the man stopped immediately, tucking his hands underneath his legs with an overly innocent smile.

She's got a reputation.

I exchanged a look of dread with Laini and Roxy. Kane and Dorian spoke in hoarse whispers. Laini shook her head, a fist pressed to her lips, silently mourning the other vampires. Roxy twisted her mouth as she watched the cart trundle through the crowd. The onlookers began moving slowly away, giving Inkarri and the other hunter a wide berth.

The safehouse was compromised. This was what the Hive vampires were terrified would happen. *Would they blame us?* My mind raced, wondering if there was some way to send news back to the Hive. If they suspected our interference had led to the safehouse being compromised, even though Kono had been captured before we reached the city, who knew how they might treat our friends who had been left behind. Injuries or not, I doubted the Hive would keep them around if they thought we'd brought trouble. And if the hunters decided to keep watch over the safehouse, the next Hive scouts could walk right into their trap.

Dorian gave a subtle gesture, summoning Laini and Roxy closer. Unfortunately, the need for distance meant I was excluded. Dorian leaned into a circle with Kane and the others, their heads bent as they fell into fervent whispers. I focused on their body language and tried to pick up the odd word by reading their lips. I could tell from their gestures that they wanted to retreat or at least get out of the area. Kane jerked his thumb over his shoulder in the direction of the falls. He had a good point—we could hide among the stinking jasmine seaweed and concoct a new plan, maybe scout the edges of the city for somewhere else to hide. Dorian cocked his head, the lines of his face sharp as he considered it. Laini lifted her hand, volunteering herself for something. If I had to guess, they planned to go back to the garden, and Laini had volunteered herself as a scout. She was the smallest vampire, so that made sense.

Leaving them to their planning, I returned to keeping watch over the fray below. The wreckage from the hunters' destruction of the house was being kicked across the street by ruler children. Inkarri and the hunters milled around, talking in low voices. The male with the braids kicked another section of the tree wall down for no reason at all. A few inhabitants of the city, mainly well-dressed Immortal rulers in a rainbow range of clothing and hairstyles, hovered around the scene, obviously experiencing some level of titillation over being present. Then came a sound that made me catch my breath, my fight-or-flight instinct immediately kicking in.

Inkarri's velek had begun to bay.

The blue-haired hunter growled. "What's this?" she asked, looking at her animal companion. The velek's gem glowed brightly, matched by the gleaming gem in Inkarri's forehead. The velek looked up at her, then swung its head in our direction, the grotesque faces in its horns writhing and screaming.

Oh crap.

I pressed my body flat against the roof, feeling the strange dips and grooves beneath me. The rest of my team did the same. The rocky material dug painfully into my ribs. The noisy street fell absolutely silent. Sweat pricked my forehead.

"What do we have here?" Inkarri asked. The velek bayed loudly in response.

The green-haired hunter sighed wearily. "Can you shut that thing up?"

Inkarri chuckled. "Shut it up? Lucra, my velek has been bound to my aura by Zeele himself, at the command of our Lord Irrikus, to sniff out prey... especially vampires. They have a particular reeking odor. He bays only when there's prey about, so we must have missed some vermin."

I could practically hear the slick, sadistic smile cross her face. The velek, for its part, refused to be silenced. It bayed noisily, the sound approaching our building. My palms grew clammy. I turned my face to the side and spotted Roxy gritting her teeth. We had spread out as much as possible in the shadows, but my heart still burned from Dorian's proximity. His eyes met mine for half a second, intense and focused, as if ready for the velek to magically leap onto the roof at any moment.

We couldn't run. They would be watching the roof now. Dorian's eyes narrowed, and his hand rose a few inches, but he made no movement with his fingers. The dancing lights above the sky, which had seemed almost fun before, shifted and cast us in a somber blue glow.

"I saw one!" a new voice cried suddenly. "A loose vampire!" It was a man's voice, dramatic and loud.

"A vampire?" a woman called out, her voice choked with panic.

The velek bayed on.

"You must save us," the male voice demanded. He let out a howl that bordered on hysterical. He gasped abruptly. "There! Didn't you see the flapping cloak? It went that way."

"Hunters, on me." It was Lucra, the green-haired ruler, and he apparently needed no more convincing.

"Damn it, Lucra, hold your eagerness," Inkarri snapped, but the frenzy of a potential hunt overwhelmed her authority.

Multiple sets of heavy footsteps thundered toward us as his comrades joined him. I reached for the handgun holster at my shoulder. Roxy went for the knives at her sides. Dorian lifted himself slightly, ready to jump into defensive mode. Shrieks rose up below. Blades were drawn from sheaths. Boots clattered against the golden street as more rulers joined the chase.

The velek continued to bay. "Silence!" The velek fell abruptly silent, as if Inkarri had flipped a switch. An echo of her enticing thrall was all she needed to quiet the animal.

The noise ascended to a terrifying crescendo of panic, then began to fade. *Did they pass us?* I stayed alert, keeping my breathing silent and shallow, straining to hear whether they were looping around the back or coming up through the house. Dorian lowered himself back down. We exchanged a shocked look. His fangs, still extended, looked almost amusing with his confused expression.

What the hell just happened?

Risking a peek through one of the peepholes, I saw that the hunters had moved away from us. Screams and shouts rang out in the distance. Lights flickered farther into the city.

The man's voice came again, pleading and hysterical. "Everyone should get indoors! It's not safe with vermin running about. Won't you think of your children? Vampires have no morals. They're as good as shrieking decays when it comes to wanton destruction."

There came the sound of hurrying feet and moving bodies. Doors and shutters began to slam, then silence fell. I raised an eyebrow at Laini. What kind of bizarre relationship did the rulers have with vampires that they could simultaneously loathe vampires and find them inferior, yet still be so afraid?

"Did you really see a vampire?" Inkarri snapped.

"Of course," the man replied smoothly. "Are you suggesting I would lie about such a serious matter?"

"I'm saying I don't trust you, Juneau," Inkarri replied, her voice acidic. "You're as slippery as a Siron toad."

"A delight as ever to see you," Juneau said smoothly. "Do give my regards to your father."

She mumbled something under her breath. The tapping of hooves sounded louder, then wandered away, accompanied by Inkarri's solid footfalls.

More clattering hooves approached, and wheels squeaked as a carriage rolled up to the building where we were hiding. Barely moving, I put my eye to the crack between two of the chimneys and saw the edges of the gaudy carriage from earlier sidle up to our hiding place.

The man, Juneau, cleared his throat. "Whoever is up there," he whispered, "I promise you don't want the hunters to find you. Whatever the hell you are, you'd better come with me."

I gaped at Laini, her stiff body unmoving. Roxy nudged me. She shook her head sternly.

He coughed. "I won't wait all day. It's either come with me or try your luck with the hunters, strangers."

Laini darted a look at Dorian. Kane began to unsheathe a large knife from his hip. Dorian flicked Kane's hand, stopping him from making any murderous moves.

"We're running out of time," Juneau called up, raising his voice slightly. "I can't very well shout at rooftops all day without attracting suspicion." He had a point.

Dorian's eyebrows rose, and a hopeful glint flickered in his eyes. He shrugged. "He's not dark," he mouthed.

Laini nodded. Even Kane's fangs had retracted, though he still wore a look of intense suspicion. Could we trust this Juneau? I glanced up the street, where a ghostly echo of sound carried over the buildings. It wouldn't be long before they realized it was a wild goose chase. A skimmer drifted up into the sky several blocks away, cutting through the multicolored mist. Dorian glanced at it, then gestured for us to follow.

Quietly, cautiously, we crawled toward the edge.

"Oh, there really was someone," the rider said softly, pressing a splayed hand across his chest. In the shadow cast by the building, I only saw the soft glint of his silver hair. He beckoned us. "Come! Quick."

Using a cast-iron trellis that started on the roof and poured down the side of the building, Dorian disappeared over the edge. Kane snorted.

"Well, it would've been nice to have a choice," he said before he too disappeared over the lip of the roof, swiftly followed by Laini.

CHAPTER FIVE

Lacking vampire abilities, Roxy and I took longer climbing down, but as soon as my feet hit the ground, a bolt of pain rushed through me and struck my chest. I was too close to Dorian, but there was no helping it. Dorian hurried to the cart, making room for Roxy and me. The carriage had been backed up to the building, and the Immortal ruler yanked the back doors open, leaning against the carriage with a little smile of affected boredom.

"Well, do the accommodations satisfy?" Juneau gestured to the inside of his carriage, the long, trailing ends of his immaculate crimson robe sweeping the ground as he did. Inside the carriage lay piles of fabrics and blankets. Trinkets hung from the ceiling. With a final lingering look at the Immortal man, Dorian entered slowly, tensed for a trap or an attack. Nothing happened, and after a moment of him rifling through the gathered fabrics, he gestured for us to join him. We crammed in behind him, batting our way through sparkling pink tulle and silky piles of multicolored ribbons.

The ruler poked his face inside, eyeing as many of us as he could see. Kane was currently drowning in a heap of black lace and tulle.

"Hide under the cloth and don't say a word." The doors shut, and darkness enveloped us.

"Lovely," Roxy grunted and dove for the red satin. I followed suit. Inside, I patted the area around me and hit something.

"That's my leg," Laini muttered.

Oops. My face hit scratchy fabric. *Why couldn't I have found silk?* I pressed myself against the material, feeling the chill emanating from the metal even with the cloth between me and the bottom of the carriage. The vehicle began to move, creaking as it went. Beams of light passed through the tiny windows at the rear, illuminating all manner of fabrics, bolts upon bolts of them.

A musky perfume rose from the cloth and tickled my sinuses. I rubbed my nose roughly, trying to contain a sneeze, wriggling away in the hope of reducing the itch. The pain in my chest surged, and I hissed as stars exploded before my eyes.

"Lyra," Dorian breathed, pained, his voice so near I could practically feel his breath.

My heart squeezed with agony, made worse by the knowledge that he was suffering alongside me. My fingers reached toward the sound of his voice. I peeked with one eye and saw his pale fingers reaching back to me. Pain exploded inside me when I grabbed his hand, but I didn't care. I clung to him like my life depended on it. The cart bounced along, the driver softly urging the velek on.

The burning surged, but I only tightened my grip, clinging to consciousness just as tightly. Dorian squeezed my hand in response. I occasionally felt him wince as the cart rolled over a bump, jostling us. I closed my eyes, sparks flying across the backs of my eyelids. Would we ever find a cure for this curse? A fuzzy recollection of Echen's story streamed through my mind, hope mixing with the pain and the sound of rustling fabric.

After more bumps and turns, the cart slowed to a creaking halt. The velek snorted. A weight shifted in the front.

"Here we are," Juneau chirped as he yanked open the doors. Light flooded the carriage, revealing the rainbow kaleidoscope of fabrics once again.

Dorian and I released each other's hands, snatching them back quickly before anyone could see. The pain still thrummed, and black spots flared at the edges of my vision. Now that I could see, I scrambled to the side of the carriage farthest from Dorian.

Kane sat up. A square of turquoise lace partially hid his face. "Are you going to kill us?" he asked bluntly.

The Immortal cocked his head to the side with a chuckle. "No immediate plans."

Laini climbed out warily, followed by Kane and Roxy, who'd also been nearest to the doors. Roxy leaned back in to help untangle me from the scratchy tulle while the Immortal watched. His red robes swirled together, shades mixing when he moved like the blurring of a phoenix's feathers. Pulling one of my knives from my boot, I tucked it out of sight up my sleeve as I hustled out into a large courtyard, creating some much-needed distance from Dorian. Each step caused the burning in my heart to fade. Kane helped Dorian out, who immediately sucked in a grateful breath of relief. The Immortal raised an eyebrow but said nothing.

I looked around, taking stock of the location where we now found ourselves. Towering jade walls surrounded us. Here, the musky fragrance grew stronger. Purple and gold lights shone upward from the ground throughout the courtyard, which consisted of a single slab of smooth stone and something like a Zen garden with sandboxes and various statues. Odd plants rose up from the gray sand at the edge of the courtyard, swaying in the air like kelp does in water but with no apparent trigger that would snap them back to place. The plants lined the tops of the walls like hedges.

I marveled at our mysterious rescuer, seeing him fully now in the soul-light. He was taller than all of us, even Kane, but easily a head shorter than Inkarri and her companions. His silver hair went down to his waist and was adorned with various minute braids and tiny jewels. His pale skin was slate gray but with a pearlescent sheen that caught my eye, a flattering shade in the underwater aesthetic of the courtyard. His yellow eyes flitted from one of us to the next, sharp as a cat. I almost expected to see a tail twitch behind him.

He flipped his hair nonchalantly. "Well, let's get started." Without any explanation, he turned toward the creature on the front of the carriage. "Secure the walls, please, Charrek."

The metallic man grunted and hauled himself off the carriage, which jolted with the sudden change of weight. Inside the carriage, bolts of fine linen dislodged themselves and fell to the ground, but the Immortal ruler paid no mind.

The ruler's servant, Charrek, looked like the other creatures I had seen in the city—brass skin, with small horns protruding from a patch of white hair. He strode toward the massive gates set into the jade wall behind us. The violet gates glowed, crafted from some kind of wood that looked like it was covered in a film of water, no doubt to complement the aquatic design of the courtyard. With a powerful tug, the creature yanked a huge bar down across the doors, sealing us in. The heavy sound sent an unsettling chill through me. I couldn't tell if we were safe, or imprisoned.

I glanced over my shoulder to see a home built like something out of a warped old book. Two dollhouse-like stories sprawled across the generous area, the exterior walls a profound blue with white curlicue trim. If I squinted, I swore every window was trimmed with the shape of seahorses in a chain. Shadows pulled back from the hooded windows and disappeared. When I turned back, he was smiling easily.

"There. Was that so bad?" he asked with a shrug. "Although I wasn't expecting so many of you. What a delight to see something new."

"We weren't expecting you at all," Roxy piped up beside me. She shot a wary side-eye at the ruler, who simply continued to smile.

He rubbed his pointed chin thoughtfully. "I suppose you're right. You may call me Juneau. I am of House Tolgroth, a noble family here in the magnificent city of Itzarriol." He bowed low to us, sweeping his hand over his chest. His long nails, each a different jewel shade, peeked out from the ends of his robes. "I happened to spot you on that dreadful building because I'm the only one who can stand to look at it. What good luck for you. Did you get a chance to see how ugly the building was? It draws the artist's eye like nothing else."

Laini, the closest to Juneau in the courtyard, stared blankly at him. She looked surprised, her eyes wide and lips slightly parted, like he'd caught her off guard. I could understand that reaction to an enormous, absurd, peacock-dressed Immortal who'd apparently just saved us all from a terrible fate.

Without warning, Juneau scooped up Laini's hand. "My lady, what a pleasure to meet you."

Kane's jaw threatened to unhinge itself and fall to the ground. Conscious of the knife still hidden in my sleeve, I stared at Juneau as he clutched Laini's hand as if she were a delicate maiden and not a fierce warrior. Dorian opened his mouth to say something, but not before Juneau stooped over and brought Laini's hand toward his mouth to bestow a kiss.

Laini blinked up at him, then a spark of clarity flickered across her face. Her eyes narrowed, and she tugged her hand free of his grasp, her nails catching the flesh of his palm. He sucked in a quick breath as a slick of black blood pooled in the wound.

"That stung!" he protested, clutching his hand to his chest.

"Don't touch me without permission," she said, with a low growl of warning. "I'll cut more than a hand next time."

His four-armed companion hurried over, moving with surprising speed despite his size. Juneau lifted his other hand and waved the creature off.

"No need to worry," he said. "It was just a misunderstanding."

Charrek stopped and went still as a statue, observing us all with sharp wariness.

Juneau's eyes snapped to Laini's face, and he smiled, appraising her with a calculating look. "You're fast," he said. "I apologize for offending you. I am excited to meet all of you, and my enthusiasm got the better of me."

Laini raised her eyebrows but said nothing. If Juneau had hoped to convince her completely, he failed. Her frown thawed by the tiniest fraction, though.

Maybe a good night's sleep will smooth things over. I bit back a stressed sigh. While Juneau could turn out to be evil, he'd saved us, and I was grateful for that.

"What do you want?" Dorian asked.

Juneau tore his eyes away from Laini as if he had suddenly remembered the rest of us existed. "An excellent question, strange travelers." His face blossomed into a wide smile. "You're welcome to hide from the hunters in my home—as long as you can keep my interest."

He trained his catlike gaze on Roxy and me with round, fascinated eyes.

"To start with, tell me about these two."

Roxy and I exchanged glances.

"Us?" I tensed, ready to let the knife slip down my sleeve. Roxy's face immediately took on the carefully neutral expression that meant she was ready to fight. Being a human in this plane too often meant being an easy target.

Juneau brought up his elegant hands and interlaced his long fingers. "Your auras are incredible," he said, as if Roxy and I were creatures to be celebrated. "I would have thought that you were just in possession of some very powerful soul energy, but there's nothing like that here." His lively gaze landed on me.

Juneau tapped his bottom lip as he looked me up and down. "Ah, but your energy is weaker now than it was back in the city. I suspect there's usually more color in your cheeks. Are you sickly, perhaps?"

Dorian grunted. I narrowed my eyes, knowing the carriage ride with Dorian had sapped my strength. However, I refused to let this Immortal see any sort of weakness. I frowned instead.

"Seems kind of a rude thing to say when you don't even know what we are," I said wryly.

"And being the rude smartass is kind of *his* thing," Roxy said, jerking a thumb at Kane.

"That's right," he confirmed loudly, making his way to stand beside Roxy and me. He glared at Juneau.

Dorian sent a pointed look toward Kane, a note of warning flashing across his face. Kane's big mouth might ruin our chances at playing the long game with Juneau. Although trust was too strong a word, I believed Juneau might actually have good intentions. He'd saved us, after all.

And if he was trying to trick us? We would play along until we needed to act. The world always thought that a soldier's job must be tiring from the physical activity. It was, but that was nothing compared to the constant churn of the mind as it tried to stay two steps ahead of a potential enemy.

"Well?" Kane prodded.

"It's because he's never had such an interesting group of people at his dinner table before," Roxy said. Her probing gaze never moved from Juneau. "What kind of people do you usually entertain? Irrikus? You seem fancy enough for such company."

Good play, Roxy. We needed to know what kind of people Juneau hung around.

The Immortal seemed oddly serene. A bit amused?

"You don't trust me," Juneau guessed.

Kane snorted. "*Obviously*. You're a ruler."

"A ruler who saved you from Inkarri and her velek," Juneau reminded him, a bite coming into his voice.

"You saw an opportunity to make a situation work to your advantage." Kane leaned toward the Immortal, teeth flashing menacingly. "It's obvious you don't like Inkarri, but that's no surprise. In my experience, rulers generally dislike each other. You don't like others getting in the way of your own selfish wants. Who's to say you didn't *rescue us*," his tone dripped with sarcasm, "just so you could turn us in to Irrikus yourself for the social benefits? And now you want us to present our friends to you like they're curiosities?"

Kane was pushing it. I would be curious, too, if I came across an entirely new species for the first time. Actually, that exact feeling was quite familiar… and it could work to our advantage.

Juneau tilted his head to the side, his long hair spilling magnificently over his shoulders and down his back. "Curiosity should never be looked down upon. In fact, I find it the highest honor among any creatures. My curiosity is a compliment. I meant no offense."

Laini pressed her lips into a fine line. Her eyebrows quirked together in a slow movement, as if she was mulling something over. What was she trying to decide in her head? She looked to me like a still boat in the water, with equal chance of suddenly turning one way or the other.

"Well, it's twice you've offended," Kane snarled and gestured to Laini. "You can play the innocent, magnanimous bystander all you want. This is a trap if ever I've seen one." He folded his arms stubbornly across his chest.

"It seems likely," Dorian agreed, but with much less bite. "Juneau, you must understand that vampires are naturally suspicious of any rulers, given our tumultuous history." Kane threw him an annoyed scowl as if to say, *Our fearless leader can't be seriously duped by this weirdo.*

Juneau exuded charm, I gave him that. Dorian was probably trying to figure out why this ruler would choose to rescue us. Kane had a point— maybe his interest was a ruse and he planned to hand us over to the hunters to improve his status—but still, Juneau could have easily called out to Inkarri and taken the credit then and there. If it wasn't for him, we would probably be in the back of the prison carriage with the Hive vampires and their allies from the exposed safehouse.

"And we're suspicious too," Roxy chimed in, spokesperson for the human contingent. "We want to know your intentions just as much as the vampires do."

"What's stopping us from killing you right now?" Laini asked, her voice sharp. "There's enough of us to do it. I'm sure you're aware of that."

My palms itched. Something in Laini had shifted on our way through the Gray Ravine. It intensified with every second that we stayed in Itzarriol. I wanted to ask her what was wrong, but it was hardly the time. *Better to wait until after this awkward exchange.*

"Well, even if we ignore the fact that I have servants ready to come fight on my behalf, your fangs aren't out," Juneau noted with a little shrug.

"So I can't be that evil. Of course, you could try to kill me regardless, but I don't think it would end well for you."

Dorian had said before that he didn't sense darkness within this strange Immortal. I peeked at Kane and Laini, neither of whom had their fangs on display.

"Just because you don't make us hungry doesn't mean you're not up to something. We're not telling you anything unless..." Kane's unfinished sentence hung in the air.

The fact was, we had nothing to bargain with. Kane could snarl his demands all he wanted, but we were fresh out of leverage. We had zero allies. Our Hive comrades, who already held us at arm's length due to their own worries, had vanished into the back of a prison carriage. After the discovery of the safehouse, the hunters would be vigilantly searching every nook and cranny for wayward vampires.

Juneau's eyebrows raised in what I imagined must be a well-practiced display of anticipation. He *knew* that we were putty—or perhaps fine pliable fabric—in his hands.

Kane said nothing, seething behind gritted teeth.

Juneau gestured toward the grand house behind us. "This is my family home." A cold sheen came over his eyes. "However, now that all my family members have finally passed away, I live here alone, in peace. You know how it is, Mother always giving you a hard time about not being blood-thirsty enough for the family line. She was eventually happy I took to fabric so well."

Something about his tone gave me pause. Had he taken out his family in order to inherit the house? I shared a quick glance with Dorian, wanting to check whether he thought this guy might be some kind of serial killer.

The pain flared again as our eyes met, making us both take a sharp breath. Beneath the pain, however, nothing in his face made me think he sensed great darkness in Juneau.

As I made my own visual assessment of our impromptu host, Juneau's dazzling robes caught my eye. His soft hands, which held no indication of labor, hardly looked like they would dirty themselves with blood. In the moment of tense silence that followed his words, Juneau brought his hands to his neck and touched a delicate string of pearls. Now that I was paying closer attention, I realized he wore several additional pieces of jewelry. I counted six rings on one hand, two stacked on his index finger. A gleaming golden skull ring sat on his thumb.

"I can even take off my magicked jewelry, if that will reassure you further that I have no malevolent spells on my person," he said. He began to remove the skull ring.

Kane scoffed. "This is what makes you untrustworthy! You're trying too hard," he said. "Why would you do this in front of vampires? We're supposed to believe that you're purposefully making yourself weak in front of us?"

Juneau smirked. "You're no fool, but you must believe me when I say that I am simply curious and more than a little bored. Nothing fun happens here anymore." His nostrils flared. "It's always the same stupid parties over and over. Celebrations of cruelty and power. Can you imagine anything so inane? I have half a mind to fall dead from a lack of intellectual stimulation. I want something from you, something to spice up my day."

"Of course you do," Kane said hotly.

"Let's hear what he has to say," Dorian said. He swept his cloak around him. His strength must have returned faster than mine. My heart beat quicker, seeing his handsome determination in the strange aquatic lights of the courtyard. There was still a slight burn in my chest, but it was much better than before.

Juneau held out his arm toward the house. "I'll let you stay here for a night under my protection. In exchange for my hospitality, I want your *stories*. I want to hear them from your own mouths." His stare quickly flickered to me and Roxy. "I especially want to know about these two enchanting creatures. That's all I ask."

"A story is all you want?" Dorian asked tightly, his jaw set as he stared Juneau down. "One story for one night."

"A story is worth more than many things," Juneau replied. "It's all I want. And if you decide not to trust me, then, as we've mentioned before, your party outnumbers me. You can jump me, tie me up, and make a tidy little escape into the soul-lit night." He paused, and I couldn't help but momentarily appreciate his dramatic timing. "It's only polite that I let you inside to confer among yourselves for a while. I'll leave you to it."

He walked elegantly toward the grand double doors of his mansion and threw them open. A wave of cooler air and musky fragrance washed out into the garden. I shifted, staring closely at Dorian and the other vampires. What did they sense in Juneau? Could there be any magic that covered an Immortal's darkness, camouflaging their nature?

Juneau gave a playful knock on the door and smiled. "Come now. Or would you rather try your luck with Inkarri and her magicked velek as they patrol the streets? The skimmer patrols will be out, too. Ugly little things." The hint of a threat lingered in his otherwise warm voice, and a tingle ran down my spine. This ruler had saved us, but could he be trusted?

Dorian's gaze swept over our group. I could practically see his silent decision in the lines of his tense expression.

We had little choice. Who was I kidding? We had no choice.

As a group, we cautiously followed Juneau inside the mansion, the doors closing behind us with a thunderous slam.

True to his word, Juneau let us have time alone in the antechamber of his home. Where he went while we spoke in low, urgent voices, I had no idea, but the vampires seemed convinced that he had actually left. We quickly discussed that we should give him a modified version of our story. We didn't have time to make up something entirely new and get our stories straight, so we would keep as close as possible to a harmless version of the truth. Some parts we could leave out for our own safety and that of our allies both here and in the Mortal Plane, in case Juneau was just trying to gather information to sell to Irrikus. We would tell him nothing of the supposed connection between the Immortal Plane and the Bureau, and not a single word about the existence of the Hive, which was of the utmost secrecy. However, we still needed to keep him entertained, so we would spill harmless details.

After we left the antechamber, we found Charrek waiting in the hall. He guided us through what felt like never-ending grand halls and chambers, through twinkling emerald tiles that changed as we moved from room to room, climbing from the floor to walls to the ceiling. They morphed into incredibly colorful mosaics formed from millions of tiles that had been lovingly carved to fit into an enormous, intricate narrative depicting alligator-like creatures crawling across endless rolling hills, slices of onyx stone, and plants I had yet to see in the Immortal Plane. Behind the reptilian horde, mounted on winged beasts made of pure embers, were an array of rulers that all looked like Juneau in some regard. The same skin, the same hair. I couldn't help but notice that each was minutely disfigured—they were all missing their eyes. I tore my gaze away, dizzy from the intricate patterns, and once again unsettled by the possibility that our host was a little insane.

Unfortunately for my dizziness, there were nothing *but* intricate patterns everywhere I looked. Each open door afforded us a new glimpse of extravagance. The servants had obediently fled and were nowhere to be found. Only Charrek led us through the mansion, staring straight ahead as he finally ground to a halt and opened a set of double doors for us. His thick bottom lip was affixed in a permanent pout, the jaw tucked forward into an underbite, but his large eyes were clear and calm as we passed him. His second pair of arms—the less muscled but more dexterous-looking pair—remained crossed at all times. *Interesting.*

Juneau sat like an Immortal prince at the end of a long dining table that stretched nearly the entire length of the walls. The polished black creation could easily seat forty people, but we all clustered together at the end by Juneau. I sat as near the ruler as I could, and Dorian, with his superior hearing, sat several chairs away in isolation. I leaned my elbows on the cold stone surface.

The dining hall stretched high above us, arching slightly before disappearing into inky darkness. Part of me wanted to slam both fists onto the table to see how far the sound would echo in the emptiness. I couldn't shake the feeling that it must be rather depressing to eat alone in this room every day, with only servants around for company.

Everything about Juneau's home made me feel as though we had stumbled into some bizarre, above-ground version of Atlantis. The walls seemed to breathe with life as dappled blue-and-green light filtered down from innumerable gems embedded in stone columns. The same kelp plants that lined the exterior wall shivered and swayed in raised mother-of-pearl planters around the room's perimeter. I squinted at the moving plants. There was absolutely no breeze in here.

Never-ending rows of portraits stared down at us from the walls. It was clear that they were family members, as with the hunting mosaic, and many appeared very much alive as they glared down at our meeting. They didn't look happy at all, and Juneau was nowhere among them. Another sign of dysfunction.

Juneau turned toward me and Roxy, whom he had specifically requested to sit beside him near the head of the table. Dorian balled his hands into fists and set them on the table. Kane let his hand hover casually near the knife on his hip. I still felt the blade tucked securely in my sleeve, ready to fall into my hand at the first sign of trouble.

Juneau leaned a bit closer, appraising me with a quick sweep of his sharp eyes. "So, tell me who you are. What's your story?"

Where could we start?

Once upon a time, I imagined myself saying, *a vampire kidnapped me at my old job, and now I have deep feelings for him.*

Juneau wanted an interesting story. We certainly had one. But could we trust him enough to tell it?

CHAPTER SIX

R oxy nudged me under the table.

I thought back to our conversation in the antechamber. We needed to say enough to pique his interest and get him hooked on wanting to hear more so we could stay here. But I really didn't want to tell him anything very personal or detailed. If he couldn't be trusted, I wanted him to know as little as possible about me and my team. A few lies might be needed. Giving Roxy a subtle nod, I let her know I was ready to begin.

I folded my hands and faced Juneau, who burned with excitement as bright as a newborn star. Studying him more closely, I saw a muscle tense in his jaw. Although he hid it well, he was on high alert for any sign of lies or reluctance. I would have to be careful. *Let's start with some harmless facts to relax him.*

"I'm a human," I said, then jerked a thumb over to Roxy. "She's a human, too."

Roxy waved.

Juneau's false calm shattered in an instant. If he'd intended to play it cool, that strategy was lost in the wind. He leaned forward with an excited wheeze. "No. *Human?*"

"Yes," I confirmed. "We came from the Mortal Plane to help our vampire allies search for some of their missing family. We think they might be somewhere in or around the Immortal capital." The best way to cover a lie was to base it in genuine truth, yet I couldn't help but register something strangely enticing about Juneau's reactions. Unlike the commanding thrall in Inkarri's voice, his had a genuine warmth that shimmered with outrage and even delight at the prospect of scandalous news, the kind that made you want to go on and on.

"Family in Itzarriol? I do hope they haven't met the same fate as those poor creatures in the house the hunters raided," Juneau said and shook his head, sending platinum silvery locks flying. Still, his face showed a little spark of delight. "I just *knew* something was happening beneath the surface of this vile city. There have been rumors I've picked up here and there, about humans. All speculation, of course." He leaned even more toward Roxy. "Is it true that your kind have no idea that vampires exist?"

"Well," she said slowly, "*we* obviously know, but… no, most humans didn't know about vampires until very recently. The information got released when the vampires came looking for asylum from your kind."

He had the decency to look shamefaced for a moment before getting swept up in his excitement again. "I've seen flashes of human experiences when I've used dark energy from souls, mostly ghastly crimes. Little bits of emotions, you understand, because we can't directly see you in your actual plane. But I never would have guessed you looked like, well, weak little vampires with dull coloring. You look positively harmless."

"You really have a way with flattery," I said, arching a brow. The naïveté of his statement made me want to smile.

"Yeah, and we'll see how harmless you think we are when I'm done with you," Roxy muttered.

Kane grinned wolfishly, all teeth and sharp angles, a hint of pride in his eyes. I glared slightly at Roxy but was secretly proud of her for standing up for us. I worried about antagonizing Juneau further, though. If he was actually dangerous, he might grow angry with us. Where was the balance in this situation? In human dilemmas, I could easily navigate unspoken social expectations. We needed more caution with our new Immortal acquaintance.

"She's joking," I assured Juneau. "But she's right. We may not be vampires, and we may not be like the humans who committed the terrible acts you've seen, but we've survived in the Immortal Plane long enough to reach your city." I said enough to placate Roxy and Kane, but hopefully kept it vague about exactly how prepared we were. If he underestimated us, it would be to our benefit.

Juneau pressed his elegant fingers over his mouth, a boyish look of sheepishness crossing his face. "Of course, of course," he murmured, apologetic.

His eyes suddenly dropped to the empty table. "My goodness, do you require sustenance?" he asked, with a note of panic in his voice. "I'm such an awful host. My mother would..." Trailing off at the end, he touched the skull ring on his finger.

A moment later, an Immortal wildling scampered through the door and hurried to stand beside Juneau. Coming to about hip height on me, the creature was covered in shaggy green moss that gleamed richly in the watery lights of the room. She wore a dazzling blue dress. Her only visible facial features were a set of shiny, curling horns protruding from the greenery and decorated with several gold and silver trinkets. It seemed Juneau liked to ensure his staff were as well dressed as he was.

"Hello, Fenru, my dear," Juneau said cheerfully and waved toward Roxy and me. "Use your lovely powers and find out what these *humans*," he gave her a conspiratorial grin, "eat, and prepare a meal for them. Make sure it's delectable. We want to make a good impression on our guests." He nodded at the vampires, including them in his statement, before turning back to Fenru. "But be careful with the wilder ingredients. I suspect they won't have the stomach for Sironese sandworms or death moss soup."

I nearly gagged, not even needing the visual. Roxy's lip curled in disgust. Despite her diminutive height, the wildling hopped up onto the table in one graceful bound and leaned toward me, her shaggy moss shaking as she cocked her head from side to side. The scent of sea salt radiated from her as she pressed a stubby finger to my forehead. Her touch was cool and pleasantly slimy, like seaweed. Two shiny black eyes appeared briefly behind the moss, the iridescent lids flickering slightly for a moment. She withdrew, then hopped over to Roxy. My teammate leaned back in her chair, reluctant, but the wildling repeated the same movement and nodded, clearly satisfied with her study.

The vampires exchanged a series of inscrutable looks, and I had an idea of what they were worried about. We humans had deliberately not eaten anything from the Immortal Plane, instead living off military rations we'd brought from the Bureau camp in Moab. There was no way to know what food from the Immortal Plane would do to a creature from the Mortal Plane, especially one as complex as a human. I very much hoped Fenru was correct in whatever assessment she made, because I was sick to death of MREs.

"I will fetch the plants with the lightest energy we have. It will be more than good for you," she said in the characteristically rough voice of a wildling. She jumped off the table and skittered from the room.

"Now that's settled, let us continue," Juneau said to Roxy and me without missing a beat. "What lands do you rule in the Mortal Plane?"

Roxy choked on her own spit. "None! We're unemployed soldiers. Try paying a mortgage with that."

"Mortgage," he repeated, as if tasting the word.

"You're too wealthy to worry about it," Roxy said, flapping a hand dismissively.

"Very few people rule lands in the Mortal Plane," I told him. "Most of our rulers are voted into power by the public." I frowned. "I mean, there are some royal families left, but they don't really rule in a traditional sense."

"Fascinating." He clapped his hands together. "Now, I have a few more questions. What color is your blood? Who is your greatest enemy in this Mortal Plane? Do you prefer the heat? Can you breathe underwater? What kind of magic can you do?"

Dorian cleared his throat loudly, speaking up for the first time since we'd left the entryway. "Juneau, before we go any further, we've given you the information you asked for. They've told you who they are. That's all any of us will say until you reveal more about yourself and why exactly a ruler caste Immortal wants to help us." He shrugged casually, dripping with charisma. "You can appreciate that as a fellow story-seeker, I'm sure."

"Oh no, I'm rather boring," Juneau replied, looking deflated. "Sorry to disappoint."

Dorian narrowed his eyes a fraction, the charisma freezing into something more menacing. "I assure you that we are *very* interested." It wasn't a threat, but a very strongly encouraged suggestion.

Juneau rapped his fingers against the table with a slight frown. "Very well. I can't put you off, can I? My adoring fans." He swept his hand upward and gestured to the mean-faced portraits. "These clods up here will enjoy the show. My name is Juneau, as you know. I'm the head of a guild that produces the most beautiful fabrics in Itzarriol, as you saw during your ride over here, and I am also a sought-after clothing designer. The makers in my guild use their powers of transmutation and the soul-energy from my harvesters to weave cloth. They turn it into whatever brightly colored fabric I design, down to the tiniest detail. The entire city trips over itself for my fabric and garments."

Makers? His harvesters? He had an entire guild under his command. Did most of the Immortal rulers have a guild? A cold sensation of unease washed over me at how casually he claimed possession of an entire group of beings. Maybe he really was no better than the other rulers.

Juneau continued. "I've lived in Itzarriol my entire life. Never needed much of anything and had no reason to leave." He exhaled wearily. "Except that everything is the same here. Every single day. I can't find satisfaction in anything. My *peers* are selfish, dull, and vapid."

Disdain dripped from his voice. The funny thing was, his arrogance was actually… palatable? His vanity was different from the cold cruelty Inkarri radiated. Juneau had an oddly objective view of the other rulers, seeing them for their true selves and not the warped standards they based their cruelties on.

Seeing he had our attention, he continued with a rising voice. "I'm not so old, even if you think I must be. Immortals have children even less frequently than vampires. I'm only three hundred, which makes me one of the younger generations in the ruling caste, you understand. But one thing all the generations have in common is how dreadfully boring we've always been." He shuddered. "Each of the castes in their perfect place? What a laugh. How insipid. Each Immortal, like a shiny, rigid cog in a machine, performing their meaningless duty for society. A society that demands cohesion and efficiency above all else. Bloodlust and cruelty are rewarded in our ranks."

I shivered, hearing his true anger break through.

His eyes hardened as he licked his lips, now practically seething. "Each Immortal wields their own unique skills for their role. We have rulers with their sway and their strategy skills, which allow them to rule over anything they see. We have the harvesters, who help cleanse souls and convert their precious darkness into the energy we use as fuel. Makers, like my dear Charrek, craft magical items with their powers over materials and bring forth magnificent cities from the very ground we stand on."

So the four-armed beings, like Charrek, were Immortal makers who crafted magical objects.

"Wildlings, like Fenru, steward the natural world with their talents for healing wounds and growing food." He sucked in an impassioned breath. "But vampires? Everyone told me vampires were abominations living on the edges of civilization, monsters who preyed on this perfect society. But I've always found you morbidly fascinating."

"How gratifying," Laini said, her voice cutting.

Juneau fell back in his chair for a moment. "I mean it in the best possible way, I assure you."

Our eyes darted to Dorian, whose furrowed brow had eased into conflicted curiosity. I knew what he was thinking, even if he didn't say it. Who *was* this guy?

Our silent speculation was cut short by Fenru's return. She whisked around the table and proudly lowered two plates before Roxy and me, covered in a variety of artfully arranged leafy greens. She stepped back and looked at us expectantly. So did the vampires and Juneau.

Roxy and I exchanged an uneasy look.

We had no way of knowing what these innocent-looking leaves would do to us.

"One bite," Fenru said firmly, sounding eerily like my mother. She had a point. If we found food we could eat in the Immortal Plane, we would be much less dependent on our swiftly dwindling rations. Starting with a small test quantity wasn't a bad idea. Even if it *was* toxic, one bite probably wouldn't kill us. I wouldn't trust the Immortal Plane food before hours had passed with no ill effects, so unfortunately, the rest of the greens had to go uneaten.

"I'll try," I said. No reason for both of us to be out of commission, if I ended up poisoning myself. Since I was already a minor hindrance, with the enforced distance from Dorian, it made sense for me to try instead of Roxy. She nodded stiffly, reluctant to let me take the risk in her stead but acknowledging the need.

I plucked one leaf from the pile, and, trying not to think too hard about what I was doing, chewed and swallowed. It was over now, one way or another. I already felt nauseous, but it was too soon to be the leaf. It was just nerves.

Everyone watching me as if I could drop to the floor in convulsions at any moment just made it worse. I leaned forward and stared at Juneau, willing him to continue.

"Thank you for indulging my chatter," Juneau said, taking the unsubtle hint. "Your timing feels like some strange fate. You see, for the last hundred years or so, I've lived alone. It's allowed me time to study politics and discuss the structure and order of the world with my servants. As a child, I thought everything fell naturally into a hierarchy, but now... society doesn't seem balanced. I've studied everything I could about the vampire wars. Long nights spent by a light in my study, trying to untangle all the political and economic and personal factors that drove the council's decisions."

His face twisted into a stormy scowl. An ice-cold sensation crept over my insides. There was such fury beneath his dramatic appearance, a hunger that searched for knowledge. In some ways, I saw bits of Juneau in myself and even Dorian. But history had taught me to doubt. Could he be trusted?

"I'd wondered what would happen if I ever met a vampire, but I never imagined I'd get the chance. There's been a longstanding policy of killing on sight, after all, and I'm no hunter to go roaming into the wilds of the Restless Desert or the deadly shores of Lake Siron. Now? I seem to have found the best source of information yet. You. Real vampires." The scowl transformed into an eager, almost manic grin. His yellow eyes sparked with life. "And *humans*! What a delight. There wasn't any mention of humans in the history books, other than merely being part of the dark energy supply chain. This is all new." He spread his hands wide and gestured to us all. "I'm sure you can understand why I'm curious."

Did he think he sounded believable? I studied his face, his eyes, his body language, trying to pick up any micro-expressions that might clue me in to his real motives. He appeared genuine, but of course, so did Alan back in the day.

The portraits glared down at us with hardened expressions, as if disgusted to see lowly vampires and humans conferring around their dining table. A ghostly sensation, like a fingernail barely touching my skin, rippled down the back of my neck. There was passion in Juneau—and determination, curiosity—but there was also something *else*. Something more calculating, something sharper, something he kept hidden away behind his bright emotions and gleaming jewels.

What was he not telling us?

CHAPTER SEVEN

"Do we believe him?" Dorian asked.

It was a short while later, and the soul-light outside had faded to a semblance of twilight. We spoke in low tones as we explored the room, checking for anything suspicious or dark. Juneau said he'd had one of his finest guest suites prepared for us. From the silent halls and uncomfortably pristine layout of the room, it didn't seem like Juneau had guests very often.

I studied the stained-glass window, which took up a giant swath of the opposite wall. It depicted a monstrous shelled beast with dozens of sharp arms sitting on a throne with an adoring crowd of equally frightening sea creatures, including massive fish with long, spiny teeth and demented squid-like beasts with a dizzying number of tentacles.

Whoever designed this place clearly had an aquatic obsession.

Juneau had asked if we wanted individual rooms, but we didn't want to be separated. And once we saw how big the place was, we realized it definitely wasn't necessary. The vast lounge area was equipped with over-sized satin-covered couches. Roxy, satisfied with her sweep of the room, hopped up onto one and dangled her feet nearly a foot above the shiny black tiles. Kane sat beside her, and even his generous leg length left his toes hanging several inches off the floor.

"I don't know," Laini said in response to Dorian's question, not bothering to hide her annoyance. She scanned the massive arches bathed in sea-green light. Towering raw pink crystals flanked the doorway, leading up to a high vaulted ceiling that seemed to be a common design feature of Juneau's mansion. "It's frustrating. He's… evenly balanced," she explained to me and Roxy, with a downward twist of her delicate lips. "Light and dark, just about the same, but not enough to make us hungry. It's a state we rarely see, because that much darkness usually deteriorates to even worse darkness. You don't often find someone walking around with perfect balance."

I nodded. "I'm not sure of Juneau's intentions at all. It's hard to get a read on him. He looks harmless, but what possible motivation could he have to help us? Pure curiosity alone doesn't seem likely. There must be something else he hasn't told us about."

"He's definitely holding something back," Kane said, standing on the couch to poke at the ever-present kelp plants that lined the gray stone walls and continued to wave unnervingly back and forth despite there being no hint of wind. "He's trying too hard to appear harmless. That makes me suspicious."

I hummed in agreement as I kept combing the room, eyes peeled for the telltale wavering of a glamor spell. An attached chamber with an arched entrance of the same pink crystal as the doorframe held a massive bed with an army of plush cushions and several intricately woven blankets. All of us could fit on the bed, including keeping Dorian and me far enough away from each other to escape any pain, but we'd immediately decided that three would sleep in the bed while the other two remained on the couches to keep watch. We'd rotate every few hours.

"If he's balanced, then he's not evil?" Roxy ventured, apparently hoping for something more conclusive.

Laini shook her head and huffed. "I wish I could say. He's not *totally* evil is all I can tell you." She glanced at the back of her hand where Juneau had bestowed his welcoming kiss. "Just clueless."

Satisfied for now with my search of the room, I clambered up beside Laini on the couch. As I ran my hand along the fabric beneath me, the silky sensation reminded me of the pure opulence of the rulers, especially Juneau. For someone who had such a critical view of his fellow rulers, he seemed happy enough to remain swaddled in their typical opulence.

"There's nothing dark about the room, either," Dorian said, doing a final lap of the space. "Just an unnecessary number of shiny, expensive things."

"It's a magical McMansion," Roxy said, shaking her head. "Reminds me of a frenemy I had in high school. Her dad's house was just *bursting* with random designer crap. Most of it was probably knockoffs, but man, did she love parading her fancy clothes and bags around school." She snickered. "She called me white trash once, so I stole her new bag and dropped it in the toilet in the second-floor bathroom."

"I don't have context for most of the things in that story," Kane said, "but I commend you for vanquishing your foe."

Roxy raised her hand, and he obediently high-fived her.

Dorian settled down as well, choosing the couch just beneath the stained-glass window.

"You can move a bit closer," I told him. I tapped my chest. "I don't even feel a buzz."

"I can hear just fine from here," he replied smoothly, lips quirking upward.

Kane took out his knife, twirling the blade so that it reflected light from the window. "I wish there was something I could grab onto to actually say this guy was evil. He unnerves me."

"Not a fan of his dramatic attitude?" Roxy asked wryly with a raised brow. "Or are you just jealous of his slick clothes?"

Kane balked. "Hardly. He's a weird guy. A weird guy with a perfect balance, like Laini said. Vampires are great at getting reads on people, but we're not made for the morally ambiguous types."

I leaned forward, placing my elbows on my knees and my chin in my hands. "Well, morality can be relative. Whoever this Juneau is, he doesn't seem hostile toward us. From the almost gleeful way he talked about his family being dead and his little speech at the end there, I doubt he cares much for his fellow rulers. At the moment, I would call that a win." Inkarri's cruel face flashed through my mind. "The hunters were so quick to find the safehouse, I really don't want to think about what they did to Kono to get him to talk. I just hope the Hive doesn't think we tipped the hunters off somehow."

"How could we have tipped them off?" Kane argued. "They caught him before we even reached the city, and they got to the safehouse before us."

"True, but the Hive won't necessarily know that," I said, almost wincing. I hated the idea that our only allies in the Immortal Plane would think we had somehow compromised their safehouse.

Laini exhaled slowly. "Not the best turn of events," she admitted. Her mouth twisted into a scowl, the anger startling on her pretty, heart-shaped face. "Things could be worse, I guess. I just wish we knew for certain that Juneau doesn't have a plan developing in the shadows. Rulers will do anything to bump up their social status. He could be faking his disdain for the system and be planning to sell us all off to Irrikus."

Laini was really beginning to worry me. In the facility, when the other vampires had frozen me out, she had been the one to smile. She'd made a point of saying goodbye and being kind to me even against the wishes of the majority. She'd always been strong and soft, and I'd admired her for walking that fine line with ease and grace. This hardness was new, and I wasn't quite sure what to think of it.

"He could be using magic to trick us," Kane said in a warning tone. "None of us would be able to sense that." He sheathed the knife. "Maybe we should make a break for it while we have the chance. Find a hovel in the city with some wildlings who aren't dark."

Dorian sat mulling something over as he stroked his sharp face. "This could be a good opportunity," he said slowly, looking up at us, his glacial eyes touched with the ghost of hope. "If we can ally with someone from the ruling caste, it would be the best way to find information. It's a chance we can't afford to waste. We need to get *some* kind of information, after everything we've done to get here. We can't let this mission be for nothing."

"You think it's worth the risk?" I asked. I wasn't sure about that myself, but I wanted to hear him out. He had played it neutral with Juneau throughout that conversation, so I couldn't tell what he actually thought about the situation.

He met my gaze. "If it means getting closer to the Immortal Council, yes. We should try to glean everything we can from Juneau, try to learn what makes him tick, what interests him, so we can give him the stories that will please him the most."

I nodded. "We need to take advantage of his hospitality to keep ourselves at full strength, too. Let's charm Juneau and humor him in the meantime. Best-case scenario, he ends up being legit, and we've made a solid ally. Worst case? He takes us to Irrikus, but we'll be ready to take advantage of his betrayal."

"I'm happy to do some snooping," Laini said. "Something about this house is too perfect. Let's see if he has any skeletons in the walls."

"Literal or figurative ones?" Kane asked.

Laini shrugged. "I wouldn't be surprised to find both. For all we know, he could have walled up his family in another of these lovely suites to starve to death."

Her face was calm as she spoke. Did she really think Juneau had done that? I'd speculated myself, but after spending time with him, I couldn't see anything to support that conjecture. It was hard to put my finger on whether Laini was truly mad at Juneau or merely furious at all rulers. Her behavior had felt particularly pointed since we arrived.

And if his family *had* been like most rulers, I couldn't even blame him for wanting them dead. I shuddered at the thought of the portraits in the dining room. He'd grown up with those people.

"Let's just stick to maybe trying to find these books he said he studied that talked about the vampire wars. If they were written by rulers, it could give us the names of some key players. If they were written by vampires, it could give us insight into what was going on behind the scenes in the government in Vanim. At least we'd have the same knowledge that Juneau has."

"Agreed," Dorian said. "We won't let our guard down, though. We'll sleep in shifts. Tonight, Kane and I can take the first watch, then Lyra and Roxy. Laini can take the last one. Everyone should try to rest up."

Roxy smacked her hands together and rubbed them gleefully. "Fantastic. I'm going to try out that tub in the connecting bathroom. I'm aching in places I didn't know could ache."

I knew the tub she meant. It was an in-floor basin crafted from a pink shell the size of a small swimming pool. It was big enough to fit eight people comfortably. The water bubbled with steam and had a pleasant herbal scent I could smell from here, calling with the promise of relaxation. As Roxy bounded off, already pulling off her jacket and hopping to yank off one of her boots, Kane's face went entirely still, and his shoulders stiffened. He deliberately looked out the window in the other direction. *Interesting.*

What did he think about Roxy? I tried to look at her in a different light, to see her through Kane's eyes. Her hard-won muscles had sculpted her body into something powerful and beautiful. The flash of her red hair as she disappeared around the corner was as eye-catching as a streak of lightning across the sky. I could see how a guy like Kane, who loved sparring and trash talking, might find himself looking at Roxy without even realizing he was doing it. She had a certain effect on people. Brash at first, but when people finally got to know her, it was like seeing the magnificence of a powerful fire up close. She navigated through life with a grin full of dark humor and a fierce loyalty to those she liked.

Dorian let out a laugh as Roxy's other boot flew out of the bathroom and rolled to a stop. "Okay. Ladies can take the springs. Kane and I will stay in the sitting room. We'll begin searching the house and learning more about our host tomorrow."

I hoped Juneau would leave the house at some point. He was technically a businessman, so maybe there would be something for him to do tomorrow. If not, some of us would have to distract him while others feigned weariness or illness in order to comb through the many rooms.

In the bathroom, I heard Roxy groan with delight as she entered the pool. I snickered to myself over her comically exaggerated happiness. It was the small things in life that mattered when you mounted a dangerous supernatural mission. As contentious as our situation was, my muscles also ached for the warm waters. It made sense to take advantage of the situation while we could.

Laini and I left Kane and Dorian to keep watch, and the two men fell into low, tense chatter.

Even without the pain to give me a clue, I felt Dorian's eyes on my back every step of the way to the bathroom. For a brief moment, I wished he was joining me instead of my female teammates, but I pushed the desire aside.

Time and place.

For now, I looked forward to finally resting my battered body—even just briefly—in this fragile oasis of peace we had found amid so much danger.

At breakfast, Juneau presented us with a stack of pancakes from his wildling chef Fenru. Despite their rather alarming dark green color, they appeared to be the real deal. I had to stop myself from drooling over the delightful smell. My stomach was thrilled to eat something that wasn't military rations. I hadn't been poisoned by the leafy greens I'd nibbled on during the awkward dinner the night before, so it seemed humans could eat some Immortal Plane food.

I took a cautious bite. The taste was slightly musty, like truffles, but they had the consistency of homemade pancakes. How had the wildling managed to conjure up something like this? My best guess was magic.

"I must work on designs today, at my workshop," Juneau announced. He ate nothing, only sipping from a tall, intricate golden beaker. "Feel free to make yourselves at home. I trust you enjoyed the thermal spring water?"

Roxy nodded approvingly, her mouth full. Her post-bath hair had dried to a softer texture than I was used to seeing, but the red locks curled in all directions. It gave her a wild appearance, but there was something beautiful in the combination with her fresh face and obvious delight.

"Well, I'm glad to hear it," Juneau said. "I hope your day is a restful one. I'm looking forward to learning more about human things when I return." He gave a small formal bow and left us, the ends of his shiny robes brushing the floor as he disappeared through the door.

We waited until his footsteps disappeared, followed by the sound of the large front doors opening and closing. Still we waited, all of us immediately slipping into a sharp, attentive mode of single-minded focus. We heard the carriage pull up, then leave, the metal wheels rattling on the stone courtyard. The external gates slammed shut, and there was finally silence.

"Time to get to work," Dorian said, eyeing the door. "The servants seem to keep to themselves, but keep an eye out for them. They'll definitely report back to Juneau. And don't go outside. It leaves us vulnerable to being spotted by skimmers or nosy neighbors."

I washed down my breakfast with a glass of water that had an underlying taste of honey, then stealthily followed my team into the hallway. A nervous flutter of butterflies disturbed my stomach. Most of my infiltration missions had involved knowing the layout of the building beforehand, but Juneau's mansion was a pure mystery. Adrenaline pumped through me as I scanned the hall. No signs of servants.

"Make sure to check your perimeter," Kane said. "I can't sense wildlings or any other creatures, so keep your wits about you."

If we wanted to know about the mysterious group of Immortal rulers and their role in trying to destroy vampires, I had a laundry list of things already in mind. We would need to acquire more knowledge about the identities of the ruling caste and how they operated. I was also interested in learning how they saw themselves, which could help us predict their next steps. I knew well enough what the vampires thought of them, but I hoped we could find something that revealed the rulers' perspective. Anything about the war would be paramount.

And of course, we would need to make sure the man who fed and took care of us was someone to be trusted. At the moment, we just didn't have enough facts to form an opinion.

"Look for anything about the ruling caste, the war, and Juneau," I suggested. "Maybe books, or anything that looks like it was designed by vampires and not Immortals. Juneau seems obsessed enough to have some kind of collection or library dedicated to the subject."

"Agreed," Dorian said. "This place is massive, so stay in pairs. A vampire to keep a lookout for dark energy and servant's auras, and a human to search through things. If someone catches you, I imagine Juneau will be more forgiving of his favorite houseguests." His mouth quirked wryly. "I'll take a solo perimeter investigation. If a servant catches you, play dumb. Like you're both lost." He paused, a weight suddenly settling onto his shoulders. "And if they don't believe you, use as much force as necessary to keep them from reporting you. Convince them, threaten them, restrain them. If we do get caught, we will have to take whatever evidence we can find and try to get Juneau to see reason. If he doesn't, we make a run for it."

We all nodded soberly. All at once, I was incredibly aware of the knives in my boots. I hoped I wouldn't have to use them.

Roxy shot him a grim thumbs-up. "Got it. Good luck, everybody."

We dispersed. Laini and I took the western side of the house. Kane accompanied Roxy. I walked with Laini down the long hallway that led to the west wing of the mansion, until we reached a point where the hallway forked in three different directions.

Laini shifted on her feet. "We'll start with the left, then take the right. I feel good about ending with the center. You search the rooms while I keep watch outside."

"Sounds good," I said and saluted her.

We slunk into the left hallway, which took an interesting turn. Not literally, but aesthetically. It was a straight path, but the blue-green shades suddenly took on a dull red tone. The tiles turned violet and shimmered as we stepped over them, our footfalls echoing eerily.

Gone were the mosaics. Instead, the steely eyes of family portraits returned. I stopped for a moment to take in the sheer number of them.

How far back did Juneau's family go? His line of ancestors stared boldly out at me. Here, they were mainly women. Their lips curled in arrogant disdain as they watched me, silvery hair coiled around their sharp faces.

"All these eyes are unnerving," Laini admitted. I nodded agreement.

I stopped at one. A woman, painfully beautiful, had her shoulders thrown back, her chin tilted up as if daring anyone to defy her. Juneau's family was blessed with excellent and *creepy* genetics. Odd, how he managed to come off as likeable while his other family members appeared to have lived for the sole purpose of terrifying small children.

We walked for what could have been hours. I stopped in any open room. I searched drawers and cupboards, stood on chairs to peer behind paintings, tapped at bare patches of wall to listen for hollow spaces. I admired the smooth edges of a doorframe made from coral. I crawled all around the base of a statue of a giant squid with horns, carefully climbing onto it to test for levers. Any books I found, I flipped through. Most were meaningless—bland romances and nonfiction studies of plants and economic reports of guild management, all written in the universal tongue. I shook my head at Laini again as we finally made our way to the last few rooms.

There were three doors left. I checked the left first. It appeared to have been some sort of music room, but I recognized none of the instruments, all of them large and contorted. I carefully went to move one to search behind it, but then I caught the sheen of its pearly surface in the light. It was bone. I left the room quickly.

"Bone instruments," I said, by way of explanation.

Laini grimaced. "Lovely."

The next room was boring. It was empty, save for a forgotten fainting couch covered in the same satin from our guest suite. My search was perfunctory, checking the walls and floors for hidden spaces.

Returning to the hall, I was struck by how the tone of the décor differed from the energy of our host. Juneau favored bright fabrics, but he lived like a gloomy merman in this place obviously decorated in the past by someone in his family.

We approached the last door. This was the only room in the hall that had a closed door. I looked back, and the hallway stretched back behind me, appearing much longer than I'd initially thought. A bone-chilling shudder rocketed through me as the door creaked open loudly, protesting my entrance. Laini winced and paused to listen, then nodded, encouraging me forward. No one was coming.

I pushed open the door.

The room was large like the others, containing only a few plush chairs and an ugly rug, the floors made of a pale red hardwood. A disappointed sigh left my lips. I stepped into the center of the room, completing a visual search before I began searching in earnest.

Laini posted herself at the door, her back turned to me.

Suddenly, Dorian's stone began to heat, the warmth increasing as I stepped into the center of the rug decorated with a pattern of overlapping swirls and diamonds. It hurt to look at the design.

Pulling out the pouch holding the stone, I stepped aside, stooping down to pull up the nearest edge of the rug. It went easily. My eyes scanned the boards made from old and deep-grained red wood. Laini glanced over her shoulder as I yanked up the rug and rolled it back, letting it land in a dusty heap.

"You found something?" she asked, her gaze flicking between me and the hallway.

"Maybe. Might be nothing."

The stone began to glow as I dropped down and placed it closer to the floorboards in the center. I crawled back, and the glow began to wane, so I moved forward once again. The stone warmed as I hovered over a particular area. I hissed, dropping the rock as the heat emanating from it became too much. The stone struck the planks, and a perfect square door abruptly emerged from the ground. At one end was a wrought-iron handle that sat in a depression in the wood. The stone stopped glowing. I pocketed it, marveling over the trapdoor.

"Laini!" I whispered excitedly, praying the servants were far away.

She quickly glanced down the hall and ducked inside to join me. "I don't see anyone around." Glancing down, she saw the trapdoor. "Oh, this is definitely something. Good job."

"It's heavy," I muttered, grasping the ring and pulling, trying to pry open the door.

Laini dropped beside me. "Here, let me."

With a soft grunt of effort, she pulled on the door. It sprang upward, and a wave of cold, dusty air hit our faces. We turned to look at each other. Below the door, a set of stone steps descended to a lower chamber.

"I'll go down first," she whispered. "You stay here. If there's something down there—" She didn't finish the sentence, but I caught her meaning. Her strength would be a better match to any monster that might be lying in wait. I had to laugh at that. I'd been training to be a soldier all my life, and she'd been an *architect*.

A moment passed while Laini stepped down into the dim light. The staircase was short from what I could see, but the steps were larger. That made sense considering it was built for rulers, and so would be designed to accommodate someone with a much longer stride.

I held out the stone, reassessing its plain appearance now that I had some definitive evidence that it was more than just a piece of rock. The harvester had said that the stone was like him, which I now suspected meant that the stone processed dark energy. But harvesters imbued it into objects. What did the stone do with all of the energy it had absorbed? I glanced down into the darkness that had temporarily swallowed Laini, wondering if she knew about the stone—if she knew *I* had the stone. Did she even know that Lanzon had given it to Dorian? My view of this little shard changed once again. How would Laini feel if she knew I had one of her dead husband's only remaining possessions, and that Dorian had given it to me the day we met?

"Nobody is down here from what I can tell," Laini whispered. "Come down."

I replaced the stone in its pouch. Now was hardly the time to explore such a sensitive, emotional topic. *Later*, I promised myself. I headed down into the hidden room, feeling my way with my free hand, allowing myself a moment of giddy excitement. We were exploring a secret room hidden by an invisible trapdoor, after all—this was what adventures were made of.

There was no railing for the stairs, only a cold cobblestone wall far plainer in design than the rest of the house. It looked like a medieval dungeon. I reached the bottom of the stairs but kept close to the staircase. The room itself was cramped and cluttered, stuffed to the brim with all sorts of intriguing items on battered wooden shelves, but these things were far from the shiny baubles I would expect Juneau to treasure.

My eyes found worn, leathery parchments and rolled-up maps. Shelves of old books held an impressive coat of dust. Ancient weapons, half-burned portraits, a box of tarnished jewelry with all the precious gems removed from their settings. Tattered clothing, jars filled with broken glass, and in the center of it all, a sagging, stuffed chair and desk with a soul-light lantern standing on top of it. Laini waved me farther into the room, and I gladly followed, my curiosity burning.

"Looks like Juneau is more than just a casual collector," I mumbled.

Laini nodded silently beside me, delicately pawing through the book-shelves.

"Texts on ancient magic," she confirmed. "Runes, various Immortal languages, vampires." The last word left her mouth in a hoarse tone. Her elegant hands plucked a battered volume from the shelf.

"He has texts on vampires?"

She flipped through the book with careful fingers. "Definitely. Looks like he wasn't lying about his obsession with us." Her eyes widened.

"What?"

"This book is very, *very* old," she told me. Her eyesight allowed her much better vision. Even with the lantern, I could barely make out the thin scrawl in the book, and even then, it wasn't in a language I could comprehend. "It's an older version of the universal language. I think I can figure it out."

I peered over her shoulder as she squinted at the page.

"It seems to be a journal? Listen to this. 'Half-Cycle in the Year of Shadow. We have called a council meeting and seen representatives from every caste. From all over the land, I saw witness to the rulers, makers, harvesters, wildlings, cleansers.'" She stopped abruptly.

"Cleansers?" I echoed. It suggested advertisements for glass cleaners promising shiny windows. Or Vonn's cryptic, messiah-like sermon about vampires cleansing souls.

"I don't understand it either," Laini muttered, shaking her head. She kept reading. "'The Council has chosen young Irrikus to join our ranks. His enthusiasm is heartening, but I worry that a cruelty grows within his heart. A coldness, unlike the rest of we rulers. My comrades tell me I'm a fool to worry, and there are other matters to attend to. I have received word that Althinia may have finally located the creature who made the standing stones.' Wait, something made the standing stones?" She stared, hypnotized by the pages.

I leaned over her shoulder. Tiny diagrams of the standing stone circles had been scrawled inside the yellowing pages. I could understand that much. "Keep going."

"'Another day has presented a challenge with this news. The creature exists outside of any knowledge that I have gathered among the castes. Those rare few who have seen him said we will know him by his shifting form and his treachery. The council met today to discuss what to do with such a creature. I suggested we gain its favor, but there are those who would like to take more strenuous measures.'"

A cold chill ran from my heels to the top of my head. What was the journal talking about? There was a creature that had somehow *made* the portals that allowed the vampires to move easily between the planes, but was apparently treacherous? Was it truly dangerous, or did it only oppose the Immortals that were written about in this journal? Most importantly, if this creature was able to manipulate the barrier enough to create portals—if it or others like it were still alive and the council had influenced them with "more strenuous measures"—could they have something to do with the tear? My heart thumped wildly against my ribs.

Laini's violet eyes found mine just before she jolted suddenly and shoved the book back in its place. "Someone's coming."

She practically dragged me up the stairs, using her vampiric speed to move us both faster than I possibly could have alone. My arm aching from where she'd pulled me, I flipped the trapdoor down as silently as possible. Scattering dust everywhere, Laini threw the rug over it. We scrambled to standing positions, trying not to appear flustered.

Before the haze in the air had the chance to settle, Charrek dragged himself into the room. A deep-set scowl settled on his metallic face as his shadowy eyes fell onto the rumpled carpet beneath us.

"My master will not be happy to know you have invaded his privacy like this," he said in a dark voice that teemed with an ominous warning. "You should not have been so foolish as to pry."

CHAPTER EIGHT

A chill crawled up the back of my neck, but I forced myself to appear calm. I stared at Charrek and his glinting, displeased features, seeing sharp intelligence in his eyes. It wasn't just the dust on our clothes or the fact that the rug was slightly off center that had tipped him off. There was something more concrete.

Dorian's recommendation to hurt anyone who threatened us played over and over in my mind as Charrek's eyes hardened. Hurting Charrek would be our last resort. Even when Dorian said it, I knew he'd want us to try everything else first.

His smaller pair of arms that had, until now, been crossed over his chest, unfurled. The fingers were incredibly long and dexterous, with twice as many joints as regular human phalanges. One digit pointed at the untidy rug beneath us. "How did you break the concealment glamor?"

"Concealment for what? I don't know what you're talking about," Laini said, feigned innocence in her voice. She faltered a moment, her eyes cutting to me. What did he mean by glamor? "I'm a vampire. I couldn't have done anything."

He studied us closely. "That spell was my own work. It's been completely neutralized."

Dorian's stone sat like a smoking gun in my pouch. It must have neutralized the maker's magic, and, earlier, Inkarri's gauntlet when she'd tried to kill me at the battle near Lake Siron. I'd had no idea what kind of power I'd apparently been carrying around.

Laini exhaled, dread radiating from her. I noticed her subtly adjust her stance to prepare for action. Dorian's instructions were obviously on her mind, as well.

But Charrek wasn't looking at her anymore. Instead, he narrowed his eyes at me. "What the vampire says is true. They cannot do magic. Which must mean it was you." He paused. "I was unaware that humans could do magic."

"I can't," I protested firmly. "There is no magic in the Mortal Plane. How could I disable something I know nothing about?" I didn't want to hurt Charrek—he was only doing his job—but we couldn't risk him reporting back to Juneau. Could we talk him out of it?

Charrek was unconvinced. Beside me, Laini took a careful step forward. "Charrek, please. Can you redo it?" she asked in a softer voice. Her violet eyes were pleading. "Please cover it for us. You have no idea what's at stake for us. I can't allow Juneau to know."

He slowly moved his gaze to her. "And you do not understand the shifting shadows of Itzarriol. It is not a place to make assumptions or plead for bargains." His grim warning carried throughout the room. "I won't cover it for you."

Laini sucked in a long, deep breath. She opened her arms wide. "Please, Charrek. We were only doing what we needed to do. We mean no physical harm to Juneau. We are in a life-or-death situation that I can't explain to you."

I wished we could tell him everything, but Laini was right. We had to be vague about why we had actually come to Itzarriol. If Charrek told Juneau and Juneau had any secret loyalty to Irrikus, our mission would be ruined.

"I can comprehend being in a difficult situation," Charrek said flatly, and I got the sense he was referring to something far beyond his experience in Juneau's household. "But you've trespassed here, after Juneau saved you from a certain trip to the sanitarium."

My palms began to sweat. Something tilted inside Laini again. I'd noticed it since we started our journey to the capital, but the way she held herself shifted. There was a vein of anger bubbling beneath her usually kind exterior. Had she been fighting inside herself this entire time? Her face twitched as though she were trying to make a difficult decision.

"We understand," I said, "and we are grateful. But please, let us tell Juneau about it in our own time. There are many things we need to discuss with our team."

Charrek sighed through his nostrils. They flared and colored the edges of his broad nose a bright red. His lips slipped into a lopsided line of resignation.

"I serve Juneau. I don't serve you," he said firmly. "You have made your decision. You cannot take it back."

Laini suddenly snapped and leapt forward in a blur. She wrapped her hand around the maker's throat and pushed him against the wall, effectively pinning him against the luxurious stone. He was only two-thirds her size, though his extra limbs made him look larger. The force caused the wall to shake, a thin layer of plaster falling from the ceiling. Some fell onto Charrek's metallic-looking shoulders.

I stiffened a moment, staring at her hand around Charrek's neck. She shuddered violently, and her eyes darkened.

"We have made our decisions because this city has taken everything from us."

Charrek didn't try to fight back. He merely lifted a hand. "I cannot make amends for what has been done to you," he said softly. "I will fight you if I must, but I suspect neither of us wants that." Charrek remained the opposite of Juneau. Where his guild master was flamboyant and dramatic, Charrek had all the calm and strength and composure of granite.

Her fingers around his throat were not enough to choke him, but they were enough to threaten. Enough to let him know that she meant it. I swallowed the grit in my throat. We had crossed a line, and there was no going back. God, I'd never wanted this. Looking into Charrek's stoic eyes sent a wave of shame over me. That line… I hadn't been prepared to cross it. Something in my gut turned. Charrek was far from the likes of Inkarri or the hunters.

"I'm not your enemy," he said, unwilling to drop his gaze from Laini's. "But I take my duties seriously. You have asked me to understand you, and now I ask you to understand this about me."

"Why are you so devoted to him? He's a ruler." She bared her fangs. Anger bloomed in her face, splotches of darkness swelling on her cheeks. Rulers had indeed taken everything from Laini, and she apparently couldn't comprehend Charrek's behavior. Honestly, neither could I.

"He treats you like property," I breathed. "He was telling us about *his* makers and *his* harvesters. What does he do to you to keep you here?" The notion of forced servitude was a stain on human history, as I was more than familiar with in my own country. It made my blood boil to see it here, alive and well in the Immortal Plane.

Charrek's eyes closed briefly, and he shook his head, muttering something incomprehensible under his breath. Light footsteps fell in the corridor, and a moment later the rest of our team entered the room. A dull buzz began in my chest.

"What's going on?" Dorian asked. Seeing me in the center of the room, he stayed in the doorway.

"Lovely," Kane muttered. "We've got the damn maker in a vise grip."

"We found a trapdoor that leads to a secret underground chamber," I explained quickly. "Charrek found us, and we're… trying to convince him not to tell Juneau."

Laini glanced at our comrades with the barest hint of a nod. The anger drained from her face slightly, as if the arrival of our friends had grounded her somewhat, but she didn't release the maker's thick neck.

"Did you find dead bodies of past guests?" Roxy asked. "Vampire prisoners?"

"No. There were plenty of books and weird old objects, though," I replied, studying Charrek's face. A flicker of his eyes could tell me if Laini and I had discovered something important. "Plenty of sources on vampires. Pretty sure it's Juneau's secret library."

Roxy's excited face deflated a little. "Well, that's no surprise. He already told us he had loads of books on vampires."

She was right. It wasn't a treasure trove or a smoking gun.

"I'm not entirely sure he obtained these books legally, though. You don't keep books like that in a secret chamber unless they shouldn't be found," Laini said. "And I'm absolutely certain the Immortal Council wouldn't be too happy to know he has them. Who else would he be hiding them from?"

Something unshuttered in Charrek's expression for a moment, and I saw the fear there. Not fear of us, but fear of the council. Almost immediately, the emotion disappeared.

"We've asked him to restore the magical barrier we unknowingly breached," Laini said. I wasn't sure if she'd seen the crack in his mask.

"What's the problem?" Kane asked. His gruff tone softened. "Can't you do it, maker?"

"I can," Charrek said, his voice bland. "But I won't."

Laini let him go with a growl of frustration. Three vampires were enough of a threat. He rubbed his neck, sighing. "You can try all you want to convince me. You won't manage it."

Laini sucked in a sharp breath. "Why?" Her voice was more sympathetic than before but carried a bitter edge. "You can tell us if you're being threatened. Are you under spells to guarantee your cooperation? Are you forced to do this? It's not worth us having to hurt you."

Charrek looked her straight in the eyes. "You can do your worst, but you'll just prove what the rulers say about your kind." He paused as Laini dropped her gaze for a moment. "It's true that rulers can be cruel. Most servants I know live in humiliating conditions. *I* lived in terrible conditions before his family passed away. Juneau is one of the few rulers that treats his guild members and servants like people. I like him, truly. He is a rarity among his kind." His gaze drifted around the cold, empty room. "Juneau is many things, and lonely is at the top of the list. He has never been understood, even in his youth. He has deep flaws, but a murky past doesn't make one irredeemable in life. The cruelties he experienced when he was young have made him into the man you see today, a ruler who detests the others in his caste." He spoke genuinely.

"You must understand why we're suspicious of his hidden room?" I asked.

He cocked his head minutely, his curved horns catching the light. "I'm sure you are all keeping secrets of your own. We all have things we are afraid of losing."

My shoulders loosened as I considered his words. That made perfect sense. The guy had a secret room full of old vampire books and what were probably illegal artifacts.

Dorian, Kane, and Laini loomed around Charrek. They exchanged glances, working out what to do with the Immortal maker. Charrek looked calmly ahead. He was stoic and loyal—a dangerous combination.

Dorian's glacial eyes swept over Charrek's throat. The pressure of Laini's grip had left behind a peach-colored bruise.

"If you intend to harm Juneau," Charrek said abruptly, "I will be forced to interfere on my master's behalf. Even though I'm no match for all of you, I will not bow to your threats."

I tried to defuse the rising tension. He had already been victimized. Who were we to add to that? "We truly don't want to hurt you—"

From somewhere in the mansion's sprawl, I heard the massive front door slam shut. Dorian gave a low growl, and his fangs peeked out from his mouth.

"There are dark presences," he snapped. "More than usual."

We could hide. But what would we do with Charrek? Laini wrapped her hand around one of Charrek's horns, holding him in place as the voices grew louder.

In the echoing halls, Juneau's voice reached us easily. Odd. He always spoke loudly and dramatically, but now his voice carried with powerful strength.

The maker stiffened. "He has activated the communication system that goes through the house. That never happens. He wants us to know someone is here. Something's wrong."

Another voice joined Juneau's. My bones chilled as Inkarri's awful tone wafted through the air with all its arrogance and evil. I froze. Had Juneau betrayed us after all? I balled my hands into fists, cursing the fact that I only had my knives on me. I hadn't thought to bring my gun along, not that it could match Inkarri's terrible strength. Our packs were still in the guest suite, and we'd left them out in the open. Damn it.

"Charrek, we have guests," Juneau called. "Could you tell the cook to make us some bleeding-heart tea? Thank you." He dragged out the last word, a phantom's call in the cavernous halls.

Charrek impatiently brushed Laini's hand away, raising both sets of arms in surrender, his expression suddenly desperate. "The tea. That's the sign," he whispered hoarsely. He caught my panicked look. "He has not sold you out to the hunters, I swear. We are being raided. Let me go, and I'll hide you in the storage room again. Or you can take your chances with Inkarri and her hunters. Your choice."

Dorian scowled, tapping his foot fervently. He glanced at me and then Laini. I could see his dilemma. If we hurt Charrek, then he would never redo the glamor over the hidden chamber, even if we dragged him inside to hide with us. If we tried to run for it now, Inkarri would track us down. If we allowed Charrek to do what he wanted, he might remain true to his word.

It was better to trust him, even if it meant putting our lives in his hands. The other options were even worse.

CHAPTER NINE

"Our host has been nothing but hospitable thus far," Dorian said
evenly. He rubbed his chin in thought, eyeing Charrek. "I think we
should trust him."

My gut said the same.

"I would rather take my chances with Juneau than Inkarri," I said.

Kane nodded, and so did Laini. She stepped aside. Charrek scampered
to the rug and flung it back with surprising speed, pulling up the trapdoor with one of his powerful arms and waving us over with his smaller,
more dexterous pair.

"Inside," he urged. We clambered down the stone steps and into the
basement. Roxy was the last inside. I kept close to the staircase, trying to
avoid Dorian, who went as far back into the room as he could. My chest
buzzed lightly with pain, but it was manageable. The trapdoor above us
shut, and an amber glow outlined the square door for a moment as
Charrek presumably reset the concealment spell. We were left with only
the dim illumination of the soul-light lantern. I crept up to the top step,
feeling my way among the cold stones. Behind me, I heard my team
shuffle into hiding spots.

I pressed my ear against the trapdoor, ensuring I kept the pouch around my neck that held the stone well away from the door. The vampires had superior hearing, but I wanted to listen for signs of trouble myself. Though right now all I could hear was the thrum of my pulse rushing in my ear. Would Charrek and Juneau betray us?

Somewhere, Roxy exhaled. "Can you hear through the door, Lyra?" she whispered.

"I can't tell," I muttered. "I don't hear anything right now."

"Should we prepare for a fight?" Kane's whisper was no louder than Roxy's.

"I'd love another round with that blue-haired harpy," Roxy murmured, her voice steely. She might have been remembering what the hunter had done to Bryce and the pain on his face when we'd had to leave him behind. Fighting Inkarri again wouldn't be wise, but the thought was tempting.

"Search for any weapons we might be able to use if we need to," Dorian muttered.

I heard the sound of books moving as I kept my ear to the door. I hoped we wouldn't regret our split-second decision. At least it was better than trying to sneak past the hunters and run out into the uncertainty of the city. We would have been easy targets in a sea of rulers and their servants. They would have vied to see who could turn us in to the hunters the fastest.

"There are some old swords," Laini whispered. "Though they'd probably break on Inkarri's armor. Whatever he's collecting, it's obviously for historical value and not practical use."

"I'll stick to my knife," Kane said. "Most of this is junk."

Metal scraped against something on the other side of the room, and I winced.

"The side of a crate just broke," Roxy said, almost inaudibly. "Does that mean he's not keeping this stuff in good condition?"

Kane sniffed several times as if scenting something. "The blood wasn't even cleaned off that blade."

Delightful.

Laini inhaled sharply. "They're coming. Quiet."

We hushed. Footsteps approached. Not just boots on the ground, but hooves—Inkarri had brought her magicked velek. Instinctively, I pressed myself flat on the steps, moving away from the door as the footsteps neared. They sounded as if they were in the hall.

"Oh, you simply must try some of this tea while you're here, Inkarri. Charrek makes the best brew in the city. Did you know that the bleeding heart has been demonstrated to increase relaxation?"

Inkarri grumbled something incomprehensible. Her voice lifted louder. "Addressing your servants by name will only make them act out, Juneau. You're a soft-hearted fool."

"Soft-hearted, perhaps," Juneau replied vaguely in a chipper tone. I could practically see the tight smile on his handsome face, his silver hair fanning around him. "Oh, you'll like this room. It was one of my dear old mother's favorites. Of course, Grandfather added the lovely squid mural —which everyone else detested, by the way—when he got into his obsessive underwater-themed remodel. The rest of the family thought squids were already overused, and I thought the entire thing was too much, but nobody asks a young boy, do they? Grandfather just locked me in a closet any time the makers came around to change something, so I wouldn't get underfoot. Sometimes they left me there for days, and I wouldn't see anyone but Charrek when he brought food. I grew to look forward to the maker's visits."

"Hm," Inkarri growled. "A charming story. Such a shame what happened to your family—from what few rumors I've heard, anyway." A snide tone slipped into her question. "What *did* happen to your family, Juneau? I can't imagine it was too terrible, since you've been able to stay in this luxurious mansion and estate and not be driven *mad* by the memories."

Juneau laughed, but it had a brittle edge to it. "Oh no, it is a truly ghastly tale. One you'd like, because it's full of absolute dread, but I don't have the strength for it today. Perhaps another time," he said. "We could discuss it over cakes in the dining room next week. My chef, Fenru, can create such delicacies that will make even you weep."

Someone smashed their foot down on the planks only inches from my head, and I flinched. It sent a tremor through the floor, shaking the door slightly. But the hardwood held firm, and somehow the step hadn't sounded hollow. Was that part of Charrek's magic? Hooves tapped back and forth overhead, growing louder and softer as the blasted velek investigated the room. God, I would be happy if I never saw another one of those things.

"Stop the simpering, Juneau," Inkarri snapped. "My velek brought us to this room, and my team will search every inch of it." Immediately, a chain reaction of footsteps sounded. She had brought reinforcements with her. The velek crossed overhead. Every stomp of its hoof felt like a knife in my heart. I held my breath as the creature sniffed and snuffed on the rug.

"Pull up the carpet," someone said. I thought I recognized the voice of the hunter with the long red-and-black braids.

Someone drew the fabric back, and I sank away from the door, retreating to where Roxy stood lower down on the stairs. She grasped my upper arm in one hand as a sign of solidarity. From behind us, light metallic sounds skittered through the quiet. Someone, I suspected Kane, had drawn his knife. I stilled, my hand around the handle of the knife in my boot, preparing myself for action.

The shuffling of hooves grew louder as the velek smelled the floor. Would Charrek's spell cover our scent?

Something dragged on the planks, and Charrek's calm voice rang out. "Can I interest you in some—"

"Get out of the way," Inkarri bellowed, the suddenness of it making me flinch even below the floor. "Tell your servant to mind his manners and know his place."

"He's not in your way. He's merely standing by with the tea I requested," Juneau said icily. "I am aware that you don't like *me* for some reason, but while you are under my roof, you and your companions will treat my staff with a modicum of respect. My servants are an extension of myself."

No wonder he felt lonely amid the other Immortal rulers. If treating other castes with respect was unusual among the rulers, I loathed to think what else they counted as strange.

"I will treat the lower castes however I please, wherever I please," Inkarri retorted.

"An interesting attitude, since without harvesters and makers your lovely magicked armor would be nothing more than scrap metal weighing you down," Juneau replied mildly. "If Lady Ernten's incredible maker hadn't riddled those big clunky boots of yours with spells, I doubt you'd even be able to walk. If you find the rules of my home too difficult to abide by, I will invite you to leave."

"How dare you." The timbre of Inkarri's voice shook dust from the ceiling above us. My eyes watered, and I tried not to sneeze. "This is one of the many reasons you are so often belittled in the upper circles of society, Juneau. And you know *exactly* why I don't like you. You're lucky it's my job to track down vampires and not punish petty rule-breakers. But mark my words, Juneau—your days of scheming and skipping around the law are numbered. You should get ready to beg for mercy before Irrikus and the Immortal courts, instead of running your mouth at hunters who are worth a hundred of you."

Someone stepped toward her. The velek stopped sniffing.

"You've got nothing on me. Nobody does," Juneau hissed. The venomous anger in his statement turned my blood cold. It was so far from the warm temperament he had presented to us, and the detached, snide politeness he'd used so far in conversation. Something about it made me wonder if he really was capable of killing his own family.

"If you want to scrub those floor planks after your velek has gotten its putrid snot all over them, I'll provide you with a rag," he continued, his tone still cutting. "Otherwise, take your pets and get out. You're not welcome here." When no one moved, he added acidly, "Regardless of what you think about it, I am still of the ruling caste. Irrikus will not be pleased if he finds out you've taken to overstepping your authority."

"Be glad that the most interesting thing about you is your dead parents' wealth," Inkarri said, sneering, "or I'd be advising you to sleep with one eye open. As it is, perhaps be careful not to send your makers out into the city alone. The city can be dangerous for the lower castes." With that final ominous threat, multiple pairs of feet thumped away from the trapdoor's location. Gradually, the footsteps neared the doorway, then faded away entirely.

I let out a tiny sigh of relief. We waited in silence for several minutes. Once, Roxy began to whisper but stopped when there was an echoing sound from somewhere deep in the house. I assumed the vampires could still feel dark presences within the house, which meant it wasn't safe yet. Maybe Inkarri had posted her magicked velek outside the room, waiting for us to let our guard down.

My mind worked overtime. Inkarri suspected Juneau of several crimes, and if she was correct, that meant our host certainly kept busy. He was apparently hiding something that would earn him a trip to the Immortal courts if she found it. But none of that had much impact on our mission. My main takeaway from their exchange was that not all rulers got along. We could use that information. Throughout the conversation with Inkarri, Juneau had become slightly more trustworthy in my book. He was hiding something, but whatever shady things he was suspected of doing, they pissed off Inkarri, which was almost enough to endear him to me.

"You heard everything?" I whispered to Roxy.

"Yeah," she said, at a similar volume. "Although I don't get what annoys Inkarri so much about Juneau. Whatever it is, it weirdly makes me like him more. Goes to show that some people must be willing to push back against Inkarri. I wonder if we'll see more of that."

I cracked a smile in the darkness. Great minds thought alike.

"Finally," Kane whispered abruptly. "They've left the house."

"Now we wait to see if our host comes to actually fetch us from his secret cellar," Dorian said, his tone dry.

My fingers felt along the edge of the trapdoor, but it refused to give when I pushed. "It won't open."

"Maybe this is how he offed his family," Roxy joked, but there was a hint of genuine concern in her voice.

"Don't be absurd," Kane said with a bark of laughter. "If he had, there would be bones down here. Maybe back there, in the far corners."

"Not helping, Kane." I pressed harder against the trapdoor, but it was no use. It refused to give an inch. Against my chest, the stone began to heat once more in its bag. I reached for it, hiding its light in my hand. If I touched the wood like I had last time, maybe it would neutralize the concealment spell again.

Suddenly, the ground creaked above us. I stuffed the pouch out of sight just as the trapdoor swung open.

Juneau looked down at us with Charrek at his side. The ruler's expression was tense, but not as angry as I'd feared.

"Well, then. Let's get you out of this dusty place, shall we?"

He offered me his hand. After a moment of hesitation, I took it.

CHAPTER TEN

Juneau's sharp footsteps echoed through the house as he led us back to the dining room. He said nothing. Charrek, except for the soft hammer strikes of his metallic feet on the mosaics, was equally silent behind us. The gaping, toothy maws of the monsters on the dining room wall were somehow even more sinister now. My body was strung as tight as a bowstring, still ready for a fight. We each pulled a high-back chair out from the stupidly large table. My team all sat together, exchanging tense glances.

Juneau casually called for Fenru the wildling chef and asked her in a polite and mild tone if she could bring us a fresh round of bleeding-heart tea. It arrived a few minutes later—minutes filled with nothing but uncomfortable silence. He took his cup from the wildling with a nod of thanks, then leaned back in his chair at the head of the table. Dorian caught my eye for a moment. I could see the lines of tension in his face deepen as he studied Juneau.

"Charrek informed me that you found my storeroom," Juneau said slowly, "an occurrence that brought me a similar level of surprise as finding Inkarri and her brutes waiting by my gates when I arrived home." The Immortal maker shifted in his place by the door. Juneau glanced over his shoulder and smirked at his faithful servant. "He isn't pleased that you somehow managed to neutralize his spell. I'm impressed you even found it. Charrek's concealment skills are some of the greatest out there. " He quirked his eyebrows. "Magic, as I understand it, is outside of vampires' powers. So, tell me, have you humans been holding out on me? Because while I feel somewhat betrayed that you would go sneaking through my house, I must admit my curiosity is more engaged than ever. I'm always in search of stories, and I'm obsessive about details." His tone was light, but his eyes hardened, his feline gaze finding me.

Although Juneau was protecting us, now that I knew he was hiding something too, the balance of power had shifted a little in our favor. "I won't apologize," I said, keeping my voice firm. "Surely, you of all people must understand the drive of curiosity. Especially curiosity that is driven by trying to protect yourself from hidden threats." His eyes narrowed minutely, but I pushed on. If he wanted honesty, I would give it to him. "I'm sorry to disappoint, but I did no active magic on Charrek's spell. Humans don't have those abilities."

The corner of his mouth lifted. "Of course I understand the drive of curiosity, dear Lyra. I am aware that you have just as many questions for me as I do for you, but I suspect the ideal way to find true and detailed answers to those questions would be to put genuine trust in one another."

He's not wrong. To my left, Roxy shrugged, still wary but not actively hostile. That convinced me more than anything. Roxy might not be able to sense darkness, but she was a very good judge of character.

I forced myself to meet our host's sharp stare. It seemed unwise to look away from a mischievous Immortal.

"We need to know if you're going to turn us in," I told him. "And I imagine your answer is, to a certain extent, influenced by the fact that we know about your collection. I'm guessing it's not entirely legal?"

Juneau didn't answer. The polite inclination of his head and the way he sat back in his chair told me all I needed to know. His little trove was full of contraband.

"What is all that stuff?" Laini asked. "There are books down there that are older than all of us put together."

"And what was Inkarri hinting at in regard to your wayward activities?" Kane leaned forward. "I'm mad I didn't discover the hidden chamber. You guys get to have all the fun."

"I suppose we all have questions," Dorian said clearly. The most important one hung heavy in the air. Would he turn us in?

Maybe I was being naïve, but I couldn't drum up any real concern over it. Something in Juneau's posture and easy state made me think he wouldn't. He'd had his chance to turn us in, and he hadn't taken it.

How delighted Inkarri's face would have been to find our pesky group waiting like lambs for the slaughter in Juneau's hidden room. Yet Juneau hadn't given us over to her. The question was, had he only spared us because it would have meant revealing his secret room?

"I will not turn you over to Inkarri and her toadies." Juneau sighed wistfully.

I tapped my fingers on the table and made up my mind. "I believe you." Dorian caught my eye from across the table and inclined his head slightly, just enough to suggest that he agreed.

"As has become very plainly apparent, I haven't been completely forthcoming," Juneau admitted. "But neither, it seems, have all of you. Caution on both of our parts is sensible, of course, and I hope we can understand that everyone was merely trying to protect their assets here. I'll come clean if you do. In fact, I'll do you one better. I'll go first."

Something in Juneau's voice hinted at relief. Maybe he was happy to finally tell someone what he kept down there. He adored collecting stories, so it stood to reason that he enjoyed telling them just as much. But I guessed that he often lacked the opportunity.

He took our silence as agreement and began without another moment lost.

"My guild of harvesters and makers creates silks and the finest fabrics the Immortal Plane has ever seen. My family's name, and now my lonesome self, is known far and wide in this city. Fabrics are my birthright. However, I also occasionally get the opportunity to collect... rare goods. Items of certain and particular interests. I appraise the item, procure it, and sell it through the necessary channels to whoever is interested in such memorabilia and willing to pay. Sometimes I keep them for myself, if my interest is piqued. That is what you saw in my little storage room."

"At home, we call that smuggling," Roxy said bluntly. "You're a smuggler."

"What an ugly term," Juneau complained. "I prefer 'specialized merchant of rarities.'"

Kane sneered. "What could be rare in a society that has enough dark energy and caste servants to make whatever dumb things you want?"

Juneau lifted an elegantly clad shoulder. "History," he said. "Historical items hold more than darkness; they contain a story. A narrative that dips back into the chaotic annals of time, which enchants the mind more than any glittering gem could. I deal in historical items, things that can't be replicated even by the finest makers. I trade in banned books, books that would be burned if Irrikus had his way. Ignorance has always been popular. Beyond books, I have a special place in my heart for old magicked items that the council has decreed unlawful."

It made sense. In a way, Juneau's loudness and extravagance, naturally drawing attention to himself, was an ideal cover for a smuggler. He had the protection of his family name and his wits to cover his back and his tracks. Inkarri's dislike of him began to gain some context in my mind. It must piss her off to no end that Juneau managed to operate right beneath the noses of the hunters, yet remain untouchable.

"And the journal?" Laini prodded impatiently.

"I take it you've skimmed through some pages?" Juneau said, then stopped to sip his tea. One never rushed a dramatic performance, apparently. I fought a small smile.

"That journal is something," he said. "It was written by a ruler who was on the ruling council a thousand years ago, give or take a few years. You know how historical records get smudged."

A thousand years ago? That was a long time, even for Immortals.

"How did it come into your possession?" I asked. If there was an established underground black market in Itzarriol, we needed to know about it. It could be a valuable source of information about the Immortal rulers, especially if it happened to be centered around knowledge that the rulers never wanted the world to see.

"Certain old families on the council have been willing to part with their historic or rare goods in return for fees and favors." He paused solemnly. "Well, *mislayings* have been arranged in some cases, if they've decided to be stubborn. Around seventy years ago, I was supposed to pass on that particular volume to a client after receiving it from a seller who had fallen on hard times. He needed the money, and I was happy to help. I'm just glad I looked within the journal first. It's been such a rich source of information." His yellow eyes glittered in the light as he rested his hands on the table. "Did you know there used to be another caste in the Immortal cities—a caste called the cleansers?"

Dorian exhaled raggedly, the quickest to understand. I glanced at him, my own suspicions forming more slowly as I connected the fact that a vampire's duty was to cleanse bodies of darkness.

Laini furrowed her brow. "I remember the journal mentioning it," she admitted with a thrum of curiosity in her voice. It was a souvenir of her genuine fascination upon discovering the journals and being able to parse the old words.

"The cleansers are interesting," Juneau said, with an excitement that reminded me of Echen, the scholar I'd met in the Hive. "From what I gleaned, cleansers used to have positions on the Immortal Council. They were appointed by the ruling caste leaders in charge of the council, and they would check the rulers of the city periodically to assess their darkness and the darkness in the city. They advised the rulers on how to keep themselves from having to be cleansed." He dropped his voice. "They *fed* on those who became consumed by darkness."

It couldn't be...

"Vampires?" Dorian asked. It sounded as if the word had fallen out of his mouth instead of being intentional. His hollow tone of disbelief sent a shiver through me.

"No," Laini said flatly. "No vampire would advise you monsters."

If he took offense at being counted among monsters, Juneau didn't show it.

"More than advised them. From the sound of it, they were part of the council," Kane said. He snarled. "There's no way. He's lying."

Laini stiffened. "I read a passage, and it did mention cleansers. I just didn't think it meant vampires." She shook her head. "You knew all this. Were you going to tell us?"

"Perhaps," Juneau said. "Whether or not I would have shown you the storage room and those very precious books would have depended on how our trust developed during your stay here." He shrugged. "But that proposed series of events is completely irrelevant now. Regardless, I assure you that this is the truth. Or the truth as far as I am aware. Once I learned about how vampires used to be part of society—how an entire caste had been cut off and discarded like a diseased limb—I started to ask questions. You can imagine that the other rulers hated that." He shifted, and a piece of his braided silver hair, threaded with dozens of tiny ruby beads, spilled into his face. "I've always felt like an outsider. You've seen how the authorities here have no love for me, especially not Inkarri, and she is more dangerous than most of those pompous, over-powered elitists. But recently I began to realize that everything the people in power tell us amounts to little more than velek manure. The balance? Our perfect roles? Garbage."

His breath hitched in excitement. It was joined by a frenzied motion of his eyebrows, which furrowed angrily as his face darkened. "It's a neat explanation that they spoon-feed us from birth to keep us compliant. They don't want us asking questions about the structure of Immortal life. It keeps everything the same. And if the Immortal Council has been lying to us about vampires, then what else are they doing behind our backs? What history are they forming right now, based on falsehoods?"

"Why did you help us?" Laini snapped, slicing through Juneau's storytelling. She pinned him with distrustful eyes, searching his face. "You still haven't answered that."

Kane eyed her warily. Even he, with his well-known snark, appeared taken aback at her tone. I wished I could read Laini's thoughts. There must be something about Juneau that primed her anger to explode. It came in surprising bursts, the catalyst something I didn't understand.

"Laini," Dorian said. It was all he said. Short and sweet, meant to reel her in. I had never heard him be short with her before. A hum of warning pulsed beneath his tone.

"It's fine," Juneau insisted, unruffled. "I saw Inkarri's velek lead her to you. Well, I didn't know it was a group of vampires and humans, of course, but I knew there was *something* up on the roof. I told you, I look at the ugly building often because I can't help myself, and I sensed something. Something *new*. Something the Immortal Council would never allow to see the soul-light again if Inkarri found it. I saw my chance to finally shake things up around here. Now that I've met you, this is my chance to get back at all these entitled sadists I've been forced to pretend to like for most of my life. We have common enemies, and with your help—"

A distinctive annoyed hiss cut off the frenetic energy of his speech.

I winced, fairly certain without looking that I knew which of my vampire companions had protested.

Dorian sat with a veritable poker face in the center of the table. He stared at Kane, who looked straight at Laini with one raised brow. Roxy sipped her tea, watching as intently as a coach at a sports tournament. Laini finished her hiss with a rumbling growl that vibrated through her narrow chest. The portraits of Juneau's family frowned down at her. Was this our Laini?

I traced the lines of our conversation, probing my memory for possible points where Laini had sparked into anger. A wave of worry washed over me and held steady. Laini must be channeling all her anger about rulers onto Juneau. Perhaps without even realizing it herself. I was no psychologist and knew even less about vampire emotions, but Juneau's proximity as the only ruler we had access to made him the perfect target for her unacknowledged grief and rage.

"You want *us* to come solve your little problems," Laini said icily. "Why didn't you do something about it yourself?"

"I've tried to do what I can," Juneau said, but it came out in a staggered tone. He opened and closed his mouth. "I can't do much—"

"Woe is you," Laini said hotly, cutting him off. "You had to hang around some rulers and pretend to like them. I'm so overjoyed that you've found the light and feel a scrap of guilt about the fact that your entire life, you've grown wealthy in perfect safety while my kind fought to survive yours. I'm sure it brightens your utterly meaningless existence. And now you plan to stick it to the council by having a grand adventure playing the hero for some poor vampires."

Roxy held her breath beside me. Laini stared at Juneau, her face teeming with cold fury. Her anger electrified the air around us. If I reached out, I feared that my hand might connect with her invisible rage and spark a fire.

She had faced the worst dreams in the Gray Ravine. Her howls and cries from that night would always haunt me. Whatever awful emotions she'd been forced to relive during our trip with the harvester were coming out now. She had kept it all pent up for too long.

"Breaking news to our fine host," she said and threw out her hands sarcastically. "We are not here for your entertainment. Nearly everyone we know and love has *died* because of your foolish Immortal garbage. Having a chip on your shoulder and a few new ideas doesn't excuse you for not lifting a finger to help us until it was suddenly amusing for you." Her scowl turned harder. Her violet eyes were rimmed with red, her entire body tense with fury.

Juneau, for his part, scoffed hotly, but I could see the wheels turning in his head as he processed her words. I wasn't sure if it had ever occurred to our host that something in life might not be about him. She was right that many of his sentiments were too little too late. The vampires had gone through devastating trials. There had been no shiny mansions to hide in when the Immortals came for Vanim. There had been only wreckage, and the sure sign of smoke as sweet, gentle Laini watched everything in her life get ripped from her hands.

On the other hand, her fury seemed disproportionate to what he'd said. It was as if some part of Laini that she had buried with her loved ones had revived to take its revenge, with Juneau as the only accessible target.

"It's not that easy," Juneau lobbed back. He lifted his hands, extending them in a smooth movement like he was trying to force the conversation back open. "What would you have me do? Would you have me lead a doomed rebellion? I'm a clothing designer who reads too many books, not a hunter. I have no weapons training or magical augmentations of strength and speed. Inkarri could snap my spine in an instant. She refrains only because Irrikus keeps her leash tight. Isn't *this* better than nothing?" He gestured wildly around him, knocking his teacup off the table. It shattered on the stone floor. Almost immediately, a wildling entered to clean the mess.

Laini stared back defiantly.

"What would you do in my situation?" he continued. "If you're going to look down on my offer to hide you here at the risk of my own *personal* safety, the least you could do is try to understand me a bit. Go ahead and make your assumptions about me, but wealth doesn't mean freedom, and it certainly doesn't mean safety. My family kept me in a stranglehold, and I only tasted free will after they died. If you're angry at this disgusting system, I'll let you punch me until you're satisfied. Or better yet, you can anonymously tip off the authorities about my hidden room, if you find me so intolerable. The guards are just waiting for an excuse to throw me in the sanitarium." He shivered violently and muttered, "Dreadful, dreadful place. I would rather die. You must understand that there are awful things awaiting those who don't play Irrikus's game in this city. Nothing is simple about a revolution."

Sanitarium? That was where Kono had been taken. I filed the information away while thinking through the rest of his argument. If rulers were also at risk of being sent to the sanitarium for eccentricities like being polite to their staff, that changed things. Although Juneau lived in splendor, he also lived in a society that demanded his constant, sustained participation in a system he despised. Irrikus was a powerful ruler who commanded complete obedience. Juneau was at risk for his life if he tried to go against the council's will, and he appeared to have few allies in this place. No wonder he preferred life here with his staff. His upbringing must have been harsh to scar even a supernatural being with immense strength.

Juneau ended his frantic rant and looked at us, his vibrant eyes brighter than ever. "You don't have to like me," he said slowly. "But you must understand that I'm better to have as your ally than your enemy. If you share with me what brought you to Itzarriol, I can help you. I have an extensive network made up of the eyes and ears of many people in this place. I'm good at slipping below attention. I'm good at protecting my own skin, and if you're with me, I'll protect yours, too."

Laini had no response to this, but her face remained hard. Kane glanced at me expectantly, as if to suggest I should jump in and help calm Laini down. *Not a good idea.* I knew a powder keg when I saw one, and Laini's grief was too profound for anyone to deal with. And what could *I* possibly say to Laini to make things better? I had been trained to hate and mistrust vampires. How was I any different from Juneau? In some ways, I was probably worse. Roxy and I used to have discussions about what it would be like to kill a vampire.

"Will you stay?" Juneau asked, spiritless. He looked worn and tired, like fabric that had thinned almost to the point of tearing. He didn't seem like he cared much about our answer either way.

Kane glanced at Dorian. I massaged my hands underneath the table, rubbing my tired knuckles. While it was true that the Immortal rulers' plotting had affected my home, the vampires and what remained of their clans were the most at risk if things here in Itzarriol with Juneau went poorly. This question was for the vampires to answer.

Dorian evaluated Laini's stony face. Her vote was clear. His gaze went to me, prompting a low buzz in my chest. Juneau followed our ping-pong game of stares and hummed curiously. Maybe he found it odd that a vampire sought my advice or that we all appeared to be making a decision together. It was very unlike a ruler giving commands to his servants.

I'd already made my choice. Why squander an ally that wanted to help us? Even if he had his own reasons, he had resources we could use for our own personal motivations. Not to mention Charrek was genuinely loyal to him. The maker risked his own life to protect Juneau. That said a lot.

He'd been useful and done nothing but help us since we'd met, at great risk to himself and his household. And now I saw him wavering, watching us with doubt. We needed to repair the damage Laini had done.

I nodded my head an inch. Dorian took my meaning immediately. His glacial eyes drilled into Juneau. We would bite off enough of our story for Juneau to chew on, enough for him to understand the strange, terrible narrative we had carried heavy on our backs since coming to this forsaken realm.

"What do you know about the war being waged against vampires in the Mortal Plane?" Dorian asked, his tone deliberately mild.

Juneau blinked twice, caught off guard by the change of topic. "I don't know anything about the Mortal Plane, only about the war against vampires in the Immortal Plane. It's the most hotly discussed topic in the city since the destruction of Vanim."

Laini tensed, and Kane placed a calming hand on her arm, though his own dark eyes burned at Juneau's casual mention of the destruction of their home.

"Which was a terrible thing, obviously," the Immortal said, catching the mood of the room. He closed his eyes and rubbed his temples, sighing wearily. "But what I do know of the war might be helpful. Okay... increased patrols have been sent out. They told us that many vampires appear to be slipping into the Mortal Plane and disappearing, which is no skin off a ruler's back. Blah, blah. What the devil did Irrikus say in that speech in the plaza? Ah, yes, they've *increased* their concentrated effort to destroy the remaining stone circles. But never ever have I heard talk about fighting vampires in the Mortal Plane."

He said "Mortal Plane" like it left a bad taste in his mouth.

"Do you dislike the human dimension?" I asked, hoping to prod information out of him. If he did, it would surprise me, given how curious he'd been about Roxy and me.

"Of course not," he said with an offended scoff. He tossed his platinum-silver locks behind him and lifted his chin. "Your plane provides us with soul-light. But Immortals going to wage war against vampires in the Mortal Plane? It makes no sense. They've already killed most of the vampires in this plane. They don't need to completely eradicate you to stop you from being a threat. Pardon my saying so, but they've already effectively ripped out any fangs that the vampire caste had."

Kane let his own fangs slip out briefly in disapproval of Juneau's flippant discussion of his murdered comrades, but Juneau had a good point. Why would the rulers go to such lengths to completely wipe out vampires in a plane they couldn't even get to?

Juneau smacked his hand on the table as this sentiment seemed to occur to him at the same time. "And another thing, how would the hunters even get there?" He stroked his chin, glancing at me. "But if your plane is under threat from Immortals, that explains why humans are here now. I mean, you're in the Immortal Plane, and I've been told that no humans could ever set foot here."

"We're here to find out information about a conspiracy," Dorian said gently. Upon hearing the last word, Juneau's eyes sparkled. "Immortals, I can only imagine the council, have communicated with humans in the Mortal Plane. We have reason to believe that—since they couldn't travel to the Mortal Plane themselves—they sought out humans to facilitate the complete eradication of vampires in both planes. We're here to find out what they plan to do next, now that they've failed."

"A complete genocide," Juneau breathed. "Spanning two planes of existence. By the soul-light, what an insane undertaking."

Laini pushed away from the table. "I can't sit and listen to this anymore," she snarled. "Come and find me when he's learned not to sound quite so impressed at the idea of mass murder." She stalked out of the room without looking back.

Juneau looked uncomfortable, remorse in his eyes. "The suffering and loss have only ever been theoretical before," he murmured. "I must admit, I've never really stopped to think about what it must be like to live through such a thing."

"It is worse than you could possibly imagine," Dorian said, voice low and gruff. He shook his head slightly, straightening up and returning to the facts. "The humans began to hunt vampires in the Mortal Plane several years ago. We believe that might be when the Immortal Plane made contact with humans."

Juneau collapsed into his chair, completely overwhelmed with emotion and information. "Tea," he croaked, and a wildling popped up with a new cup. Juneau downed it in a second. "It sounds crazy. I'm not saying I don't believe you, but it's such a wild tale."

And we hadn't even told him everything. Dorian had specifically left out the tear and the dark energy weapons, among other things. It was best to let Juneau in on things slowly while we were still establishing trust.

"Can you tell us about the Immortal Council?" I asked. "Who would have been in charge for the last five to ten years and making all these decisions about the vampires and the Mortal Plane?"

Juneau tapped his fingers on the table and began to think aloud. "Our dear Lord Irrikus himself leads it. Other than that, there are only a handful of other rulers on the council, although I'm sure there are plenty pulling strings in the background far away from public view. Those old bastards. They think themselves fit to make judgment calls for the whole continent. Anybody who gets caught poking around in their business, regardless of caste, gets put in their precious sanitarium, never to be heard from again."

"Is there anything you can think of that would aid our investigation?" I asked.

His yellow eyes lit up. "You know, I believe there is some mischief we can get ourselves into that will help you immensely." A small smile came to his lips. "But there is something I'd like in exchange for my help."

Kane grumbled. "Of course there is."

I was just glad Laini wasn't here. Kane's usual grouchiness seemed mild as milk by comparison.

"Besides the hope that I'll get to watch the Immortal Council descend into chaos and witness their bitter end from the safety of my luxurious home, I want something physical. Something real. I want human artifacts to study or sell." He shrugged, unashamed. "Once you're far away, of course. I can't risk anyone asking how I came into human possessions while I'm hiding you here. Perhaps... perhaps some of your lovely hair." He pointed to Roxy. Kane narrowed his eyes at our host.

She touched her bright red hair, which was tied back in a long pony-tail. "Um… sure? It's kind of a weird thing to ask for." Her lips twisted into a small, surprised grin.

Juneau let out a husky chuckle. "Fair enough."

"And what will *we* get?" I asked. "As much as we'd love a lock of your hair in return, I'm afraid that won't be enough. You said you could help us investigate?" It seemed a lot to ask for a lock of hair, but human hair was a rare commodity in this plane. I'd press that advantage for all I could get.

He took on a conspiratorial tone, leaning toward us. "In addition to a place to stay, I can offer you opportunities." He grinned. "You want to gather information out here, right? How about disguises and conveyance around the city? I can offer you that!" He turned to Charrek. "I *can* offer them that, right?"

"It will be difficult," the maker said, a long-suffering note in his voice in the face of Juneau's enthusiasm. I was beginning to suspect that it was just an unquenchable part of him.

"But can you do it?" Juneau asked. "We'll need to cover their aura and scent. A full-blown protection glamor over the entire group, both vampires and humans. They can't risk discovery, and I can't risk being found out as an ally of fugitives."

Charrek shook his head regretfully. "I cannot," he said and thought-fully tilted his head to the side. "But I do know someone who can."

CHAPTER ELEVEN

"Such small bodies," the strange maker said. She rolled a silky strip of fabric in her upper hands and tilted her head down to get a good look at us. "And so plain."

Charrek cleared his throat, hovering by the female maker's elbow.

It was the next day, and Juneau had led us to one of his many giant, magnificent rooms. This one was fashioned into a tailor's room with its own luxurious sitting area. Juneau had explained that this was where he sometimes did private fittings for clients, as well as all his own outfits.

Along one wall, a row of mirrors reflected the paleness of my face and new hollows beneath my eyes. I missed the warmth of the sun. Even before we'd set foot in the Immortal Plane, my skin had faded to a washed-out tan, a sickly pallor I hated seeing on myself. I hovered near one of the plush couches next to Roxy, too tense to sit. Laini, whom we had convinced to rejoin us, stood in front of the couch across from us, her violet eyes eerily lit by the glowing green coffee table between us. Kane was the only one who lounged on a couch, leaning back into the cushy fabric with a watchful eye on the maker. Dorian lurked by the door, far enough away to keep the heartburn at a minimum.

The maker swept a slow gaze over us while she pursed her lips in silence. Her skin was the same color as a pewter pendant my mother always wore. Zach had given it to her as a Christmas present. It had our initials stamped into it. A lump sat painfully in my throat, like unchewed food. It hurt to think about my parents and brother right now, when I wasn't sure I would make it back to them.

The maker had a long, beautiful face with sharp points and a pair of furry ears that protruded from her head like she'd plucked them straight off a giant bat. Her smaller set of arms crossed firmly over her chest, which rose and fell steadily, while another pair handled her strip of fabric. She had to know that our friends were vampires. And who knew what she thought of Roxy and me?

Only Juneau seemed at ease. He briefly admired the elaborate embroidery work on his sleeves before catching my eye and winking.

"We may be small, but that means you'll waste less cloth on us," I offered, trying to be helpful. Roxy elbowed me lightly with a playful roll of her eyes. Yes, I knew I was kissing up.

The maker placed her chin in her hand as her tangerine eyes flickered to my face. "Nothing I make is a waste," she said coolly. "You may call me Reshi. I know you're strange, but rest assured, the weight of a heavy purse will make me forget I ever saw you. No matter who or *what* you are, if you can pay, I'll do the work. All I ask is that you keep this transaction secret."

Dorian's arctic blue eyes caught a sheen of the room's aquatic lighting. "We will forget your name and face," he promised gravely.

Reshi dropped her chin and rubbed one side of her oval face with a free hand. She tucked her ribbon down her sleeve. "You must do everything I tell you," she warned us. "No matter how absurd you think it is. I require obedience while I work. My time is precious." Her face was a guarded fortress of composure, but her eyes kept flickering between each of us, always coming back to rest on Roxy's bright red hair.

"We appreciate you coming on such short notice," Juneau said, clasping his elegant fingers together.

"Only because Charrek asked. Otherwise you'd have had a long wait." Reshi sniffed the air with a delicate movement of her slit nostrils. "Hm.

Scents and auras will be harder to disguise. I'll need plenty of dark energy for this work—and for my fee."

Juneau opened his cloak. From an inner pocket he removed two large ochre leather pouches and handed them to Reshi. "Take whatever you need."

Reshi's thin white lips lifted into a ghost of a smile. The satisfaction of monetary compensation was apparently universal. Her lower arms held the bags while she used one long-fingered hand to pluck out a handful of small, smoothed stones from the pouch and spread them in her large palm. The rocks looked like river stones polished by years of streaming water. I marveled at the colors of the rounded pebbles—periwinkle, robin's egg blue, mossy green. They were dull, but something about their inconspicuous shape suggested power.

After a moment, she dropped a few of the stones back into the open pouch. She weighed the pouches in her hand, turning herself into a supernatural scale for a moment. "This will suffice."

Juneau's face never changed. He was a keen merchant. *He knew exactly how much to offer.*

Reshi reached into a fabric toolbelt the color of oxblood that sat around her thick waist. A variety of small pouches hung from the belt. From the largest, she pulled out a ball of mud. Yes, a ball of gray, boring mud. I stared as she took a small stone from her palm and, using her powerful arms, crushed the ball of mud and the dark green stone together. The pebble disappeared, swallowed up by the gray matter. She began to mold the mud, the extra joints in her long fingers allowing her to twist and manipulate the mass. A sliver of green melted into the putty as I watched. She pulled the clay out between her long arms, the mush becoming more flexible as she worked it. Stretch and smash, stretch and smash.

A metallic sound rang out. I struggled to follow her fast movements as bits of silver appeared in the clay. Soon, Reshi held a brilliant silver chain in her hands. Her rough hands had crafted a beautiful chain from nothing but mud and stone.

Roxy gasped. "Holy—"

"Crap," I finished. It probably sounded foolish to the makers, but Roxy and I had never seen magic done like this. We usually only saw the consequences of it—the weapons trying to kill us and the ostentatious, glittering houses of Itzarriol. I glanced over at our vampire friends, who ogled the chain. Even Laini stared with open fascination. From their expressions, it was clear they hadn't seen magic like this either.

Juneau's glittering robes and the dazzling city exteriors sprang to my mind. Had all these magnificent gems and details been fashioned from a maker's clay and stones? No wonder Juneau stayed wealthy. He must have access to the finest makers of fabric and luxurious, detailed decorations to dress his wealthy clients. And now he was helping us.

We would have to hide everything with our disguises. It wasn't enough to change the shape of a body or the pitch of a voice. We had to change everything, down to our basic foundations of scent and the frequency we emitted. The keen nose of Inkarri's magicked velek would be tough to beat, but after watching Reshi produce a silver chain from a ball of putty, my confidence grew.

Juneau's feline smile uncurled across his sharp face as he watched Reshi work. More stones and more mud, over and over. She smashed them together and stretched them out, weaving magic from the air.

Reshi smirked, pleased by our reactions to her magic. "Let's begin," she announced, and walked over to Dorian with a chain dangling from her hands. Her movements were confident and efficient. This was a woman who wanted to get her work done.

Reshi began measuring Dorian. Without words, she merely tapped certain parts of his body and pointed up or down. Dorian stripped off his cloak and lifted his arms, allowing her to measure his chest. An unexpected pang of bitterness pounded through my chest. The contact was so casual and impersonal. And it was taken for granted in a way I never could.

With her broader set of hands, she marked the measurements in a notebook. As she finished with Dorian, she nodded to herself, humming with thought. She next moved to Kane. He begrudgingly shed his cloak and presented his muscular frame.

"A perfect form for fashion," Reshi muttered as she measured him.

Kane scowled, rolling his eyes. He never liked to be reminded of his natural good looks. I held back a snicker, but Roxy didn't bother, letting out a peal of laughter.

The maker moved on to Laini next, who followed Reshi's instructions.

"I don't need one," Laini reminded us. Her stiff face relaxed as Reshi moved around her, measuring tape moving here and there. "I'm staying here to research the scrolls and journals, not going out into the city." She seemed intrigued by the journal, perhaps trying to figure out whether it was really as genuine as Juneau seemed to think it was. While we'd been trying to convince her to come back, Dorian had raised the idea that she stay behind to research it.

"It's just in case," Dorian insisted. "If anything happens to us, we need a way for you to sneak out of the city and get information back to our friends." It sounded plausible enough, but we all knew that he didn't want to take Laini on a mission in her current frame of mind. She would be a serious liability in a city full of rulers. If she couldn't convincingly act like a cowed maker or lost her temper at the wrong moment, she might give us all away.

Laini gave the barest hint of a nod, not looking at Juneau. Dorian frowned, but it was filled with concern. I suspected he was becoming more and more worried about how angry Laini had been lately. I hated that I hadn't found a good moment to approach her myself. My worry and concern for my friend had gotten pushed to the back burner with the threats of Immortal danger constantly swirling around us. There was a flame of fury lit inside those violet eyes that, even as she acquiesced, remained stubbornly lit throughout the measuring process.

Finishing with Laini, Reshi jotted down the measurements, then turned to me. "You're barely half the chain," she mumbled as she looked me up and down. She appeared to be talking to herself more than me. I eyed her pouch where the magical mud had come from.

"Do you get paid in stones?" I asked her. "They seem interesting."

Her eyes narrowed. Looking over at Juneau, she said, "They really aren't from around here, are they?"

He flapped a hand dismissively. "Nothing for you to worry about, Reshi. Just explain the stones and take the measurements."

"The stones are vessels," she informed me, gathering the chain in her hands. "They're often used as currency, but they have many uses, since they hold dark soul energy." She twisted her mouth, a glint of suspicion in her eyes as she looked over my non-vampire form dressed in worn vampire clothes. The sharpness in her gaze eased. Perhaps she thought me too poor to have ever earned currency of my own, whatever strange creature I was.

Emboldened by that thought, I opened my mouth to ask another question, but Roxy was quicker.

"You turn the stones into magic?" she asked.

Reshi glanced briefly at her and settled for a moment on Roxy's hair.

"Not quite," she said politely. She gave the same cursory look over Roxy's clothes. Maybe she would think we were some kind of curious wildlings. I prayed she didn't know much about the Mortal Plane. "I create the objects and add spells to them, but I take the magic from the stones. Dark energy is wrung from dark souls by a harvester, energy which is then packed into the stones to imbue them with magic."

Wrung from dark souls. I suppressed a shudder as Reshi wrapped the silver chain around my thighs. She clicked her tongue as she worked, diving back into her thoughts. I glanced up at Juneau, who watched with tepid interest. Measuring bodies must be an everyday affair for him.

"How did you get hold of so many stones?" I asked Juneau, feeling bold.

He lifted his eyebrows up an inch with an amused smile. "My guild of harvesters. They're out in the world where there is the highest concentration of dark souls, stripping the energy out and sending back the stones to be used in my workshop by my makers."

"Do the makers get paid in stones?" Roxy asked. "Reshi did say they were also a kind of currency. Do they make a lot?"

Juneau gave an uncomfortable laugh. "Their guild masters decide what their makers charge for their services and how much of that compensation belongs to the guild master."

The injustice that a single sentence could hold was breathtaking.

"That seems unfair." A sour feeling grew in my stomach at the implications of what he'd just said. There was a lot of pain in this world.

Juneau grimaced lightly at my remark. "Harvesters and makers must swear fealty to one specific ruling class person. All the energy and items they create are given to that ruler's household, and the ruler decides how much to return to them. It's an awful system. In *theory*, these creatures get a voice in the government through representatives appointed by that ruler's council member, and protection from..." He trailed off. "Well, protection from being harmed or stolen by other rulers."

"At best, that sounds a lot like a gang," Roxy said bluntly.

"I don't know what a gang is," Juneau reminded her.

"At worst, it sounds like slavery," she finished, her face suddenly hard. "What's making them pay the makers anything at all?"

I suspected I knew the answer to that but hoped I was wrong. *Nothing. Nothing at all.*

"A ruler shamelessly using those around them for their own profit?" Laini drawled. "What a shocking development."

"It brings me much shame," Juneau said in a voice so soft it was almost lost in the air.

Reshi pressed her lips together. Her face was an unreadable mask. Was she surprised by the direction our conversation had gone? She glanced at her notebook and cursed, pulling away from me.

"You," she said to Kane. "I've smudged my ink. Comes with having too many hands. I need to measure your chest again." He huffed but complied.

I kept my eyes trained on Juneau. "Can you tell us about the harvesters?" I prodded. "Why don't we see them in the city?" The strange smile of the harvester in the Gray Ravine sprang to mind. I tried to imagine him roaming the streets here, but it felt odd. Like the harvesters weren't meant to exist under such bright light.

Juneau pursed his lips, suddenly reluctant to answer, as though he sensed this subject would be difficult to discuss. "Harvesters mostly live outside the city," he explained. "They follow deposits of fresh souls as they come in from the Mortal Plane. Technically speaking, they could do whatever they wanted with the energy if they didn't have contracts with rulers to protect their fragile bodies. They are their own folk, utterly different from makers and rulers. But they have a job to do: produce magic energy from souls to be used as fuel and currency and materials here in the city. They have certain quotas set by their rulers, which can be quite harsh, depending on the ruler."

Reshi laughed bitterly. "This is such a precious conversation," she muttered and scanned all our faces. "No one would harm the harvesters. None of us would need any 'protection' at all if it weren't for the rulers. You can call it what you want, but however you look at this system, it's slavery. You've made your point, Juneau, though I don't know why. You can do anything you like to me. If you wanted to report me for treason, for example, there's nothing I could do about it. However, I'm sure our charming liege Irrikus would pay handsomely for information about just what it is Juneau does in his spare time." Her eyes slid to the side, regarding Juneau suspiciously. "Haven't I always done a good job for you and kept my mouth shut?"

"I'm not threatening you," he protested and gestured to Roxy and me. "They're asking questions, and I'm answering them."

Reshi smirked, but her eyes remained cold. "It would be hard to find someone else with my specific abilities. It would also be tough to find someone else who would be willing to do this task."

"Exactly. I'm not a fool," Juneau snapped. "You came highly recommended by Charrek. I'm fully aware, Reshi, that you're one of a kind." Somewhere deep down, his humanity nursed a wound. "There's no way to break the system. If anyone tried, they would be immediately attacked by all the other rulers, their servants kidnapped and forced into new contracts. We only stay in power by enforcing our control over those beneath us. The rulers would never let someone live who tried to disrupt that system." It struck me that Juneau must have realized that he was complicit in the very system that supported his warped luxury, and it hurt him. With no family left, he surrounded himself with makers and wildlings. He must have absorbed some of their stories, their feelings. If we could defeat Irrikus, maybe that would give Juneau and the makers the opening they needed to break this system of forced servitude.

Lyra, calm down. One mission at a time. Break the system after saving the day. My revolutionary spirit needed very little to light up these days.

Juneau smoothed his hair, clearly ruffled by our conversation. "You're taking part in it, too," he pointed out. "You're being paid in magic energy from harvesters. At least my harvesters work for me, which is better than working for those other bastards."

Reshi twitched her bat-like ears. "I have my reasons," she stated calmly but didn't elaborate.

I shifted from foot to foot. Who were Reshi's regular clients? Did she work in this strange underground market of whispered favors and smuggling, like Juneau did? Only Reshi wasn't a ruler in this society, and thus didn't carry the same protections. However, she'd made illegal magic right before us and hadn't batted an eye when she measured the vampires. She *must* have recognized them for what they were. Yet we'd been told by various vampires that the makers and harvesters weren't allowed to work with vampires, which meant the vampires in Vanim had no magical weapons. Being so underpowered compared to their enemies had probably been what hurt them the most during the Immortal invasion. It would be dangerous for the rulers if the makers joined forces with vampires, wouldn't it?

As for Roxy and me? Maybe she suspected we were humans but couldn't prove it. Or didn't need to. She had her money from Juneau. She presumably had a good place in this society as a highly praised maker. I shivered at the thought of commending Juneau for being kind to anyone he contracted when makers had little choice in the matter. It was only a small blessing that they'd landed in Juneau's employ, rather than another's. Charrek's loyalty was still impressive, but there was an uncomfortable edge of coercion to it thanks to this new information.

Inkarri must have her own servants. I hated to think of how she treated them. Her servants probably wished they could plot against her. If Reshi was willing to do black market magic deals, maybe other servants would be willing to work around their pledged loyalties. Or were they too afraid of the repercussions? I wished for a chance to ask Reshi if she thought there were others who might be willing to secretly resist the ways things "had to be" in Immortal life.

Reshi came back to me, satisfied by her brief monologue and measurement of Kane. "Let's finish yours and move on to the red one. I'll try to make sure my hands don't smudge the ink again." There was a faint note of humor in her voice. The urge to be extra courteous to her and to Charrek surged through me. There might be no way for me to immediately change their conditions for the better, but at least I could treat them with the respect they rarely received in their daily lives.

She lifted the chain behind me and wrapped it around to measure my chest. As her fingers made contact with the pouch hidden beneath my shirt, she gasped. Abruptly, she jerked back. The chain whipped through the air and fell to the floor.

My hand flew up to where the bag sat against my skin. Dorian's stone had grown hot. I clapped my hand on it, as if the pressure would stop it from working. The last thing I wanted was for someone to notice Dorian's stone after the whole hidden chamber debacle.

Reshi breathed hoarsely, her voice so quiet only I could hear her. "It's a stone, isn't it?"

I nodded slowly, confused.

She shook her head from side to side, pressing three hands to her mouth at once. "It can't be—"

Dorian took a step forward, his jaw clenched. "Lyra, are you okay?"

Reshi scowled, ignoring him. "Everyone out." She pointed to the door. "Now. I won't continue my work otherwise."

"I'm fine," I assured Dorian, as I saw him about to protest. "Just do as she says."

Laini sent me a furtive glance, but I nodded, urging her to go quietly too. They filed out of the room obediently.

Juneau shut the doors behind them, and I could hear him muttering as he led the group away.

"Well, that was odd. Who's up for a quick spot of tea? I'll have Fenru bring it to the best parlor. I've got the skull of a long-toothed Gray Ravine shalecat in there. Would you like to see it?"

His voice faded, and I was alone with Reshi.

"Let me see it," she said, extending one of her spidery hands.

Her eyes widened as I pulled the stone from its pouch and presented it to her. It glowed softly, but not as hot as before. Her eyes brimmed with stormy emotions I couldn't understand.

"Where did you get this?"

Her eyes narrowed. I cleared my throat, unnerved by the intensity of her gaze and her sheer size looming over me. What had made her respond like this?

"Dorian gave it to me," I said evenly. "He got it from his brother. It was a final parting gift, unfortunately."

She set her mouth in a grim line, taking my meaning. The fate of vampires was understood. "Tell me about it," she commanded.

Something in her tone made me want to tell her. However, unlike Inkarri's magical coaxing, the maker's voice was filled with interest as well as a strange urgency.

"It's an odd rock," I told her. "Downright weird, sometimes. It warms and glows at random points, but it responds most strongly when it's close to something with strong magic." I mentally stitched together a film reel of all the stone's moments. "Dorian said it helps him find me sometimes, that the stone gives off a particular frequency. He could probably tell you more about it. I don't know if he knew any of the more peculiar qualities when he gave it to me, though. I think he would've told me if he did."

Reshi nodded calmly but made no move to call Dorian. She twisted the hands of her lower arms. "The stone you have isn't odd. In fact, it's precious and rare. Tell me... where is it from? If you tell me, I will tell you what I can about it."

Everything was worth something in the Immortal Plane, but I didn't see how this information could hurt us. It was worth telling her if it meant learning something about the stone.

"It came from the mountains near Vanim," I told her.

Her eyes took on a misty look, as though she were looking back at a time I suspected came far before me. She murmured gently, "So he did make it."

He? I stared at her. She hardly registered me. The soft wrinkles beneath her large amber eyes crinkled as her lips lifted into a bittersweet smile. I'd seen it innumerable times on the faces of the vampires when they were thinking of loved ones they'd lost. Who did Reshi mourn? It would pain her, but I had to know. What if it exploded one day?

I licked my dry bottom lip. "Who made it, Reshi?"

She blinked, and her glassy eyes cleared a little. She dragged a hand down her face and sighed wearily. "A friend of mine... I would recognize his craft anywhere." The bittersweet curl to her lips returned. "He had such a signature, you know. Every maker leaves a bit of themselves on their work. The rulers are foolish and haughty. They believe themselves to be the only beings worthy of leaving their mark. They build statues of themselves. They decorate their mansions with fountains and bones of creatures they claim to have killed but haven't. They all fight and squabble to be the most individual, the most authentic, the most outrageous. But if they looked from their mansion to their neighbor's, they would only be able to see what they dislike about it, what they were unsatisfied with. They never look close enough to see the painstaking details we makers put into our work."

"And you can see the hint of a maker in the work put into this stone?" I asked, awed.

"Of course. I can feel it." She shivered and wrapped her hand around the stone. "My friend Azpai ran away from our old guild master before I pledged myself to a new guild master. My friend told me he was headed for the vampire city to try to find a new life. I remembered his lips constantly forming the word. Vanim. Vanim. Vanim. He would lull himself into such a trance just repeating the name over and over again as if it could save him." She paused. "He left one night with no warning. I found his bed cold as ice. I never heard another word from him, only a report from my master that he had been caught and punished." The smallest of tears ran down her left cheek. One of her hands brushed it away roughly.

My throat tightened. Seeing her pain threw everything from the past few weeks back at me in high definition. We were in a war that stretched so far beyond ourselves and our issues in the Mortal Plane. We were steeped in a conflict that began long before the Bureau dragged us into it. So many had lost so much, regardless of what plane they came from. I clenched my eyes shut for a moment as faces flashed before me. My brother and my parents. Dorian, Laini, Kane, Roxy. Bryce, Sike, and Arlonne, whom we'd left back at the Hive. Bravi and Major Morag, who'd stayed behind with all the others at the VAMP camp in Scotland. I swallowed my grief and opened my eyes. Reshi exhaled slowly. Her fingers uncurled from the stone. She'd never known that her friend had made it to Vanim. The overseers had clearly lied about what had befallen him, but she'd lost him just the same. She would probably never see Azpai again, even if he had survived the fall of Vanim.

I wished desperately that I could tell her something, anything to make it better. But there was nothing. Nothing but the understanding between us that life sometimes means loss. Reshi had lost her friend. The vampires had lost everything. I risked the same, if we didn't find a way to stop the Immortals from wreaking havoc on the Mortal Plane. We held the silence between us until she sucked in a breath.

Like gears sliding back into place, her face hardened. The curtain of composure drew itself over her face. She stared at me, her chin tilted upward. "Keep this safe. It's very valuable," she said and handed the stone back to me.

It felt strange in my palm, as if it had breathed a sigh of relief, a final message delivered to its maker's old friend.

"The stone can sense magic and neutralize spells," Reshi said. "That's probably what you're referring to when you say it glows. It absorbs some of the magical power that it senses and dispels the rest. It's like a sponge, but it can only hold so much. The magic within will slowly dissipate over time if not used. It can also be used as a power source for those who can perform spells."

She frowned and rubbed her cheek thoughtfully. The tear had dried completely on her pewter skin. "Although, I doubt many people would be able to use it. It's a very rare item, this stone, and it comes with a failsafe —only those with a light soul can use it. Any spellcaster with the knowledge to use this stone would be far too dark. I saw him work on a prototype before this one, but our guild master beat Azpai when he caught him working on something personal. Our master was furious that Azpai wasted his time on something like this. It's the opposite of what most people want, since it unravels spells rather than holding them together." Her stern lips softened into the tiniest of smiles. "Of course, Azpai would have made something like that. He was always contradicting himself, even his magic."

I shifted, unsure of whether to drop my gaze from her face. Reshi struck me as someone who rarely got vulnerable, and I had already seen her cry. She blinked suddenly, yanking herself back to the present.

"The stone it's made from retains memories," she explained brusquely, completely switching her tone. "It's not part of the spell, but the nature of the stone. The magic absorption and the dispelling—those two elements may interact in interesting ways. In ways that might even be frustrating."

I remembered the wall in Vanim that Roxy had leaned on, accidentally receiving a deluge of painful emotions from the attack on the city. Were my dreams of maybe-Lanzon caused by the same thing? "Could the crossover of its natural ability and the instilled magic make me dream of the previous owner?" I asked. "I never met him, but I've been having bizarre dreams of what I think is his death."

She frowned. "Possibly? You need to check with whoever gave you the stone about such details. I only know that you absolutely must keep it away from the jewelry that will make up your disguise. If the stone touches it, the stone will completely neutralize the disguise's magic. That could be deadly if it were to happen out in public." Her eyes brimmed with meaning, as if she already knew that we were planning to lurk around the Immortal capital to gather intelligence.

A wave of gratitude washed over me. "Thank you," I said and placed the stone back in its pouch. I patted it, glad for its comforting presence in my fabric.

Without waiting for another word, Reshi strode over and yanked open the door. Juneau fell in.

"I wasn't eavesdropping," he insisted as he gathered himself.

Reshi raised one amused eyebrow. "I never said you were." She clapped her top hands together. "Now, let's get everything finished."

She picked up the silver chain and finished my measurements while my team filed in the door. When she moved over to Roxy, the redhead stared at me openly while the maker took her measurements. I scanned the rest of my friends' faces. Dorian said nothing, but a muscle flexed in his jaw. It was torture not to be able to talk openly with each other right now, but his dead brother wasn't exactly a subject I wanted to bring up in a crowd. Especially not when Laini could be unbalanced by a stiff breeze.

I offered him a small smile when I caught his glacial eyes. *It's fine. I'll explain later.* We had to talk about what I suspected about the stone, too. The next chance I had to get him alone, I would tell him. No matter what.

"Good. We're done," Reshi said and placed the silver chain into a pouch on her toolbelt. She straightened her back and stood at full attention. "You can pick up the disguises from my workshop tomorrow morning." She walked over to the door, and Juneau followed her, thanking her profusely. She waved him off and hurried to the doorway.

"Charrek, please show her out the west wing tunnel," Juneau requested.

Reshi looked back over her shoulder. "I know the way," she said. "No one will see me leave." For a moment, her eyes lingered on us. "Good luck to you all."

She and Charrek went off down the hall. Juneau turned, his robes flying around him in spectacular fashion. He grinned at our group.

"We've got a full day until you can get exploring, and I have a *wonderful* idea. I'll ask you about human things all day in exchange for the disguise arrangements. Fenru will make us strange human food to make you feel at home." He tapped his chin. "I recall one man's memory in particular when I got hold of some especially powerful dark energy. He ate something like a loaf of bread, except that it was made entirely of spiced meat.

Do you know anything like that? Some sort of *loaf of meat*?" He sounded scandalized.

"Meatloaf?" Roxy asked dryly.

His eyes lit up like a boy opening presents on Christmas morning. "Meatloaf," he breathed. "Wonderful! We won't be able to make it quite like he did, since I suspect eating another human is not something humans usually do."

"Oh God, he wants us to make serial killer meatloaf," Roxy said faintly, then walked away.

A burst of nausea rose in my stomach. "No, Juneau," I croaked. "Humans are never meant to do that."

"I'm sure we'll find some replacement," Juneau said, far too cheerfully for a man who had just suggested cannibalism.

CHAPTER TWELVE

"If I have to explain the concept of school detention again, I'm going to throw myself out of that weird shark window on the third floor," Roxy lamented the next day.

I rubbed my eyes. "I would kill for some coffee," I muttered. "I'm afraid to drink whatever concoction Juneau claims has the same properties as human coffee. Remember the beans he showed us? Purple. It'd probably burn a hole in our stomachs."

Juneau had gone to fetch a scroll for us to sketch on after breakfast, which would be interesting with my abysmal art skills. The morning meal had turned into another lightning-round series of questions for us. He wanted a full layout of Roxy's high school, which she had mistakenly described as a prison during breakfast. The Immortal jumped on that description with fascination.

"Six and a half hours a day of learning?" he asked, aghast. "But your lifespans are so awfully short."

Sometimes our host said things without thinking that were less than sympathetic or appropriate. It stopped feeling like a slap in the face after the first few remarks. Juneau didn't mean to be snide. He just didn't know how to say things without taking on the tone of a privileged Immortal ruler.

I ran down the list of everything we had covered so far. In the span of five hours, we'd essentially given him a summary of a deranged internet search by a bored person. We'd discussed both world wars, Scotland's recent independence, potlucks, and social media stalking with a seven-foot Immortal wearing rainbow robes. *What is my life?*

For his part, Juneau ate up every second of it. He leaned forward in certain moments, gasping and exclaiming. He turned to our vampire friends, eager for their opinions. Occasionally, they learned things about the Mortal Plane at the same time he did.

Kane, who'd taken the last watch alone the night before, was half asleep when Juneau poked him to inquire if humans really did have the technology to dye their hair different colors using strange chemicals.

"Yeah," the vampire replied monosyllabically.

"As fabulous as mine?" Juneau asked, flipping his hair that today held dozens of different colored braids to match his multicolored robes.

Kane looked at him wearily. "Nothing could be as loud as your presentation."

I glanced up the table, and Dorian smirked when he caught my eye.

"Look, we're tired," I said. "We're running out of topics."

He lifted his hands innocently. "I never said anything," he replied.

Roxy chuckled beside me, and I shook my head, a laugh slipping from my mouth. God, our lives had shifted to something utterly bizarre. Sometimes I almost forgot the danger that lurked beneath every moment we spent in this plane. Juneau's strange but bright nature made the world lighter. For the moment, at least.

"Here's the parchment," the Immortal announced, taking a roll brought to him by a tiny pink wildling that looked like it was made of rock salt. He threw the paper down in front of Roxy and presented her with a quill.

She took it from him, cringing at the quill's fluffy feather end. "And you want me to draw my high school?"

"Specifically, the strange place where you gather to eat," he said, almost hunched over her in excitement. She laughed tiredly but began scratching a decent picture onto the page. I watched her work. Fortunately, Roxy seemed to have some half-decent drafting skills.

"It's called a cafeteria," Roxy said. "And I used to bully the bullies there and force them to give lunch money back to the little kids they took it from. And their own lunch money, too."

"Fighting injustice?" He rubbed his hands together gleefully. "How thrilling. You'll have to tell me all about it after I've fetched your disguises, which is where I'm going right now." He waved at us dramatically and bowed before leaving.

We got a brief respite of half an hour before the heavy front door slammed shut again. How on earth had a ridiculously sized, hyperactive Immortal who dressed like a paint factory explosion lived alone for so long?

"I'm back," Juneau cried triumphantly. He threw open the dining room door and grinned wolfishly. "You won't believe what a fantastic job Reshi did on these. You'll think you've gone mad."

Calling Laini from where she was poring over books in Juneau's private study, he ushered us back to the fitting room. The row of mirrors stared back at us as we clutched the small parcels Juneau handed out. Reshi had written our names on small tags on the outside of the paper-wrapped packages. I noticed immediately that she had written my name in a gorgeous golden ink, the same color Dorian's stone glowed. I ran my fingers across the tag. A shiver of excitement ran down the length of my back along with something else. Unease? Fear?

"What are you waiting for?" Juneau asked, out of breath from excitement. "Open them! Change! Put them on. I want to see you in them."

Laini cleared her throat. "Uh, do you have areas to change privately?"

Juneau waved dismissively and pressed his fingers to his mouth. "It'll happen immediately. There's no need to undress. Well, sometimes Reshi's magic strips you nude first, but not often."

Laini stared at him with a doubtful expression.

"Oh, fine," Juneau said, with a humoring smile. He gestured, and Charrek began to drag out portions of the actual wall. I watched as the maker went to the glittering solid surface and, perhaps by his own strange magic, pulled out a three-panel section. Soon, he had pulled out five room dividers from the wall and formed makeshift changing cubicles.

Roxy whistled. "Cool trick." She went behind the first one. I could barely see the top edges of her wild red hair behind the wooden panel. I took my parcel and went behind the one next to hers. We each had a few feet of room to ourselves.

"I'll leave you to it," Juneau called out. "Let me know when you're appropriately dressed."

There was a ringing amusement to his warm tone. What if we actually had to strip? Were Immortals less concerned with nudity, or was it just because he was essentially a fashion designer? He would probably love to see us naked, but just because he was so curious. I eyed Dorian's divider at the end farthest from mine. *Well, that makes two of us, Juneau.*

I sighed and untangled the package's twine. The string sprang off the paper as soon as I undid the knot, as if animated by magic. I raised a curious eyebrow as the paper unfolded itself.

A necklace crafted of shimmering blue metal lay inside. Threaded onto the delicate chain was a perfectly spherical pendant. Reshi had told us at the beginning of our initial meeting that she would construct a disguise for each of us that wouldn't be too different from our original body. She couldn't give us disguises that had a different size, bulk, or number of limbs than our own bodies. It just remained to be seen how it looked in reality.

Taking a deep breath, I placed the necklace around my neck. Dorian's stone rested safely in my pocket, away from the magic.

I first saw fur in the color of my own hair. Apparently, she'd turned me into a wildling. That made sense, since I was too short to be a convincing ruler. A scent of spiced incense rose from my body.

"What the hell?" Kane muttered nearby.

"It's—" Laini stopped herself. "*Interesting.*"

With a rush of warmth, the disguise adhered to me like a second skin. It felt like someone suddenly threw a light sheet over me, but it immediately conformed to my skin. It was strange—I wore my same clothes underneath, but the costume molded itself to me. Reshi's work was top notch. I flexed my hand and felt the disguise stretch with me.

I'd pictured clumsily wobbling around in long, flowing robes and enchanted wigs. The reality? Oh, it was much better. I gave a delighted chuckle as I stepped out from behind the room divider to join the others. My first few steps were awkward—it felt just like I was walking in a wetsuit. In the better light cast in the center of the room, I stared down at myself, then caught sight of my friends. I couldn't stop my burst of surprised laughter, followed by an all-encompassing sense of awe.

We were wearing… magic.

Across the room, a slender creature with dark blue skin and an insect-like face blinked beady, bright blue eyes at me. It twitched its head to the side in a familiar gesture.

"You have mandibles," I said to Dorian, gasping between peals of laughter.

He twitched on the hind legs of a creature that made me think of a praying mantis dressed in wide, balloon-like pants. It was him, but not. These costumes were the real deal.

"And you need a shave," he retorted with a smirk in his voice. He clicked his claw experimentally, stretching out the three fingers on his other hand.

I shook my head wildly and caught sight of my own fur flying beneath my face. Lifting my hands in front of my face, four-fingered paws tipped with talons drifted into view. They were attached to my body. *My body*. An eerie sensation came over me as I watched the paws move, operated by me and yet *not* me. It seemed that my middle and ring fingers had been combined into one digit. The fur on my paws was the same color as my hair—even my talons had the same hue.

"I love this color," Roxy said. I turned to see a golem wildling made of reddish sandstone glaring up at another beast. Her voice sounded gravelly in her disguise, as if part of the rock disguise had wound its way into her voice.

"You're as stubborn as a rock, so it works perfectly," Kane said. I watched a lean, muscled creature with curling ram horns chuckle and shake a silky dark chestnut-brown mane the same shade as Kane's natural hair.

Roxy-the-golem cracked her stony knuckles and squared up against Fluffy Kane. The two of them started carefully sparring, getting used to their new forms. When I looked up to regard my reflection, hazel-green eyes looked back at me. Reshi had managed to copy our coloring down to the minute details.

My paw went to feel the simple necklace that I knew was around my throat. When I saw my reflection, there was no trace of it. It only existed on my real body. Since vampires and humans couldn't do magic, the necklace required no activation. It really was as simple as placing it around our necks.

"I can feel my clothes on the skin and the scales," Laini muttered from the other side of me. I turned to see her disguise. It was a kind of reptilian wildling, much like our helpful aquatic wildling friends from the Hive. Her violet eyes blinked and stared in the mirror. She touched her face with elegant webbed hands, her deep brown scales shimmering beautifully in the light. "Hopefully, I won't have to wear this in the end."

My tongue turned heavy in my mouth. I really hoped Laini wouldn't have to flee without us, but it was wise to be prepared.

My wildling was naked, but I couldn't see anything inappropriate with all the fur. "These will really cover our scents and auras?" I asked, picking lightly at the fur on my chest.

"I can't smell you from here," Roxy said and cackled.

"I'd rather not find out whether it works or not in public," Dorian muttered. "I wonder how Juneau expects us to test these."

I opened my mouth to comment but was interrupted by a knock at the door.

"Are you decent?" Juneau called. "I have guests who want to see our newest wildlings." Laini took off her necklace hurriedly, instantly transforming back to herself, clothes fully intact. She slipped to the back of the room to hide. Since she wasn't coming with us, she needed to keep out of sight as much as possible, avoiding interaction with any servants besides Charrek and Fenru.

"Yes, we're... fine," I said, my voice sounding strange to my ears. Softer and more chirping.

"Excellent," Juneau said and charged in with five makers I didn't recognize. He spread a jovial hand out to our group. "My wonderful staff, look upon our newest additions." His lips widened in that signature catlike smile. These makers hadn't been around since our visit. They stared at us, their beautiful broad and sharp faces taking in our appearances.

"What do you think of them?" Juneau asked proudly, his chin held high. "They come from the far north, from a dreary little dark hovel. I stumbled upon them in my travels, and they pledged fealty to me in exchange for a place to live in the city."

The closest maker, a woman with a kind smile and melancholy eyes in a long face, gave me a sympathetic look. She bowed politely. "How wonderful to meet you. How was your homeland?"

"Um," I began and fought for words.

"Cold," Roxy blurted. The makers stared at her.

"Cold?" another asked, tilting his long, shaggy-haired head to the side. "Aren't you from the desert, dear wildling?"

She coughed. "Uh, I got separated from my family."

"I found her," Kane piped up. "Our homeland was a strange place of misfit wildlings. We all found one another. The north is—" He searched for the word but couldn't find it.

"Strange," Dorian supplied.

"Mmm, indeed," the shaggy maker said, looking him up and down. "Quite strange, but we do like novelty. You'll find Juneau is a good guild master."

"Thank you," Juneau said, positively beaming. "I'll put them to work soon." His voice teemed with humor, a silent joke with our group. We would do no work for him as servants.

The maker with the sad eyes pressed one of her hands to her face, tutting benevolently. "We never know what Juneau will ask of us next," she confessed. "Welcome to our home. I hope you'll find the City of

Perpetual Light decent enough. If your homeland was as dreadful as it sounds, then perhaps you'll find some comfort in this place of luxury."

"Thank you," Dorian said with a nod of his head, his voice not betraying his disgust at the use of the hated title of the city in which we stood. "We appreciate your kind welcome."

The makers showed no sign of doubt in our disguises. They believed us to be wildlings, poor saps that Juneau had brought in as charity cases from some weird commune up north. Even the quieter two, who hung in the back and said little, seemed to believe it.

A strange joy crept over me. The magic had worked.

We could finally start our mission.

CHAPTER THIRTEEN

When I was very young, my parents sometimes took Zach and me to the beach. Zach and I would buy popsicles that melted over our hands under the brutal sun, then dive back into the choppy water to wash off the sugary residue. My favorite part about our beach trips was jumping into the rough waves and admiring the foamy water. Sometimes, treading water, I would look at the horizon and realize how far it stretched into the distance. It felt like the ocean could swallow me up if I wasn't careful.

The Immortal Plane's ocean looked nothing like the crashing waves of the Atlantic, but the sensation of being somewhat out of my depth persisted. The texture and movement of the water was all wrong—it moved more like thick vapor than fluid, almost like liquid nitrogen. Looking out across the expanse of ocean that whirled beneath the bridge we were currently crossing, goosebumps rippled across my skin. Underneath the fur of my disguise, I shivered.

We were traveling inside one of Juneau's carriages, along a grand arched bridge that connected the island reserved for the ruling class to the rest of Itzarriol. The bridge had a low wall to stop carriages, should they swerve, from plummeting into the relentless ocean far below. From outside, a faint sound carried across the area, like a beast grinding its teeth together.

"That's just the ocean crashing against the cliffs," Juneau said brightly when I asked what it was. He'd chosen to sit in the back of the carriage with us to chat and explain things as we traveled. Dorian sat up front on the driver's bench with Charrek, watching the two massive velek in bejeweled harnesses who pulled us along at a quick pace. He'd said it was so he would have a good vantage point to gather information about the city as we passed through, but it was also to spare us the pain of traveling together. Still, tiny pinpricks tickled my chest with just the slightest pressure of pain.

The carriage was very different from Juneau's fabric-hauling cart that we'd hidden in to make it to the island. The luxurious, ornate structure could comfortably fit at least six or seven people. I pressed against the bright silk draperies, which Juneau had pulled aside so we could get a view. With our disguises on, it was no big deal if someone peeked inside our carriage as we passed. We were merely a team of wildlings with our new master, ready to serve him as he took a jaunt about town.

Nothing suspicious here, folks.

I caught sight of Juneau and Kane glaring out the other window. I followed their gaze up. A giant sign adorned the final arch of the bridge, dedicating it to the politician whose name we couldn't seem to escape.

"The Lord Irrikus Lightway," Juneau said with a roll of his eyes. Beside the hand-carved sign, another statue of Irrikus towered over the traffic in case the sign hadn't sufficiently gotten the idea across.

He just loves to remind people that he's watching. "Nobody could ever hope to forget what he looks like," I muttered.

Juneau winked. "Oh, you'll see plenty of his face while we run about town."

Our host had invited us out to show us around the city, giving us a chance to get the lay of the land and gather intelligence. Going out among the people would provide us with the opportunity to catch gossip, learn where patrols and troops were stationed, and seek out other potential hiding places to use later on.

"There's a delicious rumor going around," Juneau had mentioned at breakfast. "That perhaps Irrikus himself will grace his lovely citizens with a speech at the Makers' Bazaar today. It's a common way for the council to spread news throughout the city. Naturally, they use the busiest place around to deliver the news, but Irrikus usually sends Sempre."

"A speech," Dorian echoed with a nod. "He might drop something of interest in it."

I nodded, thanking our luck for choosing today for our visit into town.

When I was a kid, I occasionally read fantasy books about mystical courts and kingdoms in far-off fictional places. Nerves jostled for position in my stomach. Somehow, I doubted that I would find the same warmth and merriment from those pages in the streets of this forsaken city.

My furry paws rested in my lap. I stared down at them, then back out the window. The carriage rocked and bounced as it left the smooth surface of the bridge for cobblestones. The same gleaming gold streets stretched out before us, but this time the area was packed with creatures of all castes, colors, and sizes. I leaned forward with Roxy, nearly knocking into her golem head, to peer out at the passing oddities.

Our carriage crawled along as the path suddenly swam with a bustling crowd. A caravan of elderly men with long silver hair passed by us at a tortoise pace. Their lush robes swept the ground, but the rulers moved as if they were floating. Their eyes stared straight ahead. An air of arrogance drifted off them, along with an actual misty cloud of acidic flowery fragrance. Elongated panthers with mint-green coats and two sets of eyes followed in the rulers' wake. A set of three rocky wildlings parted to make way for them. A pet panther swatted playfully at one, who ducked just in time. The rulers did nothing but chuckle, barely moving their lips to do so.

"Nobody is looking at us," I mentioned, catching sight of two makers who barely gave our carriage a glance.

"And why should they?" Juneau asked, pleased. "You're just little creatures staring out at your new home. They'll think you're nothing but curious new servants, as my own staff did. You'll find that most people in this place, certainly the general population of rulers, are quite selfish. They only care about themselves and what they're doing."

"Selfish? Immortal rulers? You don't say," Kane said dryly. He took a side-eyed glance at Juneau, who shrugged apologetically.

I looked out at the passing architecture and found the usual opulence of Itzarriol, but there was something more to this merchants' area. We passed wild architecture. *Wild* because heavy hanging pitcher plants and vines crawled off many nearby buildings. I couldn't even see the underlying structure. Before it, a female wildling who looked like she was made up of thousands of floating blue and gray petals was dressed in a sash and held up a paper advertisement in the style of a scroll.

Juneau glanced at the poster. "Irrikus has dispatched his communications team to advertise the speech." He grinned. "His little minions. A ghastly shade, really." He pointed, and I followed his long finger to other wildlings down the street, all unified by their coral-colored sashes.

My heart leapt with excitement. A chance to hear an actual speech by the Immortal who was likely at the head of the plot we wanted more information about? It might be helpful to us, but I kept my hopes low. Irrikus could talk about anything today.

Roxy whistled low. "We got lucky today. It's a good thing I left my rifle back at the house."

"Your what?" Juneau asked. "And why is it a good thing you left it behind?"

"Oh boy," Roxy said, shaking her head. "We'll do guns and gun safety another day, okay, Juneau?"

Ignoring the air of slight confusion from our host, I returned to my observation as our carriage kept rolling on through Itzarriol. We passed some sort of public hot spring, where a group of shaggy-haired wildlings sat around the edges. They chatted with makers, who lounged on all sides of the large basin. One maker took a long drag of a pipe that seemed to have a soul-light attached to the bowl—for power or as a fuel, I didn't know—and blew out an astounding cloud of purple smoke that rose up and transformed into a child's serene face with a gentle smile. I was completely charmed until it opened its eyes and the face contorted into a silent scream, like it was being subjected to unbearable torment. I flinched at the sight.

It was a stark reminder that here, darkness and human souls were used for magic that was sometimes nothing more than a parlor trick. How many spells were out there at this moment, swirling around us? It surrounded us on all sides, unseen yet affecting everyone.

We passed more buildings. Some were squat, while others towered hundreds of stories above us. All manners of shapes, styles, and colors bombarded my eyes. One structure had been painted to mimic a dairy cow's coloring, which made me wonder if the Immortals even knew what kind of things they'd decorated their weird city with. If they saw these things in flashes of memories from the souls, as Juneau said he had, it would explain why this city garishly collected all kinds of global cultures together.

Above us, skimmers flew through the sky, their white metallic bodies piloted by creatures of unknown type and caste. The machines sliced through the colored clouds that swirled above the city, their approach announced by beams of small white lights and a mechanical clicking. Flying beside the skimmers, a small flock of bat-like creatures mingled with a group of honking birds that sounded like geese but resembled skinny peacocks. Their green-purple feathers fanned through the air as they flew.

Juneau suddenly sat up, staring intently at someone on the street. I followed his gaze, heart racing in anticipation of trouble, only to find a sad-eyed maker with curling horns and a feline face. He didn't look like anything out of the ordinary, with his head hung low, attending a tall male ruler who conversed with someone in a nearby parked carriage. A chained collar was fastened around his neck.

"A maker I once contracted to craft buttons," Juneau said in response to my questioning look, his face uncharacteristically expressionless. "Unfortunately, he went to another ruler after getting what he thought was a better offer."

I stared at the chain around the maker's neck and grimaced as if feeling the weight of it around my own throat. "You can't do anything for him?"

"He's contracted to the other ruler now," Juneau said with a slight shake of his head. "There is nothing I can do. If it's any consolation, he's likely getting paid more than most servants if he's willing to wear that." His long silver hair brushed me. It was unnerving how I could still feel everything even wearing this disguise.

As we got deeper into this bustling part of town, hanging lanterns illuminated shop windows and soul-lit bulbs strung like Christmas lights appeared overhead. Someone on an upper balcony threw great bolts of light into the air, which exploded like fireworks. It was light pollution on overdrive. Looking up, I felt a gnawing longing to see the sky of the Mortal Plane full of stars again. In that moment, I missed it fiercely.

On the surface, I saw an ordinary bunch of people living their lives. They laughed and went about their business in the shops. I glanced between beautiful robes and happy faces. Glittering jewelry caught the light around us, glinting wildly around necks and throats and even stretching all the way up their arms. But at what cost? One had to use darkness in order to produce such things. The number of human souls used in the wasteful consumption was only made worse by the fact that Immortal rulers were essentially the sole beneficiaries of this system. No, the *worst*, the rulers never faced any resistance to their actions.

Kane grunted under his breath, his teeth grinding together. I studied his wildling face, seeing a muscle flex tight in his unfamiliar jawline. Somewhere under his disguise, I bet his fangs were extended. I hoped Dorian would be able to control himself up at the front.

"What do you sense out there?" I asked Kane. My guess was immense darkness from the various creatures, something more concentrated, more evil than we were used to. The cruel pride of the statue's face flitted through my mind.

He growled low. "More dark souls than light out there. It's an unrelenting swell of darkness. There's no escape from it. It's overwhelming."

Juneau lifted a brow and opened his mouth to say something. Curiously, he snapped it shut just as soon as he opened it. *That's probably the first time that's ever happened...*

A shadow passed over the window.

"Look," Roxy urged.

The wheels of the carriage began to fall differently on the pavement as triangular slabs of gold ran beneath us. Our carriage arrived in a massive circular courtyard. Around us, shop buildings made of jade rose up on all sides to create a cylindrical structure with six stories. The stone shimmered in the light of a dizzying number of lanterns. Each level had a covered walkway and an awning of silky violet fabric edged with lights. Combined with the lanterns, it looked utterly magical.

Juneau grinned at our awed expressions. "Welcome to the Maker's Bazaar."

Beneath the raised first floor, an area existed for carriage parking. Wildling attendants took the reins of the velek, leading the carriage to an area where they could safely tether our vehicle.

Charrek said something to one of these wildlings, who briefly looked into our carriage. The wildling was strange. He was much taller than the others I'd seen, with a wiry body of shadowy fur and dark eyes that passed quickly over our faces. He nodded and gestured Charrek to a specific place.

"No trouble yet," Juneau said brightly as our carriage rolled into the parking area. "The disguises are working just fine."

On our way in, I took the time to study the area of the bazaar that I could see through the window. A maze of low tents with pointed tops and fabrics of shimmering blue, red, and purple had been planted in the courtyard on the ground floor. Amid these tents, a towering fountain rose to the third story. Elaborate scenes of battles between mighty warriors and small shadowy figures had been carved and sculpted from the shiny copper material. It gleamed under the amber lights around the bazaar. At the top, I spotted Irrikus in a valiant pose, flexing his mighty muscles. *What a surprise.*

I fought a roll of my eyes at that statue when I realized the attendants were about to help us get out. They looked at me patiently. Whatever their personal feelings about Irrikus were, it would be best to play an awed, respectful role while we lurked around the market.

"The fountain," Kane growled suddenly behind me.

Charrek waved off the attendants and rounded the carriage to open our door himself, but I followed Kane's gaze. What I had initially believed to be water wasn't water at all. The substance changed colors, shifting from aquamarine blue to violet to angry red. It sparkled and splashed strangely, the droplets moving like fat bouncy balls in a way that water couldn't.

Kane growled again. "It's pure magical energy, isn't it?" he asked.

"Yes," Juneau said and held a finger to his lips, telling us to be quiet as Charrek opened the door.

The attendants lurked nearby, their shadowy limbs twitching as they tethered the velek.

Kane dropped his voice so that only the people in the carriage could hear his final complaint. "It takes many, many suffering souls to create that much magic. That pointlessly showy fountain is a repulsive waste."

Charrek swept his arm and gestured for us to come out. Juneau descended first and stretched dramatically, like a cat who had just woken from a wonderful nap. Kane went next, his expression deliberately blank. I followed Roxy out and heard her swear under her breath.

The bazaar itself felt more claustrophobic than I anticipated. People jostled one another in the aisles between vendors, clamoring in delight or haggling prices. Unfortunately, the height of the Immortal rulers meant that it was difficult to see any great distance.

"Let's move a little closer," Juneau said and beckoned us to follow. Charrek and Dorian took the front. My heart twisted. I wanted nothing more than to be close to Dorian right now, but it was impossible. We had to take the utmost precaution in the bazaar with our disguises. A wildling collapsing in the middle of the street might draw dangerous attention.

Roxy, Kane, and I made our way through a haze of purple smoke, courtesy of the pipes being smoked by the group of makers. I sniffed the strong scent of heady musk. It made my head swim until I stumbled against Roxy, who'd apparently held her breath instead. Juneau glanced back and grinned. "Careful. It might be too strong for a *wildling* to breathe."

As we dove through the smoke cloud, more rising scents of exotic cooking and perfume filled the air, along with loud, boisterous music. It overwhelmed my senses. I blinked and tried to keep track of the beautiful chaos but failed. Even after we left the cloud, my head still spun in a sense of surreal wonder. I was in a city of Immortals and surrounded by magic.

"Can't see a freaking thing," Roxy lamented, glaring up at the towering figures of Immortal rulers and makers. I bit back a laugh. She was even shorter than I was, and I couldn't see much between the bodies.

I moved with her through the tent, following Juneau's magnificent robes that flapped elegantly behind him.

A woman with triangle tattoos that interlocked in mesmerizing patterns across her face offered us samples of a strange insect. The eight-legged bug with a shiny red shell had been stuck through with a toothpick and roasted over open coals. I didn't want to find out what it might do to a human digestive system. Roxy sneezed violently after another vendor sprayed her with perfume. As we moved on, a more pleasing scent arose, one which I realized a few steps later was roasted velek.

"It's like a Ren fair," Roxy muttered in my ear. She'd gone to those events whenever she'd had a day of leave from the Bureau in the autumn. I'd never been to one, but if Ren fairs were like this, I definitely should have.

I dragged my eyes back to Juneau and struggled to keep from laughing when I saw that he was also having difficulty peering over the crowd. Our host was a good deal shorter than the other rulers, though he could take solace in being the most fabulously dressed of the bunch.

A team of acrobats flipped in front of us, then soared overhead, suspending themselves on wires hung above the crowd.

"Nice to know they have some entertainment," Roxy said with a chuckle.

"Wildling," a crooning voice called beside me. "Want to come and see some horrors? We'll delight you for a mere fraction of your time, I'm sure."

I turned to see a beady-eyed maker with dark blue fur grinning down at Roxy and me with crooked, hooked teeth. The two of us shrank back as we stared up at the maker. He had painted himself to look like a human skeleton. None of the crowd had addressed us directly before, and I wasn't sure what to do. I clubbed down the hysterical urge to say something ridiculous, like, "Take me to your leader" or "Greetings, fellow Immortal."

He gestured to a ragged black tent behind him. "Come one, come all," he shouted to the disinterested crowd. "Delight in horrors beyond your imagination in the one and only dark soul energy experience. Take a journey through the horrors of the Mortal Plane. Be shocked—no! Horrified! You'll see terrors of the Mortal Plane like you've never experienced before."

As one, Roxy and I disappeared, melting into the crowd before the maker could say another word. Horrors from the Mortal Plane? I thought of Dorian's face whenever he consumed blood, and shuddered. It was disgusting that someone would view that as entertainment. The things he had to see when he fed were enough to drive anybody mad.

The bazaar swirled around us, colorful and fun, but it took on a darker edge when I considered that all this luxury came from human evil in the Mortal Plane and was built on the backs of exploited makers and harvesters. It left a bad taste in my mouth, despite the pleasant aroma of baked goods wafting through the air. An unsettling sensation of dread came over me. It was warm in the midst of the thrumming crowd, even though I didn't really have fur, but I shivered anyway.

A blast of eerie horns rose up over the crowd, startling me badly.

Roxy gave an annoyed grunt. "Guess the real festivities are starting."

The horns sounded again. From behind us, I saw a stir of movement. The crowd parted, and a carriage cut through, heading toward the fountain. Wildlings, makers, and even rulers all jumped back. I pressed my lips together as my stomach rolled with anticipation. I had a feeling that today's main guest had just arrived.

The carriage, gold and heavy with jewels, flew by us. The herd of velek that dragged it were pure black and bayed madly, shaking scarlet manes. Quickly, the crowd began to follow the carriage as it passed. I grabbed Roxy and pulled her aside so we wouldn't get crushed. Two human women stood no chance against a passionate crowd of Immortals.

"Climb on my shoulders," Roxy whispered. "At least one of us should be able to see, and I'm sturdier." Kane sidled up beside us and grabbed a crate from a distracted vendor. I scrambled onto Roxy's shoulders, and Kane balanced on the box. With the crate for Kane, and my height combined with Roxy's, we could just see over the heads of the gathered Immortals. Juneau and Dorian floated a few groups ahead in the crowd.

All eyes were on Irrikus as he exited the carriage, which had stopped on a raised platform near the fountain. The first thing I saw was his massive boot, clad in thick gold plate. His outfit was similar to what Inkarri wore, except he had commissioned his armor and cape from the finest materials available.

Kane snarled. I hushed him, but nobody paid any attention to us.

Although I hated to admit it, there was a beauty in his cruelty, so much that it nearly hurt to look at him. The planes of his face were too sharp, the twist of his lips too cruel. The long locks of his hair were gold and looked like they would cut if you touched them. His crown, twisted and curved, had been forged from gold and embedded with stones of flaming red and glittering forest green. But even without the added height of the crown, Irrikus was taller than I'd thought he would be. He must have stood at least ten or eleven feet tall. As he ascended the platform, the crown never moved on his steady head. My blood ran cold. I wasn't just looking at an Immortal ruler, but a monster.

Climbing out of the carriage after Irrikus was a familiar figure. Inkarri stared at the ground, her long blue hair braided to one side. She appeared oddly demure, even subdued. I made a note to try and learn more about

Inkarri's position with the council. She rode with them to the speech. Maybe she was their strongest hunter.

Irrikus walked on until he reached the center of the platform beside the fountain. It lifted him high enough to be seen. *By most people, anyway.* Roxy grunted beneath me but held steady. I would have to thank her later.

"Beloved citizens of Itzarriol, I welcome you to hear news from your council," Irrikus announced.

Although I saw no amplification equipment, his voice rushed out over the crowd like a mighty wind. The voice coaxed us to listen. It carried across the enormous, packed space with little effort. Was this another example of a ruler's strange vocal powers? I shuddered as I remembered Inkarri's commands to me at the lake. There was something embedded in his voice—a deep, distant pride that knew none dared question it. Who could take his power from him? No one. For an instant, I could've sworn I saw a flash of Alan's face in the tilt of Irrikus's chin.

"First and foremost, I would like to extend an invitation of the highest honor," Irrikus announced. Kane and I glanced at each other. "The council is holding a grand celebration for the public. All castes are invited and are expected to attend. It will be held at the Grand Senate in three days." He swept his hand in the air and smiled, but his eyes were cold.

"He's a party planner now?" Roxy muttered below.

"And what do we have to celebrate? Oh, there is much. Life in Itzarriol has never been better for you, my fair citizens, since Lady Izelde, Lord Orrin, and our council brought about the fall of Vanim." He grinned, a flash of white teeth that somehow beamed brighter than his hair. "But that was only the beginning. Each day, we grow closer and closer to erad- icating the leech scourge that holds us back from everything we've wished for and built. We believe we are on the cusp of our greatest victory yet. For we cannot know true perfection until we destroy this terrible pest. Under the programs that Lord Sempre and Director Zeele have developed in the sanitarium, we've been doing something *special*."

The crowd around us broke out into murmurs for the first time.

Diagonal from me now, Juneau's face paled as his gaze landed on the terrible Immortal ruler on stage. Farther up ahead, Charrek whispered something to Dorian.

Whatever they were doing, it meant bad news for us. My stomach dropped.

"We know that it is our duty to conquer all," Irrikus continued. "And what is there left to do? Sempre has found the answer for us. With the generous help of our guests in the sanitarium, he has established a way to directly affect the Mortal Plane." He let out a cut-glass laugh as the crowd erupted into cheers.

I gasped, going momentarily lightheaded, unable to help myself. It was covered by the polite clapping.

Irrikus waved, and the crowd went utterly still. A slick grin cracked his face. "We've begun to root out the most dangerous beasts from the untamed wilds at the heart of our land. With a little help, we have begun disposing of them in the Mortal Plane. It will open more of our world for development. We can create new cities and lay the foundation to improve our means of production. The harvesters will be able to tap into new areas of unharvested souls, which we have not dared disturb before for fear of the beasts. But soon, those beasts will have another home."

He chuckled, and I hated the way it boomed into every corner of the bazaar. It shook the wooden poles of the tent. Someone cackled happily behind us. I balled my hands into fists.

"And soon, we'll embark upon a project to create a wave of new, darker souls!"

More cries of celebration echoed through the crowd. Nausea and rage rose in me. A new wave of souls? That could only be accomplished by manufacturing death and evil in the Mortal Plane.

Inkarri stood motionless next to him, her eyes still on the ground. It was as though Irrikus had forgotten she existed. She looked like a toy soldier, glimmering in her armor. Thankfully, her magicked velek was nowhere to be seen.

Irrikus nodded as the latest round of applause died out. "Yes! A new wave of souls, darker than ever before, will create more energy for us *and* strike a blow to our leech enemies in the Mortal Plane. It's a tactical victory on all fronts. The humans in the Mortal Plane have no idea what's coming to them." He smiled coldly.

"With more souls than ever before, we will begin a new age. I, Lord Irrikus the Light Bringer, will lead you into this prosperity! We will have even more magical technology. Picture it: more advanced skimmers, new buildings, more art, more leisure, more light, more love, more joy for all of you! I do this for you, my people."

He looked out at the crowd with softer eyes, his gaze almost loving. The stare of a psychopath looking upon his herd of adoring captives. "The time for this dawn draws near," he breathed. His voice dropped. "Sooner than you might expect."

It was not a warning, but a promise.

CHAPTER FOURTEEN

"We need to learn more," Dorian muttered.

He paced the room in frantic circles. I leaned against one of the posts of the large bed, well out of range. We both needed clear heads, because we had to plan.

Even at this distance, however, I could see his handsome face mulling everything over with a grave scowl. I enjoyed the way his eyebrows pinched together as a strategy buzzed somewhere in the confines of his mind. For a moment, I felt transported back to our time on the run. My chest squeezed, and I leaned my head against the wooden post. Dorian's face twitched.

"Are you okay?" Roxy asked, glancing at me.

I nodded. "Of course. Just thinking." The last part of that sentence left my mouth in a wheeze as Dorian circled closer. Roxy shook her head but let it go.

"How long has Irrikus been planning this?" Laini asked. She'd left her study of Juneau's archives to come and hear what we'd learned in our afternoon outing.

"I keep asking myself that, again and again," Dorian said, clearly frustrated.

"Since he came out of the womb and declared us the scourge of the universe?" Kane suggested dryly. He huffed and dropped his face into his hands.

Without the jewelry, he had returned to his normal appearance. I swept my gaze past him to Laini. Her face remained grim, with a tight frown. *Did she find anything in the archives?* We'd need to ask her later. This clearly wasn't the time.

Dorian's ranting cut through my thoughts. "He must have been planning this for years, but why? The rulers have more riches and power than they know what to do with. They've already almost destroyed our kind."

"Almost," Laini said, a cold note ringing in her tone. "For a monster like Irrikus, that's not enough. Only complete genocide will satisfy him."

Roxy snorted. "God, I never thought someone could have *so* many statues of himself. Is he worried people might forget he's top dog for ten seconds?"

I stared down at the floor, my mind whirring. "We have to track down the Immortal Council," I said. "Irrikus *is* the top dog, but from what he said in that speech, it's mainly others who are responsible for his big plans. Lady Izelde and Lord Orrin were in charge of destroying Vanim. Irrikus said that a Lord Sempre is the one who has found a way to directly interact with the Mortal Plane. And the other guy he mentioned in connection with the sanitarium that Juneau is so afraid of, that Director Zeele guy, I'm pretty sure I heard some of the hunters mention him at the safehouse raid. I think Zeele was in charge of torturing Kono."

A shadow of triumph flashed across Dorian's face. "We're starting to find the pieces. Names are crucial. Now, we need to find out what they're planning with this new wave of souls. It sounds like it's going to be implemented very soon." His eyes hardened.

"You said this Sempre guy has found a way to influence the Mortal Plane," Laini said. "What do you think that means?" She turned to Dorian, who stared past us into the far distance. I could almost see the gears of his thoughts whirring.

A small scrape darkened the highest part of his cheekbone. A souvenir from our outing, or had it been there before? My insides twisted as I realized I hadn't even had the chance to look at him up close for the last few days. Life kept forcing us apart. I turned my attention back to the conversation. The faster we figured out our plan, the better I would feel.

"They could be planning to send something worse through the tear," Roxy suggested. "Or something else. Who knows? I still can't see what the Bureau wanted to do with the tear."

"The Bureau. The Immortal Council. What do they have to do with each other?" I wondered aloud. "It feels like we took down one group, just to find an even worse one standing behind it." My nerves jumped with frustration. I hated defeatist talk, but I needed to vent for the moment to those who understood me most.

Kane nodded with a sharp gesture, apparently frustrated beyond words.

"If they have something else in mind," Laini added with a shudder, "I can only imagine it would be horrifying."

Dorian crossed his arms. "Let's not get ahead of ourselves. We'll work on what we have before we speculate. We need to investigate Lord Sempre, if we can. And anything we can learn about how Izelde and Orrin invaded Vanim can only be helpful. It also wouldn't hurt to hunt around for information about that Zeele person Lyra said the hunters mentioned."

"Sempre, Izelde, Orrin, Zeele," Laini echoed. Her voice dripped with hatred, as if she were carving them into a hit list with an invisible blade.

I hated seeing her like this. A cloud of anger had enveloped our friend, and I suspected I could do little to help, since my own species did their part in starting this entire debacle. After all, Laini was rightfully pissed at the rulers. They had taken practically everything from her. Worse, I could feel the way my own skin prickled when Irrikus's arrogant face flashed through my mind. There had been so many lost. I shut my eyes for a moment and wished I could travel back in time. Back before the Immortal Plane, back in the compound when Dorian and I were just beginning to forge our strange companionship. I would've screamed at that Lyra to look harder at the world around her, to appreciate it while it lasted. The memory of those days brought me a sense of surreal nostalgia.

Grayson was still alive back then. Jim. Kreya and Rhome... their kids, Carwin and Detra. Myndra. Lex. How many had we lost, some for certain and others to fates unknown? I swallowed, fighting a gritty itch in my throat. Something else burned alongside the pain from Dorian's proximity—determination. It tasted grim in my mouth, but I set my jaw.

"Do you think all the vampire kidnappings have something to do with Irrikus's plans?" Roxy asked, breaking the silence. We all gave her a curious look, so she continued. "Back at the Hive, they said that hunters had recently stopped killing the vampires they caught and were instead keeping them prisoner. Hell, we saw it happen to Kono. But why the change?" She let us wrestle with the question for a moment before she gave her theory. "What if they're trying to find out how vampires cross the barrier? If Immortals could find a way to cross the barrier like vampires do, they wouldn't need the tear at all. Maybe they've found a way to survive in the Mortal Plane."

Dorian exhaled. "It's a thought."

There was a weighty silence as we considered the idea. It occurred to me how much Irrikus must hate that vampires were able to do something he couldn't. Especially when he considered them to be a sub-species. I hoped it got under his golden locks and ate him up at night. He appeared to be the particular kind of psycho who could only rest easy if he knew that he had succeeded in destroying everything that even whispered a threat to his power.

"The party," Kane said, brow furrowed as he talked out the idea as it came to him. "He said all castes were welcome. So, in addition to looking around the city, why don't we also go there? With our disguises, we should have no problem getting into his dumb giant senate building. It's where the Immortal Council does most of their business, so surely there might be records we could search, right?"

Dorian nodded. Juneau had mentioned that the council spent much of their time at Irrikus's senate, currying favor.

Laini shrugged. "It could be a good way to catch them off guard.

They'll be schmoozing or gossiping. I bet they'll be trying to outdo one another so much, they won't even notice us."

"It's not a perfect plan," Roxy said. "It shouldn't be our only plan, that's for sure, but why blow that opportunity? The enemy just waved us in for a visit. Let's explore behind their lines."

I shut my eyes and rubbed the tired lids softly, seeing spots in the darkness. Weren't we already behind enemy lines? But an excited stir crawled up my spine. Roxy might have a point. When would we get a chance like this again?

"It's a big risk," Kane said. "We have no idea what to expect in there. The senate building will be on high alert with all the castes there. I don't think we'll find them distracted."

"The guards might not be distracted, but the rulers almost certainly will be," Dorian said. He gave Kane a sharp look. "Did you have another plan in mind?"

Kane smiled wickedly. "If we could kidnap a guard, it would be much easier. Abduct them, drug them, ask them questions. We wouldn't have to draw attention to ourselves."

"Your solution is to roofie some guards?" Roxy asked. "What if someone notices they're missing?"

Laini cleared her throat. "Whatever we do, we're going to need even *more* of Juneau's help. We may not have many more favors to call in. Would the info we *might* get from one guard or the ball be worth it?"

Kane frowned, disappointed, but Laini had a point. There was no need to risk ourselves if we didn't need to. As much as an infiltration mission could bring us some crucial info, we had no guarantee that we would find anything of use, and it might be too dangerous. Laini was also right in that it would mean asking more favors of Juneau. Our lovely host was off somewhere on an errand. His clients had called with dozens of last-minute requests upon hearing the news of the party. I hoped Charrek made a strong pot of Immortal coffee for their upcoming work.

"We've already got good disguises," I pointed out. "I do like the idea of sneaking in, and the guard plan might work. For now, why not use the disguises to do more scouting in the city? We only went out once, and we have three days until the party." Gears slowly turned in my mind, scraps of information clicking together into a plan. "*Something* must have happened that prompted Irrikus to announce that his plan is going into action very soon. We should try to figure out what's made him so chipper that he's throwing a freaking city-wide celebration for all castes. It seems too charitable and inclusive for someone like him, so it must be for a reason. If we could do more pointed scouting missions, that would also give you guys a chance to feed."

Kane perked up at that. "There's nothing I'd rather do than sink my fangs into some of these creeps."

Dorian's gaze flickered to me. A ghost of a pleased smirk came to his face. "You're right. We vampires can slip out in our disguises and travel to the edges of the city to feed and scout for gossip or murmurings of unrest. Somewhere distant enough that the skimmers and patrols aren't lurking all the time. If the Hive vampires managed to feed fairly regularly, then it shouldn't be a problem for us."

"We'll have to be careful," Laini said, almost whispering. "And we should target specific people to follow. I suggest guards and hunters. They'll be the most dangerous and the most involved with the council, I bet."

"Agreed." Dorian sucked in a breath. "We'll interrogate them before we feed and see if we can obtain any memories from the darkness in their blood."

"And what will we do?" Roxy asked. "I know Lyra must be thinking the same thing as me. We don't want to just sit around while the vampires get to go out and kick ass. Put us to work."

"Juneau's collection," I said. "Laini said she hasn't managed to put much of a dent in it yet."

Laini snorted. "I read *very* fast, but Juneau is quite the collector."

"Maybe we can help find something," I said with a shrug. "We could read while they scout."

Roxy groaned. "*Lyra!* I meant something cool. That's the most boring task."

Laini laughed behind her hand. "I will continue helping, since there are a few books I've found so far that aren't written in the universal language. And don't worry, Roxy, it's the most interesting task. You'll see." A glimmer of her old self broke through the gloom. "It doesn't matter which plane you're from or what species you are—everyone has written down their secrets at one time or another. The books we'll be looking at are filled with them. What could be more interesting than that?"

Roxy could hardly argue with that.

I sneezed as I ruffled the pages before me. "For someone who loves to collect precious objects, he sure doesn't like to clean them."

Juneau had given us an unused sitting room at the very back of the house to do our research. Most of his guest suites had lain empty for years, judging by the dust. After sleeping off the excitement of the bazaar, the next morning Charrek had dragged tables and chairs to our new base of operations and helped us organize the work area while we hauled things out of the hidden chamber. Now we were surrounded by books and scrolls and notes scrawled in our various handwritings, covered in dust, and rapidly heading for mental exhaustion.

Laini handed me a small feather duster without looking up. "I suspect he doesn't let anyone but Charrek down there to grab things. I'm sure even Juneau has forgotten what he has down there." I studied her for a moment as I took the duster, murmuring thanks. The tense lines of Laini's face had relaxed slightly as we focused on our task.

"Energizing tea?" Charrek offered, sidling up to the table with a tray carrying a delicate china tea set that looked like it had come out of a mad scientist's dream. Why were there so many unnecessary spikes and tendrils? I stared at the viscous silver liquid bubbling in the kettle. Although we'd experienced no adverse effects from eating food in the Immortal Plane so far, I wasn't going to get cocky and drink an Immortal's idea of an energy drink. It could give me liver failure for all I knew.

"Uh, no thank you. But thank you for the offer. That's very kind of you."

He left it on the table anyway. Laini braved a cup but nearly gagged. Her eyes flashed silver for an instant, then she attacked the work again with renewed vigor, so it apparently worked for vampires.

I wiped my hands and rubbed my face vigorously to fight off my heavy eyelids. I'd slept fitfully the night before. My dreams were manic streams of dark shadows, Dorian's far-off cries, and being chased by someone. I never caught the face of the person pursuing me, but I saw the glint of gold in the corner of my eye.

"Are the horrifying illustrations of how to skin an aquatic wildling really necessary?" Roxy muttered as she took a break from her scroll. "I didn't think it was possible, but this is worse than the mind-numbing details of that council meeting about tracking the patterns of the soul wind so they could send harvesters to the most plentiful landing places." She tossed the parchment aside, resting her head on the table with a groan.

Catching sight of the drawing, I grimaced, quickly twisting the scroll closed. As I did so, I saw that farther down the document, someone had long ago scrawled strange symbols on the page. They weren't in the universal language, and it didn't look like Vampiric.

"Any ideas what this is, Laini?" I asked, turning it toward her.

Laini squinted at the scroll. "I can't read it, but I've found similar marks in other books, so I'm guessing it's a kind of ancient language. I doubt even Juneau can read it, since he's a younger Immortal ruler. Thankfully, most of the stuff we want to know is from a few hundred to maybe a thousand or so years ago, and all that is either written in the universal language or Vampiric, both of which I can read." She ran a nail along her open notebook, which was filled with scrawls I couldn't understand. She favored writing in a shorthand form of Vampiric, explaining that it was faster for her and would stop any Immortals from making sense of the notes, if the worst were to happen.

"Honey, we're home," a sarcastic voice called. An attractive ram-horned wildling popped into the room. "I saw that on the TV box back in Scotland."

Roxy lost a fight with a smile, rolling her eyes. "It's just a TV. You don't have to say box every time."

Dorian followed him in, also clad in his wildling disguise. I blinked. It was odd, but somehow Reshi had managed to throw a bit of Dorian into the strange costume, even with mandibles.

It was immediately apparent that he had fed because even at our safe distance of fifteen feet the telltale burn began in my chest. There was new darkness brewing in him. I pushed back from the table and moved to the opposite end as Dorian approached.

He took off his necklace. As he transformed back to his handsome self, he shot me an apologetic look. I simply shrugged. There wasn't anything we could do about it right now. We had to move past it and focus on the task at hand.

"Learn anything interesting?" Roxy demanded, thankfully distracting us.

"Depends on what you consider interesting," Kane answered. He transformed back to himself and placed his necklace in front of him on the table. "We made our way across rooftops to a guard outpost near the edge of the city. Juneau told us that it's mostly unstaffed. He's been using it for years as a place to smuggle things in and out. He slipped us a hand-drawn map to it, which we burned just in case."

Dorian leaned against the wall. "We managed to catch a solitary guard and dragged him to an abandoned warehouse. Kane kept watch while I interrogated him. He didn't want to talk at first." He gave an uncomfortable shrug. "But I can be persuasive. He told me all he knew about the military structure here. Most of the hunters are out on missions to find beasts in the deepest, wildest parts of the Immortal Plane, where Irrikus hopes to build new cities. The guard didn't know much about the tear, but *we* know that the hunters are herding these creatures through it into the Mortal Plane. Irrikus confirmed it in his speech, even though he didn't mention the tear specifically."

Kane grunted. "But he did tell Dorian that the most experienced and powerful hunters are deployed near Vanim, where they believe the highest concentration of vampire activity is. There's also a training camp for hunter recruits out there." He curled his lips in a scornful sneer. "Lucky us."

"It's where the tear is," Dorian supplied. "Like I said, the guard didn't appear to know about it. I guess they're keeping most of their soldiers in the dark."

"Like the Bureau did," I muttered. Alan and his comrades had been more than happy to do that to all their soldiers. They had manipulated us, keeping us in the dark for years. The only solace I had was that Alan currently sat in a tidy jail cell in Scotland with two other board members.

Roxy huffed. "Nice to know that bosses are jerks in this plane, too."

Dorian shifted his weight restlessly. "They have new creatures that they're magicking to detect vampires through scent. He claimed they're using other senses to work around the fact that Immortals can't perceive our auras. He didn't know anything else of interest to us."

For a moment, dread crawled over my shoulders. It was a start, but it still wasn't a lot of information. We still didn't know what was meant by this new wave of darkness they intended to unleash on the Mortal Plane. And we had no way to warn anyone back in the VAMPS camp or our teammates at the Hive. What were Zach and Gina doing now? I missed them terribly, but I wanted to succeed on our mission here. I wanted to go back with information that would help us all move forward successfully.

"We need to get closer to the top guys," Kane said. "Irrikus mentioned Orrin, Izelde, and Sempre. They're on the council and seem like they're in charge of the war plans and research going on. I'm less concerned about Zeele. It sounds like he works for Sempre anyway."

Roxy clicked her tongue. "I'm telling you guys, the ball would be a good opportunity. We have something specific we want to get information about—the intended attack on the Mortal Plane—so we wouldn't be going in blind. Some of us could do the social rounds and get drunk, pompous rulers to gossip with us, while the rest see if they can get into the council room or any personal quarters. There's never going to be another chance like this to get into the senate."

My mind whirred to life like an old film projector lighting up. I imagined us sneaking in with our disguises, splitting up, and searching their quarters. The guards would be alert, but the rulers would be out socializing. It was a decent idea. A dangerous one, but what wasn't these days? We needed to take a risk. If we succeeded, it could mean a massive turn in the tide for us.

"We can't all go," Dorian pointed out. "Someone needs to stay behind." His eyes slid over to Laini for a moment. Her explosive behavior made her the most likely to compromise the mission at this point and the best choice to stay behind. I eyed her, but to my surprise, her face was perfectly calm.

"I'll do it," Laini said. "I hate to be left behind on an important mission, but..." Her voice dropped. "We need a failsafe. If things go wrong, we need somebody to take a message to the Hive and then deliver the news of everything that we've learned to our allies back in Moab and Scotland. There's so much to cover."

I listed everything in my mind—the "wave of darkness," the scouting velek, the Immortal troops displacing beasts into the Mortal Plane, a hunter training camp near Vanim and the tear, everything we'd learned about living as humans in the Immortal Plane. It nearly made me light-headed to consider it all, and yet it still wasn't enough.

Dorian stared at Laini, one of the last of his living family in this world. He nodded solemnly. "You're right about the escape part. It's practical. We need to think about what happens if we fail."

On that note, a cold air came over the room as we sat with the task stretched out before us. I resisted clenching my hands as the tension grew. The danger loomed long ahead of us. There was so much at stake —*everything*.

"We'll plan an escape route for you with Juneau's maps." Dorian ran a hand over his hair. His eyes held an edge of warning as his gaze focused on Laini. "No rescue attempts. If something happens to the four of us, you can't risk yourself and the valuable information that we've fought to gather."

Laini straightened. "Of course." Her tone wavered with a mixture of pride and grief. For a moment, her eyes looked glassy with tears, but when I blinked, they were gone. There was nothing but determination in Laini's expression. It sent a fire through me.

We're in this together.

"When Juneau returns, we'll tell him," Dorian said.

"Tell me what?" Juneau asked as he glided in. His arms were full of scrolls. Charrek followed, clutching bolts of fabric in each pair of his hands. A length of glimmering purple lace was draped over his shoulder, giving the impression that he was clad in a gorgeous gown.

"We would like to attend the council's celebration," Dorian said. "And we need to plan an escape route for Laini, in case it ends badly. I hope we can rely on you to give us the lay of the land."

Juneau grinned magnificently and threw down his collection of scrolls. "To hell with these boring jobs! Of course I'll help." He rubbed his elegant hands together gleefully. "Let's *do* something."

"I'll get more tea," Charrek said, the barest hint of an amused smile on his face. He grabbed the scrolls Juneau had dropped and left the room. A few specks of glitter floated in the air behind him as he left, arising from the various fabrics.

Juneau threw himself down at the head of the table. "You'll need to look cool and collected when you go in." He flicked his hair behind him and brought out a blank scroll from somewhere deep within his sleeve, then pulled a fluffy feather quill from a hidden pocket. "I know a fellow who may have a map of the Grand Palace. There are great benefits to befriending your servants, you know—they talk to other servants, and dissatisfied servants are often willing to share secrets. Until then, I can draw you a basic sketch. I don't attend many parties, but when I do—"

"You're nosy?" Kane guessed.

Juneau's feline smile appeared on his face. "Oh, like you wouldn't believe. I'll tell you exactly which chambers you need to look for. All the bigwigs should be attending. Until we get a proper map, let me lay some things out for you." He began scratching at the page. His draftsmanship was excellent, given his lifetime of drawing various fashion ideas.

But Juneau's excitement turned my stomach sour. He was overrun with boyish delight at our prospective mission. I stared at the rest of our group, contemplating the grim determination we shared. For Juneau, this was his chance to finally help disrupt the system he'd never felt empowered to change. For us, it could cost our lives, and possibly the lives of those we loved in the Mortal Plane if we failed.

Dorian met my eyes, his jaw clenched with resolute passion.

We had a lot of work to do.

CHAPTER FIFTEEN

I stepped into the hot water with a pleased groan. Bubbles drifted up
from the turquoise water and flew through the air. They caught on
one another and built mountainous chains of bubbles on the surface of
the bathwater. The bubbling water lapped gently at the steps of a shimmery silver staircase. Giant spiral shells as big as I was decorated the
walls of the pool both above and below the water.

Juneau's heated pool smelled sort of like lavender, I decided, but also a
little like chemically created lemons. It was simultaneously sweet and
acidic, but oddly relaxing. I lowered myself deeper until my hair floated
up around me. When I was younger, I'd done this in pools and pretended
I was some strange mermaid with eels for hair.

As vaguely obscene as I felt to have the thirty-foot tub to myself, I had
requested some time alone tonight. As fun as it was to jump into the hot
springs with the other women, it felt like... too much right now. Roxy
would crack jokes and splash around, and Laini would stare off into the
distance.

This bath might as well have been a swimming pool, considering how
huge it was. And this was Juneau's *guest* bathroom. And he wasn't even
one of the more influential rulers.

"Opulence. Luxury. Riches." I whispered the words out into the steam. "What more could the rulers want?"

Despite having so much, Irrikus wanted more. He wanted everything. He wanted complete destruction of vampires. He would never stop. I closed my eyes and exhaled deeply, letting myself sink beneath the surface once more. Under the water, the sounds echoed differently. Water moved strangely in the Immortal Plane, even within the confines of the pool. I heard a slight tinkling of bells. Leftover human souls pulsing through the water to remind me of how all this magic worked?

I would never forget how magic was made. Despite the glittering surface, the hard truth lurked around every corner: magic required suffering. It was so unlike the fairytales I used to read as a kid, before moving on to books for junior survivalists. I sighed and came up for air.

Shelves carved into the wall carried stacks of luxurious dark blue towels. A few silk robes hung next to the towels, looking like precious gems had been melted down into fabric. I had tried one on before slipping into the pool. It was gigantic, practically a tent even on my taller-than-average frame.

As I floated, a demented sea serpent glared at me as it did battle with a tentacled creature with a crooked beak on the ceiling. What would a room in Juneau's mansion be without some warped underwater mosaic scene?

Though I tried to relax, questions crept through my brain, never far from my thoughts. Why had the Bureau worked with the rulers to eradicate vampires? How long had Irrikus been working on this? He was the one who started the process of getting vampires removed from their role as cleansers on the Immortal Council. That would make him very old. I closed my eyes and tried to recall his face, but it was impossible to guess his age from his appearance. Juneau looked no older than a cheerful twenty-seven-year-old, despite having three centuries under his fabulous belt.

Like a mental filing cabinet, I arranged everything before me as if I were a police detective trying to solve a murder.

Our scouting missions had given us a better idea of the number of hunters we were going up against. We had managed to discover a few of the areas with the greatest concentration of hunters. Most importantly, through reading Juneau's papers and interrogating various guards, we'd learned the location of several gates to the Mortal Plane. They were currently heavily guarded by hunters, but if we needed to slip through in an emergency or, worst-case scenario, Laini needed to flee alone, we knew where we could go.

The most concerning thing was that we'd gained solid evidence of hunters rousing as many terrible creatures as possible from the wild areas of the Immortal Plane and pushing them through the tear between planes. How was the Bureau handling that? I remembered the fires and the frantic scramble to defend Moab against the empty swarm that threatened to consume everything in its path. I hoped they could hold out a little longer. Before we could return to assist, we needed to learn more about the "wave of darkness" that Irrikus had preached about so enthusiastically to his citizens. He'd made genocide sound like a public health initiative.

I rubbed my eyes, wishing I had access to human coffee. I didn't know if I could read another line of faded ink on dusty paper, trying to puzzle out with Laini the sometimes-confusing turns of phrase used in the universal language. Juneau had stacks upon stacks of journals and historical scrolls. At one point, Laini had needed to lay a cold cloth over her eyes.

"I don't think I've ever read so much," she had said. "Even studying architecture back in Vanim, I didn't spend this much time bent over books."

Roxy nodded, looking miserably at her own stack. "I'm much better with practical knowledge that involves moving my body. Academia is not my strong suit."

We had been able to glean some information from the ancient sources, however. Little by little, a better picture of the history of the Immortal Plane came into focus. A thousand years in the past, vampires *had* been on the council. During that time, the current exploitative system had been much more fair, thanks to the cleansers. Vampires served as essential watchdogs who made sure society and the council never tipped out of balance. The system back then was based on the exchange of services between groups who had different types of power, rather than the victimization of all the other castes by the rulers. As we compiled our notes, I got the sense that we were uncovering a horror story one journal at a time.

"For a being who lives forever, it's nothing to enact a long-term strategy of universal domination," Laini had added bitterly.

Roughly seven hundred years ago, Irrikus rose to power in the Immortal Council and began his cruel campaign. But it hadn't started out cruel. He'd had legitimate concerns about vampires and worried that their enforcer role left them as the sole judges of good and evil. Irrikus's intentions began innocently enough. He started by voicing minor criticisms against the vampires, sowing subtle seeds of doubt. The vampires at the time had agreed that Irrikus had a point. How did they know that the vampires weren't monopolizing their position? A hundred years later, Irrikus began to change his tune. He grew more and more critical. Every scrap of power he negotiated with the vampires never seemed to please him. He became gradually obsessed with the idea that vampires were somehow plotting against the Immortal Council. No amount of assurance or evidence to the contrary stopped his paranoia. Then he began moving to undermine vampires. He stripped them of their political power and vilified them. He banned other groups from helping the cleansers at all. After that, he and his council members began to create rules that entrapped the harvesters, makers, and wildlings into the brutal system of subservience that we had observed during our time here.

Most of this information was clearly news to Dorian and our friends. In the research room, Kane had sat at the table for a long time with his head in his hands. Finally, he got up without a word, threw a single book as hard as he could across the room, and left. Nobody chased him. No one reprimanded him about the book, although Juneau winced slightly. It was justified. Everything the vampires had known about their lives, their history, and their family had been missing a vital piece. It had been taken away from them by someone who was willing to do anything to ensure his own power was absolute and untouchable. What a cruel thing, to take away the history of an entire people. Over pages and pages, I watched as Irrikus's greed consumed him. Sometimes a journal would just end with no warning, only for another document to mention that the writer had been killed or imprisoned for treason against Irrikus and the council. Everywhere but these writings, Irrikus controlled the narrative, and he had done everything he could to twist the perception of vampires and their sympathizers until there was nothing but hatred for cleansers, where there had once been awe and respect.

The same way the Bureau tried to corrupt the truth about vampires. The similarities between the rulers and my own people surrounded me and threatened to swallow me up on both sides. Humanity's role in this entire affair made my heart twist painfully. Greed spoke to everyone, ruler or not.

So much precious information had been lost through the years of persecution. I ran my hand through the water and let it drip between my fingers. Fighting Irrikus felt like fighting something we could never hold onto. I wanted to know exactly what he knew and what he planned to do. With the Bureau, I often felt like I was in the dark, but with the Immortal Council, it was like trying to pick my way through a maze completely hidden in shadows. I balled the hand into a fist.

Someone tapped on the wall at the open arched doorway that led into the bathroom. I stared up the staircase, which seemed less long and winding than when I had entered the room.

"Hello?" I asked, ducking slightly. Roxy wouldn't have knocked. Laini would have knocked, then immediately called out, asking to come in. Which meant it was probably...

"I won't come too close," Dorian said in a hoarse tone. His low voice echoed throughout the bathroom. A shiver of delight and nervousness shot through my entire body. "I wanted a word alone with you while I had the chance."

He must have been standing just outside the doorframe. The pool was so large, and he was far enough away that there was no pain at all, only a giddy sense that we were standing on the edge of something new and exciting. As I moved toward the shell-covered edge of the pool, my heart raced. His voice, his closeness—I would have sold a piece of my soul to touch him right now. The warm water suddenly made me feel light-headed, as if I couldn't get enough air.

We hadn't had a chance for a quiet moment since entering Itzarriol. Our lack of opportunity for private conversation had eaten at me since we'd set foot into this forsaken city. It had carved an empty cavern in my chest alongside the burning that occurred whenever he got close. I shook my head, trying to remind myself that keeping our distance was necessary for the mission.

My eyes fell to the significant length between the edge of the pool and the doorway. I pictured him standing just out of sight and felt a strong craving. If we couldn't touch, I at least wanted to see his handsome face in the dim aquatic lighting. I wanted to watch the tense lines of his face ease and settle into the expression he wore just for me. Something softer, more open, whenever we were alone.

"If you sit in the doorway, we should be fine," I said, voice thrumming with boldness. "In fact, you could sit on the top step leading toward the bath. There's enough room."

"I've just fed," he reminded me, but I heard the slow fall of his footsteps as he came closer. He appeared in the doorway, a towering figure mostly obscured by steam and shadow.

I kept myself half submerged, *very* aware of how completely naked I was, my shoulders poking out of the water, my wet hair clinging to my back—

"If you're sure." His voice told me that if I wanted to change my mind about this moment, I could.

But I was sure. I couldn't stop my mischievous smile. I'd been focused so intently on the mission for the past weeks, but I relished the chance to connect with him. I felt his eyes on me, drilling into me with a hunger that went far beyond blood.

"Come on in," I said.

CHAPTER SIXTEEN

You're being a fool, my inner voice reprimanded me. Too bad, I wanted to yell back. Let me be foolish for a moment.

Dorian sat on the top step. He set a little notebook down next to him.

"You look like an eager journalist," I informed him. My eyebrow quirked upward. "It's cute. All that earnestness and those cheekbones." Teasing him brought a funny bubble of glee into my throat. It wasn't often that I got the chance to talk playfully with him like this.

He smirked. Even in the low light, I could still envision his wickedly handsome expression even if I couldn't see it. It gave me goosebumps despite the warm water. "I've come to get your statement."

I couldn't help the answering smile that tugged at my lips. This might be silly, but it was fun. "I see you picked up something from our time with the journalists in Scotland."

He clicked a pen. "There's nowhere I won't go and nothing I won't do for a story." Something caught in his throat. His gaze swept over me, and I grew hyper-aware of the water hitting the tops of my breasts. "Lyra, I miss you."

The desire in his voice echoed through the bathroom, making my toes curl.

"I miss you too," I said, my tongue thick and heavy in my mouth. "You have no idea how much."

He chuckled, the sound swelling deep in his chest. "I think I do." The healthy shadows from his recent feed danced beneath his skin. He nodded. "It's been tough to stay separate for the mission, but I think we've done a good job," Dorian said. "No passing out since the lake."

Some part of me wanted to tease him about swooning over me instead of a more serious response. I didn't want to talk about the mission. I didn't want to think about the terrible history we were uncovering or the danger we were about to embrace by walking into Irrikus's palace.

"Can we not talk about the mission for a moment?" I asked. A honey sweetness snuck into my voice, laced with suggestion. I licked my bottom lip as my mouth dried. My words felt clumsy as they left my mouth, but I still liked the way they felt. "Let's talk about something else."

"Like what?" Dorian's tone teemed with something dangerous and teasing, but he was letting me take the lead, always so careful not to overstep.

I faltered for a moment, since I'd half expected him to push back and insist we be reasonable. But that was my hang-up, not his. He'd never backed down from this, not after our escape from the trial facility.

"We could talk about how good my dark vision is."

I stared at him, and my brow furrowed. What did he mean?

He let out a soft, pleased laugh, and it suddenly clicked. The darkness wasn't enough. The bubbles weren't enough. The pale pink water wasn't enough.

A low, guttural sound of approval escaped his mouth.

My face warmed. He could see... everything. My body was on full display for him. A certain towel incident aside, we'd never revealed this much to each other before. It was too risky. What if I'd passed out naked in his room at the VAMPS camp? Morag would've lost it and given us a long lecture on interspecies birth control and how we were being complete dumbasses.

I knew it wasn't the smartest decision, but I still had desires. My entire relationship with Dorian was literally defined by a necessity to stay apart.

The heart wants what it wants even when the brain knows better. I reasoned with my logical side. If I was good *almost* all the time, shouldn't I be allowed a margin of error for the other tiny bit?

My stomach turned with nerves, but my chest stirred with excitement. It was a welcome departure from the pain.

"I'm okay with that," I informed him and managed a casual shrug.

"It's an amazing view," he said smugly.

I smiled automatically, feeling it falter at the edges. Everything was so new with him. "Now you're sounding like a typical human," I informed him. "Doesn't seem fair that you get to be fully dressed though, does it?"

He made a show of scanning the room, exaggerating the movement to help me catch the shadowy lines of his head as he turned. "If I'm not mistaken, that pool is more than fifteen feet long. Mind if I join you?"

I swallowed my nervous desire. "Not at all." I turned and swam to the far side of the pool as elegantly as possible, fully aware that he was watching my naked form cutting through the water. As I reached the other end, I heard the clinking and shuffling as he descended the stairs behind me. I ran my fingers along the shells lining the area and gulped. Excitement and anxiety warred inside me. Slowly, letting the moment build for myself, I turned to see Dorian at the foot of the stairs. He'd stripped down to his waist, taking his precious time. I didn't even try to hide that I was staring. He'd seen me naked, so it was only fair. I drank him in. This was the most I had ever seen of him. Well, there was the outdoor farm shower, but I'd averted my eyes back then...

But this time?

I didn't—couldn't—look away.

Dorian slipped off his clothes in a series of agonizingly slow movements until he was completely nude. My vision was nowhere as good as his, but I could see well enough.

He was *beautiful*. Savage. Raw. Power pulsed through him. He was magnificent.

He looked back at me boldly, not an ounce of shame on his face. I reached beneath the water and braced myself against the rough edge of the pool, feeling the shells bite into my back slightly.

Not looking away, Dorian descended the stairs into the bath. Smooth as an eel, he submerged and came back up, slicking his dark hair back out of his eyes.

My chest began to burn with a small tingle, but the excited butterflies in my stomach fought the sensation with a vengeance. We stared at one another. The water grew hotter around me. A trick of the mind, or had Juneau magicked his water to respond to emotions? My mouth was bone dry as I stared at his lips, wishing they could be pressed against various places on my body.

"I wish we could try it," Dorian said.

I let out an awkward laugh as his comment sank in. At first I thought he was referring to ideas similar to those running through my own mind, but I knew he also must have been feeling the same pain. If we could figure out a way to fix the curse, we could touch and do all the things that normal couples did. We could finally come together, tangle our bodies around one another without feeling terrible pain.

"It's a cruel world out here," I said with a sigh, stirring the water with my fingers. "We shouldn't try until we get through the mission. There are too many things that could go wrong. Too many unknown variables." No matter how much I liked the idea of experimenting with a cure for the curse, Irrikus and his council loomed over us like an ever-present threat in the shadows.

A small hope rose up inside me. "We've found out so much in Juneau's journals. Maybe we'll come across more information about the curse that could help us. If you and the others weren't aware of so much of your history a thousand years ago, maybe there will be something in there we can use. After the mission, of course."

"After. I know," he said. And again, in a lower voice, "I know."

We were veering dangerously close to serious and grim, but I wasn't ready to go back to reality. Not yet. I tried to recapture our moment of lightness.

"Imagine all the things we can do once we break the curse," I said, letting my voice imply exactly what kind of things I was referring to. "Things that require no space between us." A giddy excitement rose up inside me. Dorian was my first intimate experience. There had been no time for relationships in the Bureau, and I'd never just sat around waiting for romance. I knew it would happen eventually, though I wanted nothing more when I saw Zach and Gina together. And now my body ached with the hunger of a woman who wanted to discover exactly what it meant to touch another person without holding back.

He inhaled slowly, his nostrils flaring. "I would press you against that wall. All of me against all of you. We'd finally get to feel one another."

A primal desire rose within me, making me forget the burning in my chest completely. I actually started to swim toward him, before a sharp flare killed that idea. His eyes followed my movements like a predator tracking a meal in the forest. But I was on the hunt as well. I smiled, pleased by the way I controlled his attention. "When this is over," I promised, "we'll take time for ourselves. Time to touch. Time to do everything that we've needed to do but couldn't after long, stressful days."

He gave a wretched groan, tipping his head back where he leaned against the opposite wall. I couldn't help but laugh a little, a sound he echoed.

Dorian made me nervous in the best way, but also more comfortable than any person I'd ever met. Our connection was deep, so deep that it felt natural to say these things to him. I smiled to myself. I wanted to go further with him, even if I lacked the experience.

My gaze fell to his partially visible, very naked form beneath the water. We could make up for lost time. *We will.*

Desire swelled within me, begging to be released. For a reckless moment, I was tempted to say *damn the pain* and swim toward him again. I clutched the side of the pool behind me, sternly reminding myself why that was a bad idea. If we passed out in a pool…

Dorian dragged a hand over his face. "Oh, Lyra. What are we doing?"

A raspy laugh escaped me. "Seems like we're working ourselves up into a frenzy with nowhere to go." I shook my head, water splashing on either side of me. The sweet, acidic smell burned into my nostrils, returning me to the present.

He sighed. "We're good at that, aren't we?"

"Excellent." I shrugged. "Not a surprise. We're both overachievers."

Dorian grinned. "It's been a challenge lately. We're constantly surrounded by our teammates, so there's no way to release it… not even on our own time."

The way he said the last part gave me sweat-inducing thoughts. I pushed them down, reminding myself that a cold shower didn't seem to exist in Juneau's mansion. It was all hot springs and giant heated pools.

Exciting yet frustrating.

"I feel close to you," I said and laughed at the audacity of the claim. "Isn't that funny?" I pointed to the space between us.

"Not at all," he replied smoothly. "I feel the same way. Physical distance doesn't matter when you're emotionally close."

We were far from finding a cure, but I held onto optimistic hope like my life depended on it. I couldn't bear to say goodbye to this man. Just the thought brought tears to my eyes and kicked up my pulse. In an attempt to calm itself, my mind veered from sexual tension straight back to strategy. Years at the Bureau had made me very good at compartmentalizing.

I let out a weary sigh. We had to leave the sexy tension behind. He hadn't brought a notebook in here with him for nothing—he had something on his mind. Reshi's shocked face flashed through my mind for a moment. There was something I needed to say to him, too. Somewhere in my pile of clothes near the silky towels, Lanzon's stone rested in its little bag. This was the first chance I'd had to speak with him alone.

"I need to ask a question," I admitted slowly. "It's not exactly sexy, and I've been meaning to mention it, but things have been pretty chaotic."

His face was still relaxed, but I saw him bring his desire back under control. "I'd argue that anything can be sexy if you're the one saying it. But that point aside, I'm listening."

I blushed, but the mood had shifted into something more serious. I took a deep breath. "It's about Lanzon's stone," I said. "Did you know it contained an extremely powerful spell?"

CHAPTER SEVENTEEN

"A spell?" he repeated. "Why would it have a spell on it, Lyra?" A note of worry hung in his voice.

"I know it sounds strange," I said cautiously. Dorian had originally given it to me as a method to track me, but it had soon evolved into an object with a more sentimental meaning for the two of us, and he had let me keep it.

His eyes widened. "Reshi. She—" He cut himself off, unwilling or unable to continue.

"Yes, that's what Reshi wanted to discuss the other day," I confirmed. "She *felt* the stone working against her. It absorbs magic and dispels it, too. She said it was powerful and unique. It was made by a friend of hers, Azpai, who escaped from here to head out to Vanim." My throat tightened as I remembered Reshi's grief. Her story had broken my heart, a hollow reminder that loved ones would continue to be lost in this fight with the rulers until something was done to stop Irrikus and his council. Was it better or worse, I wondered, that he'd found freedom before it was brutally stolen from him for the last time? Tears stung my eyes. I didn't know where the little soul-lights went on their cosmic winds, but it had to be somewhere better than here.

"You've seen it happen?" Dorian asked. He moved his hand in the water, and a trickle of splashes followed.

"Yes." I tucked a strand of wet hair behind my ear. "Maybe."

"You're not sure?"

"I *think* I've seen it work a few times." I paused, trying to remember. "Do you remember our fight with Inkarri, by the lake? Her gauntlet stopped working. I felt the rock heat up, but I just assumed her glove had malfunctioned. And even though she seemed surprised, I thought maybe it had something to do with Immortal technology. But then when Laini and I were searching the house, this weird portrait with some kind of glamor on it made the stone heat up and glow. And it did the same thing when I was near the secret chamber. That time it actually neutralized the concealment spell Charrek had put on the entrance."

He hummed with curiosity. "How?"

"It glowed brighter than before, and it got warmer or colder depending on how close I was to the spell," I said, hoping I didn't sound insane after our wonderful moment of sexual tension. "When I touched the stone to the floor, it undid Charrek's detection spell. But I wasn't completely sure until Reshi ordered everyone out of the room during our fitting the other day. She told me that it can even pass on memories." I swallowed. "I've been dreaming about your brother."

He looked thoughtful, water droplets trickling from his wet hair. "I had that stone for ages after Lanzon passed. I never imagined it contained magic."

"To be fair, you guys don't have much experience with magic. Maybe your brother didn't even know."

Dorian tilted his head back to stare at the ceiling mural with a faraway look in his eyes. "He was smart, Lanzon. I doubt he'd fail to notice something like that. He had a special interest in magic, despite it being relatively unknown to most vampires. I trained as a warrior, just like he did. Every day, I dragged myself back from hard hours of training to see him hunched over books. He was a true scholar in addition to being a skilled fighter." He let out a snort of delight. "Seeing all of you in the room with Juneau's works reminded me of when I would come home to him. He would be drinking something to keep him up. I would tell him to go to sleep, remind him that our parents would be furious if he didn't take care of himself. He always insisted on finishing one more page before turning out the lantern in our shared room."

I could see it easily enough. A younger Dorian, worn from hours of physical training, and Lanzon promising to turn the lantern out after just *one* more paragraph. They were brothers who never should've been separated.

"His specialty was the unfolding Immortal conflict," Dorian said, his voice tight and controlled. "He studied attacks, scout patterns, recovered Immortal weapons—virtually anything he could to see if there were new ways to develop vampire technology to use against our enemies. We could only work with magic attached to the barrier, which was limited, since nearly all of it went to protecting the city. A few wildlings and harvesters did find their way to Vanim over time, and they tried to teach us what they could of Immortal magic. My brother sought them out any time a new one arrived in Vanim." His teeth gnashed together with a clicking sound.

Were these memories he pushed down? And here I was, yanking them all up to the surface, like the bubbles in the bath around us. I tried to put myself in his position. If Zach died… even the prospect opened an abyss of grief, leaving me flinching back from the edge. Dorian must have been in freefall.

"Dorian, you don't have to tell me," I breathed, as guilt choked me. "If you—"

Dorian lifted a hand. "I want you to know." His serious gaze met mine. "I trust you. There are a few things I remember about my brother's research. Once, he was so excited because he had encountered a maker, but that maker died soon afterward. He made it to Vanim, but he'd suffered serious injuries after he escaped from Itzarriol."

My heart sank. "That sounds very much like Azpai, Reshi's friend." Every story seemed to be connected in our cruel struggle against the rulers. But if that had been Azpai who died after wandering into Vanim for sanctuary, then why had he given Lanzon the stone? It was a precious object. It was *magic*, knowledge completely stolen from the vampires.

Dorian grunted noncommittally. "It doesn't make sense," he muttered. "Why give my brother the stone? The maker had hardly any time to bond with Lanzon."

"I don't know," I said, hating the croaking sound coming from my mouth. Hearing Dorian talk about his brother did something to me. It took all the scariest parts of my mind and shook them up. I longed to call my brother, to hear his familiar voice. I wanted to hear his laugh. Irrikus had taken away the chance for Dorian to ever hear his brother laugh again.

The lines in Dorian's face grew harder. "All I know is what I saw. Vanim was attacked by Irrikus's forces. Lanzon couldn't stand the thought of Laini being in danger, and he went to look for her. I went out after him, but by the time I found him among the ruins after the bombardment, he was almost gone. I held him as he lay dying. He reached into his pocket with the last of his strength and forced the stone into my hand. I couldn't understand *why*. It made me furious in the moment. My brother was dying, and he handed me a rock, of all things. He told me to keep it with me always. Whatever else there was to know about it… that knowledge is gone, now that my brother is."

Silence stretched between us. I stared at the surface of the water and the rising puffs of steam. There was something unsaid in Dorian's message. The idea that his brother could have said something else to make it all better? It didn't matter. Lanzon had known he was going to die. He made the decision to pass on his stone to Dorian, for reasons Dorian never understood. He used the last moments of his life to give something precious to Dorian, even if he hadn't realized it at the time— something to use against the rulers.

I sucked in a breath, marveling at the bravery and clarity Lanzon had shown. I hoped, if it ever became necessary, that I would be able to do something like that. I thought about the dreams I'd had of him, how I'd initially mistaken him for Dorian.

"You two were so much alike," I said softly. "Always putting others' lives before your own."

My gaze crawled back up to Dorian, who glared at the mural on the ceiling as if it were Irrikus himself come to fight. And Dorian had given me the final thing his brother had given him. I let the realization sink in. It had been a precious part of Dorian's past, and he'd entrusted me with it.

"How are you?" I asked in a near whisper. "I mean, *really?*"

I didn't want to say, *"Don't give me the BS excuses that leaders hand out like candy to trick-or-treaters on Halloween. Don't tell me you're fine. Don't tell me that you don't sometimes wake up in a cold sweat, wondering what the day holds for us."*

My stare said it for me. He smiled bitterly because he knew he couldn't give me what I wanted.

"I'm fine," he said and shrugged. I almost laughed in frustration. "I've been holding up fine."

I gentled my voice. "Dorian, we're in an Olympic-sized bath inside the city that took everything from you. Don't give me that. We're under a ton of stress." I pointed at him. "I've seen you naked and laid bare. You might as well knock down a few of those emotional walls while you're at it."

He laughed. He laughed so hard that I worried he might bring Roxy or Kane running to see what all the fuss was about. Being caught together naked in the bath would be too awkward to explain.

"I'm not the only one with walls," Dorian replied when he finally got his breath back.

I sighed, inadvertently blowing a cluster of bubbles into the air. "I'm aware that we both have tough outer shells. It makes the leadership stuff easier." I pulled at the edges of my own internal walls. There were things I wanted to share with Dorian, fears I kept to myself. A bubble falling in the air caught a slant of purple light, the same color of Laini's eyes. "I'm worried about all of us, but especially Laini. Do you think she's okay? She seems different lately. She's focused and assertive, but… angry. So angry." I shivered for a moment, remembering her contorted face during the voyage with the harvester in the Gray Ravine, and her hiss of rage directed at Juneau.

"I'd be blind not to notice," Dorian said and mulled it over for a moment. "You have to understand, I knew Laini before all this. Before Lanzon died. Before Vanim fell. You wouldn't think it, she was so gentle and soft-spoken, but she always had that steel core. She often dragged Lanzon to things, especially when she knew there would be someone of interest for him to talk to about his research. She was great at connecting people when we lived in Vanim. And those people? Their lives slipped like sand through her hands when the barrier fell. I watched Laini fade into a ghost of herself. The curiosity was replaced by paranoia, the desire to connect with a decision to disconnect from others. She's always been kind—and it's still there, I think—but right now there's a deep anger inside her." He leaned his head back to stare at the ceiling. His shoulders sagged.

I nodded, remembering the flashes of Laini's anger over the last few days. "I was surprised to hear her rant against Juneau after he helped us, but I can't blame her for her hatred of rulers as a whole."

"I wish you could have met her before it all happened," Dorian whispered abruptly. He brought his face down, and for a moment a flicker of a younger version of himself peeked through. It was as if he were apologizing for not being his own old self. "This Laini isn't exactly the real Laini, although you guys have grown on her a lot. In some ways, I see the angry side of her as a good sign. She's finally working through her feelings instead of stuffing them down into a dark corner. I'd rather see her angry than silent and withdrawn. Is it wrong to want that? I hope it helps her heal." He grimaced, torn by his own admission.

"It's not wrong," I replied softly. "If you think this is her finally being able to express herself after everything that happened, then maybe it's for the best. We can leave plenty of space for Laini to be angry. For all of you." For a moment, I thought of Grayson. I recalled his frustrated face as he spoke to me about his discontentment among the vampires, how I'd brushed it aside, hoping it would sort itself out. There were a few times I wished I'd made more space for people's feelings throughout this journey.

"I ache for you," I whispered, unable to stop the words. I wanted him to know. I hurt with empathy for both of them, for all of them. "I think

Laini's initial reaction toward Juneau was partly about Lanzon's death. It must've enraged her to be the guest of a man who belonged to the people who took everything from you." I paused to take a breath. "I hope she rages against these guys, and that together we can stop their evil."

I sucked in a breath as I gathered my courage. Dorian had gone back to gazing at the mural, his shoulders stiff with tension.

"But Laini isn't the only one affected by this."

He slowly lowered his head to meet my gaze. Though I couldn't see him clearly, I forged ahead, staring into where I thought his eyes might be.

"You've been damaged by everything that happened to you, Dorian. Really. When I think of everything—the ghostly ruins of Vanim, the hunters, the Hive fighting for their self-preservation, losing your brother, your whole family—I worry for you. You don't have to talk about it with me, but I want you to know that I'm here if you need me." My throat tightened as the sadness and worry climbed into it. "I want you to know that I'll always be here, for as long as I can."

I was worldly enough to know that a promise of forever was at risk of shattering like glass. We were fighters. We knew all too well that sometimes life made unexpected choices for us.

He quieted. For a moment, my heart froze with a painful squeeze. Maybe I had pushed too hard. Maybe he would shut me out. He never talked about this kind of thing.

Dorian crossed his arms, the water making a faint lapping sound. "You might be right. Maybe I have locked all this away, hoping to wait until there's time. But then I think to myself that there will never be time. Maybe I'll never get a chance to open that box. We get thrown into plans. No, *I* throw myself into plans. Life has been a constant hustle to preserve what little life we have left." His voice cracked a little. "I push and I push forward because I'm afraid that if I don't, I might have to look into that box. After Lanzon passed and everything went to hell, I promised myself that I would never *ever* give up."

"You're always trying to help," I said, as tears pricked my eyes.

"I try," he muttered. "I try so hard. I helped Laini after the barrage. I convinced my parents to flee to safety with the first wave of refugees. I keep pushing so hard because if I slow down, these feelings will catch up to me and eat me from the inside out."

Something had come over him. It was like he was opening that box just an inch to give me a glimpse inside. Grief washed over me—grief and regret.

"Of course it's affected me to relive these scraps of my past. I felt something—no, worse. I felt numb. Like those memories walked right up and knocked, but there was nothing inside me for them to find. It wasn't until we got to the Hive that I let my hope grow. Some childish voice inside me thought we might find my parents there. I didn't want to tell you that because I felt foolish for wishing it."

My heart shattered completely at the pain in his voice. I hated that he'd been alone with his sadness and desperate wishes.

"When I stayed behind to help with the evacuation, I thought I would see them again soon," he said. The words tumbled from his mouth like boulders into the bath, each one spoken with urgent force. "I thought I'd find them again, but like so many others, they just... vanished. At one point, I could only get to sleep by reminding myself that my parents were well into their older years. They got a chance to live longer than most. In my mind, they never separated. I tried to comfort myself with the thought that if they had died, at least they left this life together." He exhaled, blowing out a long, weary breath. A pile of bubbles scattered like wishes into the air. "I'm no fool. I'll have to deal with these feelings eventually, but in the meantime I have to be like this. It helps me survive."

Dorian held my gaze. It was one of mutual understanding, as both lovers and soldiers who understood what it cost to move through life. My vision was slowly adjusting to the dim light, allowing me to see more of his serious yet still handsome face.

"That's understandable," I said gently, truly meaning it. "When that time comes, I want you to know that I'll be there for you, if you want me to. And... I just wish I could hold you." My voice broke on my last words. I wanted to press his body against mine and let our pain meld us together.

"Thank you." His glacial eyes pinned me to the wall in the way his body couldn't. My head went dizzy with a fierce surge of admiration and pride. This was the man I had chosen. Not quite a man, but a vampire warrior who was trying his best.

There were moments I never wanted to end. I wanted to hold onto this one until the end of time, but I didn't want to push him too far in one conversation. I promised myself there would be more like this.

After. After we're done here.

Dorian jerked his thumb toward the mural, clearing his throat harshly. "I truly wonder how Juneau thinks a person can relax or be romantic in a bath while sea serpents and tentacled beasts battle each other to death overhead."

I chuckled, grateful for the sudden levity. "Maybe this is what he likes to look at."

"*Lyra,*" Dorian complained, laughing. "I'll never get that out of my head."

"Don't worry," I told him with a grin. "I doubt Juneau is dragging his dates into guest baths. I imagine he demands to dress them in various dazzling styles all night, then realizes by morning that they're too boring for him."

We dissolved into laughter. A tiny pang of guilt struck me that we were mocking our host while enjoying his hospitality. *Sorry, Juneau.* I hadn't meant it with any malice, but just unthinkingly teased him the way I would have teased Kane, or Roxy. He'd somehow wormed his way into our little group without me noticing.

"It's getting late," Dorian said wearily. "We should probably get to bed. We have a lot to do tomorrow."

I agreed. The council's celebration was tomorrow night. We both needed to rest. In normal life, a bath turned cold to remind me to get out. Here? I could laze about in the warm suds all night.

"We can't both go back in bathrobes, or we'll look suspicious," I told him with a wink. Though I was ready to explore the physical side of our relationship, I wasn't quite ready for ribbing about it by our resident comedians, Roxy and Kane.

Dorian smirked and let his hard eyes linger on me for a moment.

Something unsaid passed through the air... something like a promise of forever condensed into three small words.

I love you.

But I couldn't find the courage to speak them here. Everything felt too raw tonight. I didn't want to break this spun glass moment. Instead, I told him, "I'm glad that I'm here with you on this mission." It was the truest thing I could think to say.

"That makes two of us." His tone softened, filling with a sweetness that caught my breath.

He slid out of the bath, and this time I watched him without tension. Dorian dried and dressed slowly, not for titillation, but just comfortable in this space filled with only us. Afterward, he rung out his dripping hair, every wonderful inch of him once again covered. "I'll tell the others I caught a bath in the opposite direction. I don't think they'll notice. Roxy and Kane were arguing over lockpicking strategies when I left."

"Thanks, Dorian."

He left, and the room felt empty without his presence. I huffed at myself, hating how hollow I felt now that he was gone from the room. *Calm down.* We had a mission ahead of us. I needed to click back into business mode. There were strategies that needed to be discussed.

Roxy and Kane were on the right track with the topic of lockpicking. I would probably find them fighting over practice locks that Juneau had given them. He actually had quite a stash of them.

I swam to the other side of the pool, diving beneath the surface one last time. I let the fear and frustration and sadness wash past me. As I broke the surface near the staircase, part of me wondered if Dorian had to do the same thing. Did we all, in our own ways, push our feelings aside into tidy compartments to make room for the difficult parts of life?

I stretched my limbs, which were lazy and heavy from their pampering and the residual sexual tension. The water trickled off my skin as I made my way up the staircase. Beneath me, the tiles were warm and dry. Near the door, I grabbed a towel for my wet hair and quickly dried my dripping body. The robes were too big, but I still wrapped one made of emerald silk around me.

Something white caught my eye. It was the paper and pen we managed to find in the Hive. Dorian had brought it with him. We'd each been given one before we left Moab. I flipped open the pages, holding it up to the dim light and squinting to read the first note.

Thank you for being so strong. Even if we can't try the cure until we get out of here, you have to know that I won't give up until I can kiss you again.

He even signed his name underneath. *Dorian.*

I smirked. As if I would wonder who left it.

My pulse picked up. He must've written that before he came in. I brushed my thumb over the note, enjoying the fluttering echo of my earlier feelings for Dorian. This was the closest thing I would get to physical contact until this was over.

I picked up the pen and sat on the tile floor, the robe billowing out around me. With the sea snakes and underwater monsters watching, I wrote my response. I would find a good time to give it to him later.

Thank you for the kind words and the <u>wonderful</u> show. I'm glad we were able to speak tonight. I'm not giving up hope either. We're both far too stubborn to do that.

I stared at the page, wondering what more I should add. How could I put my feelings into words? Actions were my strong suit. I nibbled at my bottom lip as I puzzled over the rest of the blank lined page.

No, it was perfect. It was me.

I signed it with my name below the short message, as he had done.

Yours, Lyra.

CHAPTER EIGHTEEN

The night of the party arrived, preceded by a storm rolling overhead. It sounded like the thunder of chariot wheels and horses' hooves, punctuated every few minutes by piercing, eagle-like shrieks. It made my stomach turn with nerves.

"Sometimes the souls get a bit testy," Juneau told us at dinner with a wink. "Just kidding. That'll be Irrikus's servants setting off fireworks near the senate in honor of the party. If he ever wants attention, he lets loose a barrage of those screaming irritations, and they echo throughout the lands to call his sycophants to his side."

Roxy smiled tightly at Juneau's mockery, picking at her plate of light energy vegetables. I couldn't summon up any response either as I settled into the blank, focused part of my mind to ready myself for what was to come.

In one short hour, we would enter the party and the belly of the beast. This was it—this was what we came to the Immortal Plane for. It was a chance to be close to the members of the Immortal Council who were responsible for such devastation and destruction in both the Mortal and Immortal Plane. I took a steadying breath and flexed my hands, a nervous tic to reassure myself. We were going right to the top.

Roxy and I prepared for the mission together in the bathroom suite, accompanied by Laini, who sat on a plush cushion in front of one of the many vanity mirrors. Her long hair was braided tightly back, and she did the same to Roxy's bright red locks. The braided hair would make it easier for us if we had to fight later tonight. None of us spoke, drawing comfort from each other's presence and the familiarity of pre-mission nerves.

I stared at my body in the mirror, allowing myself a second to let heat pool in my belly at the thought of Dorian's hot gaze when he'd surveyed my curves uncovered in the pool. With a deep breath, I pushed the feelings aside and brought myself back to task. We were dressing once more in the clothes we'd been given by the vampires at the Hive. The shirt was as itchy as I remembered, but the soft pants and the boots felt pleasantly like a second skin. However, as I fastened my shirt, the lump of the stone showed through the fabric of my sports bra where I'd tucked it between my breasts. I would wear it under the disguise and away from the necklace. If it touched the necklace Reshi had made, I'd be standing there in my true form with nothing but my borrowed clothes from the Hive and a knife.

We were going into the party armed, the weapons covered by the same powerful glamor as our bodies and clothes. As an extra precaution, we applied a liberal cocktail of fragrances that Juneau swore were both in style and would confuse any creatures trying to track us by scent. While Reshi had claimed that our disguises covered scent as well as aura, we all agreed it was preferable to err on the side of caution. If the worst-case scenario happened and our necklaces failed, it would be easier to escape detection if our scents matched the other fashion-conscious attendees and irritated the noses of creatures like Inkarri's velek.

As I closed my eyes against the cloud of perfume, my mind flashed with anxious premonitions of terrifying creatures pouring out from the tear and invading the Mortal Plane. I swallowed against tonight's meal of plant-based steaks, which threatened to come back up with my nerves. Invading the Bureau hadn't felt like this—for all its flaws, it was *familiar*. The Grand Senate was another story. We had little intelligence other than what we'd been told by Juneau and a few journal entries that had described the building. We'd been able to obtain a rough map from someone that Charrek knew—although he refused to say who—and we'd studied it painstakingly for the day that we'd had it, as if our lives depended on it.

A chilling sensation, the cold rope of worry, wrapped around me. *Your lives do depend on it.* It was a tiny voice, one that sounded too close to Alan for my liking. I shoved his face from my mind and finished strapping my gun into my shoulder holster.

Laini sat quietly while Roxy and I finished. She gnawed on her thumbnail, a nervous habit I'd never seen before. Would she be okay here alone? I wanted to ask how she was feeling, but after my talk with Dorian I felt like our entire group was a house of cards that could tumble at any moment. I couldn't risk sending her over the edge just before we set off for the party. Dorian was right. Maybe it was better for her like this. I'd give her space.

We found Dorian and Kane waiting in the suite, then we headed to the foyer. I kept near to Laini in the group, slipping my hand into hers and giving it a reassuring squeeze. Her lips pressed into a thin line as her eyes roamed over each of her teammates. We had our necklaces clutched in our hands. Nobody wanted to transform into their disguise before saying goodbye.

And we had to say goodbye.

If something happened, Laini could run from the city. She would take everything we knew to our friends in the Hive and back to the Mortal Plane. I hated thinking of her on the back of a redbill trying to make her way through the tear, but we had little choice.

She fiddled with the ends of her sleeve. Kane coughed.

"Well, this is less than optimal," he blurted.

As soon as he said it, a blanket of pained tension settled over the group. Dorian was far enough away, but my core still tugged with a deep ache. In the giant arching doorway of the foyer of Juneau's house, Laini looked small, but a current of ferocity hummed beneath her composed, strained face. Nobody wanted to make the first move.

Laini sighed. Her lips twitched into a sad smile. "Please be safe out there." If one of us broke down, we all might. "Give them hell." She stepped forward, and Kane enveloped her in a quick bear hug. It was the kind of embrace an older brother might give his younger sister. It made me miss Laini without even leaving her, appreciate Kane, and wish I had my own brother with me all at the same time.

This goodbye could be final.

"I'll be fine," she said as she hugged Roxy. "Even if you don't come back."

Dorian stepped up next.

"We'll do our best to make sure we do," he whispered and hugged her.

Laini wiped at her eyes. They were growing glassy, and I suspected tears might come once we left. When she was alone in the house with only Juneau's servants, she would be able to take a moment for herself. She glanced over all of us, her violet eyes brimming with all the things that none of us wanted to say.

"I won't be able to handle losing another family member," she said, looking pointedly at Dorian. "And in many ways, you're all my family."

Dorian nodded, tilting his chin up to give her a fierce look of determination. I glanced over my shoulder. Across the courtyard, Juneau faltered a step as he approached the waiting carriage. He stared at our group, taking in the unguarded moment. His eyebrows were furrowed, and his eyes were heavy with… pain? He frowned as he studied us. I turned away before he caught me watching. Maybe he hated the topic of family. It seemed unlikely that he'd been close with his own family, since he'd apparently been accused of killing them.

Laini's solemn gaze rested on me. "Lyra. I know if anyone can get out of this mission with the information that we need, it's you. Tread lightly in there." Her lips lifted in a slight grin, but her eyes stayed sad. She hugged me, and for a moment all I could smell was something fresh and earthy, a scent coming from Laini. It smelled like the morning rain in Scotland. I hoped she wouldn't have to go back there alone.

"Thank you," I told her and squeezed her hands. "I'll do my best to keep Dorian safe."

Roxy, Dorian, Kane, and I looked between one another. I nodded and lifted the necklace over my head. The others did the same. Our group transformed into our new identities as Juneau's wildlings. Fur sprouted on my hands. I was a wildling once again in a pack of fellow servants. I wiggled my clawed fingers, wishing my real nails were this sharp in case I had to fight any Immortals tonight.

It was time to go.

Laini waved as we climbed into the carriage. "Be safe."

Be safe. It was a ludicrous hope in this place, but I whispered it again as we climbed into the carriage and began our trip to the senate.

Irrikus's party had consumed everything, even the sky. As we crossed over the bridge, music reached my ears before I caught sight of the party. An airy tune floated over the festivities that spilled out into the gold-paved roads. Clouds hung over the city, and the soul-light tonight was dim beside the occasional angry spark of a magical firework in the sky. I squinted and tried to make out the watery sky somewhere past the clouds, the haze of smoke from the fireworks, and a dizzying number of multicolored lanterns. The lights hung around the senate, bobbing like fishing lures on a pond.

I felt like a sore thumb, plopped in the midst of luxuriously dressed rulers. Dorian moved easily with Juneau through the crowd. I kept closer to Roxy and Kane. Their watchful eyes roved everywhere. Luckily, this behavior wasn't out of place. Everyone appeared dazzled tonight, especially the wildlings.

Juneau swept his colorful robe, which covered his main gold outfit, around him as he walked with Dorian. It was like following a melting rainbow. He'd braided magnificent gems in his hair to lay in a tight plait on his back. A crown of golden serpents wriggled around his head. I let my jaw hang open, hoping to look like just another harried and awed servant. The Immortal rulers paid me no mind. They were far too concerned with their own greatness.

"Hold the mirror still," a male ruler snapped to his small wildling. The Immortal adjusted his hair, an elaborate updo that would put any mortal woman to shame. I kept my eyes moving. It would be bad to settle on someone for too long. They might look back.

Two Immortal rulers, possibly sisters, giggled together. They wore matching splendid gowns of dark blue. When we passed them, I realized the gowns were made to look like real moving water, complete with tiny fish swimming through the fabric. I gulped and continued walking. Juneau's grandfather, with his flair for the aquatic, would have loved those gowns.

"One of my best creations," Juneau drifted back to whisper to us covertly as we passed the two sisters.

I tore my attention away from the elaborate fashion to the tightly knit groups of guards that dotted the way up to the senate. Where were their stations? They bunched together in groups of three with their backs toward one another and eyes out on the crowd.

Juneau let out a boisterous chuckle and swatted Dorian's back as he evidently said something funny. Or perhaps our Immortal ally wanted to put on a good show. The movement of Juneau's flowing sleeves hypnotized me as the rainbow robe flew into the air and swished behind him. A guard glanced briefly at Dorian and Juneau. He rolled his eyes and merely looked ahead to scan faces back in the approaching crowd. Juneau had told us that his preferred hiding spot was in plain sight, and he seemed to have mastered the art.

Beside me, Kane growled almost inaudibly, no doubt sensing massive amounts of darkness around us. Irrikus had invited *all* the citizens of Itzarriol. Something told me that the evilest of them would find the invitation the most alluring. My eyes darted to Dorian, but nothing about his movements seemed stiff or awkward. He and Kane had fed recently on their scouting mission. I soothed myself with that reminder.

A flicker of determination arose inside me, then roared into a flame.

We had to succeed tonight.

I plunged ahead with our group as we neared the senate. I couldn't yet make it out in the haze of lingering smoke from passing makers' pipes, but the number of guards increased the closer we got. Every passing ruler and servant appeared suspect to me. I wanted to knock off their crowns and precious gems, knowing that magical spells lurked deep inside their treasures.

A female ruler scoffed under her breath when she caught me ogling my surroundings. I feigned a guilty look and darted my eyes away. Roxy stared up the road with an open mouth. I looked ahead to see what she was so awed by, and a gasp lodged itself in my throat. There was no need to fake our awe or play the part of country hicks right now.

The senate. It rose out of the haze suddenly, as if demanding that its presence be recognized and worshipped. It appeared to be made entirely of opaque, dark green glass with hints of lush violet winking beneath the lanterns. Towers stuck up like jagged, sharp teeth. Someone had carved and built strange arcs and angles into the building that didn't make sense. I tilted my head and nearly ran into Kane's shoulder. To my amusement, he had been doing the same thing. We looked like a pair of helpless birds trying to make sense of this constructed tangle.

Juneau cleared his throat. I realized I had stopped along with Roxy and Kane, utterly bewitched by the castle, and we were blocking the flow of people.

"Come now, little servants," Juneau called.

CHAPTER NINETEEN

"We mustn't be late." Juneau wagged his finger.

Except that we were already late, and very much on purpose. Juneau had mentioned that the Immortals would partake in their special stock of magical liqueur after an hour or so of the party. *Better to catch them drunk and off guard.*

I looked back at the savagely beautiful castle. Nothing inside could be seen from out here. Despite being made of glass, it had been completely magicked to show off a hazy blue shade that blurred everything on the inside. How many lives had gone into its construction? How many dark souls had been crushed and squeezed to harvest the dark energy needed to build this monstrosity? I shuddered to think. Magic was savage in this place, but it was also thanks to magic that we might be able to pull off this madman mission. My hands itched to touch the necklace around my throat.

"It looks like someone melted a million smashed wine bottles together," Roxy mumbled to me as we approached the castle.

I nodded, looking up at the ghastly building. It defied physics. Shapes grew out of the castle—or held the entire castle up—with angry edges and odd formations. I spotted a spiky snowflake on one side. On the other, a pile of glass melted down the castle's side in slow motion, then reappeared at the top and repeated the process over and over again. A crack sounded above us as a gargoyle-like face emerged from the tower closest to us. The castle was a sentient beast.

Hundreds of soul-lanterns floated by the pathway up to the castle, tethered with hooks and golden wire to a spiked metal fence. Their soul-light bathed the shiny ground in an amber glow. A steep staircase of black glass loomed before us. Figures dashed up it. Some Immortal makers stumbled down, a thick pink liquid frothing from their mouths, drunken laughs burbling in their throats. Skirting the rowdy partygoers, our little team followed the crowd up the staircase.

Through a spiked arch on the right side of the castle, I saw a white building behind the Grand Senate, right on the edge of the cliffs that marked the boundaries of the island. It was the sanitarium, according to the maps Juneau gave us to study. There were no windows carved into the bright stone. Despite its snow-white surface, the building felt like a gaping hole in the distance, ready to swallow up anything that drifted too close. It sat like a fat, white, square pebble, and yet it somehow creeped me out more than the castle.

"You see that?" Kane had moved to walk between Roxy and me.

"What?" I whispered from the side of my mouth.

He bent toward me, keeping his voice low. "That ugly white building." I could hear the furious growl rumbling beneath his words. "It's so full of dark energy that we can sense it from here."

An icy chill ran from the back of my neck straight down to my tailbone. Juneau said that the sanitarium was the last place you wanted to end up. I hoped we could avoid it in our investigation. I flattened my dry lips together as we came into view of the entrance guards. Four hunters stood tall on each side of the staircase and stared down at the oncoming crowd. Even hidden among the other partygoers, I could have sworn there was a bright red bullseye target on our backs, but the guards barely registered our presence as they motioned everyone to move along toward the senate. A grateful sigh left my lips, until I saw more guards waiting for us ahead. Thankfully, they waved us through without trouble.

If Irrikus and his council members held power beyond my wildest imagination, they must have a good reason for assigning so many guards to the party tonight. Were they expecting mischief from the crowd like thieves grabbing the rulers' beautiful treasures while they danced all night? I would consider being a thief if I had to participate in a crock system like this...

There was no more time for questions. The pulsing crowd propelled us into an enormous, cathedral-sized ballroom. Juneau's rainbow robes caught my eye in the chaos. I gravitated toward them as I stumbled out of a throng of scaly wildlings.

Kane let out a hacking cough. "The perfume on these people," he said with mild horror. I'd started taking shallow breaths in through my mouth, but that just meant I could taste it in the air.

My chest stung with a small ache as I inched too close to Dorian. Music surrounded us. A swell of bizarre honking sounds came up from a band gathered near the entrance and overpowered the original airy music. A wildling tooted away on a spiral-shaped horn. The bizarre music washed over us, and my brain tried to make sense of the brash sounds.

Something blue zoomed in the corner of my eye. Small winged wildlings flitted through the room with trays of tiny drinks in crystal tumblers. The wildlings were quick, but I saw frothy pink bubbles piled on top of the glasses. One dove toward the center edge of the room, where I glimpsed the ugliest, most intricate fountain that I'd ever laid eyes on. Violet lights flashed within the curved crevices, stacked spirals, and rough geometric shapes. Amber-tinged dark water flew up from the fountain every so often, falling back down in a dizzying array of acrobatics. More pure dark energy magic. Magic seeped into every inch of this place. *More energy wasted on absolutely nothing.*

"Oh, this is simply the nicest party yet," a chipper voice said near our group.

Two rulers leaned their heads together to chat. The steady murmur of the room grew. The bright colors stung my vision. I wanted to rub my eyes until I saw stars instead of the opulent clothing of the guests. Some of their fabrics were enchanted to glitter and gleam under any slant of light. The result left me half blind and queasy. Many, if not most, of those gathered here were our enemy, no matter how dazzling they appeared.

"I'd rather die than wear something that floofy," Roxy muttered. A female ruler in a dress like fluffy cotton pranced before us. "Is floofy a word?"

"It's the Immortal Plane," I whispered back. "We'll make it a word. *Floofy*. Now, what's your thought on the pink drinks?"

"Immortal booze." She shrugged, her rocky shoulders jerking with the gesture. A tiny pebble dislodged itself and clattered to the ground. Oh, Reshi was good at her job.

Suddenly, a flying wildling flitted before us. He extended his tray without a word, only a mischievous grin that showed off a row of small sharp teeth and beady red eyes.

"Thanks." I reluctantly took a glass, and so did Roxy.

We held them, trying to appear as polite and proper as possible, but we wouldn't drink from them. Roxy raised her glass to examine it better in the light. "A hundred bucks says that it would make you instantly vom—"

"Ladies," Juneau cut in with a dramatic sweep of his arms. "I'm off to be noticed. They'll come flocking to us after that." He plucked the glass from Roxy and downed it with a wink.

I nodded as he left in a dazzling whirlwind of colors. The plan was for Juneau to start introductions with his friends and fellow citizens, then try to involve Roxy and me in any conversation that turned to the topics of guards, hunters, and anyone involved in the Immortal Council's war effort. I hadn't had the chance to ask how Juneau planned on doing that, but his confident grin suggested he would find a way. Until then, Roxy and I would listen to random gossip and ensure that nobody noticed Kane and Dorian slinking away into a side hallway. They would use the information from Juneau's map to locate the personal rooms of Irrikus, Sempre, Izelde, and Orrin. They had memorized it. Their objective was to look for any plans or journals, and even dig through their trash cans for any hints about what the Immortal Council members might be up to.

"Good luck," Kane whispered. He grabbed Insect-Dorian, and they disappeared into the crowd. I eyed the hallway as two shadowy shapes slipped past a guard who was conveniently distracted by a tipsy female ruler with a dangerously low neckline on her strapless dress.

"Mingle in polite society," Roxy whispered to herself. "God, this is my worst nightmare. Give me a battlefield any day." Formal parties were hardly common during our time as soldiers. Although I was wary to fight, I had to admit Roxy had a point. There was something so utterly foreign about dazzling gowns and robes, especially while being among Immortal beings.

"With any luck, we won't turn the party into one tonight."

She sighed. "Do you remember when the Bureau sometimes dressed us up in our shiniest uniforms and made us go to political fundraising events? We had to blab on and on about how great the Bureau was for our nation's safety." She shook her head. "When I look out on this party, I feel as odd and uncomfortable as I did back then, except instead of looking impressive to heads of local governments, I look like a rock ripped from the desert."

I bit back a smile. "A big, impressive rock."

"You're too kind," she grumbled.

We snapped back into focus as the party whirled around us. It was nice to watch from the safety of the wall. Nobody looked at servants. You could see everything if you knew where to look. There were drunken jokers in the corners, servants shooting sour looks when a master turned his back, and sullen guards next to every exit.

"Oh, you simply must meet my new curiosities!" Juneau's voice drifted closer to us. "I found them in the northern lands. Isn't that funny?" A small circle of people surrounded him. The other rulers towered over our comparably petite host.

"Delightful. You must tell me how your maker crafts his feathers," a woman cooed. She had scarlet hair that fell down her exposed shoulders. A tube-like dress made from bright green fur forced her to waddle rather than walk—it looked like the Grinch had been skinned in the name of high fashion.

A man at her side chuckled. He was the tallest Immortal I'd seen so far. "You've found new servants?" His eyes twinkled. "You always seem to have a good relationship with your pledges." A thread of double meaning danced beneath his words.

I stopped myself from raising my eyebrows. Rumors of Juneau's smuggling must have spread beyond Inkarri.

Instead of deflating into defensiveness, Juneau's smile turned feline. "Come meet my new wildlings. They're just darling." He let out a chuckle as he waved to us. "I found them scavenging up north. Aren't they delightful?" His tone dripped with condescension. Roxy still stiffened, despite knowing his act was simply that.

Juneau leaned in toward his friends and dropped his voice. "You'll have to forgive their manners. They're quite simple. You know how the country ones are."

The woman nodded. Her mint-green eyes widened. To my surprise, she gave me a pitying smile, like I was a child. "They look wretchedly quaint."

Oof. If that was a compliment, I never wanted to hear her version of an insult.

The man nodded enthusiastically. "Fun stories here. You always seem to find the most interesting things, Juneau. Nice to meet you two."

"Hello, sir," I said in a purposefully creaky voice. The Immortal man raised his eyebrows and stared at Roxy expectantly.

She cocked her head to the side. "Nice to meet you!"

The rulers laughed, delighted. Juneau shot me a knowing look from behind their backs. As if to say, *Yes. Great. Keep acting like you're as dumb as a bag of polite rocks.*

I mentally saluted him. Roxy and I set about our work. We would weasel as much information out of these unsuspecting Immortals as possible.

Juneau turned to the man. "Artir, tell me. Irrikus is spewing off about all this new technology. Do you think he's full of hot air?"

Artir leaned toward Juneau with a sneaky grin. "I've heard rumors that suggest otherwise."

I kept quiet and still, willing my body to blend into the background. It mattered little. Artir and his companion had immediately forgotten that Roxy and I existed. We could listen to their conversation and distill as much as possible, squeezing idle gossip for the bare bits of truth.

It was time to play the game, and we just had to play it right. I only hoped Dorian and Kane had as much luck as they did skill. We would need both tonight.

CHAPTER TWENTY

My vision swam with sparkling chests and bedazzled shoulders. The rulers towered above Roxy and me, their heads tossing as they laughed merrily. The crowd wore robes of white, red, blue, green, purple, and some colors that I failed to identify. Whatever sense of style the Immortals had, they favored the loudest and brightest clothes they could get their hands on.

Artir and his companion were replaced by a new swell of the mingling crowd. I watched the figures closely. It was a practiced dance for the rulers. I was on an entirely new battlefield, one where manners and subtext were the weapons of choice. Juneau, for his part, asked deliciously loaded questions. He was a master warrior here. All it took was a casual tilt of his head as he remarked on the fabric of a woman's dress, a flicker of warmth in his voice. He spoke in low-voiced inside jokes, making fun of someone who had just walked away, which prompted tinkling laughter. The rulers soaked it up. Evidently, Juneau's attention was a hot commodity.

Roxy and I, unused to the language of subtle half-smiles and loaded gazes, found the socializing hard to decode. I focused on the faces and the body language of the rulers as they interacted. There was an air of practiced openness. They moved like dancers, at ease among one another. And yet everything was a half-truth. A woman introduced as Moppa snapped her head back like a viper as she clutched Juneau's sleeve and giggled. She waved at us and moved on, clearly done with her conversation. We awaited the next group of tipsy chatters.

"I once watched her beat a wildling half to death at the Makers' Bazaar for accidentally stepping on the train of her gown," Juneau said, whispering from the corner of his mouth.

I swallowed my immediate disgust. "Charming." My eyes stole away for a moment to the wildlings around the room. Although they held drinks, they waited attentively beside their Immortal rulers, just as Roxy and I did. The difference being that Roxy and I played a part—these poor creatures had no choice. Every day, they served these power-hungry rulers who were only in charge because they crushed anyone who posed a threat.

"We are in a pack of beasts," Juneau said, smiling as he looked out over the crowd. "Don't forget that." His eyes were cold and hard, the same look I had seen when he spoke about his family.

How could we forget, though? Roxy shifted, letting out a tiny frustrated sigh as the next group approached. Everyone appeared to be making their social rounds.

How rulers approached was one of the most interesting things. They positively glided up to Juneau, but there was always the play of a little bow exchanged between parties.

"My dear Leniv," Juneau said and opened his arms to embrace a lithe man. "I'm so pleased to see you. How go your latest designs?"

He was dressed in a well-tailored robe with geometric black-and-white patterns that mimicked the suits I was used to seeing on powerful men in the Mortal Plane. Maybe he'd gotten inspiration from a flash of human memory.

For a moment, something about his face seemed strange to me. The Immortal rulers typically had clean faces with no trace of facial hair.

When I looked closer, I realized the mustache on his full upper lip had been crafted from a pale, waxy substance that matched his hair.

Leniv twitched his mouth, which was lined in black lipstick, and played with the ends of his curly mustache. "You know how it is," Leniv drawled. He pressed a hand to his chest and shuddered, eyebrows scrunching together as if pain passed through him. "To design is to torture oneself. I sit at my table with the blank page, praying for the kind waves of inspiration to visit me. The buildings won't construct themselves. They need a guide, someone to plan their careful lines and curves." He let out a lengthy sigh.

Roxy's right eye twitched. My thoughts exactly. He talked about art as torture when makers and wildlings and all other creatures that were not rulers were unable to do art for themselves. Leniv had already revealed some interesting information, however. He was an architect, or something like it. He could have been involved in designing or building parts of the senate, perhaps even the sanitarium.

"Inspiration is a cruel mistress." Juneau smiled at him. "I find discipline to be the best solution, but where's the fun in that?"

Leniv smirked. "Exactly."

Juneau inclined his head. "What do you think about all this business with Irrikus spouting off about new technology and a new wave of darkness?" It was surprisingly blunt, but Leniv smiled. He seemed like a man who enjoyed being asked questions, to feel important.

"An old man's ravings," Leniv said with a chuckle.

I deflated slightly. Leniv knew nothing after all, because we *knew* for a fact that Irrikus was doing some of the things he claimed.

"Mm-hm," Juneau said. "A bold statement, when you're in the man's own senate."

We were thankfully interrupted by the arrival of five more people. The first, a woman, wore a dress consisting of sparkling orange flames. She wore her nails long, sharp, and painted glittery black. When she moved them through the air, they looked like scuttling beetles.

"Juneau, what are these adorable creatures?" she asked and winked at us. Her stare looked ravenous. There was something carnivorous about the way she curled her lips up, showing a slice of white teeth. A gem was embedded in her revealed canine.

Juneau swept his hand out to gesture to us. "Not for sale, Pireka." He smiled with an edge of warning. "You'll have to find your exotic meal somewhere else."

She laughed, and it sent ice through my veins. *She... ate wildlings?* "Why, just the other day I had shrieking decay. You should try it some-time. It has a wonderful bitterness to it."

Leniv grimaced. "Sounds like a one-way ticket to lying in bed for days on end."

"We were just discussing Irrikus's speech," Juneau said smoothly, tugging the conversation back where he wanted it. He took a half-inch step in front of us. Pireka blinked and dragged her hungry eyes to him. Roxy and I faded from her attention completely.

"Oh, he's been more bloodthirsty than usual, don't you think?" She dropped her voice to a low, conspiratorial whisper. "I love his dedication to caste enforcement. It's so wonderful to have everything in its place." Her black nails clacked together as she brought her hands in front of her stomach.

My insides twisted, and I bit my tongue in anger. Of course she loved the caste system. She benefited from it. She *fed* from it. This was utterly sickening. I glanced at Roxy from the corner of my eye. Despite her impressively neutral facial expression, I knew she was as enraged as I was, but letting this woman see us sweat would be a victory we refused to hand her.

"Do all scribes think like you?" Leniv asked wryly.

Pireka hummed. "Who can say? I merely oversee them. I am the *master* of scribes." She lifted her chin with a proud huff. "I don't sully myself by talking idly with my servants and makers like you two."

"To be fair, I think that must give them some comfort," Juneau said with a slick smile. "They are likely afraid you'll take a bite out of them."

She smiled playfully but said nothing. I marked her in my mind as

Pireka, the Overseer of Scribes and the Holder of Zero Information Besides Her Disgusting Appetite. She made Leniv the architect seem positively pleasant, and I'd hated him before she'd showed up. Did any of these people have actual information? I wanted to grab Pireka by the neck and shake her to see if she could give us the name of someone who actually knew something.

At that moment, a new figure broke into our circle. He was an older man and hunched slightly to Juneau's height.

"Ah, Jenka," Pireka said as he came up. "Any new scrolls you've managed to get your hands on? I'm ravenous for new material. It's exhausting to copy out and preserve the same old boring texts waxing on about Itzarriol's greatness. Well, to watch it being done by servants, anyway."

He shook his head, gray hair flying. An attending group of three of the more gorgeous makers followed him, but they stood quietly behind. "No new scrolls," he said. "Irrikus has relocated most of our resources to the technology department."

My heart thumped excitedly. Why had Irrikus suddenly taken an interest in improved technology research? *Interesting*. It matched up with his claims. I searched my mind for a way to butt into the conversation but came up blank.

Roxy cleared her throat, drawing all stares to her. She looked up at the gathered group with eyes as wide as a doe. "Juneau said we would meet the most interesting people tonight. You guys do such exciting work." She dropped her voice into almost childlike wonder, damaged only slightly by the magically induced gravelly tone to her words. "Do you ever work for the Immortal Council?"

Pireka pressed her black nails to her lips. "Oh, Juneau, you must let me have this one."

His smile was sharp. "Not a chance."

Leniv played with his mustache and let out a pompous sigh. "You'll do well to teach your servants not to speak unless they're addressed." But he turned to Roxy and leveled a gaze at her, his ego flattered enough to deign to converse with her. "All I can say is that Lord Sempre's *pets* have destroyed all the furnishings in his room again. The lord requests a new design to keep them from causing more mayhem. I don't think his project will work."

He exchanged a knowing glance with Pireka and Jenka the librarian. My skin tingled with excitement.

"What project?" I asked, copying Roxy's innocent tone.

"You'll see," Pireka cooed and gave me an appraising glance.

"Ah, they're putting out more of the cocktails in the center," Leniv said abruptly. "I hear that's the one that's blended with soul-light tonight."

Pireka grabbed him by the arm. "Come, let's refresh our glasses!"

As quickly as they came, the strange group left. Juneau chuckled bitterly and shook his head. "They know virtually nothing," he reported bitterly. "Talking out of their mouths, but the words aren't coming from their brains, every single one of them."

"You think? Leniv seemed to know something." I studied his disappointed face.

"He knew about Lord Sempre's complaint, but I have a feeling he and Pireka have merely heard rumors. They're not in the inner circle, so to speak. They would hate to admit it, but they're essentially servants to the Immortal Council members in a distant way. Pireka oversees the scribes doing the senate archival work, and Leniv sometimes works on senate projects. He mostly builds ugly buildings for wealthy rulers on the outskirts of town." He rubbed his jaw thoughtfully. "But did you see the makers behind the librarian? Their eyes widened when Leniv mentioned Sempre and his pets. They know something, but it would be too suspicious to separate them from their master. We're better off looking for our next source right now, and perhaps Charrek can send out some feelers in a few days."

Roxy and I both nodded. I wished the makers had said something, but I knew they were most likely on guard at all times if they lived in the senate, surrounded by ruler-caste Immortals. They had to stay silent or else suffer consequences. If they knew something about these "pets," then I wanted to know. What project were they a part of? They sounded dangerous, if they destroyed entire quarters. Lord Sempre was the one who ran the sanitarium. Perhaps the "pets" were from experimentation over there. The image of Inkarri's magicked velek with the gemstone in its forehead sprang into my mind. It was possible they had the technology to magic even more beasts.

What new horrors was Sempre creating at Irrikus's behest?

CHAPTER TWENTY-ONE

We repeated the same cycle for what felt like hours. A group would approach Juneau, or he would go and find one, bringing us along with him. He made conversation, sometimes pointing us out. Occasionally, a slice of gossip would come through, but usually only in vague tidbits like the one from our lovely architect and scribe.

Roxy huffed. "How are we supposed to dig for information if everyone does nothing but talk major BS just to impress each other?"

Juneau smiled with a glimmer of mischief. "The night is young. Keep up the big saucer eyes. The rulers love nothing more than admiration, and the makers will likely pity your innocence."

The time melted together. My drink went flat. I covertly poured it into the fountain while Roxy covered me. Pretending to be stupid was exhausting. Our ruse was working excellently, but I had to fight my instincts to ask well-rounded questions and instead opt for silly ones merely sprinkled with words that might lead to useful intel.

"I'm so tired of glitter," I mumbled to Roxy. Every time someone moved, tiny beams of light from their outfit stabbed me in the eyes. She nodded and rubbed her eyes for a moment.

"They really don't treat us like anything but cute animals," she said, shivering. "I always thought anything with relatively human eyes would spark some freaking empathy in people."

The guests Juneau brought to us never varied in personality. Each one was as pretentious, spoiled, and catty as the next. It was like living a high school student's worst nightmare in a ballroom full of mean cool kids. What an awful group to party with. They talked over one another for the chance to brag about an achievement, something to one-up what the previous speaker had said. Forcing myself to look impressed and interested took all my energy. No wonder Juneau refused to form deep friendships with these people.

"Oh, Hildan. Your outfit looks positively brutal," Juneau said, his tone of polite excitement the same as it had been when we arrived. He never faltered, never stumbled, never revealed any sign of the disdain he felt for those around him.

I turned to see a ruler, only a head taller than Juneau, with deeply tanned skin and long brown hair falling in ringlets to his shoulders. In lieu of a glamorous robe, he wore armor of matte black metal studded with opals. He'd slung a crushed velvet cape the color of burnt eggplant over one shoulder and matched it with a broad strip tied around his head like a sweatband or bandanna. At his side hung two swords easily as long as my body, one on each hip. He was a hunter. Brutal, indeed.

A ravishing female ruler hung off his arm, dressed in a fine gown. A few heads turned to give a longing look at Hildan as he passed with his chosen date. They couldn't take their eyes off him until they'd been caught staring. Two women appeared to be covertly trailing him as he moved, maybe waiting for their chance to dance. I studied Hildan's face. He was handsome—in a broad, flat kind of way—with an assured smile, but nothing made him any more beautiful than the other Immortal rulers. His square jaw moved stiffly as he spoke to Juneau.

"Pleased to see you," Hildan drawled in a deep, rough voice and clapped a heavy hand onto Juneau's shoulder. "How are you finding the party?"

Juneau's lips curled mischievously. "Perfectly adequate."

Something twinkled in Hildan's honey-colored eyes. "Only adequate?

We've failed the finest designer in the Immortal Plane, haven't we, darling?" He glanced at his date, earning a string of flirtatious laughs. What I would give to see the look on Roxy's face beneath her disguise. Shawls and dresses fluttered as women turned to see what had produced such mirth from Hildan and his date.

"My wildlings," Juneau said and trotted out the same cover story he'd been telling everyone.

"Northern area, eh?" Hildan turned to us with the vague hint of a smile on his face. He smelled of the purple smoke that the makers used. It itched my nose. "How do you like the capital?"

"It's beautiful," Roxy gushed. "We're learning so many interesting things."

"Yes." My mind whirred as I tried to figure out the best thing to ask him. This was my chance. We had an actual hunter in our midst. I dropped my head to one side in the most convincing display of stupid curiosity I could manage. "Is it true that you guys can control velek, like we can?"

He grinned. "You do your work herding the velek well enough, I'm sure, but yes. It's true. We've devised something even more efficient than a wildling's natural abilities. Although," he dipped toward us, "not all of us have velek. Lord Sempre is testing on some other, more dangerous creatures. I'm one of the few entrusted with one of the brand-new prototypes."

"No way," Roxy said, gasping. He nodded solemnly. My pulse raced as he lifted the strip of cloth from his forehead, then tucked it in his pocket. A red gem was embedded in the middle of his forehead. However, unlike Inkarri's implanted gem, the flesh around his was raw, as if still healing. He tapped it gently.

"When the final spells are cast into the gem, it will connect me to whatever creature Sempre and Director Zeele have selected for me. I can dictate its actions remotely. It's an incredible tool." His nostrils flared as he took a sharp, excited breath. The greatness of their technology enthralled him. It horrified me.

It was then that I noticed a pale pink stain around the hunter's mouth.

He was drunk as a skunk. This could be our chance. He seemed happy to talk and had already given us new information. My pulse quickened with excitement.

"That's incredible," I said, making sure to keep my interest in check. I wanted him to think I was an awed servant, not a spy. "What have you been able to do with it?"

Hildan licked his lips, and some of the pink in the corner of his mouth disappeared. "This and that." Unfortunately, he was sober enough to be coy.

"You never cease to impress," Juneau added. A flying server passed by, and Juneau snatched a full drink off the tray. "A toast to your greatness."

And who was Hildan to deny his own greatness? He cheered with Juneau, who took the tiniest sip of his own drink. Hildan downed his entire glass and handed the empty vessel to some poor woman behind him.

"I'll even be able to see through the gem when I tap my control bracelet," Hildan bragged. Juneau nodded. "It'll help if we ever catch those awful bloodsuckers. You know Inkarri and a bunch of the other elite hunters tracked down an entire nest of them the other day, in the city near the Illuminated Gardens?"

The Hive's safehouse. Did he know what had happened to those vampires and makers?

"Did you catch them all?" I asked, trying to sound timid and awed even as I recalled the thundering fear in my gut as we'd watched the arrests from the rooftop.

"I wasn't actually there," Hildan confessed, a slight slur to his words. "I was getting this gem implanted at the sanitarium that day, so I wasn't on duty. Director Zeele mentioned it to me as I was leaving."

"But you do catch vampires?" Roxy asked. "You're an actual, real-life hunter, right?"

I winced internally. It sounded dangerously close to an insult, but the hunter was apparently too drunk to pick up on the subtext of mockery.

"Oh, I catch them and kill them." His eye twitched. "Well, I used to. We tend to just capture them now."

Why? I wanted to ask, but such a question was too focused and direct. Hildan might be drunk, but he was still a trained hunter and might be suspicious of interest that was too eager.

"Anything that gets them off the streets makes me happy," Juneau said with a dramatic shudder. "I've never seen one up close, and I have no intention of ever doing so."

"They're ugly creatures." Hildan swept his hand over his head, rustling his hair. The gemstone in his forehead glinted, the edges where the flesh met the stone shining with angry pink skin. I tried hard not to stare at it.

"Well, you can't expect everyone to be as handsome as you are," Juneau said, laying it on thick. It earned a string of chuckles from his date, who watched Hildan with unsettling adoration. It was... unnatural. Was her attention gained through magical means, maybe some kind of charm?

"You're a good one, Juneau." Hildan let out a laugh that was too loud. "You know, I love my work. It gives me all sorts of access to interesting rumors. I mean, it's mainly because Irrikus finds me to be an excellent hunter. He's told me plenty, more than he tells the others, probably more than he even tells his own daughter. That's why I was the first hunter to be selected for the more powerful version of the gemstone technology. It's going to amaze everyone, it really is. If you'd seen some of the stuff I have... I won't pretend to understand how it works, but those researchers are just inspired. They're going to take this war to the next level. The vampires won't know what hit 'em." He hiccupped.

My mouth opened, but his date grabbed him by his powerful arm. "Dance with me, Hildan," she purred. "You promised."

Hildan shot us a look of practiced apology, which I doubted he meant at all. "Who am I to deny the ladies what they want?"

I watched as his date pulled him away to the dance floor, while onlooking women watched jealously.

Roxy growled quietly in frustration. "He was going to talk more."

Juneau rubbed his chin. "I suspect his fan club might have been assigned to him tonight. He's a good hunter, but Hildan is well known for blabbing about things he shouldn't. It takes pretty women to pull him away from spilling state secrets."

He'd already spilled *plenty*. They were improving on the gem technology they used to control creatures and were aiming for something bigger than velek this time.

"I hope he stumbles back at some point." I looked toward the dance floor, but the crowd had swallowed him and his posse up.

Roxy stifled a yawn. "How long has it been?"

Out of habit, I looked around for a clock, but there were none in the ballroom. Actually, I couldn't recall seeing any clocks since we'd stepped into the Immortal Plane. Dorian had told me before we left Moab that my own watch wouldn't work, so I'd left it behind, but the rulers must have some way of keeping time. They probably used the tears of a wildling that they'd poured into hourglasses or something equally horrifying.

And Juneau had told us the time before. I asked him for it.

"It's been four hours," he said casually. He caught the alarm in my raised eyebrows. "Don't worry. The *excitement* usually goes far into the night at balls like these." For a moment, he was back with us. He turned toward us, shielding his face from the ballroom, the mask slipping for a moment.

"Having fun?" Roxy asked dryly. A stranger might not have caught it, but I heard an undertone of sympathy in her sarcasm. It seemed she'd warmed to Juneau, too.

He let out a hollow laugh and sneered. "This place makes me want to rip my skin off."

I listened to his complaints, but my eyes wandered to the dark hallway that Dorian and Kane had disappeared into earlier. Were they safe? Four hours was a long time, but there had been no hint of panic or sounds of a struggle from anywhere in the senate.

Juneau clicked his tongue. "Snap to attention, little wildlings."

The crowd before us began to shift, people dropping into deep, elaborate bows directed toward two figures. One was Irrikus, with his elaborate crown, and the other I didn't recognize. It appeared they were making their rounds through the room and had finally reached our spot.

Juneau dipped into a bow of his own, and we hurried to copy him.

"My Lord Irrikus. My Lord Sempre," he murmured. "My warmest

thanks for the generous invitation to your party. You are divine hosts." His tone surged with sincerity, the kind that was hard to fake.

Impressive. Two shadows fell over us. The sight of them as I kept my eyes glued to the ground sent a wave of dread through me. It was like seeing a wolf's silhouette before it pounced. These were the two most powerful rulers in the whole of the Immortal Plane.

"You speak kindly, Juneau. Please, all of you rise," Irrikus said. Up close, his voice was like the steady roll of thunder in a storm.

Roxy and I slowly straightened. Irrikus gave us a quick glance, then settled back on Juneau, who twitched slightly as if the ruler's attention was a needle pricking on his skin.

"My new wildlings from the north," Juneau explained. "You're throwing an absolutely lovely party. I find the music quite delightful."

Irrikus barely looked at us. I was grateful for that, because his intimidating presence shook me more than I'd thought it would. While Juneau dove into polite conversation, I covertly peered up at the ruler of all Immortals.

He was tall. He stood at least nine feet in height, but something about his robust frame made him look even bigger. His skin was white as marble. The golden hair falling beside the paleness gave the impression he'd been ripped from some ancient Greek myth. Sparkling rings adorned his powerful hands. His neck threatened to disappear beneath the staggering number of golden necklaces. His gold eyes observed everything with a cold efficiency that made the old Bureau look downright inviting.

Doesn't look a day over a thousand, does he?

His companion, Lord Sempre, listened to the conversation impassively. His light gray skin and dark silver hair were a strange contrast to the gleaming Irrikus. While shorter than Irrikus, he was still taller than Juneau. One red eye peeked out from his bored face, covered by his side-swept bangs and shoulder-length hair. He held something in his hand, but I could hardly make it out with the crowd mingling around us. It was hard to turn my attention away from their unsettling faces. We were in the presence of monsters.

My blood boiled. I hated them. They had caused so much suffering and darkness and pain. My entire life in the Mortal Plane—and the lives of my loved ones—had been upended because of these creatures that called themselves lords and paraded around in stolen riches. My throat tightened.

Calm down. Calm down. I repeated it like a mantra. All the most painful ways I knew to kill flashed through my mind. Their flagrant embrace of darkness made me want to feed my own evil inside me. But I could never, *would* never, stoop to their level.

A tinkling metallic sound caught my ear. Beside me, Roxy sucked in a breath, as if she had just been punched in the stomach. None of the rulers noticed, caught up in their exchange of empty words.

The sound had come from behind Sempre. My gaze went past his fancy robes to see chains in his hands. Why was he holding chains?

He shifted slightly, revealing two tiny figures dressed in golden silk robes and delicate jewelry. Most shocking of all, they had jewel-encrusted muzzles and sparkling silver collars wrapped around their necks. They were attached to the chains, which I now realized were leashes. Sempre pulled on them absently, and the figures stumbled forward. One let out a pitiful cry as her head was jerked awkwardly.

I knew that voice.

My heart stopped. My mind whirled to make sense of it all. Roxy growled beside me.

Beneath their glittering makeup, I recognized the terrified faces of Carwin and Detra.

CHAPTER TWENTY-TWO

Someone had ripped the soul out of my body. Carwin and Detra were here in the Immortal Plane—in the city—with our enemies. Sempre had muzzles fastened on them. It was the last place I ever expected to see them, and yet they were here.

Irrikus turned from Juneau and glanced at me. "How are you enjoying the capital, wildling?"

His bored gaze told me he didn't really care, but my body froze. Time slowed down. Juneau's polite smile fell a hair's width.

I couldn't breathe. I couldn't think. I couldn't talk. Rage formed a vise around my throat. My jaw clenched as I stared into Irrikus's terrible gold eyes.

I clutched Roxy's cold stone arm, which shook as anger coursed through her. She had seen them, too. One of us needed to respond, but the sight of Carwin and Detra had sucked all the air from my lungs.

Juneau coughed. "You'll have to forgive them. They're overwhelmed by awe, Your Highness. They're simple creatures from the countryside and have only seen your greatness in statues."

Irrikus merely shrugged one of his massive shoulders. I had no idea whether he'd bought it, but he gestured to Sempre and looked back to Juneau.

"Maybe you'll find this amusing," Irrikus said. "Sempre, show him your new pets. "

I wanted to scream at the top of my lungs. I wanted to scoop up the children from Sempre's terrible hands. I could think of a better use for those chains—choking the air from his throat.

Sempre tugged on the leashes, pulling the children closer. "Come here, little leeches. You want to meet the little wildlings, don't you? They won't hurt you." He laughed when Carwin and Detra cringed away from our disguises, Carwin wrapping an arm around his sister.

It chilled me down to my bones. The children pulled away from me, and there was nothing I could do—I couldn't say it was me and that they would be safe. I swallowed the sour taste of hatred in my mouth. He talked to them as if they weren't beings with their own thoughts and feelings.

Detra's wide eyes filled with glossy tears, but none of them fell. Beneath the muzzles, their expressions were hollow and blank. She moved forward with her brother after a moment. I stared at the chains in Sempre's hands. Did he always drag them around this way, dressed like dolls on display? My stomach flipped, threatening to throw up today's food.

"Do these creatures make you hungry?" Sempre asked with a small smile as he stared down at the duo. He talked in a teasing tone, the one a father might use with his kid who'd asked for ice cream after dinner.

I'd never wanted to rip someone's tongue out of their mouth before. My blades were in my boots, and my gun was within easy reach in my shoulder holster. A single shot through the forehead was all it would take. The impulse was breathtakingly strong, strong enough that it almost felt like reality. But attacking now would lead to all our deaths. There was no way any of us would leave this party, let alone the city, alive.

Detra and Carwin stared at us. I prayed that they would recognize us somehow and be comforted. But how could they? Our disguises covered everything. Reshi had gone to great lengths to make sure of it.

Detra furrowed her brow for a moment in confusion. "No?" she asked.

She sounded so unsure of herself. Her soft voice broke my heart into a million pieces. Every second of this exchange passed by with an agonizing ache.

Sempre and Irrikus shared a look. Concern or mild surprise? I couldn't read it. Maybe to them, lightness in itself was incriminating? *Imagine being that evil...*

Our host stared at me, his eyes pleading for me to say something. The faintest hint of sweat dotted his upper lip.

"Pleased to meet you," I managed, hoping I sounded foolish and awed.

Juneau let out a chuckle of feigned ease as he stepped in front of me. He stooped to get a better look at Detra and Carwin. It gave me some distance from them, which might have been his intent. The panicked fury dimmed slightly inside me. I blinked, feeling the haze of rage clear a little.

"They're precious when they're young, I see," Juneau said and drew himself back to full height. "I never thought much about the children before. It must be difficult to take care of them as they get older... As you can see, I also take an interest in *unusual* creatures. If you ever find any more, will you let me know?"

Irrikus gave a throaty laugh, and Sempre smiled coldly. "Of course," he replied in a silky voice. The condescending warmth dripping off his tongue said everything. Juneau would *never* be of a level to afford exotic luxuries such as pet vampires, or so these two council members thought.

All night I had watched and analyzed the subtleties of the social code that passed between these rulers like flowing water. They could hardly help baring their teeth at one another underneath the niceties. Everything was a competition. What was worse than being a hateful creature of unimaginable strength? Being an *unlikeable* all-powerful person. There was not a shred of decency left in their towering bodies. I hated them for their chain leashes, for their grand plans, and even for their snubs to Juneau.

"We have others to speak to," Irrikus said simply and drifted away. Sempre led the children after him. I watched, horrified, as he stroked Carwin's hair and ruffled it like he was a kitten.

"I'm fast enough," Roxy muttered furiously. "I can cut those fingers off."

I balled my hands into fists. Juneau swept his robes over us, partially shielding us from the room. He leaned close and pressed his lips into a grim line.

"I know they're the worst thing to walk this plane since the creation of life itself," Juneau said, quietly furious. "But we have a job. Irrikus pisses everyone off on some level. Get it together before you jeopardize us all."

A hollow sensation filled me. We couldn't leave Carwin and Detra behind, but Juneau was right. We couldn't risk the mission right now.

"You know those children?" he whispered, putting the pieces together from our expressions.

Roxy's lips twisted hesitantly. Although Juneau had provided a safe place for us here, should we tell him about our pasts? He had done a lot to win our trust… perhaps it would be better if he knew everything we were up against now.

"Yes," I said, and a new wave of terrible rage washed over me. "Where their parents are, I have no idea. They must've—" They could be here in the senate. My stomach dropped. Had Sempre taken the kids as pets and thrown Rhome and Kreya into that awful white square known as the sanitarium? My fingers went numb. They might not even be alive anymore.

"Are you all right?" Juneau asked. For a moment, the dramatics melted away from his expression. He scanned our faces with a touch of genuine concern.

I took a deep breath. We had made it this far. Roxy and I could keep up our ruse a while longer. The more we learned at this party, the sooner we could plan a rescue for Carwin and Detra. The first thing I would do? Take those disgusting collars off their necks.

A streak of light cut through the air, and it wasn't soul-light or a decoration. It savagely lit the room, prompting everyone to look up. A chandelier made up of glass trembled violently above us.

More light streaked through the chamber as gem weapons began firing. The band came to a discordant halt, their instruments shrieking into the chaos. Someone screamed, shortly joined by other voices. The relaxed atmosphere was shattered in seconds. Near the corridors, party-goers shoved one another and ran at full speed toward the exits.

Juneau stretched a hand, warning us not to run and get trampled. He swept us against the wall.

"What's going on?" I asked him, standing on my toes in a futile attempt to see where the commotion had started.

"I get the feeling Kane and Dorian are nearby," Roxy said grimly. "Let's get closer."

"It's unwise," Juneau said, then saw my stony face. He dragged a hand over his cheek and gestured covertly to the stage. "Fine. Look. Stay to the wall. We can't be caught up in this. Try to make sure Irrikus isn't looking."

The stage had stood empty a moment ago, but my mouth went dry at the sight of Irrikus and Sempre sitting stoically among a few other figures on their thrones. Their crowns glittered in the ballroom light. The Immortal Council had officially gathered, not appearing concerned in the slightest by the intrusion.

We moved toward the commotion with Juneau leading the way. I dodged flying limbs as more panicked celebrants fled, screeching about vampires. Someone had set up a dais toward the front of the room, the grand structure draped in gold fabric. The elegant chairs set out for council members were currently empty. We hurried toward the dais, seeing more gem lasers concentrated in that area. Juneau clenched his hands into fists as more shots blazed the length of the room. We arrived at a giant arching doorway that led to a grand corridor attached to the ballroom. It ran straight ahead for several yards. Footsteps thumped wildly against the tiled ground.

Juneau hissed, "This isn't good."

I peered past him to see a group of guards and makers spilling from the end of the hallway. Hunters closed in on two figures. I closed my eyes against the sight of Dorian and Kane, free of their disguises and completely surrounded. After everything we'd been through, we'd finally failed at the worst possible time.

A handful of panicked guests had been caught up near the doorframe and were currently cowering behind a group of guards in a state of alarm. A man yelled when he spotted Dorian's extended fangs. The ruler's face paled considerably. Someone pushed the man from behind, and the entire throng of people changed course to the main entryway. The pale-faced man smacked me hard on the shoulder as he rushed past. I gasped. The force had pulled my necklace tight against my neck, making me suddenly aware of how fragile my disguise was. I turned back to the scene as another cry rang out.

"Push them into the ballroom!" cried a hunter. As one, they charged Dorian and Kane.

Dorian gracefully dodged an oncoming hunter. Kane hit one with a right hook. But the guards and hunters had gauntlets similar to the one Inkarri had used during our fight at the lake.

Kane dodged a beam from one, only to skid into the path of a tall, burly hunter who let loose a continuous stream of light from his gauntlet. Kane dropped to his belly, and the light struck a wall across the ballroom, sending a huge chunk of green glass smashing to the ground.

A woman screamed, her horror rising above the panic. "You've crushed him!"

Some poor soul would never attend another party.

The guards glanced over at their mistake. Irrikus's army was less prepared than I thought they'd be. It was an amateur mistake. Dorian used the distraction to launch himself at one of them, and Roxy tugged on my arm as the fight drew closer to us. We ran with Juneau out to the edge of the ballroom, just dodging another hunter as he went flying into the air from a blow by either Dorian or Kane.

These guys aren't as strong as Inkarri. When I squinted at the fallen hunter's weapon, I saw that the light of his gauntlet flickered weakly. Maybe only the elites got the super-charged weapons. If so, Dorian and Kane were taking on the B team, and that meant...

"My Lord Irrikus!" Inkarri's amplified voice rang out. "Alarms were tripped in your private chambers. We found these leeches disguised as wildlings."

The A team had arrived.

Inkarri appeared in the doorway. She tossed her blue hair back and gnashed her teeth together. Her boot came down on the ground, causing a terrible scraping sound against the tile. She stared straight ahead, her eyes moving past the vampires she sought.

I followed Inkarri's gaze to the dais. Sempre and Irrikus stared into the crowd with a cold fury. They glared down at Dorian and Kane, who had been forced onto the now empty dance floor. My worst nightmares melded with reality. A fight against Immortals was the worst-case scenario. We might all perish in this room today.

"More guards," Inkarri shouted into the crowd. From outside the senate doors, a new group of lackeys rushed inside. Her pale cheeks turned purple with rage. She slammed her foot on the floor with a blow powerful enough to crack the tile. "Close the doors! No one is getting in or out, *especially* wildlings."

I looked at Roxy and found her looking back in silent agreement. The commotion was a good distraction. We left Juneau and darted toward the fight, staying close to the edge of the crowd. Some still tried to run for the doors even as guards attempted to close the immense entrance. Others in the crowd grew brave and kept close to the action. I looked back for Juneau, but he had melted into the crowd. Had he run? I felt a soft pang of regret, but I couldn't think about him now.

Three guards surrounded Kane, their swords drawn. Their blades glinted violet, similar to the light given off by the gemstones. When they lunged for him, Kane moved in a flash. He growled, jumping and spinning between the guards. One slashed at the vampire but missed, instead striking another hunter across the face. The two of them crashed together, toppling to the ground.

Inkarri charged at Dorian. He ducked out of her way, but she nearly caught him with her speed. Her eyes blazed with fury—she wasn't focused. For a moment, she stole a glance at the dais. Dorian used the opportunity to shove another hunter into her. They collided, and Inkarri growled.

"I'll take your head," she cried. They clashed in a whirlwind fight, crossing paths with Kane's battle. A deadly dance began to unfold in the middle of the ballroom.

What could I do? I itched to help the men, but Immortals would outmatch me easily in hand-to-hand combat. A pistol might take care of one, but then it would blow my cover in a ballroom full of them. I had my knives in my boots. I eyed Inkarri's neck. It could work, if she got close enough in a crowded fight, but the chances were astronomically low.

Kane narrowly dodged a blast of gemstone light and swore. Roxy shifted beside me, practically vibrating with the strain it was taking to not rush in. Our position was clear. There was little we could do if we wanted to keep our cover. We were forced to stand by and watch helplessly. I frantically scanned the room for anything that might help.

Kane shoved one guard off him with a violent headbutt.

An enraged growl left Inkarri's lips. "Stop tripping over yourselves! If you've been drinking on the job, I'll kill you all myself."

My hopes lifted slightly when I realized the issue between the rulers and the vampires. The rulers were fast and powerful, but they were *huge*, and several had definitely sampled the pink cocktails from earlier. The vampires were smaller but far more nimble and, more importantly, sober. Kane smashed a third guard to the ground, but I could see his heaving chest. He and Dorian couldn't keep this up much longer.

More guards poured into the room, further demonstrating the hopelessness of the situation. Their boots struck the tiled floor like charging animals in a stampede. I gasped as they fired wildly into the gathered crowd. I ducked and pulled Roxy with me to dodge a blast of lilac light.

"They're panicking," I whispered to her. "They'll take out half the guests just to kill two vampires."

Dorian cried out with a pained grunt as Inkarri smashed her foot into his stomach. He flew several yards from the force of the kick but jumped back up. He curled his lip in disdain as Inkarri smirked.

"Regretting your stupidity yet?" she asked. She licked her lips and balanced the blade of her blue glass knife comfortably in her hand.

Dorian snarled but said nothing. Like Kane, his breath left him in ragged gasps. A cruel smile bloomed on Inkarri's face as she lifted her hand to show off the gem embedded in her palm.

"Remember this?" She aimed her gauntlet at him.

The lights flickered. An electric current of tension surged through the air as Irrikus released a terrifying roar. It froze the entire scene. Inkarri paused, her eyebrows knitted in frustration at being stopped.

"Such *insolence* in my senate," Irrikus spat. Dorian faced him. Irrikus's nostrils flared. "There's no good in any of you." He rose from his throne and stepped off the dais. His crown glittered like knives as he approached.

Inkarri gritted her teeth together tightly. "My lord, I have this under control." Unfortunately, her blade and raised gauntlet supported that claim.

My throat burned as I watched Irrikus walk toward them. His steps held the terrible promises of violence, war, and suffering. He glared stonily at the younger hunter. "If that were true, daughter, they would not have made it this far. Retreat with your guards."

Daughter? Another puzzle piece slid into place as I observed them together. But what was he doing? He'd just stopped his best fighter from doing her job.

Inkarri seethed. "With *respect*, my lord, I can handle this." She held her blade defiantly. "Let me finish my work." She turned away from Dorian. Only Irrikus existed to her right now.

"Your way isn't working," Irrikus complained hotly. "So I must take care of it myself."

What the hell were they doing? A soldier never had a full-on discussion until the enemy was—

Dorian leapt forward, kicking Inkarri in her distracted face. She let out a pained cry as she flew back into the wall. He lunged for her to press his advantage, his hands wrapping around her throat.

"STOP!"

Irrikus's cry actually shook the walls. Glasses on abandoned trays shattered. All the tiny flying wildlings fell to the ground as their wings froze in place. Dorian winced, faltering and stumbling to a stop before Inkarri's groaning body.

Inkarri's coaxing voice was powerful, but something in Irrikus's tone demanded absolute obedience. The same sneer I had seen on his statues now rested on his face. It brimmed with danger. My mind reeled as the Immortal's command sank into me against my will. My joints felt stiff as everything except my eyes stopped moving. Such power shouldn't exist.

"You will stop," Irrikus boomed. "You will keep your limbs still like the pinned insects you are."

Dorian shivered, his arms slack at his sides. He wavered and drifted slightly, frowning in confusion, but something furious raged behind those glacial eyes. Kane tried to move his hand but only succeeded in wiggling his fingers. Somewhere beneath the surface, Dorian and Kane fought the sway of Irrikus's voice.

I tried to shake myself from the trance, but it was no use. *Move,* I told my feet. They carried me a step in the direction of Irrikus and stopped again. It was like trying to run in a dream. I bit my lip hard enough to draw blood, hoping it would snap me out of it. Instead, I tasted pain and iron while my body stayed frozen.

"Mmm," Dorian murmured. His lips fought to produce sound.

Irrikus lifted one haughty eyebrow and laughed with contempt. "Don't try to fight it, vampire. You might be able to resist Inkarri, but not *me*. I command all in this senate."

Dorian growled. "You won't be able... to keep us... forever." He somehow managed to force the words out.

Irrikus chuckled, shaking his head. He tapped the crown on top of his head. "I'm afraid I can do whatever I want." His golden eyes hardened. He waved his guards over. "And I don't *want* to keep you forever, scum. A short time will serve my needs. Guards and hunters, you are free to move. Vampires, keep still for now. I like to watch you struggle against my will."

As horrible as our situation was, I couldn't help feeling relief. Whatever the guards intended to do to the vampires, it didn't look like they would kill the men in front of us.

Kane glared murderously at Irrikus. He tried to lift his fists, but his arms shook terribly. His body fought against him for the entire movement.

Inkarri struggled to her feet. "Father, I can subdue them—"

"You have disappointed me enough already." Irrikus sneered. "Let the guards do their work."

Inkarri's face contorted. She stared at the ground. The crowd whispered around me, but I couldn't make out anything they were saying. I focused on Dorian and Kane.

"Surrender," Irrikus ordered. He waved the guards toward the immobilized vampires. They moved in on Kane first, who managed to break free long enough to snap his fangs at them.

"You'll… never take me alive." He struggled to speak, but it sounded genuine.

My breath caught in my throat. If Kane killed himself rather than fall into Immortal clutches, would Dorian do the same? I couldn't watch him die today, at their hands or his own. Roxy breathed heavily beside me with her hands balled into fists.

My body drifted toward them an inch, fighting against the terrible thrall of Irrikus's voice.

Suddenly, the sound of a chain jerking to the end of its length cut through the air.

"Uncle Dorian?" Carwin called out in a high voice.

Dorian and Kane broke free from the mental domination. Their heads turned in the direction of the dais, where Sempre pulled back on his chains. Detra and Carwin fought to jump off the stage, straining against their leashes.

"Uncle Dorian!" Detra cried. She broke into wordless sobs that climbed to the high ceiling. My hand reached out instinctively. I wanted so badly to grab her and her brother.

The sway broke completely. Dorian rushed the dais, Kane in his wake. The guards pushed them back with raised weapons. Dorian snapped his teeth, fangs flashing in the light.

"I'll drain every single one of you to get to them," he said, his voice holding a promise of death.

Sempre looked down at his abruptly animated pets. The children's dead-eyed composure was gone. Carwin and Detra reached out for Dorian and Kane, crying and struggling against the leashes. With a huff, Sempre yanked them back, and their tiny bodies tumbled into each other. My heart twisted as I watched Sempre grab a glass dagger from his belt.

"Vampires," he said in a clear voice, "would you like to see these lovely children die tonight? It can be arranged." He yanked a snarling Detra closer using his leash hand. Carwin cried out and pummeled the ruler's legs with his tiny fists. Sempre smiled icily. He lifted the glass blade to Detra's neck. She screamed when the knife pressed into her skin.

Dorian's anger against the rulers was almost tangible, scorching the air. But still, he slowly lifted his hands in surrender, his stricken eyes on the children.

CHAPTER TWENTY-THREE

I rrikus watched with a pleased smile as two burly guards marched up to Dorian and Kane.

Roxy grabbed my hand and squeezed. There was no way we could help them right now. The only chance we had was to get out of here, then figure out how to mount a rescue. My thoughts flashed by with dizzying speed. We could circle back to grab Laini and take a redbill to the Mortal Plane, go to the Bureau with what we'd learned. We could get Bravi and a few others, bring them to Itzarriol, and break Kane and Dorian out. I would just have to trust them to survive that long.

"Tell us, vampire. Who brought you here?" Irrikus said. His low voice sent a shiver through the crowd.

Carwin and Detra sobbed. Sempre scowled and whispered something to them in a low voice. The children stopped squirming. Anger blazed through me at the sight of their terror.

Irrikus clapped his hands at the silence. "Who brought them here?" he bellowed and glowered at Dorian. "Do you have accomplices? Tell me." The sway pulled at me, but I zipped my mouth shut.

I reached over and gently grabbed Roxy's arm to tug her. The sway of Irrikus's voice had broken. We needed to get out of here. Surreptitiously, we worked our way through the crowd. Smaller than most, it was easy enough to duck down and weave our way through the bodies.

Don't turn around. I begged the crowd to stay where they were, standing witness to the ruler of Immortals and his fury. If Roxy and I could make it to one of the corridors or doors, we could try to hide and wait for them to open the castle again. Maybe there was a servants' door somewhere.

"Juneau brought strange wildlings into the party!"

The voice, from the dreadful Pireka, sent shards of ice through my body. Roxy and I pushed forward, keeping to the wall, trying to stay out of sight. We couldn't stop, even as the crowd turned to look for Juneau.

"My wildlings?" Juneau called from near the dais, offended. He let out a scoff, but there was a hint of hollowness. An effect of Irrikus's sway? Juneau raised his voice. "My wildlings would never cause such a stir. It's outrageous to suggest such a thing."

"He's always causing trouble," someone else yelled.

"That's not true," Juneau cried. His voice shook.

Irrikus growled in disbelief. "Your wildlings *were* strange... where are they?"

I didn't look back, hoping Juneau could talk his way out of this. He could claim we'd been separated by the crowd. The door finally came into sight. A crowd surged around it. If we could just make it outside, we could find a way back to Juneau's mansion. One foot after the other, I prayed the crowd would focus on him. There was a small side hallway. If we could slip past the two burly guards by using the fight as a diversion, then maybe...

Suddenly, what felt like a thin cord wrapped around my wrist. I had time to see a familiar red-and-black braid, tipped with a hook, pull tight around my limb, before Roxy sucked in a sharp breath and stumbled backward like she'd been yanked. I turned to look into the furious eyes of the hunter we had seen capture Kono, his blue eyes like those of a hungry wolf.

I took a deep breath, then exploded into motion. Grabbing for one of the knives in my boot, I whipped it up, cutting through the hunter's restricting braid. The hair fell to the ground as he howled.

"They're trying to get out!"

Roxy shoved me. I sprang toward the door, but guards descended on us, blocking the door with their hulking bodies. I drew back, ready to use my knife, and ran into Roxy, who grabbed my shoulders to stop me from rushing in. The Immortal guards surrounded us, their armor glinting.

The party was over, and so were our chances.

I turned back to the dais, panting. Irrikus glared in our direction, but it was Sempre who spoke. He moved forward with the children at his sides and gently ran his hand along the top of Carwin's head.

"I would advise you to stop, or I'll be forced to find new pets to train as energy detectors."

I let the knife drop to the floor with a clatter and slowly raised my hands, palms out. Roxy did the same. My humiliation and panic paled in comparison to my rage as I considered Sempre's words. He was using the children as energy detectors as though they were simply trained dogs. I forced myself not to look at Dorian and Kane, knowing that would only give Irrikus the confirmation he so desperately wanted.

The hunter I had escaped from a moment before descended on me, yanking my arms behind my back so hard that my shoulders cried out in pain. I hissed as his braids bound my wrists tightly but gave no other reaction, not wanting to give Irrikus the pleasure of watching me struggle. Beside me, a wildling guard grabbed Roxy. She muttered a barrage of curses that would have made a sailor blush.

The hunter, his braids hissing eerily, pushed me forward with a rough shove. "Move, scum."

He led me out of the room. As he did, I heard the crowd stirring behind us. Somewhere in the mess, guards herded Dorian and Kane as well.

"My lord, I swear to you that I can make this right," Juneau said evenly, with an eerie calm to his voice. "I can bring you another, if only you forgive me."

Juneau had sold us out in the end. This was no longer a fun game for him. The scumbag would trade Laini to save his own skin. My only hope was that Laini's unfaltering suspicion of our former host had led her to plan her escape as soon as we left for the party.

But there was no escape for us. The ruse was up.

Nearly a dozen guards herded the four of us to a simple stone-lined room several hallways over from the ballroom. Dorian scowled as a guard stepped in front of him. It was strange to see his face and remember that Roxy and I still resembled wildlings. The guard motioned for the burly fellow restraining Dorian to bring the two vampires up front.

Dorian jerked away as the guard from behind released him, but the guard in front was a smiley fellow with quick movements. He never stopped smiling. He easily snatched Dorian's wrists and held them together. The other guards, supervised by the hunter with the hooked braids, did the same to the rest of us. As the hunter shoved me toward one of the guards, I watched them all, looking for weak links. Most of them watched with utter fascination, and none had swiped a cocktail while on the job.

The smiling guard in front of Dorian pulled a bundle of green wire from his pocket. It unsettled every cell in my body. His grin grew even bigger, as if he'd just presented us with a fine toy. He snapped off a piece and handed it to the next guard, then quickly wrapped the scrap around Dorian's neck. To my shock, the ripped ends melded together with a crackle of light and transformed into a single ring of metal flush against Dorian's skin. Fury and dread rose up inside me, twisting my insides until my lungs squeezed with pain. Immediately, Dorian began to stagger as if he were drunk, a groan of pain slipping from his mouth.

Somewhere in the back of my brain, any final hope I had of trying to escape during transit slipped away. Restraints or cuffs we could have worked our way out of, but these collars seemed to be far worse.

That meant that now was my last best chance to escape. As a female wildling covered in dark purple scales stepped up to attach my collar, a final, desperate surge came over me. I wouldn't go down without a fight. In a blur, I drew my pistol, flicked off the safety, and fired three rounds at the hunter. Dark blood sprayed, and he toppled backward. Even with the silencer on, the sound was startling in the small room. Chaos immediately erupted. The female guard dropped the wire and leapt for me with a yell. I scrambled back, letting off another shot at her torso, but it ricocheted off her gray metal breastplate. Roxy pulled her own gun from her thigh holster, firing at the guards as she backed up. One or two went down, but she soon disappeared under a pile of wildlings and another hunter.

Kane fought to reach us, but two guards wrapped several loops of wire around his neck, and he crumpled to the ground. I managed to get off one last shot, sending a wildling reeling away with a wounded leg, before the scaled female pinned me to the ground and slammed the hilt of her dagger into my wrist. My hand went numb, and the gun fell away. We grappled on the ground, twisting together, and then there was a spark and a snap. My hands lost their fur, my clothes appeared, and my necklace tinkled to the floor.

There was a moment of shocked silence before the scaled wildling wrapped wire around my throat, her lips curling in a sneer of fury. She smirked when I winced as the collar adhered to my neck. It was tight. If I tensed my neck and strained against it, I could feel it start to bite like a garrote.

"I will enjoy thinking of Zeele hurting you," she hissed.

Roxy snarled when the same female guard found and broke her necklace, stripping away her stony form, but the woman merely wrapped wire around her neck without comment.

I was yanked to my feet by another guard, and my head swam as a wave of nausea rose. My limbs were heavier than usual. I glanced over at Dorian, who was now propped against the wall. Kane was pinned to the floor, pawing at his collar with his fingers, but it was no use. No matter how he fought, the collar refused to budge. He shook as he tried to regain control over himself.

The body of the hunter I had shot slumped against the wall, his creepy braids limp. At least I'd managed to take one of them down with me. I yelped as the guards shoved Dorian and Kane toward us. My chest caught flame as our proximity broke the fifteen foot minimum, then closed in on ten. The air left my mouth as the guard again pushed him closer. I staggered against Roxy. The scaled wildling stepped up to separate us.

"She's leaning, not fighting," Roxy said defensively, wrapping her arms around me.

The woman's cold eyes narrowed. I forced myself to straighten, but the pain seemed to double. Dorian huffed, and I looked over in time to see all the color drain from his face. He snapped his fangs at the smiling guard, who was delighted by the mysterious increased pain. They hadn't worked it out yet. They likely thought their magic green wire had merely taken some time to work or worked better on some than others.

My heart seared as the pain stabilized but didn't decrease. The guards began to push us from the room. I took a final look around at the blood and scuffle. What a mess. We had come with high hopes of finding vital information, but things had unraveled completely and turned out far worse than I ever imagined. The presence of Carwin and Detra pushed everything over the edge. If I looked down, I envisioned toeing the edge of a cliff and knowing the drop might not be far off.

"Move," the woman guard snapped.

My head swam as the guards' rough handling inadvertently forced me closer to Dorian. A bead of sweat slipped down the side of my face. My mouth was dry. It went even drier when I realized they were leading us through the senate, toward the back. They were going to immediately send us to the sanitarium. Our guards took us down a cobblestone staircase that descended to the roiling water of the uncanny ocean. A small pier of shimmering stone protruded into the waves, where a large, sleek barge made from pearly white wood waited for us.

"On," the woman barked.

I'd love to tell her *where* she could put all those orders. I blinked through tears brought on by the heartburn, and my eyes fell to the water. The vaporous substance around the boat was an ominous welcome to the island.

They lined us up on separate benches in the center of the boat. It was only by luck that Roxy managed to fake a trip and put herself in front of me in line, which meant there was an extra bench between Dorian and me. I breathed a small sigh of relief when I sat on the wooden seat. The burning abated slightly.

I licked my dry lips as a guard at the front gave the order to push off. Before us, the giant, forbidding white building corrupted the other side of the island like an ambitious fungus. The female guard saw me looking and grinned with satisfaction at the flicker of fear that crossed my face.

"The sanitarium," she drawled gleefully. "You've earned yourself a one-way ticket."

CHAPTER TWENTY-FOUR

The sanitarium grew larger and larger until we reached the base of the cliff where it perched like a patient leopard waiting for prey to pass below. The immense white walls sent a shiver of fear down my spine. Somewhere deep down, I knew that prisoners who entered the building never left its walls.

"Off the boat," a guard called. They marched us up a narrow staircase with no handrail that crawled up the cliffside. It was old and wet, reeking of copper. For a moment, I wished Bryce, Sike, and Arlonne were with us. Arlonne would be silent, emanating strength that I could imitate. Sike would make a joke or wink at the other captives to cheer us up. And Bryce would have an idea and the experience to pull it off. If we hadn't separated, would we have even been caught in the first place?

"Up, up, up," the scaled wildling commanded, bringing me back to reality. I didn't really want my friends to be here, doomed with us. I was fiercely glad that they would have the chance to escape to safety in the Mortal Plane. At the sight of my small smile, my guard pinched my arm. I didn't give her the satisfaction of a reaction.

My legs were heavy as we climbed the staircase. It felt like weights had been adhered to the soles of my feet. I glanced up to see Dorian and Kane struggling, their bodies shuddering against the added invisible resistance that the wire caused. It was unlike my own collar, which merely felt like an uncomfortable weight that threw me off balance. The collar must be incredibly painful for them. If the fight hadn't already worn us out, this trek would do it.

We reached the top of the staircase. The sole advantage of the climb had been that there was more distance between Dorian and me, but now the guards lined us back up. Even with Roxy and Kane between us, my vision blurred momentarily.

A small door stood in the nearest wall. It was barely larger than the average Immortal. Maybe eight feet? It opened as we approached. White shimmery walls greeted me on the inside, so sterile and blank that my eyeballs felt as dry as bones. A new group of guards, made up entirely of makers, awaited us in the narrow corridor. They were much smaller than the rulers, but their arms were thick with ropey muscles that said not to test them. They wore open-faced helmets, allowing us to look at their wide, beautiful faces and red eyes. Their armor covered everything except their upper arms, possibly a specific gap to show off powerful physiques. Even their weaker, second pair of arms had disappeared beneath armor.

"Watch these carefully, especially the small creatures in vampire clothing," the female guard said. "They fought back when we restrained them. That one," she pointed to me, "killed Arton with this." She handed over the gun and necklaces carefully. "The necklaces hold a powerful glamor which made them look like wildlings. The other was used to kill Arton. It's some kind of magic I haven't seen before. Let Director Zeele know."

"They will be searched thoroughly," one maker guard promised in a low, growling voice. Unlike the senate guards, his voice lacked hatred.

The female guard released my arm and gave me a cutting smile. "Enjoy your stay."

The sanitarium guards lined us up against the wall and told us to face it. We obeyed.

"Bring the unknown creatures to the front inspection room first, then the vampires," a cool voice said behind us.

"You can turn around," the guard closest to me said gruffly. Two guards grabbed Roxy and me and led us to a small room. The security collar stayed on, and I stood in front of the guards with nothing but my real face. No magic, no weapons, no allies.

The guard beside me raised his eyebrow at my strange appearance but said nothing.

"Interesting," the man from before said.

I glanced over to see two rulers standing by. They wore light breast-plates over white robes so pure that I nearly lost them in the walls behind them. One man gazed at me intently with electric green eyes. The other was a woman who stared at Roxy's hair with a sharp look.

"I was told to inform you that these creatures used unknown magic to kill a hunter," the guard said to the green-eyed ruler, handing over the necklaces and the gun.

"Search them for other weapons," green eyes commanded. He dropped the items into a plain white bag.

The guards obeyed, the first staying with me and another going to Roxy. He began to pat me down and feel around the edges of my Hive clothing. The final knife was removed from my boot, and he sliced off my shoulder holster, throwing it aside. My heart thumped wildly in my chest when I remembered Dorian's stone in my sports bra. The guard pulled back, and for a blissful second, I thought he was done.

Then the guards cut off our belts and jackets and pulled off our shoes. My hopes fell, but surely they wouldn't search my bra. Even Immortals had to have some sense of decency, right?

As if to answer me, my guard dug into the front pockets of my pants and flipped them inside out. He whipped out a small blade and cut the pocket off, then pawed it to make sure nothing was hidden. I eyed the silver knife nervously. Without pause, he resumed his pat down with his smaller, dexterous set of hands, and he went *everywhere*. As his hands skimmed over my chest, he frowned. My lips twitched irritably as he prodded my sports bra more closely, though to his credit, he didn't seem to derive any pleasure from it. I glared at him, but he stared back without a hint of shame.

"I need you to give me that," he said simply.

I scowled and begrudgingly dug into my bra for the stone. As I placed it in his palm, I was relieved to see that it looked like a simple rock, no glowing or strange colors. He handed it to his colleague, a female maker. She squinted at it until one of the white-robed rulers, green eyes, stepped up.

He gently took it and studied it. "Interesting." A faint impression of Juneau came to mind, but this ruler's fascination seemed more controlled, impersonal. He pocketed the stone.

I memorized his face. Light brown skin, ear-length black hair with a greenish tint that splayed around his face in wild curls, and those bright eyes.

He didn't move away when he noticed me staring. In fact, he looked closer, and his interested gaze slid over to Roxy after a moment.

"I can see your auras clearly now," he muttered. "You're not vampires. No, no… you're quite different, aren't you? You're… more valuable."

My guard placed his hands at his sides. "Shall we lead them away, sir?"

The green-eyed ruler waved his hand. "Yes. I shall attend to them personally. Put them in my interest group."

The other ruler gave a polite cough. "Ah, Director Zeele, are you sure we shouldn't…"

Zeele. I finally had a face to put to the name. Director Zeele who worked with Sempre on the projects here at the sanitarium.

The director lifted a finger. His eye twitched. "Shall I remind you that I'm the only one authorized to work on Lord Sempre's personal projects? The vampires can go in the vampire holding cells. These creatures will go in my interest group." He waved her off.

She pursed her lips but said nothing more.

We were led back out to the main room. Mere moments after we arrived, however, Kane and Dorian were marched off into the hall. I turned to catch a glimpse of Dorian before he was forced from the room. His eyes surged with raw fury and pain. I knew there must be similar desperation written all over my face. Our exchange sparked through the air, an unspoken message between us—we had to get out of here.

The guards hustled us into the hall. Zeele turned left to follow us, while the woman went right with Dorian and Kane. The hallways here were brightly lit by long glowing tubes, the kind of white that almost seemed purple or blue if you squinted. The tubes ran along the corridors, far too bright after several days in dim soul-light. I shielded my eyes until they adjusted. The corridor stretched on like a never-ending hospital ward. Behind me, I heard Dorian and Kane's footsteps fade into nothing. My heart fell, but the burning completely disappeared from my chest.

The white suddenly changed to tunnels cut from slate-colored stone. The corridor widened before snaking down to a massive chamber with several doorways that led to other rooms. All along the back edge of the chamber were a series of holding cells along the rock wall. It appeared to be some kind of observation room. The ceiling and front of the cells were made of yellowish glass. My breath caught in my throat when I saw a large group of figures packed into the cell. There were vampires, a few wildlings, and even some makers among them. A lone ruler averted his eyes as we passed by one of the amber windows. They were all in rough condition with ripped clothes, bruised faces, and hungry eyes. I shuddered at the thought of Zeele and his colleagues watching them all day.

Roxy and I were marched past the big chamber. I could've sworn I saw one of the Hive vampires from the safehouse raid press his face to the glass, but the guards hustled us along. There was no time to try to remember his face. Wherever they were taking us, it couldn't be good.

Zeele had mentioned we were being put with a special interest group and that he was in charge of Sempre's personal experiments. What the hell did that mean? Detra and Carwin flashed through my mind. Maybe Zeele had helped him obtain the children and trained them like dogs.

The guards stopped abruptly, and I nearly ran into the one ahead of me. The chamber in front of us was smaller than the others and had far fewer creatures packed inside.

"Ready?" Zeele asked. The guards nodded, and Zeele placed his hand on the glass. It sank into the window. Abruptly, the guards shoved Roxy and me forward. I stumbled into the window, slipping through it like it was chilly Jell-O.

We staggered inside. Instantly, Roxy spun and jumped back for the glass. Zeele snatched his hand back, and her head smashed against the suddenly solid surface with a sickening crack. She fell to the ground, cursing in pain. I stooped down to comfort her as Zeele gave a sharp laugh of triumph. Soon, he and the guards vanished back down the hall, leaving us in the cell.

Angry tears spilled from the corners of Roxy's eyes. She clenched her head between tight hands, not bothering to stand. A bright red spot began to bloom on her forehead. The sight of seeing tough-as-nails Roxy cry blurred my own eyes with bitter tears. I wrapped my arms around her and gave her a tight hug. I hated to see her like this. I hated this entire mess. Dorian, Kane, Detra, and Carwin deserved better than cruelty at the hands of their longtime oppressors. Roxy deserved to be safe and kicking butt somewhere in the Mortal Plane, heading home every few months to see her precious siblings.

And yet we were here, imprisoned in the sanitarium.

The absence of burning in my chest made me feel hollow. Dorian was somewhere far from me now. I shut my eyes for a brief moment as an entirely different kind of pain consumed me.

The two of us sniffled a little, pulling ourselves together when we registered that we had an audience. I became aware of the number of bodies present in the small room. Tensing, ready for anything, I turned to see who we had been left with.

"Lyra? Roxy?"

The last thing I'd expected was a familiar voice. The timbre of his hopeful tone reminded me of someone. I squinted in the room's dim yellow light to see a figure moving toward us from behind the group of six vampires.

A male vampire limped closer, taking his steps with great effort, but something about the silhouette also snagged at a memory. He drew near, and my heart raced when I finally made out his features as he emerged from the shadows.

"Rhome?"

CHAPTER TWENTY-FIVE

"**R**home!" Roxy cried, blinking in a daze. The nasty welt on her forehead had quickly turned dark and angry under the yellow light. "Wait, is this my concussion talking?"

"I can't believe you're here," Rhome breathed and shook his head. He smiled, but he was thin and worn, like a sweater that had gone through the washer too many times. There were tired lines under his eyes that had never been there before. As he limped the last few steps toward us, he stumbled. I reached out to steady him.

"We're so glad to see you," I said, then shook my head. "I mean, these aren't the most ideal circumstances, but it's good to know you're alive."

He chuckled weakly. "'Alive' might be too generous. But I'm still going. Barely." He dragged a hand through his hair. It had always been streaked with silver, but now there was a new chunk of gray in it. Roxy stared, knowing the trauma he must have gone through for this change to have taken place.

"You look different," she blurted.

His sad eyes swept over us. "I feel different."

He waved for us to follow him and led the way to the back of the chamber. Most of the vampires were gathered there, as far from the window as possible. Rhome moved slowly from some kind of injury in his left hip. My stomach sank with dread. There were no blankets, no amenities, no water—just cold, unforgiving glass and rock.

The other vampires varied in age, gender, and state of damage. None looked familiar to me, nor did their appearance suggest that Zeele selected a certain type of vampire for this cell. They could have come from the Hive. I hadn't met everyone there. Were there other groups hiding in the Immortal Plane? I offered them a small smile, but it wasn't returned. Most kept their gazes averted. A woman who appeared close to my age stared at the wall with dead eyes. Her greasy hair was splayed around her, unkempt and knotted. An older man sat next to her and stared at his bare feet, which were bruised and cut.

Something was wrong, something that went beyond the obvious signs of torture. I studied their faces, looking at the young woman in particular. The barest of shadows flickered on her face. They were *starving*. A hole dug itself in my gut, leaving a space that immediately filled with numbed sadness. I'd hoped to never see another starving vampire.

Something had shredded the bottom of Rhome's pants. The fabric hung like party streamers starting at his knee. Between the ribbons of material, I could see that his legs were covered in scratches. Whatever had done this to him had seriously sharp claws.

He looked over at Roxy. "You're not the first to have made that mistake with the glass, but it's a mistake you only ever make once," he said. "The glass is only permeable when the butchers put their hands on it." He jerked his chin at a passing white-robed figure.

Butchers. Even though their white robes weren't literally stained with blood right now, I got the sense they were morally drenched in the stuff.

Roxy leaned back against the stone wall with a weary sigh of acknowledgment. She wouldn't be trying that again.

"What happened to you?" I asked. "Dorian said they lost you and Kreya in the Immortal Plane."

The last I'd heard, Dorian and the other vampires had tried to rescue Rhome and Kreya after receiving word that the estranged husband and wife were under attack by hunters. Unfortunately, the team had failed, rushing back from the Immortal Plane just in time to end the battle between my human team and a Bureau contingent that had their own shrieking decay. After experiencing the Immortal Plane myself, I understood how easy it would be for the Immortals to capture vampires who got separated from their comrades.

Rhome settled against the wall with a sigh, wincing as his hip hit the ground. "I went to scout with Bravi and Vonn. Kreya managed to find us not long after we came through the tear. She was frantic. She said that she and the children had been hiding in a tiny cabin in the mountains near Vanim. She thought it was abandoned, and it served as a perfect hiding place for a while. There was a cellar and a series of underground tunnels that Carwin discovered via a trapdoor."

"Where near Vanim?" I pressed. It was pretty ballsy of Kreya to stay there with all the hunters in the area.

"Right under the tear. Nobody thought to look at it because patrols were thickest there. Her plan worked brilliantly, for a while."

I supposed it made sense, in a crazy sort of way. She would benefit from their complacency, and also had a quick escape route back to the Mortal Plane in an emergency. I reluctantly admired her sheer weaselly cunning, but clearly something had gone wrong. Those kinds of tactics never worked long term.

"The cabin had originally housed a dozen or so digging wildlings with some darkness in them. She killed them all to feed the children."

Roxy raised her eyebrows, and we exchanged a look. I hadn't realized Kreya was capable of that. Clearly, sparring with her back at the facility would have been worthwhile.

Rhome caught our look and smirked. "Kreya was the fiercest fighter in Vanim before the city fell," he told us proudly. "She used to teach the fighting arts. She trained Dorian and Lanzon both." His eyes darkened, and he looked away.

I plucked at the loose threads where the pockets had been cut out of my pants. "What happened next?"

"Turns out, a hunter patrol found the children while she was out hunting and took them, figuring there must be someone else nearby, since they were clean and fed. The hunters were combing the area, and while we were trying to avoid them, we stumbled into Kreya by accident. She asked for our help to attack the group of hunters." He closed his eyes and gave a deep, shuddering sigh. "I would have done anything to get the kids back. No matter what she and I have disagreed about, protecting our children always comes first, no matter what." He paused for a moment, running his thumb along his bottom lip. He nodded as if to convince himself of his own words. His lip was scabbed, like someone had split it recently.

Roxy pulled her knees to her chest. The bad news was coming.

"Plans are short lived in the Immortal Plane. The fight got messy. Kreya and I told Bravi and Vonn to flee and try to get reinforcements. She and I barricaded ourselves in the tunnels under the cabin, hoping we could last a few hours before Bravi and Vonn came back with help. When Dorian and the others arrived, we thought it might be okay." He pressed his face into his hands.

I gently reached up to touch his shoulder, shocked by how thin it felt. "You don't have to explain if you're not okay after all of... this."

Rhome took a deep breath. "No, I want to tell you. The hunters used the kids to force me and Kreya to surrender. Dorian and most of his team managed to escape to the Mortal Plane, with some losses, as I'm sure you must know. As soon as we got to the sanitarium, we were separated. Kreya and I were brought here along with the kids..." His breath hitched with pain. "Initially, Kreya was in this group instead of me. I got put in a holding cell with what they call *low-interest* vampires. I haven't seen Carwin and Detra since they brought us in."

Roxy and I exchanged a look. He had no idea that his kids were in the senate across from the island. It would crush him to hear the news, but he deserved the truth.

"We've seen them," Roxy said gently.

Rhome opened his mouth, but nothing came out. How many nights had he tortured himself, wondering what had happened to his children?

"They're in the palace," I relayed. "They're being held by Lord Sempre, a member of the Immortal Council. He's, uh, keeping them as... well, as pets." Part of me wanted to soften the blow, but Rhome deserved the truth about his children.

"They're alive?" Rhome pressed, the lump in his throat bobbing.

"Yes. They're alive, and I'd even go so far as to say relatively safe." I didn't add *for the moment*. "Sempre is training them to sense darkness for the ruling caste."

He sighed. "As sick as it is, I'm glad. If they're serving a purpose, it could keep them alive. I lost a lot of hope when they moved me to this cell after Kreya—" He stopped abruptly. A pinprick of dread touched the back of my neck.

"What happened to her?" Roxy asked tentatively.

Rhome rubbed his eyes with grimy hands. "I... I don't have the strength to talk about that yet. Please. Tell me what is going on in the Mortal Plane. What are you two *doing* here? Where's Dorian?" He took in a ragged breath. My gut twisted violently. Kreya might be dead.

Roxy and I shared a worried look. So much had happened in the last few weeks, I didn't know where to begin. It felt like a year had passed since we came to the Immortal Plane, let alone anything before that.

"Well," I said with a sigh, "I guess I'll start with when Dorian and the others came back. We were in the middle of fighting a shrieking decay around the ski resort."

"There was a shrieking decay in the Mortal Plane?" Rhome asked, aghast.

I nodded grimly. "We have a lot to catch you up on."

And so, I recounted the tale of Vonn's betrayal, storming the Bureau, the faceoff on the roof, and the aftermath of revealing vampires to the entire planet. Most of the vampires inside our cell stared blankly at the walls. A few glanced in our direction, but they seemed more focused on Rhome than on us. Part of me wondered if they'd gotten burned out on welcoming new prisoners only to have them disappear.

Rhome leaned back with a look of disbelief. "That's... a lot to take in." He blinked. "Bryce has a *sister*?"

Roxy grinned. "We went through some wild adventures while you were gone. It's a pretty exciting tale until…" She looked around the chamber. "Our plan was to *not* end up in prison."

"Don't worry. You tried your best." Rhome gave her a bittersweet smile. "That's all we can do."

I wrapped up the story with our latest exploits. Rhome seemed excited by the prospect of the Hive, but disappointed to hear that their safehouse had been raided. None of the other vampires stirred at my whispered mention of the Hive, so I assumed they either weren't aware of it or were determined to keep their mouths shut under any circumstances. I left out details of their location. I didn't want to burden Rhome with any extra information that the butchers might find interesting.

Rhome wiped a hand down his face. "You're lucky that the researchers only make occasional rounds in the middle of the night. Your tale is… well, convoluted."

Roxy snorted. "It's straight-up bonkers. We've gone through the craziest things. Like when we were in Vanim, I made the mistake of touching a wall, which gave an instant download of the thoughts and feelings that occurred there." She shuddered. "It was awful."

Rhome's eyebrows dipped, and his eyes filled with sadness. "I miss that place. Or I suppose I miss what it used to be. That place used to be filled with so much joy and determination and bravery. So many good memories."

We all took a moment of silence, processing how that was definitely no longer the case and perhaps never would be again.

"You mentioned that the researchers usually take off in the middle of the night," I said. "How do you tell the time in here? I've got no idea of how days and night pass here in the Immortal Plane. Do you guys have some sort of internal sense?"

He gave a hollow laugh. "In here, you can't see the sky, so there's no way to see if it's soul-bright or soul-dim. But the internal clock of this place relies on when the butchers start coming to take people from the cells. Dread and anticipation are good timekeepers."

As if they had heard our conversation, white-robed figures spilled into the chamber outside the cells. The young female vampire flinched and drew closer to the wall beside the older man as they passed by our window. An older woman stared numbly, watching the group of prisoners that followed the Immortal butchers. Behind the vampires, the same muscled maker guards that had escorted us in used what looked like magical prods with spiky blue glowing ends to keep the prisoners walking. The vampires—shackled, muzzled, and bound at the feet—passed by slowly. Their collars, the same monstrosities made from glowing green wire, rested tight on their necks. I caught sight of a few of the vampires' faces and regretted it immediately.

Shadows filled their faces, but instead of showing strength and health, the shadows looked sinister, like when Dorian had been overwhelmed by shots from the Bureau's X-75. I pressed my nails into my palms as my frustration surged. There was nothing I could do. The burly makers pushed the vampires onward, their red eyes in their sharp faces focused on the prisoners, while the white-robed rulers chatted casually.

I wanted to pound my fists on the glass, but that would only invite trouble. The starved vampires in our cell needed peace more than chaos.

"Their foreheads," Roxy breathed. She tugged on my sleeve. "Look."

I followed her covert pointing to the two vampires walking at the back of the group. Just like the velek and Inkarri and Hildan, these vampires had gems implanted in their foreheads. Unlike the others, these jewels were red. I suspected that if I got close enough to see, I'd find the flesh around the gems was sore and swollen.

Scraps of information slotted together in my head, a horrifying possibility taking shape. I dropped my mouth close to Roxy's ear, not wanting any of the vampires to hear.

"You know how Hildan said they were experimenting with the gems, connecting hunters with creatures more powerful than velek…?"

She gave a look filled with disgust and anger. "You don't think…?"

"What better way to hunt your prey than by masquerading as one of them?" I murmured.

I desperately hoped I was wrong, but if I wasn't, then for Kane, Dorian, and all the other vampires here, death wasn't the worst thing that could happen to them.

CHAPTER TWENTY-SIX

S till shaken by what I'd just seen, I lifted my hand to my neck. Sweat
  pricked at my damned collar. I tugged on it, testing its strength.

"What exactly do these collars do?" I asked. Obviously, I'd experienced
some of it for myself on the long walk from the ballroom, but I didn't
want to get surprised if I tried a jumping jack and it zapped me or
something.

Rhome ran a finger around his neck. "They dull your senses and take
away balance, coordination, and any sense of people's auras. The woozy
feeling is the worst. It's like walking on a sinking ship."

"It seems to affect vampires more than it does us," I told him. "Roxy
and I have a hard time with it, but Kane and Dorian looked like they were
really struggling."

Rhome nodded, understanding. "My theory is that the collars react to
the dark energy in vampires' bodies, making it sicken us. My main
evidence is that the more they starve us, the higher they turn up the
power. They have to adjust it for vampires they're purposefully starving,
or else we become desensitized to it."

"They can increase the effects?" I asked.

"The researchers and guards often increase the intensity as punishment," Rhome said, flinching slightly from remembered pain. "It'll put you on the ground. I heard a rumor from someone in my old cell that the high intensity killed an older vampire."

"So it's kind of like a magical shock collar," Roxy said, sounding thoroughly unamused by our predicament. "And it's not working on us because we're human and don't have a lot of dark energy."

"I wouldn't want to test that," Rhome cautioned. "You really don't want to draw their attention. Especially Zeele—he seems to have a special love of sadism. He's a favorite of Lord Sempre's. I always hear him drop the name when he wants to gloat to another butcher."

I mulled over Rhome's theory. The collar made my limbs heavy, and it gave me a dizzy feeling, but it wasn't awful. I traced the metal. From what Rhome said, I didn't want to find out what it felt like when they turned the intensity up. We would have to wait for an opportunity to take advantage of it and hope that we wouldn't overshoot our capabilities.

"Do you know what the hell is going on with the vampires they just marched by?" Roxy asked. "The gems in their heads?"

Rhome averted his eyes. "That goes back to what happened to Kreya." His voice wobbled. "I wasn't permitted to see her for a long time. It was awful. I had no idea what they were doing to her. Finally, not too long ago, a white-robe came to my old cell to tell me I was being moved into the experimental group. Part of me was terrified that Kreya was dead and they were moving on to me next, but when they brought me here, she was waiting. They placed us in a cell next to this one. I was so excited to see her, but she was… different." His glassy eyes told me that he was reliving that meeting. My stomach dropped with dread, feeling the weight of inevitable grief hanging over my head.

He met our stares. "She was full of dark energy. Far too much, even more than when Dorian was hit with that dark energy weapon. But somehow they'd done something that kept her from completely falling apart. I don't know what they did, but it wasn't stable. She was teetering on the edge of losing control the whole time." He rubbed his weary eyes. "Eventually, they put us together in one of the intense research labs for observation. I don't know why. I didn't understand what was happening, but she was manic. One moment, she knew me and spoke of our children. The next, she whispered about conspiracies, raving warnings about shadows trying to grab her through the walls. I woke up once to her clawing at my arm, muttering about needing to dig it out of me. I had to fight her off." He lifted up his arms. Dried scabs over deep wounds covered most of his forearms. "Ordinarily, I wouldn't have been a match for her, but she'd lost all her skill."

Memories of Dorian's hands around my throat at the Chicago HQ when he'd been overloaded with darkness sent a shudder through me. It was pure torture to be attacked by someone you loved, even knowing they had no idea what they were doing.

"She said the white-robes injected her with dark energy. Put it straight into her blood. She claimed she couldn't sleep because all she saw were nightmares of the Mortal Plane. One day, she lost it. I don't remember what set it off. She grabbed me, started tearing at my clothes, screaming that I was trying to hurt her. She wasn't Kreya anymore."

"How long ago was this?" Roxy asked. "Those scratches look pretty fresh."

"Old enough… maybe three weeks? The collars affect vampire healing somehow. Dorian and Kane will catch on to that if they have to deal with experiments or get into a scuffle with the guards."

"What happened to Kreya?" I asked.

Rhome sighed. "I desperately tried drinking some of the dark energy out of her. I didn't know what else to do. But the researchers obviously didn't want that. They were watching the whole time, and the guards finally forced us apart. In the struggle, my hip was dislocated." He grimaced.

Roxy nodded with a sympathetic frown. I put my hand on one of his, anger and sadness fighting a war in my heart.

"I'm so sorry, Rhome."

He shook his head. "I don't know what happened to Kreya after that. It was the last time I saw her. Honestly, I think the only reason they brought me into this *interest* group was to test her reactions to a—" His voice broke terribly. "A loved one." He clenched his eyes shut for a moment.

Roxy snarled and beat her fists on her thighs. "Every time I think I've found the baseline for how damn awful rulers are, they surprise me. To do that to two people who love each other is unforgivable."

Rhome let out a sad laugh. Melancholy settled over him as he shrugged. "It is unforgivable. But I don't know how much of the horror was manufactured by them, and how much they were just taking advantage of bad feelings that were already there."

Part of me could understand where he was coming from. He was angry and hurt, a man who had lost his family twice—first because of the wife he no longer felt a deep connection to and second because of his sworn enemies. But Kreya's decision to go back to the Immortal Plane was the only thing he could fault her for. It wasn't her fault the hunters found her.

"How can you say that, Rhome?" I asked. "I know things have been awful recently, but you can't blame yourself or Kreya for any of this."

The dullness of his eyes was haunting. "Lyra, what Kreya and I had was damaged long before we ended up here. She took my children away from me and endangered them because she thought she knew best. She made a decision and refused to listen to me. Yes, the white-robes changed her, but Kreya was upset with me long before this, and I was furious right back at her." He took deep gulping breaths, his voice cracking and spitting on the next words. "She brought them *here*, and now you're telling me that they might've been safe in Scotland if we'd worked together like I asked her to. I *begged* her to stay, to take me with them, anything. You tell me I can't blame myself or Kreya, but I do. I do blame her."

His pain was raw, laid bare before us, and his open face resonated with an acceptance of his grief and agony.

"I barely recognize the woman I love anymore," he said wearily. "The worst thing is that I'll never know whether it was the trauma of the past few years that forced us to this point, or whether part of her was like this all along and we would have fallen apart even if everything had stayed the same."

He had a point, but how does one navigate a strained relationship when survival is top priority? There were no easy answers here. He would probably have to continue working through his anger with Kreya before he could find some peace.

"She made a stupid decision, but she was a mother bent on trying to protect her kids," Roxy said softly. "People can do awful things when they're trying to protect their kids in what they think is the best way possible."

It was a rash choice, but things were chaotic back then. So much had already changed since that fateful day when we escaped the Bureau the first time.

"In hindsight, bringing Carwin and Detra back to the Immortal Plane was foolish, but at the time we didn't know where we were going to end up," I reminded him. "The Bureau was hunting us, too. We didn't even know if we'd be alive the next day." I swept a strand of hair behind my ear as frustration rose within me. We'd had to face down so much in such a short space of time, and it wasn't fair. "Taking the children from you was a terrible thing to do, but that was a situation with no easy answers. The Kreya you've known for longer than this dark version of her might still be in there somewhere. We can't give up on people until we know for certain they can't return to who they were."

He stared at me. I wasn't sure what he thought about it, but I spoke from experience. When Dorian was overwhelmed by darkness, it had taken four vampires to drain away the excess dark energy, and for a little while, it wasn't clear whether they were going to be able to help him.

Rhome bowed his head. "Perhaps you're right. Only time will tell... though I don't know how much time any of us has left." There was something else in his statement. Something like, *I don't even know if I'll ever see Kreya again.*

Roxy groaned in pain and frustration. "When will our lives stop being so exhausting and high stakes and terrible? A few months ago, I didn't know vampires still existed or that dark energy was even a thing. Now?" She made a quick gesture at the surrounding chamber. "I'm a lab rat for Immortal mass murderers on an entirely different plane of existence. It feels like dark energy seeps out of every crack in this damn building, and I'm not even supposed to be able to sense it."

"Definitely," I agreed. My skin erupted into goosebumps at the sight of the white walls. It was like feeling someone was watching you constantly. "Kane said he could sense it from the palace. Could it be generated by the number of auras inside? Or by the awful acts being committed here?"

Rhome frowned. "I can't be sure. I've been here for so long, it's just painful background noise now. My fangs barely extend anymore. But I don't think any creatures—Immortal rulers or otherwise—could contain this much darkness. I feel it pulsing all around us. It's exhausting."

I pressed a hand to my forehead. Either the nonstop talking or the collar had made me lightheaded. How could the sanitarium have such a strong dark energy signature? If the white-robes were overloading vampires with dark energy, like they did with Kreya, that could create an uptick in the darkness that the vampires sensed. But where was it all coming from? I couldn't see Zeele opening his veins for science, and vampires would be used to feeding on rulers, so they wouldn't be overwhelmed. They'd probably just thank him for the snack.

Perhaps it was connected to the new technologies that Sempre and Zeele were working on. If my suspicions were correct, then they were planning to link hunters and vampires through the gems somehow, stripping away the vampires' control and forcing them to obey the hunter. They would likely need lots of raw dark energy straight from the harvesters to create the spells needed for such a thing. They probably had it stockpiled somewhere, the way a fort might stockpile ammunition.

"Is there anything else about the outside I need to be caught up on?" Rhome asked.

I exchanged a knowing look with Roxy. We should have made a tidy presentation because there was a lot to go over.

"A lot of scandals," Roxy confirmed.

"We've been gathering information on the Immortal rulers to figure out what their plans are after the Bureau failure," I said.

"It looks like Irrikus is planning to use the Mortal Plane as a dumping ground for the monsters from this plane so he can build more cities and access more souls," Roxy added.

Only a few hours ago, our knowledge of these developments was exciting and valuable. Now we were a danger to ourselves and our allies. If we were tortured, there was so much we were at risk of revealing. Even if they weren't interested in what we knew, all our hard work to gather this information might be for nothing. What use was it, if we died in the sanitarium? I could only hope that Laini had made it out and was running for the Mortal Plane as fast as she could.

Some of the vampires had listened to us halfheartedly throughout the long night, but most of them still stared at the walls. At our mention of Irrikus, however, an older woman sat up from where she was huddled on the stone floor to glare at our group.

"Shut up. I can't rest with you three blabbing about dark energy and that monster, and plans, as if you're going to get out of here," she said with a sneer.

"They're trying to help—"

The woman cut Rhome off with a fierce scoff. "It doesn't matter who these weird humans are, or why they're here. You shouldn't let yourself get worked up. Newcomers won't change anything. You can't fall into the trap of thinking every new arrival might rescue us." Her voice rang hollow, void of hope. "We're all going to die here. Get used to the idea."

Our trio fell quiet in the face of such furious nihilism. The woman exhaled roughly through her nose and returned to trying to sleep.

Rhome dropped his voice to a whisper. "If it was anyone else, I wouldn't bother with fresh hope. But I know the two of you, and I know Dorian and Kane won't give up. We might be able to figure something out together."

His trust lit something inside me that glowed like a candle. "We *will* find a way to escape. Somehow. Someway. I don't know what it looks like yet, but I won't give up either."

Roxy punched the air wearily. "That's the spirit."

Fatigue finally hit me as our conversation wrapped up. All the adrenaline and shock of the past few hours finally drained away, and my eyelids were drooping. Using my arms as a pillow, I rested beside Roxy on the cold, rough ground.

I slept fitfully, dreaming of the dead hunter's blood on the wall and of the tear expanding unstoppably over my home, nightmares pouring forth to destroy everything I knew.

Eventually, a rhythmic thudding cut through into my unconscious state. I lifted my head, and my bleary vision made out a figure and two green dots near the yellow glass.

Zeele stopped pounding on the glass and grinned coldly. "Come to the window, humans."

"Yeah, that's not happening," Roxy muttered.

Zeele let out a short chuckle. "Oh, we'll fix that attitude soon enough. You know, I'm impressed that your bedfellows didn't feast on you at all during the night. They must be awfully hungry by now."

My body turned icy, and goosebumps covered my skin as Zeele's gleeful smile practically split his face apart. His electric green eyes were far too alive and joyous as he stared at Roxy and me.

"I hope we can get them interested in taking a bite soon," he breathed. "I've changed the experiment roster just for you two. Isn't that flattering? You're first on my list."

CHAPTER TWENTY-SEVEN

The guards came into the cell to grab Roxy and me. Zeele watched with poorly contained excitement, clutching a clipboard made of a shining metallic substance to his chest.

This was the man who had hurt Kreya and Rhome, who had tortured Kono so badly that he'd given up the location of the safehouse. This was the Immortal who worked as Sempre's right hand in his twisted research. I stole as much time as I dared to memorize every line of Zeele's face before the guards shoved me forward.

"Walk," the guard behind me muttered.

I wanted to snap my elbow back into his sternum, twist out of his grasp, and make a run for it. I wanted to kick out Zeele's knees, open the cells, and let the hordes of starving vampires descend on him in a flood of bloody revenge. But I kept my mouth shut. Rhome's limp was engraved in my mind.

My weapons were gone. Dorian's stone was gone. Dorian himself was gone. Brute strength alone would not get us out of here—it was going to take guts, intelligence, and patience.

I studied everything I could about the place as they led us back up into the white halls. The guard pushed me occasionally when I slowed, but maybe a precious extra second would allow me to see something I could use. But there was nothing much to see. The white hallways stretched forever into more white halls. There was no apparent rhyme or reason to the layout.

They'd probably designed it this way on purpose. Mounting an escape plan or riot was significantly more complicated in a white maze. But the researchers and guards navigated the building without getting lost. They must have had some way to make sense of the endless tangle. If we managed to escape, we needed to know how to actually *leave*.

I paid close attention to the walls, but nothing stood out. No signs or arrows to speak of. There were no control panels or even any joining lines from slabs of bricks. There was nothing to indicate that the sanitarium wasn't built from one solid block of white stone.

At the end of a ponderous hallway, the guards snapped for us to turn. The corridor we segued into continued to narrow until it ended at two double doors made of black wood. A guard stood to each side. Much like our current security detail, they merely gazed at us with impassive frowns. They stepped forward at a sharp hand motion from Zeele, heaving open the black doors like they were the gaping maw of some primeval horror. Roxy and I were forced forward. I was sure her pulse was hammering as frantically as mine was. The doors rumbled closed behind us.

The room was square and white. The lack of design was less irritating and more disorienting. The rooms and hallways were already beginning to blend together in my mind. They had no defining features to cling to. Well, there were a few differences from the other areas of the sanitarium we had seen, but they were far from reassuring.

More guards stood beside a behemoth contraption that looked like a wizard had tried to recreate a computer after looking at one once through a dirty window. I couldn't even begin to understand how the combination of glowing gems, shards of glass, and carved runes worked together with whatever spells had been woven into the device.

The machine hummed lightly at a pitch that wasn't electronic but almost tinny. I tore my gaze away to take in the rest of the chamber. A row of tall dark chairs faced a yellow tank. The armrests had straps adhered to them, the kind meant to secure someone to the chair. The legs had similar restraints. Silver wires ran from the machine to the tank, which was made of the same pale amber glass as our prison cells. Above the tank was a sign in an Immortal language.

Roxy sucked in a breath. Every part of me went still. We both recognized one symbol in particular. Laini had pointed it out to us during our research at Juneau's mansion. It was a character similar to a swirling M with arrows at the end of each loop. She said it was often used to signify extreme danger. The symbol sat neatly on both ends of the sign with other incomprehensible scribbles in between. That could only mean bad things.

Zeele snapped his fingers. I watched as a wildling, a strange addition to the maker guards, hurried over to him.

"While we prepare the chamber," Zeele said impatiently, "find these two some light-plant food and water. Lord Sempre has informed me that these strange creatures are humans. Apparently, they are awfully high-maintenance creatures, and I'd be upset if such rare research subjects expired. Could you imagine? What a waste."

The wildling bowed—his gray fur shining like gunmetal in the harsh light—and hurried out of the room, the frayed hem of his plain brown robe brushing the floor. Zeele began to poke and calibrate something on the machine, not paying any attention to the little wildling when he returned a few minutes later. From a satchel around his waist, he brought out two dry, bluish rolls. I could tell they were stale. The wildling offered us each one. We stared at each other, uncertain.

Zeele looked over and sneered. "Don't be foolish. I wouldn't poison you and *then* experiment on you. It would ruin the validity of it. I do want you a bit stressed, though." As he finished speaking, a tiny smile bloomed on his face.

I took a roll, as did Roxy. We ate them slowly, choking down the musty offering. The wildling brought out a small canteen of water. He grunted after I took two long swigs and motioned for me to pass it to Roxy.

Okay, I guess they're really trying to keep us alive.

While Roxy finished off the small bit of water, the aftertaste turned sour in my mouth. Did Zeele have the other prisoners watch his experiments? Cold dread washed over me, and my stomach burned as I turned back to the yellow tank. There were no instruments adhered to the wall—no drills, no lasers, no gas nozzles inside that I could see. Perhaps he was testing the physical limits of vampire bodies in there. Somewhere deep inside me, something clicked. The experiments in the sanitarium were not so different from what Alan had done to vampires in the Mortal World. For God's sake, he'd cut off Arlonne's arm without painkillers just to see how she responded. The thought made me sick. I desperately hoped we wouldn't face a similar fate.

Don't you dare throw up those precious calories, Lyra.

I licked my dry lips and wished I had eight more bottles of water. Zeele clapped his hands as the doors opened once again. This time, a familiar figure walked in. He wore simple robes of silver and dark blue, his chest covered by a light breastplate of beautifully engraved leather. A small crown sat atop his head.

Lord Sempre regarded Roxy and me coolly as Zeele gave an excessive bow. He splayed his hands in an animated display of surprise.

"My lord," he said, his tone fawning. "I'm honored by your presence in our research chambers. What can I do for you?"

Sempre lifted a hand in the universal sign from a powerful man that everyone should stop talking. "I don't normally come to the sanitarium. I trust your work." Zeele beamed. Sempre continued, "But with these two humans, I want to supervise more directly. The results of these experiments are very pertinent to my personal research. This could be groundbreaking for us. It will be interesting to see if it is possible to influence humans directly, rather than carefully trying to shape the Mortal Plane's circumstances via our useless intermediaries. Don't you think?"

Zeele bobbed his head up and down like an excited puppy. "Of course. You're absolutely right."

I had a feeling that if Sempre suggested setting Zeele on fire, he would've had the same response. They *crafted* situations in the Mortal

Plane, which meant it had to do with the Bureau. So far, Sempre hadn't deigned to look at where Roxy and I were carefully guarded off to the side.

It was interesting to note that the rulers seemed content to talk in front of us. Perhaps they didn't think us capable of understanding their discussions. We were likely the first humans they had seen in person, and they didn't know who we were, as far as I could tell. To them, we were just two random—if somewhat dangerous—humans who had gotten caught up in a vampire plot. Very little about their actions suggested they considered us a threat, even though I had killed the hunter Arton. It would be useful if we overhead something good, but it might mean the rulers didn't intend to leave us alive.

The guards chatted softly in the corner. Zeele cleared his throat irritably. "If I can have everyone's attention, I'd like to speak about how useful I hope to find the human test subjects. But first," Zeele leaned toward me with a hard look, "how did you come through the tear?"

I kept my mouth shut. Roxy looked up at the ceiling. A silent message passed between us: *Tell them nothing.*

Lord Sempre smirked tightly. "No matter. If they don't want to talk, they'll still be of use to you."

"Of course they will. Mortals can survive in the Immortal Plane for extended periods, as the dirty state of these creatures and their infiltration of a ruler's abode suggests they've been here for several soul-light cycles. The tear is a long way away, even with help from vampires. So perhaps Immortals—not just the leeches—can spend time in the Mortal Plane without harm. We threw a maker over, and they failed to fare well for long. A ruler might have more time, but not much."

Rulers running wild in the Mortal Plane could only be a bad thing. Dorian had told me that it was impossible for Immortals to leave the Immortal Plane. Only vampires, and maybe the creature who made the gates between planes, could do that. It was the entire reason we speculated the rulers probably reached out to the Bureau. They couldn't hunt the vampires down in the Mortal Plane like humans could.

Sempre tapped a long-nailed finger against his thin lips. "Better to risk proxies than our own kind to do such dirty work," he said. "That's why we let others make the sacrifice for us." The arrogance radiated from him. Maybe he wished it was his own face adorning the statues around the city.

Zeele pressed his clipboard against his chest. His cheeks flushed. "Absolutely. I would never risk one of our precious members when their body could go to my other research. Except for the traitors, of course." He turned his eyes to us, but his attention was still focused on Sempre. "I'm curious what we will find in our study of these creatures. I hope to find a way to increase darkness in average humans."

The anticipation in his tone made every inch of my body buzz with attention. Rhome's description of Kreya following their experiments with darkness made my skin crawl. Would we end up in a similar state? We might just end up weighed down with darkness as we were corrupted. Well, if such a thing were possible. I looked around the room, internally begging the walls for some sign of what was to come. But there was only the slight hum of the strange machine and Zeele's heavy breathing for his own sick research.

"Darkness is always the answer, isn't it?" Sempre asked, but the question was rhetorical.

Irrikus's dreadful speech about a new wave of darkness came back to me. What would happen if the rulers and their human allies succeeded at removing vampires as a threat to their plans? Darkness would become the only answer, as both planes would soon be overrun with it. We couldn't let that happen, but right now there was nothing we could do. I glanced at Roxy out of the corner of my eye, wondering what thoughts ran through her head. Her red hair had tangled, falling out of its braid thanks to our stone beds.

We needed a plan to make a break for it. While Rhome's observation that the collars didn't work as well on us was correct and the Immortals had yet to notice, we were still trapped in this labyrinth of a building with no idea where Dorian and Kane were. Fear battered my ribs even harder than before.

"I never imagined that humans would come to us," Zeele said with a laugh. He seized Roxy's arm. She flinched and tried to pull away with a growl, but his long fingers were a vise. Leaning in, he gave an unsettling smile. "Lucky you. You're first on my list, Red."

Roxy began to struggle, pulling back as he drew her toward the tank in the center of the room, but a guard came to assist Zeele. I was dragged to one of the observation chairs, my arms, torso, and legs strapped tightly in place with a series of thick leather straps and locking metal bands. When Zeele placed a hand on the strange yellow glass, it lightened slightly, once more becoming permeable. The guard shoved Roxy. She stumbled inside and wheeled around as Zeele yanked his hand away again. She thumped her fist against the glass but didn't make the same mistake as last night.

Zeele waved at her with a satisfied smirk. His eyes darted to Sempre, who gave a nod of approval. Sempre and Irrikus both had lapdogs ready to prove their loyalty.

There was a faint metallic scraping as Roxy's foot knocked against something lying on the floor. She crouched, picking up a knife. Then she picked up another and another, all of varying sizes and designs. She stared at me as an unspoken question passed over her face. *What the hell?*

A door opened from a solid-looking wall on the other side of the room. Several guards struggled in, dragging a furious and fighting Kane between them. Zeele tapped the glass again as they approached, and our vampire friend was shoved unceremoniously into the tank. Exhausted and dangerous, Kane looked up at Roxy, his irritated expression morphing into one of disbelief. His eyes dropped to the knives.

"You've got to be kidding me," he groaned.

Zeele let out a mocking laugh. "You're fairly smart for a bloodsucker. Most just hopelessly gaze at the instruments, thinking someone else will arrive to remove their organs."

Sempre watched with the ghost of a smile.

"Now," Zeele said, taking a pen from the top of his clipboard. "Fight one another."

Roxy slammed her fist against the yellow glass. "No way!"

"Same," Kane added icily. "You'll never get us to fight."

"Just so you know, everyone who stands in that tank says the exact same thing." Zeele shrugged. "Let me make this clear. Fight, or I'll torture you to entertain myself while you're wasting my time." He flipped his arm, the robe falling open along his forearm to reveal a collection of dozens of bracelets. He tapped one of the bracelets, then dragged his finger over the metal band.

Kane let out a yell of agony as he crumpled to the ground. Roxy gasped for a split second, then her knees buckled. She let out a pained wail, clutching her head.

CHAPTER TWENTY-EIGHT

"S top—" Roxy's cry broke. My heart slammed against my chest.
"You can't do this," I said.

Sempre gave me a frosty stare but said nothing. Zeele never looked away from his work. Instead, he simply repeated a similar action on his strange bracelet. Roxy and Kane gasped for breath, sucking greedily from the air. Their only words were curses too explicit to detail and ones which I doubted Zeele understood.

"Do you understand your predicament?" Zeele asked, almost kindly. There was something unsettling about the way he looked at them. "Your collars should be adequate so that you can fight. I'll give you enough extra leash for you to put on a good show."

He wants a good show to impress his awful boss. All eyes focused on the experiment tank. Roxy sucked in a long, heavy breath as she grabbed one of the knives. She tossed a short one to Kane.

"That one's about as long as your attention span," she said with a tiny snarl. But the corner of her mouth quirked upward, like it was a secret shared between friends. He snatched it out of the air and rolled his eyes.

"Blades are for cowards," he said. "Let's grapple. Show these limp-wristed softies what real fighting looks like."

Roxy tossed aside the knife she had been weighing in her hands and grinned. Zeele's eyebrows pinched together for a moment, a flicker of peevish annoyance at Kane's flippancy crossing his face. Seeing that his pompousness could be hurt, even just briefly, brought me a petty satisfaction. He'd made a gross miscalculation if he thought he was going to have cowering subjects for this particular experiment.

Roxy and Kane launched themselves at each other. Kane went for a sweeping kick, and Roxy let out a barking laugh as she dodged it. The collar slowed him down. It made his movements about as fast as mine.

"Predictable as hell. You always go for the legs first. I'm convinced it's in your DNA or something," she said. She darted forward, attempting to fake him out and duck to the left, but he caught her.

"And you favor the left, weakling."

They came to blows, but it was just like their training in Scotland. When Roxy and Kane fought, it was more like a dance between two people who had been told their entire lives to stop being so destructive. Their violence had the grace of a thousand repetitions. Each inflicted harm to the exact degree that they intended, or brushed aside their partner's attack like it was a suggestion, changing directions like switching the subject of a conversation. Their friendship was forged in fighting.

I glanced at Zeele and Sempre, gauging their reactions. Zeele noted things down quickly on his clipboard. Sempre seemed more interested in watching Roxy's movements, staring at her in a way that made me want to tackle him. Was he sizing her up as his new pet?

As the fight progressed, Zeele occasionally let out a mocking little clap, reminding them that he was still there and that they were under his control. Every time, Roxy gritted her teeth, once even whirling around to land an open-palmed slap against the glass. Kane uncharacteristically did not press his advantage, instead waiting for her to get her temper back under control before throwing his next punch.

I took the opportunity to look around at the others. To my disgust, a few more white-robed researchers had joined us and appeared equally pleased by the performance. A few times, Zeele pressed something on his bracelet to adjust the collars. During those moments, Roxy and Kane would twitch and snarl. All the white-robed researchers wore bracelets, but not all of them had so many. On Zeele's right forearm, I counted twelve; eight on Sempre's left arm, the one I could see from my chair. The guards wore one or two, the bracelets molded into their armor. From watching Zeele control the glass and the collars, my guess was that the bracelets were connected to the spells used to control things like the doors and collars. I filed the information away for later.

"You're dancing around like a delicate ballerina," Kane snapped. "Too afraid to hit me? Or…" His lips curled, mocking.

"What? You think I'm tired?" Roxy's eyebrows lowered menacingly, but a wide grin spread across her face. "See if you can handle this, you overgrown tree." She went for his legs, despite her earlier criticism.

I winced. This was a move Roxy called the X Special. She and her siblings had apparently regularly performed it on one another to decide TV remote privileges when she was younger.

Kane let out a surprised grunt as she tackled him. They both hit the ground with a thud. A laugh ripped from his chest as he flipped her with a swift movement, hovering over her and pinning her wrists down. "Let it go, firecracker. We're done here." *Not with that weak mount, you're not.* If he were smart, he'd be pressing down with his whole body to immobilize her. I'd watched him do it before, but this time he held back. It seemed he'd gotten shy.

Roxy apparently agreed with me. She drew both her feet up to her chest and, her thighs working like pistons, slammed her feet into his chest. *That's why you secure the hips.* Typical Roxy—there had to be a dozen escapes from that position, and she'd chosen the most dramatic one possible. Kane groaned as he flew backward, the weight of the collar making him less of a sparring partner than she was accustomed to.

She knelt over him on the floor, pinning his hips and shoulders with textbook form as his ragged breath left his chest. Her own chest heaved. Dark circles smeared under her puffy eyes. She glared up at Zeele.

"We done here?" she demanded.

I tugged at the metal bands holding my wrists in place, testing them, but they didn't so much as bend.

Zeele marked something on his clipboard, then stepped toward the tank. "Use a knife on him."

Roxy's exhaustion collapsed into disbelief. "What?"

Zeele pointed at the knives. "Stab him. We've provided plenty of instruments to choose from. Cut him, or..." He lifted his wrist and tapped a bracelet with a sickening smile. "Did you know that with enough power, one of these collars can actually kill you?"

Roxy dropped her pained gaze down to Kane. He stayed still beneath her, making no attempt to remove himself from the vulnerable position.

She glared at Zeele. "You sick freak. I hope someday you find out what it's like to be trapped and helpless in one of these boxes."

The researcher let out a dramatic sigh and hovered his finger above the bracelet. "You're useless to me if you don't cooperate, so I'd be happy to demonstrate the full range of the collar's capabilities for your friend here. Maybe it will make her more participatory."

"Do it," Kane said suddenly. "I can handle it."

Roxy grabbed a knife, and for the first time ever, I saw her hands shake while holding a weapon. Taking a sharp breath, she held his forearm still with one hand and made a shallow cut. It was a scratch, really, and caused only tiny streams of blood to trickle onto the scuffed stone floor of the tank.

Kane didn't react at all.

"Continue," Zeele commanded, leaning forward in interest. Behind us, the machine chittered and whirred.

She moved to his shoulder. From the angle of her knife and the swiftness of the cut, I knew she was being as careful as possible.

"Stab him," Sempre instructed, breaking the eerie silence he'd held since the terrible trial began. "Somewhere nonvital, since we don't want to waste a useful subject. I can see you're a warrior of some kind, human. I'm sure you know how to do such a thing."

Roxy stared at the blade that now glistened with Kane's blood. She dropped it, rising to her feet and leveling a withering glare at the researchers. "Go die in a hole."

Blood streaked across the sharp points of Roxy's cheekbones. Her glare gave her a wild kind of allure. I blinked slowly, wondering if somehow a supernatural warrior goddess had made her way into the cell. But no, it was just Roxy... the way she'd always been. She was fierce, strong, and ready for a fight.

Less impressed than I was, Zeele pressed the bracelet as soon as the refusal left her mouth. Roxy gasped in pain and dropped to the ground, curling into a ball, smearing her cheek in some of Kane's blood. Kane snarled in agony and pressed himself face-first into the ground. His body shuddered and convulsed.

"Stop it! They did what you asked. Stop!" Unable to keep calm any longer, I openly fought my restraints, but it was no use. The white-robes had all the power in here, and they knew it.

When my friends' bodies went limp with unconsciousness, Zeele opened the tank, swiping another of his bracelets and setting his hand on the glass. The guards dragged Roxy and Kane out, strapping them into two of the chairs. My heart slammed against my ribs as I watched the guards restrain them.

One guard yanked the purple circlet helmet from Kane's head. "This will be good data."

I pressed my lips into a flat line. Irrikus's wave of darkness speech played over and over again in the back of my mind, skipping like the world's worst broken record. Would this treatment darken their souls over time? The researchers wanted to push humans toward increased darkness, after all. Anger climbed up my throat. From what Rhome had said, the butchers had somehow succeeded in doing such a thing to Kreya. The Bureau's use of dark energy weapons was the first time I'd heard of injecting darkness into vampires. I now suspected they might have been inspired by the research here.

I turned my attention back to Zeele and Sempre, who had their heads together in conversation. They seemed to be working on the theory that simply encouraging dark behaviors or injecting darkness by force would lead to... *something* in vampires and humans. It was almost laughable. They regarded darkness more as a fuel source for magic or soul corruption than as a complex moral issue. As far as I was concerned, forcing people to hurt each other didn't turn them evil, it just revealed the depths of the rulers' own darkness.

Roxy gave a painful moan next to me as she returned to consciousness, and I reined in my speculation. She muttered something and squinted at the scene before us. There would be time to ponder the Immortals' flawed understanding of darkness later. Right now, we had to survive.

Zeele strolled up and placed a hand beneath my chin, shoving my face up. He squinted at the collar around my neck.

"Let's take care of this." He reached around and broke the collar. It turned back into the original wire, which he handed to the wildling. The wildling scurried over, and I raised a curious eyebrow as I watched the wildling place it in a container and label it. For later study? My aching head enjoyed the relief of freedom from the collar, but it was short lived.

The wildling handed a roll of electric violet wire to Zeele. He tore off a piece and wrapped it around my neck. It adhered and transformed into metal once more. The wildling replaced the roll of wire in a cabinet beside the strange machine. As Zeele fussed with the placement of the wire against my neck, one of the pockets in his robe twitched open. Inside, I saw Dorian's stone. My pulse staggered. Making the smallest of movements, I tried to wriggle my fingers as much as I could with my wrist still held in place, to try to coax it into my hand. But it was too far, and he pulled away a moment later.

"Time for more research," Zeele announced.

Since they'd brought in Roxy and Kane, would they want me to fight Dorian next? My stomach twisted. If it was Dorian, knives would be the least of our problems. Our proximity and the pain from the curse would knock us out long before either of us caused physical damage to one another, and who knew when either of us would wake up this time. I really, *really* didn't want the sadistic Zeele to learn about the curse. Even if he didn't know the cause, I was certain he would find a way to torment both of us with it.

"Your turn," Zeele said smoothly.

I forced myself to remain calm, even as my mind raced. I took a steady breath and looked to Sempre. Maybe there was a way out of this situation, at least temporarily.

"My lord," I said evenly, ignoring the sharp look I could feel Roxy giving me as I used the Immortal's formal title. "I think you might know my uncle."

Kane had stirred awake as well. His sharp eyes hit my skin like knives.

Sempre flicked his hair behind his shoulder and gave me a bored look. "I know no humans."

Nice try. I had his full attention for the first time.

I leaned forward an inch. "Are you certain?" I asked, with a beat of urgency to try to make myself seem important. I twisted my lips into dramatic hesitation. "I'm sorry, my lord, if I'm wrong. From your status on the Immortal Council, I assumed you would know about the communication between the Bureau and the Immortal Plane. Perhaps I'm mistaken?"

I felt a flicker of satisfaction as I watched Sempre stumble on his pride. If you can't punch, pit them against one another. All I'd done was suggest I knew more than he did and given him a pitying look, and I had him.

His eye twitched, and a cool expression stole over his sharp face. "Of course I know about that," Sempre snapped. He puffed up his chest, likely an unconscious move to remind me of his size and position.

Excitement stirred in my chest, but I had to tread carefully. "Then you must know Alan Sloane," I said slowly.

Sempre watched me without moving a muscle, but something in his eyes glimmered with interest. I was good at reading people, but Immortals often behaved in ways I couldn't decipher. He continued staring. Good.

Zeele hovered uncertainly in front of me, eyes flickering between me and his superior, anxious to begin his experiment. With a dismissive movement, Sempre waved him away.

"Speak," he commanded me.

I had his attention. Now it was time to get him invested. Time to open my mouth and lie, lie, lie. "I was close to the heads of the Bureau before I fell out with them," I confessed dramatically with a little shrug. "You know how these things go. However, since I had a vested interest in the process, my uncle kept me in the know."

I swallowed my pride and plowed ahead.

"I really don't want to fight my comrades or get hurt," I groveled. I let my head hang low. "I don't want any more pain. I'll give you whatever information I have if you spare me from the torture." Glancing at my friends, I saw they were both staring at me with angry, hard eyes. Surely, they knew I was acting?

Sempre chortled. "How delightful. And why would you betray your companions?" He placed a fingertip on his cheekbone and regarded me.

The memory of Juneau's pleading over the crowd haunted me. "I'm sure you understand. It's only reasonable to use the information you have to your advantage. I don't want to suffer."

Roxy hissed under her breath. Her face was streaked with Kane's blood and bruised from her sparring. She bared her teeth at me. A small trickle of blood escaped the side of her mouth.

"What the hell?" she snapped.

Sempre looked between us and smiled far too wide for my liking. Kane was giving me a more calculating look, but I could see doubt in his eyes. It made me sick.

Roxy spat blood onto the floor. "You're *betraying* us? You coward. You're nothing but a self-serving liar, just like your psychopathic uncle."

The uncle barb went straight through my chest like an arrow. I gritted my teeth, praying it was all for show.

"Release her," Sempre said evenly. The wildling undid my restraints slowly and carefully. The entire time, Roxy glared at me, whispering ugly and furious things. Kane ignored me, which somehow was worse—it was as if he had simply accepted that such an act had been inevitable all along.

"Bind her hands," Sempre snapped to the wildling. Zeele deflated, disappointed to see one of his humans being marched off, but he couldn't argue. The wildling obeyed, binding my hands together in front of me.

"Follow me," Sempre said and began striding away in a swish of silken robes.

I refused to look back at Roxy and Kane as I walked after him. They *knew* I wasn't a coward. They *knew* I wouldn't sell them out to be spared. They *knew* that this was an act.

All I could do was hope.

CHAPTER TWENTY-NINE

Sempre led the way, and I was escorted by two guards. It made sense —I'd been part of an infiltration team and had killed a hunter less than a day before. Of course Sempre would be suspicious of me, but I had my foot in the door. That's what mattered.

We marched down another long white hallway until we arrived at a dead end. Sempre placed his hand on the white expanse, and his long, gnarled fingers were briefly outlined in a golden glow. The wall began to fade. It was there, and then it wasn't. The guards pushed me inside the new room, still following the Immortal lord.

What first caught my eye was the opposite wall, which was constructed from an opaque, reflective crystal. Unlike the other room, the interior here was glamorous—dark wood furnishings, softer lighting provided by lanterns gluttonously stuffed with souls, and a floor made of black marble shot through with twists of white and gold. A long table almost the width of the room had a series of drawers running just beneath the lip. Cabinets lined the walls, but I suspected they were locked, given their shiny keyholes. An alcove in the left side wall held a tableau of the members of the Immortal Council captured in gold, Irrikus at its center.

Everything was pretty ordinary except for the chunks of crystal wrapped in wires and attached to metal spikes. Set into the crystal, in no apparent pattern, were small green, blue, and red gems. These antennae-like constructions had obviously been deliberately placed at either end of the large crystal wall. I briefly wondered if it was a mirror, but my reflection flickered slightly as if there were something on the other side.

Sempre approached the wall, reaching for one of the many gems on golden chains around his neck. He touched a shimmering green gem the size of my thumb, and the window flickered to life. The crystal expanse divided into evenly sized panes bordered by a thin, glowing periwinkle line. Each square was immediately filled with a different still image.

Most pictures had a hazy red tint to them, but some were tinged with blue or green. Many of the squares showed prison cells from the sanitarium, the yellow glass wall turned greenish in the blue-tinted light. Two other squares looked out at the base of giant textured pillars in a large room I didn't recognize. From the scale and detail, I was certain it was Immortal Plane architecture, however.

Every ten seconds or so, the picture flickered, like an image from slow CCTV footage, then changed. Although I couldn't read the symbols used, a timestamp of some kind changed every time the picture did.

My eyes moved to the sinister red squares, catching on certain details. A gnarled tree growing determinedly up through a large rock. Scraps of familiar mountains at the edge of the screen. A compound filled with old military barracks. Bile rose up in the back of my throat.

It was the VAMPS camp. The image looked like it was coming from the exact mountain path that I used to run.

They know.

My pulse raced, and I tried to calm myself as Sempre turned to survey me with his cold gaze, one half of his face obscured by his hair as always. They knew about our camp. They had *surveillance* on our camp. Zach's smiling face flashed through my mind. I pumped the brakes before I was bombarded with the faces of each of the camp inhabitants. Fear for them would paralyze me.

How did Sempre get these images? Immortal Plane magic couldn't function in the Mortal Plane, just as Mortal Plane technology couldn't operate in the Immortal Plane. I had no idea how the Immortals were doing this. The selection of the colors triggered a memory, but I couldn't put my finger on it. The red snapshots of the VAMPS camp were particularly unsettling.

Sempre took a step toward me, staring intently at my face, his intent clear. A scent of sour sweetness drifted off his stupid hair.

"Do you recognize this place?" he asked tightly, pointing to the top row of red.

I glanced back at the screens, instinctively wanting to lie and say no, but he wasn't stupid. He knew I had recognized the VAMPS camp, so if I told him the opposite it would erase whatever shred of self-interested trust he had in me, and I'd be back in that tank, back at square one.

"Yes," I whispered, hating the way I sounded as I said it. Small. Defeated. The worst part was, it wasn't entirely for show. Reaching into every corner of my brain, I scraped together a story. "It's one of the vampires' bases in the Mortal Plane, I believe."

Since I couldn't lie, I would mislead him. He didn't need to know that the other bases were abandoned. If he wasted time trying to track them down, that would buy some time for the VAMPS camp. More than that, I wanted him to be scared, as frightened as Detra and Carwin in their terrible muzzles. I wished he could be dragged around on a leash until he wept with shame.

"The vermin have more bolt holes?" Sempre asked, raising his chin to give me a withering look.

I bluffed. "I'll only tell you if you can guarantee my safety, and maybe get me some food." My stomach chose that moment to let out a ferocious growl. I pulled a long face. "It's been so hard. I don't want to suffer anymore. I won't last like this much longer." I darted my eyes away from him and dropped my gaze to the ground, hoping I looked woefully pathetic.

Sempre threw his head back and laughed. Before I could prepare, he pressed down on a bracelet.

The pain knocked the air from my lungs. Nausea twisted my stomach as I cursed and fell to my knees. The screens blurred into a fuzzy trail of smearing color. I slammed my bound hands onto the tile and gasped for something—air, Dorian, any sort of relief. After the initial shock, though, it wasn't actually unbearable. Uncomfortable, not debilitating. My pride surged for a moment, a voice in my head that wanted to pretend like this failed to hurt. I didn't want Sempre to have his sadistic satisfaction.

If it was this bad for me, it must be hell for the vampires. Sempre was watching me closely.

Screw my pride. I needed him to assume that I was just as debilitated by it as the vampires. Surrendering to the pain, I shuddered and made a grand show of my poor muscles giving out, letting my face slam against the freezing tiles. The pain ricocheted through my jaw. Sempre let out a delighted chuckle as I writhed on the ground.

"Please," I begged. It wasn't difficult to make my voice shake. I retched, letting it struggle through my tight throat. "I can't take anymore. Please make it stop."

Let him think the collar had destroyed me. Let him think I was weak. He would come to regret it.

Sempre luxuriated in my pain for a moment longer, and a wave of real lightheadedness passed through me. I coughed violently, balling my hands into fists and slamming them into the marble floor.

Arlonne's reminder suddenly came floating back to me. In the shadowy recesses of my mind, I heard her say, *Make your weaknesses into strengths.* She would know—she still fought like a hound from hell in battle, even after Alan took away an actual piece of her.

Okay, Arlonne. I would wail my way through half-real pain and do everything it took to get my team out of here.

Sempre clacked his nail on the bracelet, and the pain dampened to its previous low level. I took a blissful gasp of air, blinking up at the ceiling in a daze. Sempre looked me over. For a moment, I swore something beneath his silver hair glinted, but I must have been seeing stars from the pain.

"That was just a taste," he promised with an edge to his voice. He meant it.

I pulled myself to my knees and cradled my bruised cheek in one hand. I nodded slowly and muttered, "Of course, Lord Sempre. I'm sorry, my lord." My tongue felt heavy and slick with acidic poison as I pretended to be cowed.

"We won't be rude again, will we?" he asked.

I glanced up through my damp lashes to see him tracing a finger between his bracelets. The thought of him pressing the bracelet again sent a genuinely horrified shudder down my spine.

"No, my lord." I took a labored breath, making it far shakier than it needed to be. "I'm sorry for my impudence."

Stroke that ego.

"You're going to tell me the things I want to know," Sempre snapped. "For no other reason than that I want to know them. Understood?"

I cowered like a frightened dog. "Of course, of course."

He hummed. "Tell me about your relationship with vampires."

I clenched my fists tighter. "They're... not like anything I've ever known." It was true. I tried to recall my feelings about vampires before I met Dorian and scrunched up my nose. "When my uncle originally revealed to me that they were real, I was disgusted that we'd allowed them to live for so long." Although I'd known about the existence of vampires since my parents fought them, I wanted Sempre to think my relationship with Alan was much closer than was exactly true.

"And yet you've aligned yourself with them? Followed them into the Immortal Plane and helped them infiltrate the home of a once respected ruler?"

Crap. How could I explain this away?

"I was part of a plan that my uncle devised to wipe out all vampires on the Mortal Plane." I could hear my own words streaming out of my lips, but they felt disembodied. *Lie, lie, lie.* "However, the final stages of the plan fell apart, and I had to go undercover when Alan was captured."

"Yes, I saw you at the meeting that was attacked so mysteriously." He gave an icy smirk.

My heartrate doubled. Sempre had seen the press conference and had as much as admitted that the council was behind the attack. I glanced at the screens again.

"Why did you come to Itzarriol? What was your purpose?" Sempre asked, circling the large table, his steps loud in the still room.

"My uncle gave me vague details about his allies in the Immortal Plane," I said, stringing together scraps of truth among the lies. Alan had given me little more than riddles and mockery, but we'd pulled info from enough other sources to make a rough guess. "I was supposed to accompany the vampires, learn their goals, and then either report back to my uncle's allies in the Mortal Plane or betray the vampires directly to the Immortal Council, my lord. Luckily, the infiltrators were caught without requiring me to give up my cover."

He came to a stop on the other side of the table and was silent for a long time, his eyes never leaving my face. I let my earnest desperation and fear show in my features.

With a sharp movement, he began to walk again, heading toward the alcove that contained the statue. "Tell me about the locations of the vampire camps. You said there were multiple. Do you know where they are?" The last bit sounded like an accusation.

I cleared my throat, wishing I had a dozen bottles of water to guzzle. I knew exactly what I could say that would be true enough to satisfy Sempre while still protecting my friends.

"A camp in the Canyonlands. They burrowed there like rats after they crossed through the tear. They favor deserts for the space and desolation. There are very few humans in the area, so they're able to hide, going out only to feed. I suspect the desert's landscape and stone structures make them think they can hide well there," I said, unrolling the half-truths from my throat like a scroll only I could see.

"Ah yes," Sempre said with a bitter chuckle. "I've seen a few glimpses of this land among mortals. It is a ghost of Vanim, with a reddish tint to the dirt. How nostalgic of the leeches." He sniffed, which I took as an indication that I should continue.

"They're no longer in the camp that I was taken to, but I suspect they have other hideouts in the area. There is a camp in the mountains where it's cold all year round. The redbills they use favor higher altitudes. I believe they naturally prefer to nest in these areas." I had no idea what the natural patterns of redbills were, but it sounded reasonable. I whispered in my heart for Drigar to forgive me, wherever he was, for surrendering their mountain nest.

I studied Sempre. He tapped his foot, digesting this information. I doubted he knew enough about redbills to call me on my BS nature fact. The vampires would have hidden anywhere that promised them some relief, but I wanted Sempre to think I'd given him important information about their habits, something he could use.

I felt a sick sort of admiration for Alan. I detested my uncle, but his self-assurance meant his ego was not easily manipulated, despite his talent for exploiting that weak point in others. It made me wonder if he'd somehow thought he could fleece the rulers after doing some of their bidding.

"Any other places?" Sempre asked.

So far, it looked like I was getting away with this deceit.

"They've been granted political asylum by Scotland, as I'm sure you know. They're well-protected by the Scottish military," I said, trying to warn him off. "But... not all the vampires are staying there. My lord, vampires are able to travel far and wide, thanks to their connection with natural creatures and ability to travel through portals in the barrier. I suspect that there are hundreds of others, but I don't know where."

That was the most blatant lie I'd told, but he had no way of disproving my claim. In fact, if I was right, he and the other rulers were likely worried about just such a thing. Maybe they had reason to be. I didn't know everything, after all. There *could* be other vampire groups that I didn't know about, in both planes, surviving by keeping their heads down.

He sneered condescendingly at my final point but said nothing. The tile floor was cold and hard beneath me. It was time to amp up my performance of weakness.

I pretended to struggle as I pointed at the screen showing the camp. "The Mortal Plane is a vast land, my lord, just like the Immortal Plane." In truth, I wanted an excuse to look at the screens openly. My eyes focused on another image. I squinted. I saw human faces and a group that looked familiar. They were on a red screen.

The faint outline of a man came into view. A man I had once seen frowning at me across a conference table in Chicago HQ. They looked like... the original Bureau board members? I looked for any details that might give away their location, but unfortunately, real life didn't work like TV. They were in a generic conference room, which was frustrating. They were supposed to be on the run, but they didn't seem to be very inconvenienced.

I pointed at them. "Those were some of the people running the operation."

Sempre huffed. "I know *that*," he said irritably.

Was this screen their way of communicating? I searched for anything that resembled microphones or speakers or an unknown magical device that might allow two-way communication, but nothing stood out. It looked like Sempre was just watching, but there might have been something I was missing.

"The human governments are searching for those board members. They want to arrest them and put them into the human version of the sanitarium." He probably already knew this. Maybe the rulers had even arranged some kind of safehouse, though that seemed suspiciously generous of them. Unless they thought the board members could continue to help them somehow. Again and again, the issue of *how* the rulers successfully interacted with the Mortal Plane continued to haunt my mind.

"Lord Sempre," someone called out. Three white-robed researchers surged into the room.

I continued my feigned suffering, letting my muscles shake as my head lolled forward weakly. I peeked at them from the corner of my eye. Sempre's lips twisted into a displeased scowl as he regarded his subordinates.

"What?"

"If you have a moment, we need—" The one who was speaking cut himself off when he spotted me on the ground. Whatever he wanted to say, he wasn't sure whether he should blab in front of a prisoner.

Damn. If only they'd seen me a moment later.

Sempre cast a weary look my way. His lips curled in disgust as I gave another shudder.

"Let's step into the corridor," he said coldly. They walked away, robes swishing. Sempre gave me a death stare with his beady red eyes before he left. The white wall appeared again as a solid barrier between the butchers and me.

Go time.

I quickly forced myself up despite the protestations of my exhausted, underfed body. Even with the collar's low setting, I felt sick. This could be, and in fact probably was, a trap by Sempre to test me. I stared at the wall, frozen for a moment by indecision.

I only had a few moments alone in an obviously important chamber here in the sanitarium. It was too good an opportunity to pass up, even if it was a trap. Who knew what Sempre had hidden in this room?

CHAPTER THIRTY

Even with the temporarily solid white wall haunting me like a phantom, I began to move through the room. First, I went for the drawers beneath the long table, quickly tugging them open and digging through the contents. Pages upon pages—covered in the Immortal scientific diagrams and notes that were slowly becoming more familiar—were clipped together in packets that threatened to spill as I rummaged. I had no idea what they said. They had graphs and tables containing some sort of math, but it made my eyes blur just looking at it.

My bound hands found the last in the series of drawers beneath the table. I pulled it open. A flat crystal array slid smoothly outward on a tray. From the surface of the table, a 3-D projection bloomed to life.

It was a giant map made of layers in green and violet with indications of regional topographical formations. My eyes roved over the map, trying to make sense of why it seemed familiar. All at once, I recalled standing next to Morag at some point, hunched over a map to study the area where our VAMPS camp was located.

"You can always tell where northern Scotland is. We've got the Highlands with all those lovely mountains and glens," she'd explained.

As I stared at the map, it dawned on me that the green layer I was looking at was the area of northern Scotland near the VAMPS camp. It was overlaid with a similar structure in violet, which I assumed was the portion of Immortal Plane that existed parallel to Scotland. A Mortal Plane-to-Immortal Plane map.

I tried to soak in every last detail of the map. My throat tightened when I saw a spot on the violet layer highlighted with dozens of glowing teal dots. That location roughly aligned with the stone circle where Kane and his party had been ambushed. That hadn't been a chance encounter; the rulers had more information than we ever thought.

Scanning the map, I saw more clusters of dots pulsing in various locations, some of them moving slightly, like the image of a car on a navigation app. I leaned forward to study them, my nose nearly brushing the map.

The Immortal Plane map, a bright violet, contained a massive cluster of red dots as well as a smattering of green and blue. Green, teal, and red. I frowned as I ran over the colors in my mind, neurons firing slower after being deprived of food and water.

Concentrate, Lyra. What are these colors?

I glanced over my shoulder at the white wall and quickly closed the drawer, afraid Sempre might walk in at any moment. Time was running out. I quickly inspected the crystals in the corner of the room, again finding the same colors: teal, red, and green. I reached up to touch one of the gems. It wasn't warm or cool to the touch. It just… existed.

Gems and crystals. I glared at the tinted screens. Why only these three colors on the screen? The red reminded me of the awful gems I'd seen stuck in the vampires' foreheads yesterday, the ones the guards marched by our cell.

Wait…

My eyes flew to the teal gem. It was the same shade as the jewel in Inkarri's forehead, and that of her magicked velek. The pompous vampire hunter, Hildan, and his drunken bragging about his new red gem flew back to me like a slap in the face. He'd boasted that he would be able to see through a matching jewel connected to another creature, one more advanced than a velek. My heart squeezed terribly for a moment.

Were all these "surveillance cameras" actually coming from gems on the foreheads of Immortal Plane creatures? The redbills could travel through the tear easily enough. Why not other animals? But I had only seen the red stones on vampires so far. My insides twisted viciously as I considered the possibilities.

A single red dot pulsed in the Scottish area, signifying some Immortal Plane creature lurking in Scotland. The only entry point for the Immortals was the tear, so they must have crossed the Atlantic. That would have taken weeks unless they'd somehow hitchhiked on a plane.

A sniper had attacked our group at a press conference. An animal couldn't do such a thing, and the shooter had escaped with unbelievable speed. A red-tinted screen showed the VAMPS camp, a color I had only seen on the gems placed in Hildan and vampires' foreheads. Was it possible the white-robes had been able to send a puppet vampire through the barrier while maintaining control? An Immortal would have the speed to flee like the shooter had after the shots rang out. The vampires said the shooter had an unusually dark energy signature.

But Hildan had only had his stone inserted a few days ago in an experimental procedure that was part of Sempre and Zeele's work for Irrikus.

I shook my head. Whatever creature it was, the VAMPS camp was no longer safe. If the rulers had eyes on the camp, then they weren't far off from doing something about it.

I glanced back to the image of the Bureau board members. If there *was* a way to communicate with the other side, I could send a warning to Zach and Morag. I could tell Bravi to move their location. I could—

"Looks like you failed the test," Lord Sempre whispered icily in my ear.

I whirled around as his fingers smashed down on the bracelet. I gasped and lurched backward as he turned the collar up. My head swam, and I fell against the crystal wall. Its sharp points dug into my back.

"You thought you could flatter and lie and scheme to get what you wanted?" Sempre gloated as I sank to my knees. He crossed his arms and tapped a finger against his face. "Humans are even less intelligent than I thought."

I merely gasped for air as the pain struck over and over.

He laughed deeply. "Your kind thinks they can use us, but we're always one step ahead. How arrogant, to think you could outwit beings who have lived for thousands of years. Your uncle was the same way." His red eyes lit with pleasure at my pain. "He was so happy to lap up any ridiculous information we fed his greedy face."

He snapped his fingers. The wall disappeared, and guards charged inside.

"Take this useless creature and isolate her from the others," he barked.

The guards grabbed my arms roughly, dragging me through loops of hallways. The lights became less frequent, the roof lowered. The room we finally barreled into was dim and damp, lined with tiny cubicles constructed of glass.

Covering my head with my bound hands was the only thing that stopped me from breaking my head against the stone wall of my new cell when the guards threw me in. Sempre reduced the pain from my collar with a sneer before stalking off.

I laid my head against the icy ground and sucked in a grateful breath. The ground felt better, safer. The guards faded away down the hall. I looked at slate-gray wall and awful yellow glass blocking me in on every side, including up. The room was barely large enough for me to lie down. Trying to drag myself into a sitting position made my body ache, so I didn't bother.

My mouth was dry as leather. I turned my aching temple to the cold stone floor. Every breath seemed to spark a new echo of agony.

A tiny trickle of water oozed down the wall. Desperate, I scooted toward it. Every ounce of pride and dignity fled as I lapped at the tiny, almost nonexistent stream. It was brackish and slightly bitter, but it moistened my mouth. I longed for water bottles as big as my head. My dry throat felt cracked. I rolled onto my back and let out a sob.

A tear slicked down my cheek. I didn't have the energy to press my hand against my eyes, to beg myself to stop. They kept coming. The hot, salty tears burned my cheeks as my carefully constructed floodgates burst open.

My entire life, I'd tried my best to save everyone, but right now I couldn't save anyone. Not even myself. I burned with self-hatred. I hated the rulers more. There was nothing I could do to stop them. It had been stupid to try to trick Sempre into giving me information. Look where it had gotten me. The tears continued to fall. At least before, I'd had Roxy and Rhome for support. But now they both probably thought I was a traitor.

The thought sent a cold chill over me. Roxy had snarled the entire time the guards had dragged me away from the research lab. My heart twisted painfully. *I didn't betray you, Roxy.*

Would she tell Rhome with venom in her voice about how precious, ex-golden child of the Bureau Lyra Sloane had betrayed them all? A steady weight built in my lungs as I let every terrible hypothetical march through my mind's eye. Rhome listening intently to Roxy, unable to believe his ears. Would Kane tell Dorian of my apparent betrayal? Would he understand that it was a ploy? Assuming he was still alive. Our captors could've killed him in some other experiment by now. Every last tendril of hope plummeted into the depths of my cracking spirit. I flexed my fingers as if I could feel the last bits of my strength leaving my weak and numb hands. When had it gotten so cold? I shivered violently.

"Please trust me," I whispered to nobody. Then I cried until it hurt. Snot ran down my face, and I roughly wiped it away on my sleeve. I needed to stop crying. I was already dehydrated, and this would only make it worse. Part of me was grateful that they had left me alone. I never wanted anyone to see me like this—helpless and angry with no way out. What would my brother think if he saw me now?

I sobbed again, thinking of Zach. The rulers knew about the VAMPS camp. Somehow they had eyes on it, and if the Immortal Council had sent the sniper to the Edinburgh press conference, then my brother and everyone else at the camp was in terrible danger.

Would I die here? If I died during one of Zeele's experiments, then Zach and Gina and my parents would likely never find out what happened to me. If Laini hadn't managed to escape Juneau and take news of our capture back to the Mortal Plane, then there was little chance my family would ever receive any closure over my death. Sike, Bryce, and Arlonne would never know what happened to us. Dorian, if he was alive, might never know what became of me. I'd just be lost. I forced an inhale and then an exhale.

Juneau had manipulated us from the start, joining our mission to amuse himself, then bailing when it stopped being fun. That Immortal jerk knew precisely how to play the vulnerable card. He'd never fit into ruler society? I let out a hollow laugh. What a joke. He was a perfect ruler —out to save his own skin no matter what.

We'd done so much, risked everything for information that might never even make it back to the Mortal Plane. Dorian and I had put off trying any cure for the curse until we were safe and had more time. Now I deeply regretted that decision, no matter how sensible it had been. There was no time left, and we'd never had any of it together. It was all for nothing, in the end.

CHAPTER THIRTY-ONE

The tears came slower, but they were steady. I coughed. My lips burned from dehydration and the dry air of the sanitarium.

Wrapping my arms around my legs, I pulled them tight to my chest. The next wave of desperation and doubtful inner voices came crashing down. Terrible thoughts surrounded me like enemy soldiers.

I took a deep breath. A fat tear trickled from the corner of my eye, but nothing followed it. I concentrated on the rise and fall of my chest. Counting my breaths, I made sure to exhale for an extra count of two. The adrenaline rushing through me began to lag. I imagined it like a faucet and envisioned my steady hand turning the handle until the gushing flow reduced to a trickle.

I always strove to keep my emotions in check during a mission, focusing on my responsibilities to my team and our objectives. But right here, in this desolate and desperate place, I was no longer a soldier. I was a ghost of my former self, trying to reconstruct my identity in a conflict that stretched far beyond my ability to comprehend it. The various causes and moving parts of this mess were still beyond my understanding. I had scraps, shreds of the whole. And now I was unlikely to ever see the full picture.

An hour passed. Or maybe two. I counted the seconds until I lost track, then started again, over and over. The sobs and ragged hiccups of grief faded. My breathing calmed.

You're stronger than you think. You've been through so much the last few months. Most people would break under these conditions. It's okay.

I mean, who wouldn't have a meltdown after being shoved into solitary confinement to face every wretched inner demon they'd stuffed down over the course of several months? I brought my bound hands up to rub my temple on the side that wasn't puffy and aching. My headache still pounded against my skull, raging against the waste of precious water.

I wasn't dead, so this wasn't over yet. I chose to believe that there was still a future—for me, my team, and our mission—outside of this stupid cell. There were always options. It didn't look good right now, but I would never give up.

"I always find a way to make something work."

Talking to myself was calming. My voice had regained some of its strength, though it was still dry and scratchy as sandpaper.

I rolled over again toward the wall and sucked the drizzle of water running down the stone. I needed to eat something and drink water soon, before I lost my mind.

My stomach growled at the thought of food. I would trade a year of my life right now for my mother's lasagna and a serving of my father's apple pie. He liked to carve elements from the periodic table into the crust. What a nerd. I missed my family with every beat of my heart.

For the first time since I'd been flung in here, I let my mind go quiet, turning my awareness outward and trying to gather whatever knowledge I could from my surroundings. Pressing my ear against the floor, I heard the faint pulse of crashing water. These cells were near sea level, maybe in the base of the cliffs. Now suspicious, I looked more closely at the liquid running down the wall. It most likely was seeping through from the strange not-quite ocean, the one we had seen when crossing the bridge from the rulers' island. It probably wasn't wise to keep lapping it up. According to the maps that I'd studied in Juneau's office, the main river that emptied into the bay containing the rulers' island and the sanitarium was the one we'd traveled along in the Gray Ravine. At least I knew it wasn't toxic to touch. I just didn't know if it was good for a human to drink.

Rolling onto my back again, I lifted my hands to my mouth, hoping to find a weak point in the wire to chew through. Just as I was examining the restraints for some sign of a seam, the sound of something stirring nearby caught my attention.

I froze, peering through the wall of yellow glass to my right. The glass distorted what lay beyond, like privacy windows used for bathrooms. It almost entirely obscured everything beyond it. My puffy eyes hardly helped. Using all my strength, I rolled into a sitting position against the back wall.

Now that I was straining, I could see into the cells on either side of mine. One was empty, the other... was not. Somebody moved inside the cell to my right. It was a relatively large humanoid figure, but the proportions seemed strange. Perhaps it was a creature I hadn't encountered before, or maybe the glass was just distorting the shape. Scooting closer, I leaned forward and squinted.

The ghostly, somewhat masculine face and form of this creature came into better focus. He was little more than a reddish smudge through the hazy glass, but I could make out chains wrapped around most of his body. Solitary confinement *and* full-body restraints? God, the sanitarium staff must have been terrified of him.

Suddenly, a hand slapped the wall right in front of where I was peering through, and I fell backward, startled.

"Hello?" I said. Anybody who was an enemy of the sanitarium could be a friend of mine, even if he had poor social skills. "Can you hear me?"

There came a sharp scraping sound, and I watched as he began to draw something on the wall that divided us. Abstract shapes in all kinds of colors began to appear on the hazy glass, creating an elaborate art piece. Where did he get the materials?

I pressed my face against the glass and saw that the abstract shapes held a passing resemblance to creatures and buildings and plants, but the details were unfamiliar.

"Hello?" I called again. There was no stir. I frowned and tried tapping the glass. Nothing. I could hear him, but that didn't necessarily mean he could hear me. They might have done something to him.

Keeping my face close to the glass between us, I watched as this mysterious other prisoner continued to decorate the wall. After watching a while, I realized that he wasn't drawing with any materials. He was instead scratching his designs into the glass with what I thought was a knife at first but soon identified as his finger. Or it had once been a finger that was replaced with a blade at some point. I couldn't tell whether the sharp tool had grown or been fitted directly into his hand. Unnerved, I stopped knocking. It didn't seem to be helping, anyway. He either couldn't hear me or couldn't care less.

I sighed, letting my lips puff out from the gesture. My head, which I'd kept propped against the glass, rattled slightly, picking up vibrations from the creature's carving. I closed my eyes and hoped that if he could hear me, he might change his mind about communicating.

Time passed slower than the lazy trickle of water on the wall. I abandoned the yellow glass for a few minutes to inspect the confines of my cell, but found nothing except a crude drainage hole which, from the smell, seemed to be the extent of the bathroom facilities. Desperate to pee, I struggled to lower my pants with my bound hands. Getting them up again was frustrating, and when I returned to lean against the wall, my face was red with humiliation and anger.

It was getting more and more difficult to ignore my need to secure food and water. I pressed my head against the yellow glass.

"You got a dollar for the vending machine, pal?" I muttered dryly.

My unknown companion didn't reply, of course. He just kept at the walls with the dogged determination of someone who had nothing better to do with their time.

I sighed and let my hot breath fog the glass for a moment. It was an inconsequential amount of water, but I keenly felt the waste. Should I risk licking the wall again? I decided against it for now. Surely the guards would come by with food and water soon. Sempre and Zeele had been clear they didn't want to kill us.

It had to be night again by now. Did the guards clock out and return to homes in the city, or did they all stay elsewhere in the sanitarium? I imagined nice housing for the guards of Itzarriol, but it seemed unlikely that Irrikus would be so generous.

Somewhere far away, a door opened. I barely heard it. Then another opened, closer this time. More figures filled the cell beside me, all of them dressed in white robes. This particular group of white-robes included a rare maker, walking behind all of the rulers. A group of guards hung back in the hall. The creature stopped scratching, something resigned in the slump of his form as they surrounded him. The guards undid the chains, the weighty links dropping to the stone floor in an invasive cacophony of sound after so many hours of silence.

I leaned my ear against the glass, not caring if they saw me eavesdropping. A guard barked something. I caught the tail end of it.

"Prisoner One."

I stilled. They didn't necessarily number their prisoners in order of admittance; they could have an entirely different system that I wasn't aware of. I tried to think about every prisoner who had been unfortunate enough to pass through the sanitarium's door and swallowed a painful lump of shock in my throat. Could he truly be the first?

"It's time for you to fulfill your duty to the city."

My ear felt frosty as I leaned against the glass, but I ignored it. His fate might not even be relevant to my own mission, but I desperately wanted to know about Prisoner One's duty to the city. What could he do that warranted his release? I stared intently as the guards yanked my mysterious cellmate to his feet.

"I was in the middle of my art," the prisoner said. So, he'd been ignoring me after all.

His voice was deep and resonant, cracked with stress but no hint of real pain. It was like someone who had forgotten to drink all day was speaking. He sighed wearily, as if the guards and the white-robes annoyed him.

"You're mad," one of the white-robes snapped. Another said something in a foul tone, but it was too low for me to make out. The others laughed; the sound made me wince.

The prisoner merely lifted his long limbs and extended his hands. The guards threaded another chain through the shackles on his wrists, tugging him out into the open section of the chamber. The little group walked past the transparent front of my cell as they exited, and I greedily gathered details of Prisoner Number One.

He was not very tall, probably shorter than my height, with sienna-red skin. He was bald and had no visible body hair. He was indeed wrapped in chains, many etched with glowing glyphs. His clothing—a graying shirt and loose, equally gray pants—looked old and worn. His feet were bare.

One of the guards, a scarlet-skinned ruler, saw me looking and struck the glass with the butt of his sword. It made a harsh ringing sound. "Eyes down," he snarled. "Or I'll turn the collar up."

I ducked my head, listening as the door to the chamber opened and closed. A more distant door opened and closed. Then, there was complete silence. My mind turned slowly, replaying the details I'd observed, when something odd struck me.

His hands, long and elegant, had been bound in front of him, all fingers clearly visible as the guards marched him past my cell. There had been no sign of the blade I'd seen fitted to replace one of his fingers.

CHAPTER THIRTY-TWO

I woke to a boot smacking me square in the stomach. My guts reeled as my eyes flew open. I vomited up bile.

"Up, human," a guard barked.

Dazed, I looked up at him through bleary eyes. He hovered over me with a scowl. It was the scarlet skinned ruler who'd taken Prisoner Number One out of his cell however many hours before. Another guard, an insect-like wildling, stood beside him. The Immortal shuffled his foot as if mulling over whether to give me another kick. I scrambled up, deciding to make sure they didn't need to. Would they give me water today?

My empty stomach groaned loudly, and I licked my dry lips. There was the copper hint of blood in my mouth from licking the wall. It reminded me of buying jawbreaker candies with Zach when we were kids. Our tongues would bleed as we tried to get to the centers. It made our mother furious.

While the guards looked me over, I noticed that Number One was back in his cell and had resumed his carvings. Whatever had been done to him was over and done with by this morning.

"Back to the research room," the guard snapped.

They marched me out into the hall, and I fell into the role of a well-behaved prisoner. After getting caught red-handed, I expected punishment beyond simply being thrown in solitary. In the less desolate light of logic, I was confident Sempre wanted to keep me alive for at least a while longer, regardless of whether he believed any of the information I'd given him. I *also* suspected he didn't think I had a chance of escaping the sanitarium. And if that really was the original prisoner of this place back there in solitary, then he was statistically correct.

I curled and uncurled my numb hands in their bindings as the guards led me down indistinguishable white hallways to a familiar set of black double doors. The guards who flanked these doors gave a small nod to my captors, and the doors slid open. A puff of cold air streamed out, even chillier than the hallway. I tried to stop myself from shivering, but my body betrayed me. Unfortunately, Zeele and his white-robes saw the bodily reaction as they swung their attention toward my entrance.

Zeele smirked but said nothing. He marked something down on his clipboard. I wanted to smack that smirk right off his face. What was he writing, anyway? *Subject appears to be cold because she hasn't eaten a full meal in several days.*

I bit my tongue and felt my anger rise. I detested Zeele's face. His smiles sickened me. Even without food in my stomach, the white-hot rage at torturing living beings in the name of research made me want to throw up.

He interlaced his fingers, many glinting rings knocking together. The sleeve of his robe hung open to reveal his collection of bracelets, one of which was to control the collars. A wave of terrible fear came over me. My body *knew* what that bracelet meant.

If only I could snatch Dorian's stone back…

"We're going to have a very special experiment today," Zeele said. When he smiled, the whites of his eyes grew so much that his electric green irises didn't touch the tops of his lids. Louise once told me that she read there was a Japanese word for it on the internet. It was easily the most unsettling part about Zeele's current expression, despite his megawatt smile.

I kept my mouth shut. Zeele shifted slightly and regarded his white-robe comrades coolly.

One of them snapped to attention. "Uh, what is it, sir?"

Big fish in a little pond. Zeele could lord around his role in the sanitarium when Sempre was out of the room. How lovely for him.

Zeele brushed an imaginary piece of lint off his chest plate. "We're about to witness something fascinating, something that I've only heard the faintest rumors about. It was only by luck that I discovered something *delicious* in Juneau's gaudy mansion."

One of the white-robes snorted, but I refused to turn to see who. My eyes drilled into Zeele's terrible smile.

He snapped his fingers, and the doors opened. Two guards shoved in a familiar figure, his dark-haired head bent forward. My heart cried out... and then it began to burn.

Dorian!

He barely had the strength to lift his head to give me a pitying look, his eyes soft when they found me in the room. The collar made him weaker than I was, but they must've already run some tests on him, too. Had they made him fight Kane yesterday? Or pitted him against Roxy, who was forced to once again cut up one of her friends?

His eyes held pain, but only the physical kind, suggesting that either Kane and Roxy had believed my act or simply hadn't had the chance to pass along news of my apparent betrayal. Even then, I was certain Dorian knew I would never betray him. After all we'd been through together? The white-robes would have to put a gem in my forehead before I betrayed my friends for real.

Zeele swung his eyes between us and grinned. "Would you like to know what I found at Juneau's home?" he asked in a sing-song voice. He pulled something out of his pocket.

A bead of sweat began to form beneath the edge of my collar. Dorian's proximity caused a small burn, but it was nothing... yet.

"Someone foolish enough to leave behind paper notes while hiding from the authorities. Someone stupid enough to write their names. Does this look familiar to you, Dorian and Lyra?"

Every hair on my arms stood to attention as Zeele waved around a small notebook. It was the small Bureau notepad Dorian and I had used to write letters to one another. I shut my eyes for a moment as dread and rage swallowed me whole.

I wanted to lunge at Zeele and attack him with everything I had. The one time Dorian and I had opened up about our feelings for each other in one of our small stolen moments, and Zeele had now tainted it. The notebook was like a slap in the face, a reminder that even Dorian and I could make mistakes. We were foolish not to have burned the notebook. We were foolish to have used our names. We were foolish to have trusted Juneau.

Dorian and I both looked broken and weary. We had no energy left for performances or protestations.

"We nabbed it the night of the ball," Zeele gloated. "A pretty little treasure in Juneau's house. How kind of you."

My heart sank into my stomach. But... if the guards raided Juneau's house and found the notebook, they should've found Laini. If they'd found her, they would've immediately dragged her here to the sanitarium, and Zeele would be reveling in another capture. My shoulders lifted an inch as a sudden hope filled me. Maybe Laini got away after all!

Zeele let out a mocking laugh as he thumbed through the pages. "You two are so sweet. Immortals aren't so sentimental." He snapped the journal closed. "We *were* going to send dear Dorian to be harvested, but this has provided other opportunities. We've heard of the vampires' curse in far-flung legends and ancient scribbles from the time when leeches actually dared to ingratiate themselves as part of the Immortal Council. Still, now we have the perfect opportunity to test those age-old theories." His cheeks warmed pink from his delirious happiness.

Dread replaced the blood in my veins. Zeele knew nothing of the curse's effects, so if Dorian and I passed out, would they be able to wake us from the coma? How stunningly cruel that it could be love that killed me. I tried not to react, but I couldn't resist looking at Dorian.

He staggered to the side for a moment, weakened by the collar and our proximity. The guards righted him. Our eyes met. His eyebrows lifted with the ghost of alarm, expertly concealed despite his own fatigue. I tried to send him a silent signal of equal parts panic, worry, and frustration. Anger scratched at my chest, a demon trying to escape, alongside the rising burn from the curse.

"Into the tank," Zeele ordered cheerfully. The guards pushed Dorian past me. For a moment, we were so close that my legs threatened to buckle, but the guards moved him away before it could happen. Zeele, however, made a note of the reaction on his ever-present clipboard.

"This is going to be interesting," he said and nodded. "Restrain the vampire to the chair."

One of the restraining chairs had been placed in the yellow chamber where Roxy and Kane had fought yesterday. The guards roughly shoved Dorian into it and immediately tightened the bindings around his wrists, torso, and ankles.

Zeele sidled up beside me. "Are you afraid?"

I refused to reply. He hummed, unbothered.

"Affix the monitoring circlets," he commanded the other white-robes.

Two moved to Dorian while one came to me. They took out spools of purple wire and wrapped it several times around my head. The makeshift headband sealed itself, the wire resting tight against my skin and dirty hair. I looked up in time to see them finish doing the same to Dorian.

"We're going to start by testing the effect of proximity, since that appears to be the most obvious symptom of this… affliction," Zeele said. His hand latched tightly onto my right arm. "You'll stop when I tell you to. The circlets, as well as the researchers, will be gathering comprehensive data of all physical reactions." At this, he walked me six inches toward Dorian.

Helpless, I followed his demands. The burn began to grow to a constant pain. It was low enough that I could keep my reactions calm, but I saw Dorian flinch. The collar, in addition to the curse, meant he was weaker than usual. My eyes blurred with angry tears that I blinked back. I would never let Zeele see me cry.

Zeele scratched something down on his clipboard. The other researchers lurking nearby nodded and muttered among themselves, tapping at the machine in the corner as it hummed and crackled. Zeele prodded me to move forward again, two more steps this time. Every step of the way, the guards hovered close behind me while Dorian's guards flanked him.

The burning in my chest began to grow like a campfire starting to catch ablaze. Dorian paled. I hissed. Zeele stopped me and repeated his notes.

"Again."

I inched closer to Dorian. The pain bloomed into an ache, then exploded from an ache into a twisted tangle of agony. Zeele dragged me forward until my nose brushed the yellow glass. Then he took an excited breath and opened the glass.

"Walk."

My legs barely holding me up, I stumbled right up to Dorian. Zeele watched me closely and turned to Dorian, enjoying the sight of him squirming against his restraints. Dorian gnashed his fangs together and cried out as I brushed against his knee.

"Fascinating," Zeele said.

The pain seared me from the inside out, and shadows began to bleed into the corners of my eyes. I writhed against my restraints, the wire digging into my wrists. My joints were turning to wet sand, unstable and abrasive under my skin.

And then Zeele shoved me into Dorian's lap.

I gasped as I collapsed onto Dorian. The very threads of me were being unpicked one by one as the explosion of agony rocked through my body. Using the last dregs of my strength, I threw myself backward, falling to the ground. Dorian was whimpering, such a horribly unnatural sound for him. It tore at my burning heart. Then the world swam with darkness, and the shadows overtook me.

The last thing I could process was Zeele leaning over me and whispering, "This has just begun, *Lyra*."

When I woke up, it was to a vaguely acidic taste in my mouth. A cold droplet landed on my cheek. My head ached, and I felt like I'd been hit by a truck.

"Wake up." Someone slapped me. The force of it snapped my face to the side.

I lifted my weak, shivering hands to my stinging cheek, eyes opening to see a hazy vision of Zeele. He held an eyedropper to my lips, sending another drip of liquid into the back of my throat. It burned a little, but I felt a spark of awareness returning. I groaned.

Zeele emptied the rest of the dropper, and I gagged, jerking upward. Big mistake. Pain swelled in my head.

How long had I been out? Not three days, that much was clear. But then again… how would I have been able to tell? The room would look the same no matter what; the researchers would all look the same in their white robes. How could I be sure?

I glanced to my left, and the familiar burning in my chest moved to the forefront. Dorian sat in his restraints in the tank. I was just outside the yellow glass.

Catching my eye, he forced out through teeth gritted against the pain, "It's only been a few minutes. Don't worry."

Zeele glanced between us. "Is it usually longer? Interesting. Let's see how long it goes for next time." He looked over to a researcher. "Make a note of the time it takes for the human to return to consciousness each time. Include that we're using blackfish bile to invigorate the nerves."

The researcher nodded, making a note on their own clipboard.

"Let's reset and go again," Zeele said. The guards dragged me to my feet. Dorian's head drooped, his shoulders heaving.

"No," I whispered hoarsely as we returned to where we'd started on the other side of the room.

Zeele latched onto my wrist. "Oh yes." His grin made me sure that I looked into the face of a shark rather than any sort of being who appeared remotely like a human. "Again."

Over and over, we performed the torturous walk. Dorian screamed like he was dying the third time I was shoved into his lap. The fourth time, I fought so much that the guards had to force me toward the glass box. By the fifth time, I was so weak that I could no longer walk. They dragged me instead, my boots scuffing the clean white floor as they moved me closer to Dorian, step by step. Zeele continued taking notes. The scratches of a pen nib on paper became a maddening soundtrack to my nightmare.

The sixth time, I began choking on my own spit. I heaved. Zeele snapped to call a wildling, who threw a cup of water on me. Delirious, I gasped and tried to wipe the water into my mouth. Zeele snatched my arm and began to drag me toward Dorian again.

Every time, the pain came like an awful promise, doubling, tripling, folding in on itself until there was no beginning and no end. There was just pain.

CHAPTER THIRTY-THREE

My memories blurred. Sometimes I was blindfolded. Sometimes Dorian was blindfolded. A few times I had to carry a heavy weight. Another time, while I was blindfolded, I heard them untie Dorian and order him to hold two weights in the air without dropping them.

My body ached. A thought drifted in and floated away in my exhausted brain. I tried to snag it, holding it tightly to my consciousness.

Think, Lyra. What could I do to stop this? How could I use Zeele's experiment against him?

There were around thirty seconds between dropping me onto Dorian's lap before one or both of us fainted. A wild idea crystalized in my mind. It was desperate and dangerous and all I had left.

I could use those precious seconds. I could push past the pain.

Hold it together.

Zeele shoved me. As soon as I landed in Dorian's lap, I aimed my head toward his shoulder.

"Feed on me," I begged, pushing toward him rather than away. "Feed on me, Dorian. It's our only hope to fix this."

The brush of his lips on my neck sent a jolt of pain through me, followed by an immense wave of pleasure. It was the bittersweet taste of our romance that I'd learned to love.

"Remember," he whispered hoarsely. His fangs scraped the delicate skin of my neck. "No matter what happens, remember that I love you, Lyra."

He sank his fangs into the pulsing vein. Cold exploded in the space between my neck and my shoulder. Pain, a new kind of pain, slammed into me, raking along every nerve in my body. It overtook the burning in my chest. I screamed. Time trickled by. It felt like ten minutes passed. The guards yanked me away.

Zeele yelled, "No! Take her back!"

Don't faint. I chanted the thought over and over. My mind swam in a delirious mixture of pain and relief. An ache that surged up from my bones as my body bucked and rolled. Was it the bite or the curse? I sucked in a gasping, desperate breath. Distractedly, I noticed that I was on the ground, but I couldn't feel it. Darkness began to creep over my vision.

No, no, no.

I didn't want to faint. What if I didn't wake up this time?

Zeele hovered over me. The shadows began to eat away at him, too. Instead of disappointment, he smiled like he was looking at a shiny penny he'd just found on the street.

"She's lost a lot of blood… I have an idea."

I closed my eyes. Everything slipped away.

I gasped awake to crackling heat in white and yellow, then flames. They crawled up my arm without burning. My delirious mind screamed as my half-baked consciousness fought to wake up. I looked down at my arm. There were no flames.

In front of me, my hands were not my hands. They were large and rough. When I looked down at them, they were detached from me, and yet I *knew* they were my hands.

I grabbed someone as they appeared in front of me. No, wait—they'd been here the whole time. A distant buzz of sound surged into focus. One of my hands wrapped around their throat. The other, I smashed into their face over and over again. The person was screaming, sobbing. A woman? I tried to force the hands, my hands, to stop their violent assault, but I wasn't in control.

Thoughts that weren't my own floated to the front of my mind: *I'll show you. You think I'm weak?*

I gasped as a new surge of heat came up my arm, but the hands continued their vicious beating. My mouth opened to scream, but nothing came out. A disgusting wave of self-hatred hit me, trying to rip my chest open. The guilt came after as the sobs began to wane.

"Please stop," I whispered to the air and the hands. I needed the images to disappear.

I blinked as the hands abruptly faded away, my vision bleeding white and yellow. I was in a yellow-tinted chamber. I tried to focus, but the fire crept through my body. I stared down at my left forearm.

A crystal needle was in my arm. The needle pumped a dark red substance into me. The thick red liquid swam with shadows. My head spun.

Vampire blood.

The memories of the brutal hands haunted my mind, but I tried to push them away as the horror of what was happening to me here and now swept over me. They were pumping vampire blood into me. My stomach turned, and I groaned as heat pulsed in my arm again.

Guards grabbed me. A blurry Zeele pulled the needle from my arm. The increased heat stopped, but the fire continued spreading through my body.

Time folded and sprang open again. We were somewhere else now. White walls stung my eyes. I blinked for what felt like an hour, and when I opened my eyes again, we were back to the original yellow chamber. As my vision focused, I could see Dorian slumped against his restraints.

"New wire," Zeele snapped.

One of the white-robes rushed up to replace my headband of purple wire. I tried to touch the area, not realizing that my other one had vanished. The researcher batted my hand away with a smack. I hissed.

The cycle began again, but everything had changed inside me.

The collar made me woozy. The guards had to help steady my shaking frame. I took a step forward, and the room spun. The woman's crying and the sound of fists hitting flesh replayed over and over. I closed my eyes, but it didn't stop the terrible images inside my mind. Were they memories? Was this what Dorian and the other vampires had to suffer through when they fed?

They moved me closer to Dorian, who looked out at me weakly, his face pale. His eyes were guarded, waiting for the inevitable spike in agony as we were forced together again. The guards brought me to stand in front of Dorian.

The information finally trickled through to my scrambled mind— there was no heartburn.

There was no heartburn.

The collar made me dizzy, but the pain was nothing compared to before. We had an advantage. We could use this.

I met Dorian's gaze, begging him to understand the panicked but pain-free look on my face. Zeele and the guards faced him. They couldn't see my face.

"No pain," I mouthed.

Dorian's eyes glittered with a spark of recognition, then he suddenly writhed in his chair. Wailing, he snarled and struggled, breath tearing in and out of his throat. For a brief moment, I wondered if it was only me and he was still experiencing the old debilitating pain... but then I saw the minute nuances of his apparent suffering. This Dorian was a performance. Whatever fix had worked on me seemed to have worked on him, too.

An odd sense of relief washed over me despite our circumstances. I waited for one second, my skin prickling, waiting for Zeele to react, and then I began to scream as well.

"Closer. Perhaps the blood has just delayed the effects," Zeele said, delighted.

The guards pushed us toward one another, and I mimicked the symptoms of the curse, bucking and shuddering. The guards pushed me onto Dorian again. Spasming, I collapsed halfway over Dorian's lap, leaning against the side of his chair. I let my eyes roll back into my head, hoping Zeele would buy the performance.

Hidden from the guards' perspective, I let the hand hidden by my body squeeze Dorian's hand. He squeezed back. My heart felt light for the first time since they'd brought us to the sanitarium. Dorian's body went slack. I followed his lead.

A strange exhilaration passed through me. I was *this* close to Dorian with no pain. I could have sung my happiness… away from Zeele.

The guards wrapped their hands around me again and dragged me away as I played limp and kept my eyes shut, forcing my mouth to relax open. A set of hands removed my circlet of purple wire, and I listened to everything as they pulled me out of the tank. Covertly, I peeked out from beneath flickering lids.

They dragged me past the end of a corridor, and I saw the feet of several white-robes gathered near a doorway. Someone inside said, "It's the tear…" My ears perked up instantly. I tried to make myself as heavy as possible for the guards to drag. They grunted.

"We need to speed up our plans," a hoarse voice said. I heard a fist slam into a palm.

"The vampires won't be malleable yet."

The other scoffed. "It won't matter."

I cursed inwardly as the guards dragged me away from the conversation, and my ears filled with the sound of my body dragging on the tiles.

Cold metal bit into my back as the guards hauled me onto a table. I made a show of groaning and fluttering my eyes open, finding—to my horror—that I was on some kind of operating table. A bright lamp hung overhead, the light spilling over my body.

Zeele whispered something to the guards. They hadn't seen me open my eyes yet. I closed them again, pretending my eyelids were just fluttering.

Observe and wait for your chance. They hadn't restrained me yet, but I'd spotted various restraints attached to the frame of the table. One guard left, but two remained—the scarlet-skinned ruler and the humanoid insect wildling that had brought me from my cell this morning.

A few minutes passed. Zeele wrote something on his clipboard. He spoke to the remaining two guards in low whispers. What were they doing?

Down the hall, a giant thump sounded as a scuffle broke out. My heart froze for a moment. Was Dorian trying to escape? The two guards snapped their attention toward the hall.

"Investigate it, idiots," Zeele hissed. The guards ran out. My heart began to beat faster and faster, anticipation making my palms sweat. I could feel the moment of opportunity creeping into the room. I waited.

Zeele wandered over to the table, huffing under his breath about the difficulty of finding good employees.

"I thought the effects of this would be more interesting," he muttered to himself with a disappointed sigh. He shuffled some papers on his clipboard. "So far, the darkness hasn't affected her much. Unfortunate. It would have been an interesting development to take to Lord Sempre." He left me and strolled to the other side of the room. It sounded as if he grabbed something from a table.

My nerves surged. Was it a knife? Was he going to embed a tidy little gem into my forehead too?

Over my dead body.

I half opened my eyes when I heard him moving around at the opposite end of the room. Beneath my lashes, I could see him leaning over a metal tray. A minute later, he dragged a small silver cart over to the operating table. As he drew closer, I saw a familiar lump in a pocket on his chest. I knew the size and shape well. It was the magic-imbued stone Dorian had given me. My heart slammed in my chest. The moment arrived, washing over me with a wave of energy that sent sparks down my spine.

When Zeele turned his back, looking for something on the cart, I surged into action. Leaping to my feet with a speed that I'd never felt before, I reached over his shoulder to snatch the stone from his pocket.

Instantly, it heated in my hand, sparking to life like a fire. I clapped it to my neck, and the collar surged with heat before springing open and falling to the tabletop as nothing more than a length of harmless wire. The constant low-level wooziness disappeared.

The Immortal opened his mouth to cry out, but I didn't give him the chance. After a strike to the solar plexus, I yanked him toward me by the hair, hooking my arm around his neck. Bryce had taught me how to perform a chokehold, and he'd taught me well.

"The goal is to cut off blood flow to the brain by using the pressure of your forearm and upper arm to constrict the sides of the neck, rather than the upper arm across the front of the neck, lass. You get your enemy like that, and they'll go down faster and easier. It clamps veins and arteries, rather than trying to crush the trachea and cutting off air to the lungs." He grinned with the joy that only a seasoned warrior could have. "You'll find that your victim won't understand what's happening until it's far too late."

Zeele was a researcher. His muscles were strong because of Immortal genetics, but they were soft and underused. *An ideal target.* I was ready to deliver some payback.

The choke worked. He gasped for air and wriggled against me, trying to buy time until he could break away. His hand stretched out for the metal table. I kicked it gently away and let it roll to the other side of the room. There would be no loud noises to bring his precious guards back to do his dirty work. Sure enough, he soon went limp in my arms.

He slid toward the floor in his flowy white robes like he'd melted. I hauled him up by his shoulders, surprised at how light he was. It had been the same with Inkarri, even with her armor and weapons. Was this lightness a trait of the ruling caste?

Switching our positions, so he now lay on the cold surface of the table, I grabbed the restraints before he could move. With great pleasure, I strapped him down tightly by the wrists, ankles, and all along his torso. He wasn't going anywhere fast without help. I ripped a long strip of his robes from the bottom hem and stuffed some in his mouth. I used an extra length to tie around his mouth like a gag.

"How does it feel to be on the receiving end?" I asked hoarsely, wishing I could be here when his panicked eyes flickered open. "You won't be able to scream."

I took a deep breath, relishing the role reversal. I never held grudges, but I could make a special exception for Zeele.

It was time to move.

CHAPTER THIRTY-FOUR

I only had a few precious moments. Snatching up a scalpel—it was as long as one of my knives and wickedly sharp—from Zeele's tray of torture tools, I dashed toward the door. As I approached, however, the door swung open, and two armored guards charged into the room, followed by a wildling.

"Prisoner!" a guard croaked.

The wildling gasped. "Master Zeele!"

I crouched in a defensive position, holding the scalpel in front of me. The guards stopped and tapped at bracelets on their wrists, trying to activate the green wire collar.

Taking advantage of their ignorance, I stumbled forward and feigned a pained gasp as I collapsed to the ground, making sure I landed close to their feet. The guards grumbled in satisfaction as I went down. The wildling let out a sigh of relief. The guards loomed over me and lowered their blades.

In my hand, the stone began to heat, sensing magic nearby in the armor of the guards. Preparing myself for another burst of movement, I waited for them to take another step forward, then shot my arm out and tapped the stone to the first one's armored boots. I repeated the action with the other guard, then scrambled backward.

The stone glowed, but I had no idea what magic it was absorbing. For all I knew, I could have just removed an anti-rust spell and nothing more.

The first guard, a burly fellow with crimson eyes, went to step toward me but couldn't seem to raise his legs. The metal clanked, and he growled and grunted, succeeding in moving forward only a few inches before he toppled over.

The other guard, with a large, sinewy build like Kane's, tried to do the same, but he was entirely stuck in place. Grabbing a heavy drill off the tray, I leapt for the unrestrained wildling, swinging the metal base into the side of the creature's head. He let out a pained groan before crumpling to the tiled floor. The wildling was out. One of the guards swung at me with a sword, but I ducked the blade, the blow sloppy from his inability to move. Leaping up onto the more agile guard's back, I yanked him backward and performed another chokehold, restraining his struggling body with my legs tight around his waist. While he struggled against inevitable unconsciousness, and then finally fell to the floor, the crimson-eyed guard tried to crawl away, the weight of his unmagicked boots weighing him down. A blow to the back of his skull with the drill finished the job.

I hadn't left fighting behind when I'd walked away from the Bureau. If anything, I'd signed up for something far worse.

"Serves you right," I told the unconscious bodies, my chest heaving. Turning back to the chaos of the room, I planned my next move.

First step was to bind the hands of the three unconscious creatures with some of the wire they'd used on me, though it didn't activate to drain their strength. I also stuffed wads of gauze into their mouths to stop them from raising the alarm, and bound the wildling's feet, just to be safe.

My next problem was getting out of the room. The guards had closed the door behind them, and after a quick investigation of the entryway, it looked like I wouldn't be able to get through it without some sort of key. I turned my attention to Zeele's bracelets.

I tried to yank them off, but they clung to his wrist as though melded to his skin, and I could see no fastening to open them. My hands began to sweat as I weighed my options in a split second. More guards would likely come soon, drawn either by the commotion down the hall or by realizing Zeele had been missing for more than a few minutes.

Everything in me slowed, my heart rate steadying. I knew what I needed to do, and a scalpel wasn't going to be enough. The bulkier guard carried a two-headed throwing ax on his belt. I pulled it free and returned to Zeele's immobile body. Sliding the restraint out of the way on the arm wearing the row of crucial bracelets, I gripped the handle of the ax tightly.

It would be karma for his years and years of torturing others. And it wasn't that I *wanted* to do this; it was a necessary choice in a desperate situation. Nevertheless, as I raised the axe, there was a thrill of anticipation crackling through my bones as I imagined the shockwaves from the strike traveling up my arms. Deep down, there were ugly shards of anger in my gut as I reveled in the vengeful suffering I was about to inflict upon him. For a second, I caught my reflection in the metal surface of the tray of surgical instruments. My pupils were huge dark pits, wiping out the hazel irises. My face looked pale and haggard. It was me, but sharper, more dangerous, driven to this act by desperation.

I needed to save my friends. I needed to save my family. I needed to save the entire damn Mortal Plane. There was no time to feel guilt. I had to get out of here.

I brought the ax down as hard as I could, aiming for the wrist joint.

The blade was lethally sharp, and the wrist came off in one clean slice. I stood to the side to avoid the spray of blood. Zeele exploded into consciousness, screaming into the gag.

He thrashed on the table as much as his bindings allowed, a dark mirror of Dorian's actions only a few minutes earlier. I reached over and held him down. Some of his blood got smeared on my cheeks and in my hair, strangely cold against my skin. Zeele let out one last muffled cry against his gag before fainting again, affected by the shock and the blood loss the same way a mortal would be.

The tightness of the restraint around his arm acted like a weak tourniquet, slowing the flow of blood. I didn't have time to loosen it, so he would bleed out more slowly than he otherwise would have, a thought that gave me a cold satisfaction. Covered in blood, I slipped the bracelets off the bloody stump of a wrist and wiped them clean on Zeele's white robe. They slid over my hand easily enough but hung too loose on my arm, clattering together like I was shaking a bag of cutlery with every step.

I needed pockets, but the guards had cut them out of my pants, and right now I had no boots. There was only room in my sports bra for Dorian's stone, and my clothes were spattered with blood. I couldn't go wandering the halls like this. I turned back to the guards and the wildling to see if they had anything I could use.

The wildling wore a jerkin made of woven leather that fastened at the front with a series of hooks and eyes. I yanked it off the unconscious creature and fastened it around myself. My ribs protested, weak from the torture I'd so recently endured. After slipping the bracelets into a low pocket, I pulled the guards and wildling to the back of the research room where they couldn't immediately be seen from the door. There wasn't much I could do about Zeele, still strapped down and bleeding on the table. For now, I threw a sheet over him, hoping it would be enough.

I snatched anything else that could be useful. From the sinewy guard, I grabbed his weapon belt and secured the bloody ax to it. There was already a dagger attached to the belt, and I left it on. I skidded in my bare feet as I hit a puddle of Zeele's blood. I grimaced. The wildling's boots might fit me. The other two pairs were too large and useless now that I'd removed the spells that lightened the heavy metal. The wildling's boots were a bit big but serviceable. I wiggled my toes and tried to ignore the squishing blood.

The glint of the leaner guard's gem gauntlet caught my eye. I stared at the four passed out bodies for a moment, horrified. A weighted quiet filled the room—a silence I had created with my own violent energy. I swallowed, brushing aside the dark thoughts that surged for a moment, and grabbed the gauntlet off the guard. It wasn't too bad a fit. But could I operate it?

Guess we'll find out.

The proximity to magic made Dorian's stone warm where it was pressed against my skin. The gentle heat comforted me as I gathered myself, feeling more confident now that I had some semblance of armor and weaponry.

Adrenaline rushed through my veins... or perhaps it was the newly introduced vampire blood. It moved me forward with a surge of strength I hadn't thought possible. It felt like I could rip metal apart. Hunger pains no longer plagued me. I could only taste the coppery, acidic scent of Zeele's blood in the air.

I crept quietly to the door the guards had come through and pressed my gauntlet hand against the wall. Nothing happened. It would take Azpai's stone too long to drain a magical item that it couldn't touch. Taking out the handful of bracelets, I pressed them all against the wall, hoping one would spark the necessary magic to get through. With a soft swoosh, the door swung inward, revealing a white hallway. I held my breath and stepped out as quietly as possible, heading left down the hall, trying to retrace the route we had taken a short while before. The wildling's boots were quiet, much softer than the boots of the guards with their distinctive metal clink.

My aim was to get back to the hall and the room where I'd heard the voices discussing plans. My throat burned. Even with vampire blood pumping through my veins a mile a minute, I was desperate for some water.

I'll dunk my head into a bath full of it the first chance I get once I'm back in the Mortal Plane.

With thoughts of fresh waterfalls, I crept forward. Nothing was more nerve-wracking than the slow crawl of the white walls beside me. I knew the direction Zeele had brought me from, but it was difficult to tell which turns we'd taken and how far we'd come—there was no trace of voices arguing about the next steps of final plans.

The hallway forked, and I followed a path at random. I tried to focus on the comforting warmth of Dorian's stone against my chest. Only a few dozen yards later, voices began to ring out, rapidly coming closer.

Glancing around for somewhere to hide, I spotted a set of double doors to the side, one of them standing slightly ajar. With only half a second to check whether the room was occupied, I dove inside.

The room was an experiment lab similar to the one where Zeele had performed his tests on us. However, this one appeared to be out of use. A thin layer of dust covered a cabinet to my left. I crouched beside it, keeping myself hidden but with a clear line of sight through the cracked door.

The voices grew louder, and I watched three guards pass by, their metal boots clinking against the tiles. Stumbling behind two of the guards were two vampire prisoners who were obviously on their last shreds of strength. Their heads hung low, and I could hear their labored breathing from my hiding spot. The guards grunted, annoyed.

"They get smaller every batch, it seems," one of them remarked. The other two laughed.

A sour taste settled in my mouth as I listened to the ragged convoy continue onward, staying motionless until I was sure the guards were well past me. Once the hall was silent again, I released a relieved sigh. But a new problem occurred to me: I needed to find a way to be invisible in this place, since I obviously wasn't a wildling or a ruler. It was only a matter of time before someone found Zeele, and then all hell would break loose.

My gaze landed on a medical gurney that had a white sheet draped over it. Tentative, I tested its movement. The wheels rolled silently. Well, well, well... maybe I could do something with this. As an added measure, I found a set of white robes complete with hood stored in the cabinet. Concealing my human form as best as I could, I pushed the gurney out into the hall, continuing in the direction of the buzzing sound.

The guards were long gone. An eerie silence hung in the overly bright space. The cart moved silently, but something about the quiet made me shiver. Any moment, someone could pop out of a wall or from around a corner.

Stopping at a new four-way intersection of corridors, I pressed my ear to the wall again. The buzz was louder. My heart gave an excited skip as I began to make out low voices coming from an open door, one of which had the airy arrogance of Sempre.

I quickly tucked the gurney into an alcove beside the door, climbing as silently as possible beneath the sheet. Bodies were probably pushed around here all the time. Holding my breath, I began to listen. My nerves were jangled and shivery. Over the rabbit-fast beat of my heart, I could just make out the heated conversation in progress.

"Of course we are moving ahead as planned." It was Sempre.

I strained to hear more and wished I had vampire senses to help. A chorus of voices said something in response that I couldn't catch. The voices swelled in volume as if the speakers had moved closer to the door or were becoming more impassioned. I focused and shut my eyes, begging my hearing to heighten.

"I don't care what those other idiots on the Immortal Council are saying. We've got to speed up the timeline," Sempre snapped. "As much as I hate saying it, we're in danger." He sighed wearily.

"You think the mortals will cause problems?" someone asked him in a higher, needling tone.

Sempre let out a bark of laughter that was not at *all* amused. "I'm no fool. We may have caught two, but there are undoubtably more already in the Immortal Plane, or they are preparing to send in more. And now that the humans are working with vampires… well, that could start to cause us some problems."

A third person groaned. It sounded like an old wooden door creaking open after not being used for years. "But we haven't recovered our assets yet. They hold important knowledge of the Mortal Plane that we need. If we start the wave, we put them at risk."

Assets in the Mortal Plane with important knowledge? That could only mean the Bureau board members. So, the rulers were pushing up their timeline because they were worried that people were planning to start moving into the Immortal Plane en masse? Perhaps our presence had caused more of a stir than we'd anticipated.

"Assets is a strong word," another said. "They're almost worthless now. Besides, Sempre, didn't you say that one of the little mortals brought in from the ball claimed it had some useful info? Not the belligerent one, the other one."

I grimaced. It wasn't difficult to guess which of the two humans was the belligerent one.

"It was a waste of time," Sempre said icily. "It was just hoping to snoop around and avoid Zeele's experiments. Not that it helped the meddlesome creature much. Zeele is having an enormous amount of fun with it as we speak." His voice shifted, and I could picture him pacing around the table. "Every minute we waste discussing this, we lose more advantage over our current position." His voice lowered into a hiss. "Think of Irrikus."

The threat of Irrikus caused a tense silence. I cursed Sempre for his threatening words. *Come on, give me a little more here.*

The third voice sighed, as creaky-sounding as ever. "His wave of darkness will happen soon enough."

"Soon enough?" the needling voice repeated. "We haven't done nearly enough experiments to be sure the revenants will respond to long-distance control."

"It's time to spread chaos," Sempre said. "We cannot spread chaos if those fools take away our advantage."

The needling voice gave a nervous wheeze. I imagined a white-robed ruler clutching his chest as he stared at Sempre. "My lord, to be frank, only a few of the revenants are truly able to be manipulated at this point. The rest are—"

"Are what?" Sempre asked hotly.

"They're uncontrollable menaces!" His comrade gave an anxious sigh. "I wouldn't trust them not to turn against us like angry shrieking decays."

Sempre snorted. "The two-faced human confirmed that this location was part of the vampire base. I'm assuming from her reaction that it's a significant one, which gives us something to go on."

His comrades fell into a hush. At least the conversation told me something about Sempre's knowledge. He was suspicious of most of my claims, but my stomach twisted as I realized that I'd confirmed the Scotland location for them.

Sempre spoke again. "We need to strike soon." His voice rang out with the kind of arrogance that came only from years and years of rarely being challenged. "It doesn't matter if our army of vampires isn't fully under control. If the revenants lose control in the Mortal Plane, all sorts of darkness will follow." He chuckled.

Oh God, they really had been working to control the vampires through the crystals embedded in their foreheads. Except now they were calling them revenants? An army of controlled vampires forced to spread darkness in the Mortal Plane. I felt sick as I thought of Kreya and the other vampires I'd seen.

"The more evil the mortals believe the leeches to be, the better for us. We will get closer to our goal no matter what. We'll send the larger teams of revenants to Moab and the Scotland facility simultaneously, hitting both in one move." Sempre clacked his nail against something, probably one of the monitor screens. "The nests that those rodents have been building in the Mortal Plane will be dealt a huge blow. The humans will lose all empathy and fall back into their fear and mistrust of vampires. The politicians will wring their stupid little scared hands and piss themselves. They won't give a damn when the resistance leeches come crawling to them, saying it's not all vampires, that those doing the terrible acts are revenants being controlled. They'll have nowhere to go on either plane."

"Of course, my lord," the croaking voice said.

My entire body chilled to ice. This dwarfed the schemes that Alan had been building. Sempre had an army of vampires driven mad with darkness to sow fear and discord in the Mortal Plane. Pushing monsters from the hellish depths of the Immortal Plane wasn't enough destruction for them? What was clear was that the Bureau was no longer necessary for their plans. The Immortal Council, particularly Sempre, would be able to influence the public opinion of vampires all on their own.

Rhome's awful tale of Kreya and her manic whispers about Immortals injecting darkness into her now made perfect sense. The rulers wanted the vampires as dark as possible. They wanted the vampires to be utterly deranged when they let them loose in the Mortal Plane.

I shuddered when I remembered Dorian's deranged face during our fight at Chicago HQ. His black eyes still haunted me in certain moments. And now the Immortal Council had control of an army with *that* level of darkness that they planned to unleash upon unsuspecting humans.

Zach, Gina, Morag, Bravi—they would all be in the compound. Would they see the oncoming vampires and mistake them for potential allies? No, the other vampires would sense the darkness immediately. My stomach turned. The vampires would fight and maybe try to feed off their fellow kin, but there would be too many of them. It took four vampires to drain Dorian before. And the red gems controlling the revenant vampires might make things harder. I had no idea what effects the jewels would have on the mad vampires.

"In the end, it won't matter," Lord Sempre said with an ominous but pleased tone. "The Immortal Council wins."

His arrogant proclamation sank into my bones with a chilling promise of things to come.

CHAPTER THIRTY-FIVE

My pulse staggered. Even if Laini had made it back to the Mortal Plane, she had no details of Sempre's plan. Only I did, and I was currently trapped beneath a sheet, listening to the very man who wanted to destroy everything my team and I had fought so hard to protect. I resisted the burning voice demanding I run in there and tear them all apart, with my teeth if necessary. Digging deep into my well of practiced calm, I let my mind slip into soldier mode.

The Immortal Council planned to invade the Mortal Plane with vampires driven mad with darkness, which the rulers were referring to as revenants. Most notable was that the rulers had some level of control over these revenants using the magic-infused gems inserted into the vampires' foreheads. Never mind that apparently this army of revenant vampires wasn't quite ready. Sempre and the other council members were worried that humans and vampires were becoming too closely allied, so they planned to plunge the Mortal Plane into madness and destruction.

The VAMPS camp could reasonably handle a few revenants, but what if there were familiar faces among the black eyes filled with evil? Our team of humans and vampires back in Scotland wouldn't understand what had happened. Worse, the current vampires at the VAMPS camp might panic, thinking the assault meant that Dorian had gone to the Immortal Plane and officially failed.

The silence crept over me, and I stopped breathing for a moment, wondering what they were doing inside the room. Had someone seen me? I needed to keep my chest as still as possible. Dorian's stone was still warm. I considered digging it out from beneath my shirt and bra. I wanted to be ready to de-magic any surprises.

I took a breath and held it. How many vampires did Sempre consider to be an army? Fifty? A hundred? The Hive had informed us that the hunters had recently switched from killing vampires on sight to capturing them. But how long had they been collecting vampires to turn into revenants? The last human year? Or had it only been since the Bureau collapsed a few weeks ago? Maybe even prior to that if Alan and the others let them know there were complications with the genocide plan.

They could have started the plans simultaneously. Perhaps Irrikus and Sempre believed the Bureau to be enough but wanted an extra safety net for themselves. If they'd collected vampires in the sanitarium through their use of aggressive hunting patrols and sniffing out of Hive vampires, how many did they have? My worried thoughts sent a dreadful shudder through me. I needed to find Dorian and the others, fast. I let my breath out slowly, trying to keep my breathing shallow.

Rushed footsteps rang out from down the hall. I stilled again, trying to look as inert as possible. The guards rushed past me into the control room without stopping. My heart thumped loudly in my ears.

"The prisoners are escaping!" someone cried in alarm.

"What?" Sempre hissed.

"Zeele has been attacked and injured," another reported breathlessly. "One of the mortals cut off his hand and stole his control bracelets. And there's a vampire loose in the halls."

My neck stiffened. I could still smell Zeele's blood on me.

"Did they take all his bracelets?" There was a note of fear in Sempre's voice that I found momentarily satisfying.

"Yes, my lord."

There was a moment of loaded silence. "I'll send someone to secure Prisoner Number One down in solitary. Even if they don't understand the binding magic on the bracelets, there's a chance they'll be trying to track him."

"Yes, my lord. Right away."

Sempre growled. "What are you waiting for? Alert the captain and go find the vampire and the mortal, fools!" He stomped farther from the door, but I just managed to hear his parting words to the guards. "I'll be there shortly with reinforcements."

Two pairs of feet passed me as the guards ran back out of the room.

"We'll go find the captain of the guard," one of them yelled back. Their retreating footsteps faded away. Another stampede of footsteps sounded as the rest of the group rushed out of the room, thankfully paying no mind to the gurney, and instead running in the opposite direction. By my guess, only Sempre and a few white-robed rulers remained in the room.

Sempre said something I couldn't quite hear, and then whatever doors led to the control room closed. Silently, I listened, waiting until all footsteps had faded before scrambling out from under the sheet. The gurney remained quiet as I hopped off.

I crept past the control room doors, heading in the direction the guards had gone, then broke into a run when I reached the corner. I whispered an internal note of thanks to the poor wildling back with Zeele. His leather boots were soft and muffled on the floor even as I ran at full speed.

My feet slid slightly as I rounded another corner, fighting off the disorientation caused by the labyrinth of white corridors. The sounds of grunting and fists striking flesh reached my ears. I hurried to find the source of the scuffle.

Just around the next turn, Dorian fought wildly against four guards. He smashed a fist into one guard's helmet, then pulled the armor off the maker's head to land another blow. The guard stumbled back, but there were three more surrounding Dorian. He snarled, fangs flashing. Against the white walls, the shadows beneath his skin looked black as ink. Beads of sweat dotted his furrowed brow. Weary circles clung beneath his blue eyes. The collar was still dampening his abilities.

The three guards around Dorian lifted their arms, and I took a sharp intake of chilled air as I saw they each wore a gauntlet. Dorian flinched and sank into himself for a second, fighting to take a step forward. He swiped at the guard closest to him, but the Immortal dodged easily. The guard on the ground tried to scramble to his feet.

Four against one.

Dorian clicked his teeth together and let out a snarl of pain. Sheer willpower was all that was keeping him on his feet and fighting. I pushed myself into a run, fumbling with the gauntlet around my own arm. Copying the action that I had seen Inkarri and the guards do, I raised my arm, squeezed my fingers into a fist, and released it, aiming for the guard closest to Dorian.

Red light crackling with menace tore through the air. The magic bolt smashed into the guard, sending him down with a pained groan. His two comrades turned.

"Escaped prisoner—"

Still charging forward, I cut off the cry with a series of vicious shots that smashed into the guards. My magic bolts seemed to be self-aiming, hitting my targets easily. Was this why the hunters appeared so powerful? The gauntlet did most of the work for me, perhaps improved only slightly by my years of weapons practice. The thought of such a weapon in the hands of hunters made my blood boil with rage. They had no particular skill or talent. They relied on magic and cruelty. The nagging guilt over chopping off Zeele's hand faded. Rage destroyed any semblance of pity I had for these Immortals. They had targeted vampires for generations to ensure that they would stay at the top of the magical food chain.

The guards fell like dominoes under my barrage of red lasers.

"Dorian!" I cried. He lifted his gaze. As soon as he found my face, he grinned. My heart soared as no pain sparked in my chest. I could have cried from happiness.

"Lyra," he whispered hoarsely. His eyes dropped to the gauntlet on my arm and the blood spattered over my clothes. "Are you okay?"

"I'm fine. But I heard Sempre talking. They're going after the VAMPS camp using vampires doped up with darkness."

Dorian's face paled. His fingers brushed my gauntlet-free arm as if testing to see that I was real. For just a few precious seconds, I threw my arms around him. He clung to me just as desperately, then pulled away, cocking his head to the side with a jerk.

"More are coming." He stooped to grab a utility belt filled with knives from one of the fallen guards. "There's somewhere we can go. I just cleared a room around the corner."

I followed him as he led me down the hall to the left. The doors were open, and he waved me through as he kept an eye out for more approaching guards. The room was like most of the experiment areas: white walls, rolling trays of instruments, glass tank in the center, chairs with restraints, cabinets lining the side wall. An awful creeping sensation ran through me. How many experiment rooms were in this place?

"The cabinet," Dorian blurted. "Watch your feet."

I stepped over an unconscious researcher who had a small puddle of blood beneath her. It stained the sleeve of her pristine white robe. I tore my gaze away, momentarily mesmerized by the shining black blood.

Dorian opened the cabinet door and hopped in. I squeezed in beside him. It had no shelves, luckily for us. We scrambled to the back, pushing aside a mismatched pile of rough crystals. They tumbled off one another until finally coming to rest next to a spool of green wire. I jammed my elbow against a large crystal that looked in danger of falling and shattering, kicking the wire away from my leg.

Dorian pulled me against him as I eased the door shut behind us. A sickening quiet fell over us. Dorian's hot breath was in my ear. My heart slammed over and over again, waiting for the dreaded arrival of the guards. Dorian hovered a hand protectively over my shoulder. The smell of Zeele's dried blood filled the cabinet. I tried to push the scent from my mind, reveling in the absence of pain. I leaned my head against his chest, my right shoulder pressed into him. My left hand steadied the handle of the ax so it wouldn't knock against the metal cabinet.

I tried to bring up the stone to his collar, but my elbow caught the metal side. The contact let out a clank. Dorian gently grabbed my hand. "Soon," he said through gritted teeth, his voice strained lightly.

Soon.

How long had I wanted to be close to him without pain? Too long. I breathed in his scent, desperate for something to erase the awful smell of blood on me. My muscles warmed as I felt him shift against me with his steady breathing. Adrenaline and desire mingled, sending my heart rate off the charts. Heat pooled low in my belly. I shut my eyes, hoping it would do something to calm my heart.

I loved being close to Dorian like this. My head swayed lightly from the chaotic sensations inside me. I wanted to press against him more, but my ears were straining to hear anything from the outside. His breathing grew heavier. Or my hearing became better. It was hard to tell in a situation like this. Our awkward position didn't help soothe the clamoring urge I had to kiss him. I pressed my nose to his chest instead, drinking in the scent of him underneath the sweat and dirt.

My body began to move on its own, begging to touch him, inhale him, taste him. After everything—the memory of the ax slicing through Zeele's wrist flashed before my eyes—I wanted to do something with all the white-hot rage and despair inside me.

Suddenly, Dorian's arm tightened around me. Butterflies rose in my stomach. Footsteps clattered outside, muffled by the two sets of doors between us.

"I think the noise came from here," a guard said as she came into the room.

"You think, or you know?" snapped another. "I thought it was farther down the hall…" His voice trailed off, unsure.

"I don't know," the first guard confessed. I pressed my lips tightly together and prayed that they overlooked the closet. "There's a body!"

I heard them stoop to turn the body over.

"Drag her outside. Medic teams are sweeping the halls. They'll find her soon enough." The second guard sighed gruffly. "The prisoners are probably nearby."

"There's weird mixed energy," the first guard said in a soft voice.

The second guard scoffed. "We are looking for vampires! They don't have auras, stupid. Who knows what weird stuff is in here that could be giving off light energy!"

I could practically hear the first guard's ego deflate. The guards left the room, taking the researcher with them. The doors shut behind them. I pressed myself against Dorian and took a slow breath after a few seconds.

Dorian let out a relieved sigh. Before I could stop myself, I leaned into him as best I could in my cramped position, needing to feel his touch. Releasing the handle of my ax, I reached up to pull his lips down to mine. My blood sparked to life with all the warmth and desire that my body had desperately missed for the last few weeks. With no pain, there was nothing to stop me.

Instead of protesting, Dorian swept me against him, twisting as quietly as he could to get a better hold on me. Our kiss was fierce, filled with all the frustration we'd kept under lock and key during the mission. It was everything I wanted to say. My hopes, my dreams, my worries—I poured everything into my touch. He tensed, finally forcing himself away, a ragged breath leaving his mouth. I nestled against his chest and savored the sensation of him holding me.

"I won't apologize for that," I whispered.

He let out a low chuckle. I loved the vibrations it sent through his chest.

"I wouldn't ask you to," he said, his voice deep with longing. "But we need to move. I wish we could stay like this, but we *are* in the middle of breaking out of prison."

The reminder washed over me like a bucket of ice water. I pulled away a few inches, remembering all the exciting developments I had to tell him. My fingers found the collar around his neck.

"We should get this off you. I used your stone—Lanzon's stone—to dispel the magic in my collar and the guards' armor," I relayed to him. "The armor is magicked to be much lighter for the guards to move more easily, so if I can remove the spells, they're at a disadvantage. And if I can get to the other vampires' collars, I can get us some reinforcements that the guards can't control anymore."

"It's that powerful?" Dorian asked, almost doubtful.

"Definitely," I said and tried to squirm to reach inside my bra, but as soon as I did so, the collection of junk behind me began to shift with a disconcerting amount of noise. I froze, realizing I was holding it still with my body. I bit my bottom lip. "It's in my bra. I know how it's going to sound, but... I need you to reach in and get it so we can touch it to your collar."

Dorian let out a long, husky sigh that sent an excited shiver straight down my spine.

"Do you know what you just said to me?"

"Yes," I confessed and grinned, knowing he could see my mischievous expression even in the dark. "If it's going to be *too* terrible for you, you don't have to do it. But it might be nice to have your collar off before we pop out of this cabinet. There could still be guards in the halls waiting for us."

He hummed, amused and frustrated. I bit back my grin from growing even further. For a moment, he said nothing; there was only the sound of his labored breathing in the vulnerable shell of my ear. My excited shivers multiplied. An electric current surged from the top of my head straight down to my longing core.

We could steal a few moments in this cabinet...

A sharp voice cut into my thoughts. *World domination, Lyra. Prison break.*

Right, right.

I froze as Dorian's warm hand skirted over my hip and slid slowly up under my shirt. His fingers trailed across the bottom of my sports bra, brushing against the solid shape of the stone. There was a very subtle trembling in his fingertips from the effect of the collar... or our proximity. He hesitated for a moment as he nudged under the lower seam of the bra before reaching between my breasts. The touch of his fingers on the soft skin there made my breath catch in my throat as an explosion of warmth filled me. I leaned into the touch as he teased me, taking his hand back out without the stone, cupping the full weight of one breast in his palm. I inhaled sharply, desperate for air as sensations I'd never truly felt before hit me like a tidal wave.

Before I could react any further, he smoothly slid his hand back into my bra, grabbed the stone, and quickly pulled it out.

"Not as terrible as I was expecting," he quipped, the words murmured into my ear making me shiver once more, his eyes dark pools in the sudden light of the stone.

I exhaled, my lips puffing out with a mixture of relief and deep, deep displeasure. "Rude. And so very mean."

"You're welcome." He hissed in anticipation as he brought the glowing stone up to his collar. It glowed softly, absorbing whatever spell was on the wire. The awful contraption fell from Dorian's neck, and he let out of a huge sigh of relief. His body immediately relaxed against mine for a millisecond before he dropped the stone and grabbed me.

I gasped as his hands pressed on either side of my face, and he pulled me into a fierce kiss. He kissed me hungrily for a moment before pulling away. It was glorious. I wanted to respond, but we had work to do. Instead, we panted together in the shadows.

"This is so nice," I whispered, grabbing the stone again.

"We'll do it again and again once we're out of here," he promised me.

Once we're out of here.

"It's not going to be easy," I said. "But we have to make it. We need to get word back to the Bureau before Irrikus and Sempre and their plans destroy everything we've worked so hard for."

I knew his glacial eyes were sparking with determination. "Then we're not going to let that happen." He took my hand and squeezed it. "When has anything in this madcap journey of ours been easy? And we've made it through everything that's come before. Together."

"So let's do this," I said. "Together."

I pulled away from him and gently eased the door open as quietly as possible. I looked back to see a slice of his handsome face lit by a dim ray of light.

It was time to throw a wrench in Sempre's plans.

CHAPTER THIRTY-SIX

Dorian leaned his ear against the silver double doors for a moment. He grunted with satisfaction. "I don't hear anyone. It sounds like they've gone up ahead."

"We need to get out of this area as quickly as possible," I said, rolling the warm stone between my fingers. I would hold it, in case we came across any more rulers. "They're going to drag every available guard here and to the cells. I did cut Zeele's hand off, after all."

His eyes widened in shock and respect. "You did what? Actually, let's talk about that later. The most important thing right now is making sure we don't get caught again." His lips twisted downward. "Sempre will likely be headed for wherever they keep the revenant vampires, right?"

"Possibly?" I guessed. "He seems set on releasing them. His research colleagues were not pleased. They said they didn't have full control over the vampires yet. Maybe a few, but not with any level of confidence." I quickly explained what I knew about the gems and how Zeele and Sempre had been working to connect hunters to vampires, rather than just creatures like velek.

Dorian, looking sickened, let out a hollow laugh. "Leave it to rulers to think up something so horrific and then not be able to control it." He tapped the door that the guards had closed behind them. "Any idea how to open this thing?"

Dorian raised an eyebrow as I pulled out the handful of slightly gory bracelets and pressed them to the door. We took off down the tunnels, Dorian continually scanning for any fluctuation in darkness.

"It's everywhere, but I can feel what I *think* is the prison cells." He pumped his arms, and I worked hard to follow him. Now that he wasn't slowed down by his collar, I appeared drastically slower even with my manic energy.

In some ways, the vampire blood flowing through my veins gave me a sensation of absolute power. Like I could leap as far as I wanted and tear through anything with just my bare hands. But something churned beneath the energy, as if my human limits thrummed just below the surface. The current power was temporary, that much was clear.

When I was in the Bureau, they did a scientific trial among my team to test supplements for improved performance. The scientists wanted to use low-level stimulants on their younger, healthiest recruits. I remembered the intense sensation as the lowest dose hit my system. My mouth went painfully dry and my hands shook, but I could run hard for an hour without stopping and beat my powerlifting personal best. Bryce nixed the entire thing after a few weeks, hating the zombie-like stares he saw all of us wearing when we crashed from the high.

This? It was ten times more powerful and undoubtedly far more dangerous. At some point, I would crash. What that would look like, I didn't know—it wasn't like any of us had experience with what happened when a human was given a transfusion of vampire blood. We would just have to be sure that we did what needed to be done before that point.

I followed Dorian, trusting his sense of direction and knowing that it was our only hope for getting through these white halls.

"There's a collection of presences down below," Dorian whispered. "We're close."

The halls were still miraculously empty as we ran. This was less than reassuring, however, as it meant that most of the security staff could be waiting for us outside the vampire cells.

"Heads up," Dorian snapped as we rounded a corner. Three guards, two rulers and a wildling, were in the middle of the hall. I clutched the stone in one hand. With my other, I took out the double-headed hand ax.

With our collars off and desperation fueling our every step, this fight was very different.

I immediately went for the boots, skidding into the fray on my knees as Dorian knocked the guards to the ground. They fell like bowling pins, and with a quick tap I made damn sure they stayed down. The stone glowed hot in my hand as I made contact with each boot. The guards struggled to get up, flailing with their weapons. Any blows that came too close, I parried with the hand axe, at one point striking the metal breast-plate of one of the rulers hard enough that it bent inward, cracking a rib as it went.

Dorian rendered each guard unconscious, the blows resounding with a crack. I tapped the various other pieces of their armor and sucked the power from the gauntlet one of them wore. He stopped me from absorbing the last one, pulling it over his hand. Then we continued on, leaving the bodies in the hall.

Twice more on our route to the cells, Dorian barked out a warning before we headed into a group of guards. Dorian and I operated like a well-oiled machine. When the gauntlet failed to work for him, he flung it away without pause. He took the guards out by hand when possible, skill-fully using the dagger from his stolen weapons belt when necessary. I focused on neutralizing armor with the stone, fighting back with my ax as needed. The guards exchanged panicked looks after the stone's magic stripped them of their advantages. None of them cried out a warning. It all happened too fast.

A sense of joy surged through me each time we overpowered a new group. I smiled smugly as I elbowed a wildling in the throat and took out his feebly gripped sword. Nice try, rulers. In the end, Dorian and I had far superior training and skills. It was good to know that without their precious gauntlets and the collars, the rulers fell much more rapidly to our prowess.

Thank God Bryce always told us never to cut corners.

And the best part? There was no pain as Dorian and I fought side by side.

He smirked at me as he hovered over the unconscious bodies of two guards. "It feels good to be like this again."

"You took the words right out of my mouth," I told him with a laugh. My body felt like it could do this all night, no matter how many guards I needed to fight. My muscles hummed with power. I sucked in a deep breath before we began sprinting down the hall again.

"Yes," Dorian whispered with victory as we skidded into the stone halls that marked the beginning of the cell section. The white halls gave way to slate-gray surroundings. He was right on the money.

Abruptly, Dorian caught my arm. "Get on my back."

I hopped on without another word, and he took off. As I wrapped my arms around his shoulders tight enough to hold on but not enough to choke him, I felt the stone begin to get even hotter in my hand.

"They're up ahead," I said. "The stone is picking up on the magic."

He nodded, and I steeled myself. For a moment, I looked back. When was Sempre going to show up with reinforcements? He could've alerted Irrikus, and the entire palace guard could be on their way right now. Speed was of the essence.

Only two guards were on duty in the main cell block. Slipping off Dorian's back, I let him keep his pace and crash into the maker that stood by one of the largest holding cells. The vampires inside the cells stirred at the sudden explosion of movement. Landing in a roll that brought me to the feet of the other guard, an insect-like wildling I was sure I had seen before, I tapped the armor with one hand, delivering punches with the other. Once the guard was immobile, feet all but stuck in place, I leapt up onto their back, wrapping my legs around the narrow thorax, and performed a blood choke. Dorian was avoiding punches from two sets of arms on the other side of the chamber, and the vampires in the cells were starting to murmur and shuffle to life. I knew if I could just get this guard down, I could open all the cages and release them from the collars.

The chokehold wasn't working, however, and it occurred to me that the anatomy of an insect wildling was probably different from most other things, so it wasn't as affected by the hold. The insect wildling was still clicking and jerking, fighting to remain upright. A very sharp claw reached back, snapping at my face, and I felt blood well across my cheekbone. With a grunt, I threw my weight backward, hoping that if I could get it on the floor, I could figure out some way to restrain it. As I did so, there was a sickening crack from its neck, and its body went limp, both of us tumbling to the ground.

Stunned, I lay pinned beneath the corpse, an unexpected pulse of regret rushing through me. But there was no time for that. Wriggling free, I yanked all the bracelets out of my pocket just as Dorian downed the maker guard. I pressed the whole handful to the glass, watching as the yellow glass dissipated into the permeable layer.

"Come on!" I cried.

Dorian reached inside, his hand passing through the wall to show them that they weren't dreaming. A tall woman stood up in the front. My heart twisted upon seeing her. She was starving, her rust-colored skin stretched tight over high cheekbones and hollow eye sockets. I could see her questioning, frenzied eyes thinking that it must be a hallucination.

"Now!" Dorian snapped, his voice rumbling with such command that it rivaled Irrikus.

Then, stumbling forward from the back, a familiar figure came into view. Pitch-dark skin, pale lavender hair, and a tattered cloak. *Kono*. One eye was swollen shut, there was a stiffness to his step, and he looked hungry, but he was alive.

"Do what they say," the Hive scout said to the others, speaking so fast that his words slurred together in his excitement.

The tall woman began helping an older vampire man to his feet. He looked around with age-clouded eyes and finally settled on Dorian's face, blinking.

"Are we being saved?"

"We're trying," Dorian said. "Everyone out. Out!"

The prisoners rushed through the yellow barrier. The tall woman and Kono helped the older man along. I counted fifteen in all as they came through. One by one, I went around and released their collars. Many flinched and gasped as the pain they had been continuously enduring disappeared. Kono gripped my arm, emotions crowding his face.

"Thank you," he said. "I doubt you came all this way for me, but I am forever grateful that the two of you came back down here for us."

I squeezed his shoulder. "I'm so glad we found you here. But we still have others to find."

"Then I shall help you find them," he said in his rumbling bass voice.

With a nod of thanks, I turned back to the others.

"You're free," I told them. "If you want to help us free everyone else, you can. If you don't, you should get out as soon as possible."

Two dark-haired younger vampires bolted for the exit tunnel. They would have to grab the bracelets off one of the unconscious guards along the way in order to escape this place. I tried not to think about what they might have to do to get those bracelets. The tall woman stood by the older man who was tugging anxiously at his limp braid of dark blue hair. They'd decided to stick beside us, likely not trusting their own strength.

I held the stone tight as Dorian quickly counted the group behind us under his breath.

"Six," he whispered to me. "And maybe four of those can fight. Let's try to keep track of who came with us."

I nodded, but my thoughts were on the stone. How many spells could it hold? It was already getting uncomfortably warm, and who knew how many more guards there were to disarm? How many more collars to dispel? There were so many unknowns, but there was no other way to go but forward.

The tall woman's eyes dropped to the dried blood on the bracelets in my other hand. She said nothing, but her eyes flickered with understanding.

Blood had already been spilled. This escape was real.

CHAPTER THIRTY-SEVEN

As a group, we hurried to the block of cells in the next room, repeating the process there: take out the guards, open the wall, remove the collars, and let the vampires choose their next course of action.

Again, the vampires stared at us, astonished and untrusting. This time, the tall woman, who introduced herself tersely as Alona, helped. She vouched for us, reassuring the more suspicious individuals as Dorian ordered everyone to hurry. As I released the collars, vampires in the other holding cells around the chamber began to pound on the glass, calling for their own release. Half usually decided to stick with us, while half tried their chances elsewhere.

"They might return after they've grabbed some weapons," Dorian muttered to me. "Or after they've fed on some dark guards."

He was right. A few came back, their refreshed faces an odd contrast to the blood around their mouths. I swallowed the grit in my throat as we came closer to the "interest group" pen. Would Roxy and Rhome still be here? Where was Kane? Fists pounded on the yellow glass as we came down the length of the hall.

"Help us!" came the muffled cry, over and over.

"We're going as fast as we can," Dorian shouted.

Hands kept pounding.

We reached Zeele's favorite cell, and I immediately saw Roxy's face pressed to the glass. She spotted the two of us among the growing cohort of revenge-hungry vampires and let out a giant sigh of relief.

"Lyra," she shouted with a grin. "I was starting to worry you actually went and betrayed me." She wiped a hand dramatically on her forehead, then tapped the glass. "Care to let me and my pals join the team?"

"Sounds good to me," I told her with a smile and pressed the bracelets on the glass.

Roxy turned to help anyone inside who was weak after their torture. Again, we ushered everyone out, but thankfully this group had waited by the glass. Rhome was nowhere to be seen as I went around releasing collars.

Roxy smacked my back playfully as I let her free from hers. "You jerk! You probably had all the fun without me."

"If by *fun* you mean intense torture and a continuous fight for our lives, then we sure have," Dorian said dryly. "More importantly, where are Kane and Rhome?"

Roxy frowned. "They took them a few hours ago. I don't know if it's for experiments or what." Her eyes fell to the gauntlet on my arm, and she whistled. "Nice firepower. Now we can finally get even with those Immortal creeps. If you'll excuse me." She eyed a fallen guard at the end of the hallway and began swiping his gear. Some of the vampires from the earlier cells must've made their way down the hall and taken out any guards coming from the other direction. Roxy swiftly grabbed a gauntlet and some armor around her size.

"Did you see which way they took Kane and Rhome?" Dorian asked.

Roxy yanked on the pair of gem-studded boots, surveying the motley crew of prisoners behind us. "Deeper into the prison chambers." Her tone was filled with the particular kind of dread reserved for discussing the unknown fates of comrades.

"There are cells deeper than this hall," the old man from the first room said. "I've been here longer than most, seen folks come and go. This place goes down a few stories."

My flame-haired teammate kicked at the ground with her new boots, breaking away chunks of stone. "I'll choke the life out of these guys."

"That's the plan," Dorian said with a sharp smile. He turned his blue eyes to the prisoners. There were around thirty who'd decided to stick with us. Some were on the weaker side and were looking for a less confrontational route out of the sanitarium, while others were actively ready to help with the prison break. The number of successful rescues we'd already achieved had energized the entire group.

Kono stepped forward. "What can we do?"

"Do you know where Lord Sempre is?" someone in the crowd asked urgently.

"Where's Zeele? I've got some things I'd like to hit him with."

"Has Irrikus been alerted?"

All these vampires knew who ran the show in the Immortal Plane. I looked over their faces, most of them pale and worn from starvation, torture, or both. If we failed, the Immortal Council would kill us. Or worse, they might take over our bodies to create more revenants. Did these prisoners know what happened to their friends and comrades?

"Can we actually escape?" Alona asked, narrowing her dark eyes as she glanced between Dorian and me.

"I can offer no guarantees, but we have to try," Dorian said firmly. The conversations stilled to a hush. "Listen to me. We need to move through these halls. Attack every guard you see. Take their bracelets to open any prison cells along the way. We need to release everyone if we want a fighting chance at escaping. Take nonmagical weapons. The gem gauntlets don't work for vampires, so don't even try."

Roxy slapped a hand on my arm and pulled me closer to her. "We have to find Rhome and Kane."

"Of course," I said. "The question is, how? They could be anywhere in this labyrinth. There are so many layers we haven't even searched yet." Worse, what if they'd been dragged somewhere to be turned into revenants? My fingers buzzed with energy, desperate to do something. I interlaced them and worried my knuckles, thinking over what we knew about the sanitarium.

Where should we go?

Something popped into my brain. I started.

"Zeele said something about how he'd been planning to harvest Dorian. But I don't know what they would be harvesting."

Roxy furrowed her brow. "You're sure they said *harvesting*? Like a freaking plant?"

"Yes," I said, but I was only half listening to her. Zeele had infused vampire blood into me, and I doubted any of the vampires in here had willingly donated. "Maybe he meant taking the vampire blood."

Dorian, Kono, and several others gave me confused looks.

"It's the only thing that makes sense to me," I said, taking a deep breath before I gave away the next piece of information. "He gave me a transfusion of vampire blood, so they had to have collected it at some point." My mind raced with the memory of Zeele and his gleeful proclamation.

There was a moment of complete silence, and I noticed several of the vampires giving me a more intense look than before.

Dorian hummed in thought, but I could see a muscle jumping at the hinge of his jaw. "Vampire blood is full of darkness." Dorian looked at the ground below us. "The strongest concentration of dark energy is below us right now. I can feel it. We need to head deeper."

It was another risk to go down deeper to search for the darkness. It was one thing to free more prisoners, but now we were talking about searching for whatever beastly core lay at the center of this entire thing. My heart pounded.

"That's the direction they took Rhome and Kane," Roxy said. There was real fear in her voice. "Oh God, what if they've harvested them already?"

Dorian looked at me. "Now," he said fiercely. "Now is the time to find out what they're doing with all this dark energy. Let's go!"

He was right. It was now or never.

The gathered vampires nodded along with our plan with grimly determined faces.

"We might find more prisoner cells," Dorian told them, "but we might find something worse." He paused. "If you have any doubts, leave now," he warned.

The group wavered for a moment, but nobody left. Something like real hope fluttered to life in my gut. For the first time, it felt like we had a solid group.

We descended deeper into the tunnels. The stone seemed to soak up the sound, probably designed to absorb the screams of tortured prisoners, but now it served us well. Any guards we found, the vampires descended upon in packs of two or three at a time. As more guards went down, vampires ripped the bracelets off their wrists. Nobody resorted to chopping off limbs, although they probably wanted to. Vampires ran up to touch the bracelets against any holding cells we found.

"Careful," Dorian called out. "Some of these have beasts in them. Look before you touch."

Indeed, we passed some chambers that held a variety of creatures. Something aquatic and shiny with far too many legs, its cry partially muffled by the yellow glass. Water and slime dripped down in puddles around it. A tiger-like beast snarled and flashed a mouth full of sharp, spindly teeth reminiscent of an angler fish as we passed. A few cells held innocent-looking velek who had gems embedded in their heads. They stared out at us.

"Sempre has a way to use the gem as a camera," I told Dorian and Roxy as we hurried through the halls. "He's got feeds showing the gemstone's point of view from a bunch of creatures and possibly vampires too."

A wolf creature the size of a moose with bristling quills across its back and shoulders rammed itself against the wall with a frantic yelp. The bright blue gem in its forehead wept blood and pus down its face.

Roxy scowled. "They would no doubt tear our heads off given a chance, but I feel bad for them. Nobody deserves to lose control of themselves."

Some cells were empty, but they still showed evidence of having contained horrible sights. Shackles were attached to the wall in some areas. Beds of nails rested beneath blinking screens. A small yellow tank held a bubbling black liquid.

"Resistance trials, I'm sure," Dorian spat and curled his lips in disgust.

We passed a monstrous shrieking decay trussed up in a harness. It stared silently at us, apparently too weak to stand.

"It's like the one we fought near the resort," Roxy said with a violent shudder. "Except they're not even taking care of this one."

"Rulers are inherently selfish," Alona said behind us. She said nothing more, staring at the ground as we moved along.

I briefly surveyed those of the group who were keeping pace with us instead of charging ahead to take down guards. The pain in their eyes made my heart ache. The things they must've seen here…

Farther and farther down, the chambers became larger and larger. Some of them were empty. Some contained more terrifying creatures. My vision began to blur over the yellow glass. Every chamber I looked into felt empty once I realized neither Kane nor Rhome was inside.

"We're getting closer," Dorian assured me.

All around us, the vampires had their fangs out. Some of them hissed, beginning to react to the proximity of the darkness. I tightened my grip on Dorian's stone.

"I can sense it," someone seethed behind us. Their starved faces turned desperate as the darkness increased. My skin jumped nervously at the sound of several pairs of fangs gnashing together in hunger.

Roxy smirked. "It used to horrify me, but right now nothing would make me happier than seeing these guys take out a bunch of dark jerks."

My gut twisted into a pretzel of worry. And if we didn't find any dark guards down there? It might just be vampires injected with darkness. Our ragtag team needed to know that they might soon be face-to-face with friends who had been forcibly turned into mind-controlled revenants.

Dorian glanced warily at me. Perhaps he was thinking the same thing. He took a deep breath, and explained to the group what we might find down there. A few vampires reacted the way I might have expected, with tears and outrage. The larger part of the group seemed numb to any further horrors that the rulers had inflicted on vampires, which unexpectedly brought tears to my own eyes. I wouldn't have expected the lack of reaction to be more upsetting to watch, but it spoke to so much more pain beneath the surface.

The hallway forked. Dorian hovered toward the right. "This way."

I glanced at the other, smaller passage, which reminded me of the tunnel the guards led me through to solitary confinement. I paused, dropping to the back of the pack. If Sempre's paranoia had anything to with it, Prisoner Number One was probably drawing on the walls of his cell somewhere, surrounded by guards. Recalling Sempre's reaction to the news that I'd taken all Zeele's bracelets, I pulled the metal bands out. Something about this creature was important. So important that Sempre was concerned that I'd taken Zeele's bracelets in order to track the creature.

Sorting through the bracelets, I peered at each one carefully. There had been something about binding magic that, while I didn't fully understand the mechanics, didn't take a genius to figure out. My guess was that one of the bracelets connected to some kind of magical tracking device on Prisoner Number One. *There.* I felt a rush of satisfaction as I held up a slim silver bracelet made of seven woven strands. At three points, the wire held a setting for a tiny black gem. As I lifted it toward the leftmost tunnel, it glowed a soft purple.

Torn, I looked between the rapidly disappearing group and the empty tunnel. As much as I wanted to get answers to my questions, we didn't have time to investigate right now. No, our priority was to find the source of the darkness.

I rushed after the group, stuffing the silver bracelet into a more secure pocket than the others. Dorian raised a curious eyebrow as I returned to my spot beside him but said nothing as we continued down the hall.

A short while later we reached the tunnel's end, our march stopping at a massive red glass door.

A vampire with twin braids walked up to the door and pressed a bracelet to it. Nothing happened. She frowned. Someone else tried the same. I stepped up, the crimson reflection of my tired face staring back at me. I lifted my collection of bracelets to it, hoping one of them would work.

With a dull rush of air, the doors opened slowly from the bottom, rising up by some invisible means. Light spilled from the room out into the tunnel.

At the last second, Dorian grabbed my hand and squeezed it. I just had the chance to squeeze it back before he let it drop, and we all poured into the room.

CHAPTER THIRTY-EIGHT

Everyone stopped and stared.

The chamber had a vaulted ceiling stretching several hundred feet above us. It was filled to the brim with amber soul-lights. They floated at the highest points of the ceiling as if trying to find a way out.

On the floor, vampires were packed together like sardines in small holding cells of yellow glass. When they moved, it was like sad shadows flickering together. Disgusted bile rose up in my throat.

At the center of the room was a garden of towering plants that were at least two stories tall. They had no leaves, just pale orange, textured stalks that were as thick around as most of the redwoods I'd seen. At the top of each plant, the trunks extended with multiple hanging vines that ended with giant bulbous heads encased in glass boxes similar to the cells. Inside the boxes, mouths like monstrous Venus flytraps snapped their teeth lazily. The flesh of the plants pulsed and vibrated, like angry bees were trapped beneath the strange texture. I shuddered, disturbed.

"What the actual hell?" Roxy puffed beside me.

Dorian threw his arm out and herded everyone behind him.

"Nobody releases the vampires until I say so," he commanded, keeping his voice low. We hadn't been noticed yet, but whatever this place was, none of us had been prepared for it.

I studied the scene before us. The chambers holding the heads sat on platforms reached by metal stairs. At ground level, white-robes siphoned vials of something thick and dark from distended sacs on the sides of the plants. On the upper levels, closer to the chambers with the plant heads, more researchers and guards milled around. There was a low buzz and crunch in the room, possibly coming from the plants clacking their teeth together.

Movement caught my eye on the platform closest to us. The researcher had their back facing us, so they hadn't seen our group enter. I watched in horror as the white-robed researcher, with the help of a white-furred wildling, dragged a weak and struggling vampire to one of the chambers. They swung the vampire back and forth twice for momentum, then threw her into the plant's waiting mouth.

Someone behind us let out a grunt of disgust and pain.

The liquid in the sacs made sense now, along with why there was such a concentrated amount of darkness down here—the white-robes were feeding the vampires to these plants in order to harvest the dark energy in their blood.

Roxy clapped a hand to her mouth. "I'm gonna be sick."

Dorian stared at the scene, his face pale. The shadows beneath his skin swirled wildly, spurred on by the presence of all the darkness around us. The other vampires had been chomping at the bit as we approached, but now a collective horror had dampened their natural urges.

I grabbed Dorian's elbow. "We need to release the vampires. Now!"

"Dorian!" Rhome's voice shouted from somewhere in a holding cell. We whipped our heads in the direction, but it was hard to hear him over the buzz of the chewing plant. "They've got—"

"Kane!" Roxy screamed. She lifted her stolen gauntlet and shot an acid-green energy blast at a guard.

I snapped my head up to see a guard trying to shove Kane into one of the plant mouths. The laser smacked the guard between the shoulder blades, sending him stumbling backward into the gaping maw of the plant. He let out an ear-shattering scream as his bones were crushed with a terrifying crack. Kane looked over at us, his bound hands pressed to his chest as he processed his near death.

Immediately, guards rushed at Kane with raised weapons. He stumbled toward them, but the damned collar was still around his neck. He lunged at one guard, tackling her to the ground. Roxy ran up to help him, firing her gauntlet as she went and earning a series of screams as guards reeled from the hits. With the aid of her new magicked boots, her strides doubled in length, and she quickly reached the fray on the platform.

Now that our presence had been revealed, our group scattered, starving vampires tackling guards and researchers. I followed Dorian as we dashed toward the source of Rhome's voice.

"Rhome!" I called for him over the chaos. Above us, people began to scream. Gauntlets were fired. Vampires from our group swarmed up the stairs, pushing guards and researchers into the ravenous mouths of the carnivorous plants.

In response to my call, a hand waved wildly from the center of a holding cell. Rhome fought his way through the crowd. He pressed his hands desperately against the yellow glass, face wet with tears.

I slammed the bracelets against the glass, and the vampires poured out. The first collar I released was Rhome's, the wire falling to the floor. He let out a relieved sigh and slumped against Dorian. There was a raw ring around his neck where the wire had been chafing.

"I thought they had him," he wheezed. "I'm so tired."

Dorian clapped him on the back. "I know, friend, but we're almost out of this."

I looked out into the room. After seeing us free the other vampires, some of our team began pressing their bracelets against the glass of the holding cells. A stream of grateful vampires flooded the room, some immediately leaping into the fight while others took off running. Rhome screamed over the chaos, directing vampires toward me to have their collars removed. Heads snapped to attention at that. Good. We would be able to streamline the process somehow.

Above, the other members of our group continued fighting guards.

My pulse raced as I spotted a crowd of our prison escape squad taking shelter behind the far side of the glass pen. The freed vampires milling near me yanked at their collars. I tightened my grip around Dorian's stone as an immense sense of power and relief came over me.

Things might be turning our way.

Some freed vampires needed no help with their collars. They had enough anger and adrenaline to run up the stairs and help take out guards. A few ran back up the tunnel, and I couldn't blame them for trying to escape. I only hoped that some of them were Hive members determined to take the news back to the vampire haven.

I scanned the crowd after the last cell was opened. Dorian was ushering more vampires toward me, and Rhome was directing weak or vulnerable vampires to shelter in an alcove behind the cells. Many vampires were feeding ravenously, a few dragging guards and researchers over to those too starved to move. Chaos abounded in this terrible heart of the sanitarium.

As I began releasing collars as fast as I could, the stone continuing to heat in my hand, a chilled breeze invaded the room. Rhome was staring at the entrance, such shock in his eyes that I immediately turned to follow his gaze. The red doors were still open, and a small group of robed figures was marching in.

They came calmly. That was the worst part.

They had an air of absolute tranquility. They didn't rush as they entered the thick of the chaos. There was no screaming or taking defensive measures. No, they simply marched forward.

Seven figures in all. It was difficult to tell at first that they were vampires. Filled with oozing shadow, every inch of their skin was a soulless, unnatural black. Their eyes? Black. Their fingernails? Black. The only distinguishing features of these revenant vampires were the long, sharp white fangs glinting from their mouths. It was like staring into a pit that had no end.

In the center of their foreheads, red crystals glinted like sparks among charcoal.

They were joined by two beasts that towered above the group. I guessed them to be twice the size of horses, with none of the beauty. They looked like lions made of soot and ash and nearly extinguished embers, skin cracking with fine lines of orange as if magma boiled just beneath the surface. Birdlike wings covered in sooty feathers were folded against their sides. Their distended faces ended in crooked beaks with sharp, spindly ends. I'd seen these creatures before, I realized, in a mosaic in Juneau's mansion. It had done a poor job of representing their vast size.

Each beast had four smoldering orange eyes that looked out at the scene, unblinking. The eyes cemented the vampires to the spot. Everyone on the ground level froze and stared at the new group.

The beasts were fitted with harnesses and muzzles forged from gold and precious gems. They reminded me of the muzzles worn by the shrieking decays, except these muzzles were meant to absolutely cement the beasts' teeth together. Palms sweating, I tried to form a plan in case these beasts had acidic attacks.

"I guess we know what Sempre was busy doing," Dorian whispered beside me.

The new force came to a standstill as my gaze crawled up to the riders. Sempre sat atop one beast, wearing an expression that said he couldn't care less about the prison riot happening right before his eyes. My insides curdled with worry like bad milk. That couldn't be a good sign.

Behind him sat Prisoner Number One, his long arms chained together. As it had been before, his sienna skin was crisscrossed with chains. In addition, a collar sat around his neck, and a metal cage was strapped over the crown of his head. He stared at the ground, but I saw his fingers twitching as if drawing on the walls of his cell again. However, despite his distracted actions, his vibrant purple eyes with no pupils at all flickered like the gems in the vampires' foreheads.

Zeele sat on the other creature, looking less pleased than Sempre. It might have something to do with the bloody stump of his arm wrapped in bandages and the red-splattered robe.

Should've killed him. I cursed my vindictiveness. If I'd thought anyone would get to him in time to help him, I would have given him the fast death that he didn't deserve.

Dorian elbowed me urgently and pointed. I followed his gesture to see that Sempre had pushed his hair out of his face. A red gem gleamed in the center of his forehead.

"The gem," I muttered. "He's in control of the revenants, not hunters."

"No," Dorian said harshly.

I realized he was pointing lower, toward the vampire closest to Sempre. My heart broke. We knew one of the vampires in this lineup.

It was Kreya.

CHAPTER THIRTY-NINE

"K reya," Rhome whispered. He sounded like someone had punched him straight in the stomach.

Kreya's black eyes stared out of her slack face, fangs glinting where they peeked out of her mouth. She failed to flinch or even glance in Rhome's direction.

What had they done to her? I glared at Sempre, who surveyed us like a bored overseer. The Immortal snapped his fingers, and the sound somehow filled the entire room. The vampires and guards who had escaped the snapping jaws of the plants thus far froze. Every eye in the place turned toward Sempre, which he apparently preferred. My hand tightened around Dorian's burning stone as I narrowed my eyes at him, using the pain to focus my rage.

"Now is the time to surrender," Sempre announced in a booming voice. "Before you're all destroyed." His words reached every nook and cranny, sinking into every part of the room with a magical power that told me he was using the influence ability we'd seen demonstrated by several rulers so far. The plants shivered in the wake of his commanding voice. His tone held sway, but thankfully it wasn't as powerful as Irrikus's voice. I shook it off, and my loathing for him remained rooted inside me like a stubborn weed.

My eyes darted to Kreya, who had yet to blink. What Sempre had done to Kreya and the others with Zeele's help was beyond redemption. I'd take the researcher's other hand as revenge.

As if echoing my thoughts, the vampires broke their silence with screams of fury at Sempre's demand. Voices flew up from all levels of the room.

"It's the beast!"

"Sempre, the head butcher!"

"Get him!"

A swell of recently released prisoners charged toward Sempre and the converged revenants. Desperately, I flew into action. The remaining vampires hanging near us barely reacted as I ran up to them with Dorian's stone, eager to join the attack.

I hurried to press the stone against more collars. Most were done, but there were still a few I could free while the rulers were distracted. The more of them I could release, the better our chances.

My eyes kept floating back to our enemies, my own hunger for revenge swirling through my bloodstream. As I hit each collar, the stone grew hotter and hotter in my hands, soon glowing bright amber. Pain radiated out of my palm as my skin began to blister. Knowledge of magic stones was not my specialty, but in my experience it was rarely a good sign when things that were not meant to be hot became very hot. When she'd examined it, Reshi had only told me the stone would suck up some magic. She didn't say it had a limit or what might happen if that limit was reached.

Kreya—who was sneering slightly to show off the length of her fangs —and her group of revenant vampires stepped forward to meet the oncoming charge. They hissed and growled in guttural warning tones as the other vampires attempted to break their line. Sempre smirked with delight and folded his hands calmly in front of him.

"You should be more careful." He tutted. "Someone is going to get hurt if we're not careful." Then he snapped his fingers again.

The revenants lunged toward their recently freed kin, and my heart leapt. Blood spurted through the air as Kreya sank her fangs into someone's neck, ripping away a chunk of flesh. My mouth opened in an involuntary cry as I saw it was Alona, the tall woman from the first cell. My eyes stung with angry tears.

Three vampires attempted to pile onto Kreya, but she was helped by a revenant beside her. Something about the young woman seemed almost familiar, but her movements were too fast for me to keep up with. In a blur of violence, she smashed her fists across a younger vampire's face. He cried out in pain and reeled backward, knocking into several others.

Looking back as I rushed through removing the last few collars, my heart fell as I was reminded of Dorian during our Chicago fight. The sane vampires outnumbered the revenants, but it was no use. The revenants moved and snapped and smashed with extraordinary strength. They were compelled to protect Sempre and Zeele with their lives. Kreya and all the others would have to be bled of darkness just like Dorian had been in the cave and then again on the Chicago rooftop. But who knew if that would help? There might be too much darkness in the revenants to be drained even by this number of vampires.

Releasing the final collar, I spun and fired a shot from my gauntlet out toward the battle, aiming for a revenant who was currently grappling with Kono. Slightly farther away, Kreya tore through the shirt of an older vampire man, who soon lost his throat to her quick movements. The revenants attempted to pull his bleeding form toward them, but two vampires snatched him back. They pushed the weaker vampires to the rear of the battle, and Rhome ran toward any with collars still on, shoving them toward me.

A vampire was flung into the staircase, screaming in pain as his bones crunched on the metal. My nerves twisted into a frenzy, but I forced myself to keep going.

Dorian dropped back beside me and swept his eyes over the situation. "This is worse than madness."

I knew what he meant. Sempre controlled these revenants, and they weren't lashing out wildly. When Dorian had gone mad with darkness, he was like an animal. But Kreya moved like a well-trained beast. And her trainer? Sempre, who sat smug and safe on his incendiary mount. A sinking sensation settled over me as I recalled the conversation between Sempre and the researchers. One of them mentioned there were only a few vampires they felt reasonably confident about controlling. Did Kreya and these vampires fall into that category?

We had to stop Sempre if we wanted to stop the revenants, but as I reasoned back and forth over potential strategies in the span of a few seconds, my eyes caught movement.

Zeele, his mount bullying through the line of vampires, moved farther into the room. Three revenants attended him, leaving four to protect Sempre. Once the line was broken by Zeele's mount, Sempre followed, bringing the battle away from the door and closer to the snapping plants in the center of the room.

Dorian snarled under his breath. "I'm going for Sempre," he snapped.

Before I could protest, he leapt over a line of vampires who were being driven back by a coalition of revenants and guards. A ruler guard came charging at me from the side, and I lost sight of Dorian as I engaged in an encounter of my own.

Tapping the stone to the Immortal's armor helped me somewhat, but I still took a painful blow to my ribs that knocked the air from my lungs. Rolling to the side to avoid her plunging sword, I fired a blast from my gauntlet directly into her face, sending her reeling backward, screaming. Three vampires leapt on her falling form, sucking the darkness from her before she went still forever.

Kreya snatched up her opponent and hurled the poor woman right into Dorian's path as he fought his way to her. He skidded to a stop and growled at the revenant who had once been his friend. The woman Kreya had thrown crawled past him toward Rhome, who directed her toward me. Her desperate eyes searched mine as she shuddered beneath the collar's weight. I brought up the stone, releasing the wire, and she slumped against another vampire nearby, who gently eased her to the ground.

Kreya stepped up to Dorian, drool dripping from her mouth along with a streak of blood.

Dorian shook his head. "I'm sorry about this, Kreya."

Kreya charged him. Dorian lashed out with a punch, but she dodged it with wicked speed. She dropped her shoulder to bring him to the ground, but Dorian hurled her off. She flew violently back into the root of one of the plants. Sempre frowned. His eyebrow twitched in annoyance as he regarded Dorian.

The plant let out a strange gurgle as Kreya struck its base. Her eyelids fluttered for a moment before her terrible black eyes glared once again. She growled low under her breath like an animal, then hurled herself at him once more. This time, she managed to catch Dorian a second early. He stumbled back, and she nearly bit into his shoulder. He grabbed one of the knives from his belt and shoved it between her teeth. Her fangs collided with the metal with a painful clatter. She shrieked, grabbing at her face.

The other revenants drew closer, but the vampires gathered around Dorian. Perhaps emboldened by Dorian's ability to fight Kreya, our prisoner side wanted to fight the other three revenants.

How could I help most efficiently? Even with vampire blood coursing through my veins, I was much weaker than Kreya and her fellow revenants.

You're the only one who can operate the stone, a stern voice reminded me. By this point, I was surprised Sempre hadn't been drawn to me yet. It glowed like a miniature sun inside my hand and burned nearly as much.

"Kreya!" Rhome cried over the chaos.

She flinched for a moment, losing her focus in her fight with Dorian. Some strange battle waged on her face. Something thrumming beneath the surface fought to emerge but lost. Her eyes were black as coal and cold as ice.

She was lost to the darkness.

My blood surged with heat, my anger stoking the darkness flowing through my veins. The things they had done to Kreya... Kreya who must somehow be trapped deep inside that prison of her own mind, screaming for her children.

Dorian smashed his teeth together furiously as Kreya suddenly lunged for him. "Wake up," he snarled. "I don't want to hurt you."

Dorian was the better fighter, but Kreya was unencumbered by sentiment. Her fists smashed into Dorian, nails trying to sink deep into his skin. A few of them succeeded, ripping at Dorian's upper arms until his shadow-rich blood stained his white shirt.

"Dorian," I whispered hoarsely. Two more vampires fled from the chaos toward me, yanking at their collars. Rhome covered me as I pressed the stone to their necks. It felt like I held a burning ember now. I tucked the stone into the weapon belt as the heat became too much. Would it last much longer?

"She doesn't recognize me," Rhome muttered helplessly. His eyes darted to the other revenants with her. Four stayed back, close to Sempre, and the two with Zeele were fending off a constant flow of enraged vampires as they tried to enact their revenge upon the head researcher. Kreya and Dorian fought in the center of it all, a ring of empty space around them created by those who didn't want to get involved in this brawl.

Dorian would try to pin her down and drink from her to lessen her darkness, but just him feeding wouldn't be enough. He couldn't drain enough dark energy from her body to make a difference on his own.

Kreya reeled back as Dorian batted at her, shredding the front of her robes with the knife in his hand. To inexperienced fighters, it might look like he was trying his best to hit her, but I knew better. He was trying to get her to do something reckless in her fury. If she got close enough to him, Dorian could pin her and render her unconscious long enough to hopefully drain her of some darkness and get her away from Sempre.

Friends fighting friends. What had we come to? My white-hot stare landed on Sempre and Zeele. No, what had we been *forced* to?

CHAPTER FORTY

Another vampire fell back toward me nursing a wound on his hand that he'd sustained in the fighting. His panicked eyes met mine. "Are you destroying the collars?" he asked, voice wheezing like an old wooden house in a storm.

I nodded, turning my back on the Immortal rulers to shield the burning stone from their view. One touch, and it was done. I tucked it back in the small pouch of the weapon belt, turning to face the room once more.

Before I could locate Dorian, Roxy, and Kane in the battle, a terrible screech ripped through the room. I covered my ears with a hiss as the high-pitched sound sliced through my thoughts. Pain pounded in my head, and my muscles began to stiffen and lock up. What the hell was this?

Beside me, Rhome fell to the floor, convulsing. The young man I'd just freed hit the ground and covered his ears, gagging. A snake of red crossed my vision, followed by pulses of purple and green. Soon, an acidic rainbow swarmed through my head. I stumbled to the ground, trying to dislodge the colors and the buzz left behind by the sound.

Rhome covered his ears as best as he could and wrenched me upward as he got back to his feet, letting me lean on him. I sucked in a desperate breath as the colors began to drift away. Every part of my body thrummed with alarm.

"I was afraid of this," he said, looking past me to the mounts. "I thought the muzzles might be to keep them permanently silent, but I guess not."

The muzzles were indeed now cracked open slightly, fiery breath smoking between the metal plates.

Rhome began tearing at his shirt. "Those creatures are ash wraiths. Their cries cause distortion and eventual madness if they keep screeching. In the wild, they only use the ability for hunting, but it seems the rulers have found another purpose for it. They must be wearing something in their ears to protect them." He was seething, and a muscle popped in his jaw as he began to wind the strips of his shirt around his head to cover his ears. "Vampires are particularly susceptible to it, since we're so closely connected to the creatures of the Immortal Plane."

It was clear that the vampires were more affected. Many were still writhing on the ground around us. Some of them must've also known the ash wraiths, because they were doing the same as Rhome, ripping at their shirts to wrap strips of cloth around their heads.

A vampire with a buzzcut rolled away from the nearest ash wraith, groaning. A sturdy vampire woman snatched him up and dragged him past Rhome and me. Our numbers had dwindled. Some were making a break for the doorway, but the remaining guards had moved to block the exit. Many looked helplessly at the mounts, fear beginning to replace anger in their eyes. We were getting disconcertingly close to being trapped.

Dorian recovered well enough to snatch Kreya into a headlock, pushing through his pain to latch onto her.

Sempre pulled a lever on his saddle, and the muzzle opened fully to reveal a hooked golden beak. The ruler snapped his fingers, and his wraith darted forward, striking at the remaining vampires with its claws and newly released beak.

"Fall back," Rhome screamed. "We'll never win if we have our eyes plucked out."

Drawn by the sound, Sempre and Zeele looked over, finally catching sight of me. Zeele's electric green eyes drilled into me, burning with hatred.

The wraith struck one poor man, sending him flying backward to land at Rhome's feet.

"A gift," Sempre said with a chuckle. Zeele laughed beside him, but it was forced. If he had his way, I would soon have both my hands on a chopping block. A hand for a hand in the Immortal Plane.

I helped Rhome grab the man who'd fallen at our feet. His oily blond hair fell over his face as we yanked him up. Blood poured from a gash in his chest. Rhome hauled him toward two lingering women.

"Get him somewhere. Those who are injured, try to stay out of the way unless you want to die a pointless death."

The blond vampire swallowed, his throat bobbing. "No," he croaked. His eyes shone with determination. "I'd rather die fighting."

"Then prepare yourself," Rhome muttered, watching as the ash wraiths advanced another step, breaking up the line of vampires even further. "I don't know if we're going to get out of here alive, but we're sure as hell going to try." His stare returned to Kreya.

In the light of the hundreds of souls above us, I saw Rhome in a new way. The sanitarium had inadvertently forged a diamond by capturing Rhome, who already had the workings of a leader within him. The lines of his face had hardened from starvation. Even with his lingering injuries, he would do everything he could.

Sempre's wraith darted forward, prepared to strike once more at our throng of former prisoners, but flashes of light from a gauntlet streaked through the air. They smashed into the wraith and pushed the beast back.

Preparing to fire my own gauntlet, I spotted Roxy up on the stairs near a group of wildlings and two imprisoned rulers we had freed. She grinned, her fiery hair splayed around her like a halo as she lifted her stolen gauntlet. The wildlings and rulers had also taken gauntlets, and they were all aimed at Sempre and Zeele. The wraiths growled behind their muzzles, the metal rattling under the force of the vibration.

"Aim for the face," Dorian shouted. He finally had Kreya pinned to the ground, but she shoved him off as he turned to yell at Roxy.

"Aye, aye!" Roxy cried back and let out a barrage of shots.

The arcane beams slammed into the wraiths around their heads and necks. The beasts shuddered and tried to move away. With a savage growl, Sempre drove his heels into his mount's sides, urging it forward.

As each shot landed, Prisoner Number One made no attempt to defend himself or get off the saddle. Any wayward rays that struck him appeared to do no damage, his many chains sparking with light as each blow landed. Sempre and Zeele, however, had to duck several times, cursing in a language I didn't understand. I made a note of the difference—Prisoner Number One was warded in ways that not even the rulers were. He was basically wearing a magical bulletproof vest. Why was this creature so important to Sempre?

The ash wraith suddenly snapped its head back as Sempre released a switch on the back of the saddle. There was a flash of light at the side of the wraith's head, then it opened its beak and let out an ear-shattering shriek. I clapped my palms over my ears, sweat slick against my skin. The cry squirmed its way through any opening and tried to pierce my brain. I fought the colors and sounds, knowing to expect them now.

A few vampires weren't fast enough and fell to their knees, moaning and groaning. The wraith charged forward as defenses plummeted, its glowing eyes promising vengeance. Keeping in line with the ash wraiths, the revenants moved forward too.

Dorian snarled as Kreya landed a swipe across his face that knocked him onto his back. Kreya hovered above him, her dark eyes bleeding shadows.

Leaping up onto a table, I released a shot from my gauntlet, aiming for a revenant coming in from the side to help Kreya in her attack. The revenant yelped and rolled away before immediately leaping up again with a snarl. The hood fell back, and my glimmer of recognition from earlier grew into heartbroken surprise. It was Myndra, Sabal's missing twin sister. Her long dark hair had been shaved off and her face was gaunt with hunger, but I was certain. Perhaps the sigil of comfort and remembrance Sabal had painted on her door in the barracks hadn't been in vain.

Without warning, Rhome took off, throwing himself between Kreya and Dorian. Kreya stumbled backward, her lips curling into a frustrated sneer. Rhome swayed slightly, his limp causing him to favor one side.

"Please," he begged. "Please, Kreya. I know you're still in there somewhere."

Kreya hesitated, her sneer melting into a furrowed brow. She shook her head and grunted. Her nails raked across her bare scalp, drawing thick black blood.

"Stop hurting yourself," Rhome said in a voice so soft and caring it threatened to rip my heart from my chest. Smaller fights continued to whirl around them, but I could see that for Rhome, it was just the two of them.

Dorian scrambled to his feet, dark energy dripping from his mouth where he'd managed to grab a mouthful from Kreya. He remained ready to strike if needed, his eyes never leaving the revenant.

Kreya snarled like a desperate animal with her leg caught in a trap.

"Please," Rhome said again. "I don't want to hurt you. You're supposed to be helping me find the children, remember? Carwin and Detra are somewhere in the palace. Sempre is keeping them as pets."

Sempre bristled on the back of his wraith, which he'd managed to rein in for the moment. A flicker of worry passed over his pompous face. Was he thinking back to what his researchers had told him about the link to the revenant vampires being unpredictable?

Which fire do we put out first? I glanced from Kreya to Sempre to Myndra to Zeele. Roxy and her band of new friends hovered on the upper levels, clearly thinking the same thing.

Kreya let out an abrupt roar of fury and launched herself at Rhome.

I needed to be closer. I darted through the crowd—some of the vampires were still engaged in occasional sporadic bouts of combat, but most were watching the wraiths. Without even asking, whenever I spotted a collar I'd missed, I simply snatched up the stone and pressed it to the vampire's neck. The collars fell away and the stone burned, leaving a welt in my palm after I tucked it back into the weapons belt.

The last vampire, a short woman, patted her neck and stared at me. "It's gone?" Her eyes filled with tears.

I nodded. There was no time to explain to her. I turned back to the fight. Kreya grappled with Rhome, her fingers digging deep into his bony arms as she attempted to throw him around. He shuddered, weakened on one side and generally exhausted.

Should I join the fray? My skin would be sliced open like ribbons beneath Kreya's fury. I stared at the other revenants who still hovered near Sempre and Zeele.

Before I got the chance to help Rhome, Dorian leapt forward onto Kreya's back. He clamped his arm around her neck to keep her from tearing at Rhome's throat.

Rhome stumbled back a moment, putting a protective hand near his neck, fingers coming away bloody from where she had already made contact. His eyes darkened as he watched Kreya struggle against Dorian.

An expression I'd never seen before passed over his determined face. His fangs flashed as he stepped forward.

"I'm sorry," he said, the words reaching everyone in the sudden lull that fell over the room.

A slight movement caught my eye as Sempre reached for a lever on the saddle. The wraith's head reared back, and I saw its beak begin to open.

"Rhome, look out!" I yelled.

But Rhome was single-minded. With a cry that was almost a sob, he dug his nails into the flesh of his wife's forehead, ripping the gem away as Kreya let out a piercing scream of pain.

She screamed and screamed, and I saw the gem sitting in Rhome's hand, dripping with gore and surrounded by spidery wires.

Everyone froze as Sempre began to echo her screams.

CHAPTER FORTY-ONE

Kreya's and Sempre's cries rose together, but soon Sempre's swallowed hers up completely. The inherent power in his voice sent his wail of agony echoing throughout the room. It was followed by a deafening hush as shocked faces stared at the Immortal ruler.

Our small team from the Mortal Plane only had eyes for Kreya, who was now blindly staggering away from Rhome. She clutched at her head and wept, drops of blood flying from between her hands as she shook her head frantically. The blood was inky darkness, slight flecks of red all that remained of her regular blood.

The wraiths bucked and jerked, reacting to the sound of Sempre's cry. He was pawing at his face, no longer controlling his mount, and without the muzzle to keep its mouth closed, the ash wraith let out a piercing scream of misery.

I clutched at my ears, feeling the bone-shaking effects as bodies around me buckled to their knees or writhed or tried to flee. The sturdy woman I had just freed from her collar ran past me with ragged breathing.

My stomach soured as my vision began to blur, the vampires around me becoming little more than smudges. Red flashed, and I shuddered as bile rose up the back of my throat. Something about the wraith's cry sank deep into my nerves. No amount of training could counter the effects of an Immortal beast like this.

Sempre finally stopped screaming and sucked in a sharp, pained breath, yanking a lever on the saddle to shut the wraith's muzzle. I stumbled to my knees, losing the fight against the weakness. I tried desperately to keep my slick palms on my ears as I breathed. The air was filled with the scent of spilled blood and the musky stench of the monstrous plants.

Through the madness, I saw that Kreya no longer pawed at her forehead and had covered her ears. Trails of shadowy tears stained her face, and she groaned. Blood dripped steadily from the shallow indentation in the center of her forehead. Rhome, his ears covered, had managed to resist the worst of the wraith's cry but had fallen to his knees. The bloody glint of Kreya's stone peeked from his hand.

Dorian was still standing, hands clamped over his ears. His lips curled in horror at the sight of Kreya and Rhome covered in blood.

Focus on Sempre.

I struggled to my feet, keeping half an eye on Myndra. If I could do something similar to her, it would take another revenant from Sempre.

Sempre gnashed his teeth, nothing but loathing and hatred pouring from his narrowed eyes. Those among the vampires who had fared best with the wraith's cry looked at him. Even through the haze of chaos, I could practically hear the flicker of invisible light bulbs sparking above our group as we all came to the same conclusion.

Lord Sempre was connected to these revenants. He had been wounded while still on his mount. If he could be hurt, he could be killed.

The remaining guards sensed the shift in mood and started to rush forward from where they had been barricading the door, but the vampires were faster, surging toward Sempre and Zeele's mounts with renewed vigor.

On the upper level, Roxy stomped to gain the attention of her scattered gauntlet crew. A few of them remained in commission. One ruler and two wildlings were ripping their clothes to cover their ears. Roxy motioned for them to follow her, and they hurried down the steps, utterly unnoticed by everyone but me. She brought them to hide behind the base of one of the plants. Poking her head out to glance at the situation, she caught my eye and grinned.

Her hands went to her shirt. She ripped half of it, revealing her muscled midriff. She began to tear the fabric into ribbons, layering them together and tying them over her ears. I did the same. As I quickly tore at my clothes, my only concern was whether I would be able to hear the battle.

Balling up several strips over my ears, I wrapped another piece around my head to hold the pads in place. The material of the Hive shirt worked well, blocking out the low-rumbling moans and Kreya's continued sobbing.

With my hearing mostly secured, I rushed into the fray. The stone burned my newly bare stomach through the weapons belt, a constant reminder that I was carrying a volatile ace up my sleeve.

The wraiths needed to be neutralized. Even if we dispatched Sempre and Zeele, the animals seemed prone to screech when threatened. Perhaps we could jam the mechanism on the saddle that opened and closed the muzzle. If we could keep it shut, that would help us immensely.

Seeing me hop into action, a flurry of vampires followed, scraps of fabric tied around their heads to block out the sound. We probably looked like a group of starved, savage bandits to Sempre and Zeele. I curled my hands into fists as I ran toward them. Good. Let them see the raw brutality that their cruel actions had inspired.

As I drew close, Myndra lunged for me, but I managed to side-step her long enough for Kono, who had joined me from the heart of the fray, to tackle her. As the two of them spun away in a tangle of violence, I saw that *blood* leaked from her ears. The revenants had endured the full brunt of the wraths' cries with zero protection. As cruel as it sounded, I hoped Sempre's callousness would be the oversight that cost him this fight. In his disdain for his pet soldiers, he'd forgotten to protect his most potent weapons.

My body burned with fury, and I pushed on through the melee.

Another revenant tried to grab my legs, but two vampires, a set of twin teenage boys, quickly pushed him back.

"We've got your back," one of them cried.

It was close and loud enough to hear through my makeshift earplugs. They pinned the revenant to the ground, both diving in to feed. A wave of hope and adrenaline crashed over me. My fingers buzzed to snatch Sempre off his wraith.

A film reel of something dangerous flashed through my mind. I raised my gauntlet in Sempre's direct line of sight and let out a flurry of blasts aimed right at his wraith. The cloth over my ears muffled the explosions as they fired from my palm, and I watched as they made contact with the wraith. On impact, the saddle lit up with ghostly engravings similar to those on the chains wrapped around Prisoner Number One. I could make out a few glyphs here and there, but nothing significant. Still, if they were magic and we took them away, we took power away from Sempre.

I fired off another round of shots at the wraith, watching as it tossed its head, fighting with the harness to avoid the attack. The wraith let out a smaller cry than before, and while the shockwave rolled through the room, those of us who had covered our ears were slowed for less time than before. The sound only made me pause for a few seconds before I pressed onward.

As I drew closer and the wraith stopped its scream, I found my voice.

"Sempre," I shouted, ensuring my voice was as loud and venomous as possible. "Aren't you just infuriated that your precious prisoners are going to finally take their revenge? After all your monstrous talk of sending revenants to the Mortal Plane to cause chaos, you're going to die here before you even have a chance to prove you're more than a pet pulled along on a leash by Irrikus. All this time spent killing vampires for dark energy and feeding them to these plants because you're secretly terrified of them. Some part of you must hate that the only thing that gives you power is monopolizing your greatest enemy."

I fired at his wraith. Sempre's silver hair was blown back as he avoided the blast only by wrenching the wraith to the side. The burning beast swiped at me with its talons and beak in response, but I pulled back, firing off another blast as I went.

Sempre snarled. "You disgusting little bug." Although everything else was muffled, his voice rang out crystal clear in my mind, the ruler's sway cutting through my covering. "You're too late. The plans of the Immortal Council *will not* be stopped. The first wave of revenants is already on its way to the Mortal Plane."

He laughed. It echoed in my head with horrifying volume, as if his lips were just beside my ear. I gnashed my teeth together. Zach, Morag, Gina, Bravi—everyone at the VAMPS camp was in danger. Driven to a frenzy, I lunged toward the wraith like a wild dog.

"If I catch you, I'm sewing your mouth shut," I yelled and fired at the wraith. Even at close range, the warding took most of the force out of the blow. It took the hit with a pained squeal, then charged toward me.

Diving aside, I led with my shoulder to roll smoothly and immediately leap back up to my feet. As I did, Prisoner Number One stared at me with wide eyes like he was trying to say something. But what?

Sempre leaned his head back to laugh with all the warmth of an icicle. "My revenants will clear out your base in Scotland very soon. Surprise attacks are such fun, aren't they?" A menacing smile crossed his face. "Moab will be next. I'll be headed to the tear as soon as I deal with you and your stupid riot."

I wrenched the hand ax from my belt. The wraith hesitated, all four glowing eyes on the weapon. I raised the gauntlet. "You're sick."

Sempre shook his head at my words. "Your mortal mind can't understand, can it? This is the natural order. Vampires are dirty leeches. Humans are fuel. You're nothing more than a meat puppet meant for evil." He lifted his arms, the billowing sleeves falling open. "The darkness grows within your kind because they are stupid and greedy. I've seen memories of your wars, your crimes, your depraved acts. We watch you fight one another like simpletons. It's so easy. Why else would you be so easy to influence? So easy to bait? You and your kind cause nothing but suffering and hate."

He sat atop his wraith, no doubt seeing himself as an Immortal messiah preaching his sick prophecies. The vampires not currently engaged with any of the revenants glared at him.

Fury burned through me, the flames of my anger licking at my skin. Blood oozed into my mouth as my teeth cut into my tongue. I stared at him, my vision going dark at the edges as I surveyed his most vital points. My body begged me to charge him, but something held me back. The wraith clacked its beak, and I gripped the ax tighter in my hand.

Behind Sempre, the prisoner stared hard at me with his eerie violet eyes. I froze for a moment. It was as though he were warning me to stop. Sempre wanted me to attack him. Of course he did—and I wanted to do it.

What was so valuable about this prisoner that Sempre rode to battle with him atop an ash wraith?

I grabbed the ax handle hard, feeling my knuckles whiten. "Prisoner Number One," I yelled. "I don't know why they're keeping you here, but we'll help you! I know you want more than these walls. We can free you!"

My shout reached him. Something sparked behind those odd eyes, but he remained as silent as a statue.

Talk to me. I pleaded with my eyes as best as I could.

Sempre snarled and rolled his eyes. "Oh, please. This thing is merely a shell, so there is no point in appealing to him. He's been insane for a hundred times longer than you've been alive." He sneered, and the ugliness of the expression warped his terrible beauty. "He'd just as likely tear your face off as help you."

Prisoner Number One said nothing. He merely kept staring at me. Then I thought I saw his finger change minutely, the tip becoming reminiscent of the blade I'd noticed earlier as he traced something in the air.

Sempre saw the hope still lingering on my face and spat in my direction. "Idiot."

I raised my brows in a mocking response. He was agitated, which meant I had scratched at some truth. Somewhere deep down inside, I knew Prisoner Number One was the sanitarium's greatest treasure. He *did* something that Sempre and Irrikus needed.

A revenant came at me from the side, his hollow black eyes glaring at me. His face was gaunt and dark as pitch, transformed by the shadows beneath his skin. He snarled at me in a blind rage. I jerked myself back as he swept his arm toward my throat.

A shock of blue light from one of the wildlings using a gauntlet struck him in the chest. He let out a pained growl as he flew backward into one of his allies. More vampires pushed into Sempre's dark forces, but the revenants were being joined by more guards. Our strength remained in the sheer number of prisoners we had released, and we didn't have time to stand around talking when more guards were undoubtedly on their way.

Sempre's nostrils flared as he regarded me coolly. "It's time for your little rebellion to end," he snapped. "I have things to do."

His hand flew to a copper lever at the side of the wraith's harness. My body tensed, knowing what would happen next as the lever released the muzzle on the wraith.

I slammed one hand against my head, covering my closest ear as much as possible. The ash wraith opened its crooked beak and screeched its terrible cry. The cloth over my ears helped, but it wasn't enough to completely block the sound.

With a shake, I brought up my gauntlet to aim at the wraith's mouth. I winced and released my clenched fist, the light blazing from the gem and slamming into the wraith's open mouth.

Everything happened in a flash. The cry of the wraith shifted abruptly into a stomach-turning gurgle. A wet spitting sound erupted from its smoking beak, like fire being hit by water. The wraith scrambled backward, clawing at the ground and trying to regain its balance. It let out a pained little cry with none of the usual effects as it skidded into the base of one of the carnivorous plants.

Sempre tried to hold on, but the wraith bucked and twisted with such ferocity that he flew out of the saddle as the creature smashed into the plant's base. Prisoner Number One rolled off its back, narrowly avoiding being trampled by its clawed feet. Sempre tried to land on his feet but stumbled. It gave me precious few moments to act.

I rushed toward Prisoner Number One where he had landed several yards from me, curled on his side. I raced through the whirling battle, leaping over fallen bodies and avoiding blows from guards and revenants. I had to get to the prisoner before Sempre did. I needed to set one final prisoner loose.

"You little—" Sempre descended into a string of foul-mouthed curses in the universal language.

I dropped to the prisoner's side, shaking his shoulder gently. His sienna skin was papery under my touch. He shook his head woozily and tried to pull himself up. His violet eyes were blank, the lack of pupils even stranger up close. I took a deep breath as I gently placed my hand onto one of his gangly arms.

"I'm not going to hurt you," I promised as I helped haul him back to his feet. When he stood, he was around my height. He stared at me neutrally as I lifted my gem gauntlet to the side of his head. "Trust me. Please." I had no idea if he even understood me, but he put up no resistance.

I turned. Sempre was headed our way, a slight limp on his left side. His face contorted into a furious grimace of rage. Blood trickled down from the corner of his mouth. "You. How dare you." He stopped when he saw my gauntlet placed against the creature's head.

"Call off the attack in the Mortal Plane," I yelled. "Or I'll shoot your most important asset." I squeezed the prisoner's arm, praying he understood that I was trying to bluff Sempre. If my hunch was right, this creature was important… important enough for Sempre to listen to me.

Behind Sempre, Dorian and Kono were joined by Kane as they circled two of the remaining revenants like wolves. Rhome crouched beside Kreya, whose face I couldn't see. Across the room, Zeele was pulled off his mount by a mob of vampires, and surrounded by them. He somehow broke free, and ran. The rest of the vampires were either drinking from fallen revenants or were picking off the last of the current guards.

Sempre pulled his lips into a tight grimace and dusted off his silver-and-blue robes as if dusting off my threat. Drawing himself up to his full eight feet, he folded his arms. Even with his injury, he wanted to establish his dominance.

Bracing myself for a struggle, I made a move to clench my fist, hoping it would scare him. Sempre's mouth twitched, and I saw panic flash across his eyes as his gaze darted to Prisoner Number One.

"No," he said firmly, then added, "You won't move, human."

His voice echoed through the room. The force of it stilled my entire body, my feet rooting themselves to the ground. His powerful influence brought a cruel but furious smile to his face.

"I'll shoot him," I said, my voice trembling as my body felt the effects of the thrall in Sempre's voice. I tried to make another threat, but my throat tightened. Beneath my fingers, the metal of Prisoner Number One's collar pricked my skin.

"Oh, I don't think you will." Sempre narrowed his eyes. "Release the prisoner. He's mine."

CHAPTER FORTY-TWO

My traitorous body began to tremble as I resisted Sempre's order. My fingers slackened around Prisoner Number One's collar. I willed my body to resist the call to push him forward to the awaiting Immortal ruler. If Sempre wanted an easy surrender, I would give him hell instead.

Sempre clenched his jaw and glared at me. "I. Said. Release. Him."

Resist. Don't give in.

I took a ragged breath, my core muscles seizing, desperate to force me into movement. The power in Sempre's voice slithered into my ears, commanding my brain to move my body, but I refused to let the prisoner go. He might be our only chance of survival. I glared hard at Sempre, who watched and said nothing as his expression darkened. Did it upset him to see a mere human resist his powerful call? I hoped it made him furious.

As my mind and heart raged with the chaos of this inner fight, I could barely see Prisoner One out of the corner of my eye, but I felt the movement as he gently turned toward me with a tilt of his head. Still fighting the command from Sempre, I glanced at the creature I was ostensibly holding hostage. Meeting the pupil-less eyes that regarded me, I hoped that breaking eye contact with the ruler wouldn't compromise my resistance to his will.

For the first time, Prisoner One finally had a small spark of life in his eyes. He looked as if he'd just woken from a very long rest as he blinked slowly, a shadow of engagement shining in those lavender eyes.

His fingers twitched, always seeming to trace some unknown shape or sigil in the air.

"Shoot me," he whispered. "Do it. Anything is better than being stuck in this place for another moment. I just want to be free. Please."

The desperate request hit me like a punch. His voice rumbled, a deep bass with a scratchy quality that made it sound as though he'd been in need of a drink of water since his capture. My muscles stopped turning against me, the command nullified by a cold sensation of sadness that crept over me. Slowly, my body relaxed. I managed to turn my head toward him, the call of Sempre's demand forgotten.

"I won't kill you," I said. My eyes fell to his collar. "But I will free you."

Snatching the stone from the pocket of the weapons belt, I pressed it against Prisoner One's collar. It was thicker than any of the others I'd dealt with so far and was made of a blue twisted metal cord.

"No!" Sempre bellowed, not entirely understanding, but recognizing that it wasn't good that I was disobeying his direct command.

The collar shimmered and sparked. The stone flashed with heat in my hand and seared my skin, causing me to let out a yelp of pain. Then, with a definitive clatter, the collar fell to the ground, dull gray smoke twisting up elegantly from the metal.

Prisoner One swayed for a moment, his fingers gently pressed to his bare neck, which was marked with a deep brown ring. His lips parted, and I tensed, unsure what to do or what was happening.

"You fool," Sempre growled, and for the first time, I saw genuine fear in his face.

Prisoner One shook his head from side to side, weaving like a snake as he reveled in his release. His eyes widened, dazed, and he let out a low chuckle as a grin spread across his face, revealing huge sharp teeth stained yellow with time. "Oh," he said, tipping his head back. "Oh, I had forgotten what this feels like."

The stone burned in my hand like a tiny sun, rays of light spilling from between my fingers. I had to surrender a strip of cloth that was covering my ear to be able to keep holding onto the stone. With some slight relief from the pain, I surveyed the rest of Prisoner One's body, taking stock of the chains and the shackles etched with glyphs that restrained him. Would it overdo the stone if I used it one more time? It already felt dangerous.

A surge of energy rushed through me. I had to try.

Sempre growled as I lifted the stone again. "Stop! I command you. Stop!"

His cries buzzed at my ears like annoying gnats. I grinned, delighted to find my body no longer struggled to resist Sempre's orders. It was like a mental shield had slammed down over my will, protecting me from his sway. Dropping into a crouch, I struck out with the stone at every lock, buckle, and fastening I could see. First, I took out the restraints around his ankles, which I saw had worn into his skin over time, just like on his neck. No doubt the sores would heal in time, but the scars would be a permanent reminder of the many years he'd lived as a captive of the Immortal rulers in this awful place. Moving upward, I tapped the burning stone to the restraints around his waist, which connected to chains hooked to the restraints on his arms. A few rapid taps, and the whole construction fell apart.

With each touch, the stone's heat seared into my hand. My adrenaline kept the worst of the pain at bay, but now I felt like I was floating outside my body. I moved with a crazed quickness, desperate to release the prisoner from Sempre's clutches for good.

Sempre took a step forward, but several vampires immediately blocked his path, snarling. He struck out at them, but they nimbly avoided his grasp. "Stop!"

Sempre was powerless to control me.

Prisoner One shuddered as I started neutralizing the multicolored gems set into the chains that were strung all over his body. Each one shattered as I touched it, the removal of the magic exploding the jewel. Several shards sliced into my arms and bare stomach, leaving hairline trails of blood along my skin. As I cleared the spells, it occurred to me that the prisoner must be extremely powerful if the rulers had loaded him down with this many protections.

Too late to turn back now.

With a final crackling spark, I finished with the last jewel, and the prisoner gave a startled gasp, abruptly dropping to his knees. The stone burned painfully in my hand, but I couldn't seem to drop it or put it back in my pouch. My fingers grasped it tightly, ignoring the agony as the already raw skin of my palm continued to be scorched. I didn't want to let it go.

Slowly, a sensation—different from just mere adrenaline—began to prickle across the back of my head. Blood rushed to my face, my eyes stinging with heat. I breathed in, dizzy, and as I did, the creature before me appeared to shift and change. Was this... was this what an aura felt like? The air around him shimmered like a ripple across a pond. He was all at once stranger, wilder, and yet more familiar than before.

I let the sensation overwhelm me for a moment, then reached to help the prisoner. Before I could take his hand, the heavy point of a boot smashed into my back with sharp pain. I gasped, feeling one of my ribs crack from the force of the blow. I rolled several times, blood pounding in my ears in response to the pain. Somewhere, I heard a muffled yell as Dorian called out my name. The overwhelming sensation of this strange new perception stopped as the world swirled around me.

Gasping for breath, I closed my eyes against the pain. When I opened them again, Sempre was standing over me, his face red with rage.

"Do you have any idea what you've just done?" he asked, livid and breathing heavily. "You maggot beneath my boot, you have no idea what you have just unleashed."

I opened my mouth to reply when a whooshing wail of victory ripped through the room.

It was reminiscent of the roar of an enormous bonfire exploding to life. It surged through the entire chamber, vibrating the yellow glass around the plants, making the metal stairs and catwalks shake from the power of the cry.

A giant clawed hand snatched Sempre from the ground. I stared at its sienna-red scales and long, knife-like talons as the hand tightened around the ruler's chest. He shrieked with pain, struggling to free his arm from the clawed grip and pull his dagger from his belt. Flailing as his torso was crushed, Sempre stabbed the massive hand, driving his blade into one of its fingers, but there wasn't so much as a twitch in response.

My eyes followed along a lengthy outstretched arm that connected to a giant reptilian body of the same sienna color. Enormous wings stretched from the creature's back, briefly shading its face for a moment but not concealing the sharp teeth with deep yellow stains. Its eyes were dark purple and devoid of pupils. The beast glared at Sempre, who wailed as the creature squeezed him again.

I craned my neck to take in the brutal majesty of Prisoner One's new form. It was wild but truly magical-looking. What agony it must have been to be confined like that by the rulers, trapped in a puny remnant of his true form. Head still reeling, I stared up at him, unable to believe my eyes. How could that gangly prisoner transform into such a magnificent beast?

Sempre screamed for his revenants. "Kill him!" He stabbed at the fist again.

Two of the remaining revenants managed to vault past Kane and Dorian, who were distracted by the new creature just like everyone else. Myndra, bleeding slightly from her neck, attempted to grab the creature's massive clawed leg, but the beast merely let out a snort. It whipped a long tail I hadn't noticed before, smashing away the revenants and sending their bodies across the room with shocking force. Myndra let out a pitiful groan as she struck the wall alongside her comrade. They sank to the ground, motionless.

Silence fell over the chamber.

Scrabbling to my feet, a seed of fear started to bloom in my chest, and I backed away from the monster as my survival instincts kicked in.

The beast paid me no mind. He looked down at Sempre and gave him another tight squeeze, shaking the ruler like a rag doll.

"Nine *hundred* years in shackles. You of all creatures should know how long that is," he hissed icily. His nostrils, horizontal slits in his face, flared as he let out a long exhale.

Sempre stuttered, blubbering something between shaking lips. He could find no words. He shivered violently in the creature's grasp, reduced to a mute in his terror.

The beast laughed, the hollow chuckle vibrating like thunder through the chamber and echoing off the vast vaulted ceiling above us. "Oh, don't worry. You will."

The wings gave a mighty flap, the downdraft knocking me to my knees once more. With a burst of speed, the creature who had once been Prisoner One flew toward the far wall of the prison. Sempre screamed— for help, for someone, for anything.

There was a gut-churning tearing sound, and despite the creature not touching it, a portion of the wall ripped open like paper. Amber soul-light spilled from the tear, further illuminating the chaos inside the chamber and accompanied by fresh air that cleared the stench of blood and death and fear. Everyone watched the creature hover in front of the hole, the tear too small to allow passage for his giant frame. A crunching sound reached my ears as the creature began to change. His form rearranged, bones popping and cracking, skin undulating into new shapes, form elongating until he took on a long and narrow snake-like form. Sempre was still clutched in his clawed fist, and his shriek was the last sound I heard as the creature slithered through the hole and disappeared. The last thing I saw was his pointed oxblood tail as it vanished from sight.

Only a few seconds passed before an itch exploded in my brain, a throb that started in the front of my head before sliding slowly to the side as if a magnet were pulling a steel plate around the inside of my skull. Somehow, I knew it was the creature, the energy I was sensing a match for the beast I had unleashed.

A hunch was beginning to form, a line from an old journal Laini had read to me days ago.

You shall know him by his shifting form and his treachery.

I needed to run after them. If what the journal said was true, then he might be the only thing that could help mend the tear between the planes.

My nerves burned frantically as I stared at the amber-light-filled tear, desperately trying to think of how I could go after him. Someone caught me by the elbow, pulling me from my whirling thoughts.

"Lyra," Dorian breathed. He pulled me to him and hugged me tightly, backing off with an apology when I winced from the pain in my broken rib. "What was that thing?"

I looked between him and the tear in the wall, my hunch solidifying into certainty.

"Dorian," I said, taking his hands in mine. "I need to go after him. I think… I think that was the Gate Maker."

CHAPTER FORTY-THREE

"What?" Dorian stared at me, stunned. His clothes were torn, and deep scratches marred with rivulets of red peeked through the rips. I hovered my hand over them as if I could touch them and heal them somehow. He looked like someone had sent him through a shredder.

I shook my head as the itch to follow Prisoner One grew more intense. I gently pressed a hand to Dorian's chest and let the world around us fade away as I breathed in his scent, leaning in to rest my head on his chest. My muscles relaxed, the pain from my cracked rib and burned hand receding into the background for a blissful moment.

"I saw him in solitary confinement," I explained, pulling away again so he could see my face. "The prisoner. Sempre sent guards to take him out during the night. They said something about him doing his duty, whatever that means. I knew he must be important to Sempre, so I took a risk to free him. I wasn't expecting that, though."

"I don't think anyone was," Dorian noted, looking around at everyone left with us in the chamber.

I did the same. Most of the guards and researchers were dead, their blood staining the stone floor. Over on the other side of the room, I saw Roxy and Kane going through the bodies, gathering weapons and armor that could be of use while avoiding the corpses that were surrounded by hungry former prisoners. Those vampires that weren't still feeding on sanitarium staff were staring at the gaping wall, probably enjoying the feeling of clear air on their faces for the first time in who knew how long. A few of them regarded the revenants, several of whom were laid out apparently lifeless—it seemed that it was possible to drain even the immense amounts of dark energy from their bodies if there were enough starving vampires to do it. The two who had been struck by the trans-formed Prisoner One were still in crumpled heaps on the ground where they'd landed. The remaining three were imprisoned in one of the cells, snarling and battering against the glass.

Dorian eyed them warily, then turned back to face the tear. "I don't know of anything in the Immortal Plane that can shapeshift to that extent. Unless there are some powerful unknown spells at work." He frowned, plucking a shard of gem from my forearm. "How do you think he tore open the wall?"

I tried to play back the sequence in my mind. The ripping sound happened before the actual tear, and I hadn't seen him touch the wall to pull it open. I imagined these walls were as stable as any of the others in the sanitarium.

"I'm guessing magic of some kind," I said. "I think this is a creature with the ability to create portals in the barrier that separates the Mortal Plane and the Immortal Plane. If I'm right, then getting through a basic wall is probably not that difficult."

I looked back to the wall. Some of the vampires had joined us, but nobody dared to venture past the point where Dorian and I stood. The wall looked like it nursed an angry wound, split open by whatever powerful magic the creature had used.

"We should go after it," Dorian said, his voice rising. "Lyra, this could be our chance!"

The itch in my head wanted to jump on his suggestion, but before I could address the logistics of how we would go about that, a soft cry caught my ear. Rhome was hunched over Kreya far behind our group, holding her and rocking back and forth as she twitched and wailed.

"Sempre claimed that he'd sent a group of revenants to attack our friends and family in the VAMPS camp," I reminded him. "If they're like Kreya and are connected to Sempre through the gems, then there's a chance that if he dies, they might lose their urge to create havoc. But considering how much darkness is in them and what it's done to their mental state..." I trailed off, unable to finish my thought as I stared at the blood staining Kreya's hands. She continued to press them against her forehead.

Sempre's disappearance was unlikely to stop the attack if it had already started, which meant we needed to get back to the Mortal Plane as quickly as we could. The first thing to do was to secure the area and find a way out of here. I looked around the room. We also needed to gather all our friends and any possible allies interested in escaping to the Mortal Plane.

Weaving together memories of the interior of the sanitarium, I began formulating exit strategies while I surveyed the situation in the chamber. The two revenants who had been thrown into the wall—one of whom was Myndra—were now on their feet surrounded by a group of vampires but weren't currently putting up any kind of fight.

I stared at the two figures swaying in the center of a circle of vampires. The revenants looked around with wild eyes and furrowed brows. The vampires watched them warily, flinching and getting ready to pounce any time they saw one of the revenants so much as twitch.

Myndra was shaking and clawing at her face, hissing. The vampires gave her plenty of space. She snapped her teeth together and grimaced, some internal pain bothering her. A red gem matching the one Rhome had pulled from Kreya burned in the center of her forehead. Fangs extended, she curled her lips, seemingly unable to decide whether she should jump forward and sink her fangs into someone or curl into a ball. She looked utterly lost.

"Poor Myndra," I muttered, staring at her. Her cheeks were hollow, her electric green eyes turned solid black by whatever tortures Zeele and Sempre had performed on her.

Dorian squeezed my unburned hand and began to walk in her direction. I went with him.

Her companion, a gaunt-faced man, began to look around wildly at the crowd of vampires. Balling his hands into fists, he knocked them against his chest as Myndra continued to scratch at her own skin. I pressed my lips into a fine line. Our approach agitated them, but we couldn't let them loose again.

As I took another step, Myndra suddenly froze, her face going slack as she began to pale. No, she wasn't paling—she was disappearing. I choked back a startled gasp as Myndra and the other revenants rippled like someone had submerged them underwater before they vanished from the chamber completely.

"What...?" a sturdy female vampire asked, uncertain. "What just happened?"

Her words sparked a chain reaction of disbelieving outbursts from the vampires. Where the hell had the revenant vampires gone? I turned to Dorian, who stared back at me.

"Did they just—?" I couldn't even finish the thought.

Dorian blinked. "I think... they just traveled to the Mortal Plane without a circle. It's the only reason I can think of that a vampire would disappear like that."

"What's going on?" someone asked from the crowd.

I pressed a hand to my head and looked at the empty spot where Myndra and the other vampire had been. "The Mortal Plane? How could that happen?"

Dorian glanced at the tear on the wall and then at the place where the vampires had disappeared. "It takes so much energy to phase to the Mortal Plane like that," he said. "It could go so badly. Only insane vampires would try it. That's why everyone is freaking out."

He lifted a hand, drawing the attention of the gathered vampires. "Everyone. Let's calm down. We need to regroup." He picked someone from the crowd, a lanky young man with dull brown hair. "Can you take stock of any injuries?"

The youth nodded and hopped to it. I was thankful that nobody challenged Dorian's authority in this situation. It wasn't surprising, since we had been the ones to free everyone, but I hoped this sense of cooperation would last while we figured out what to do about Prisoner One.

I glanced at our comrades and saw many of them nursing wounds. Slashes, cuts, bruises, and a few appeared to be limping on bad injuries or clutching broken arms to their chests. The revenants had fought like hell, and now they were simply... gone.

"If they're filled with darkness, that could've made the process easier. Or at least *possible*." He frowned, his handsome face twisting as he mulled something over. "This means they're more dangerous than we thought. But if they went through here, then they'll still have to travel across the ocean in the Mortal Plane to get to the Immortal Plane parallel with Scotland. Maybe there's still time to warn them if we find some redbills and fly for the portal that would bring us out near the VAMPS camp." His voice ended on an upbeat note of hope, but I frowned as I digested the information.

We had to warn our teammates. If it was already too late, then we had to get there so we could help with the fight. We needed a way to get there fast. I glanced at the tear over my shoulder.

Dorian turned toward me and began to say something, but a jarring commotion rang out behind us, cutting him off.

"Let us out!" someone shouted.

I whirled around to see more prison cells lining the wall on the other side of the room.

Dorian cursed. "There are more?"

We hadn't spotted them in the chaos, and the structure of the room kept these other areas in a blind spot. We took off toward the cells without another thought. There would be more collars to undo, and I hoped the stone could handle it.

A small group of vampires crowded around the three cells, and I spotted one lifting a stolen guard's bracelet to open the wall. Another group had already been liberated. The vampires were spilling out, rapidly blurting questions at their fellow kin, their collars still in place. It was chaos—I could barely make out what was being said.

Then came one distinct shout. "Stop!"

Jumping up onto a crate to see over the crowd, I spotted a familiar pair of terrified green eyes. During the skirmish with Sempre, Zeele had managed to get inside one of the yellow glass cells along with his ash wraith and a guard. The guard was now dead and being picked at by the wraith, while Zeele was shouting furiously at four collared vampires who were clawing at the glass. Their fangs were extended, and their eyes were wild with hunger as they terrorized the very Immortal who had spent his time starving them. They wanted Zeele, full of darkness, to feast on. It was lucky for him that none of his immediate attackers wore any kind of bracelet to get through the glass.

"Filthy leeches," Zeele screeched. "Every last one of you. You're disgusting. Just wait until reinforcements come."

He was trying to wield some of his former intimidation, but it was like watching a puppy trying to be menacing. The wraith scraped its beak over the guard's body on the ground even though it couldn't open its beak more than an inch with the muzzle on.

Dorian pushed his way through to the front, and I followed along behind him until we were standing in front of Zeele's pen. Seeing the ruler's frightened face sent a mixture of fury and delight through me, but my soldier's logic sliced through the furious thoughts of revenge. Zeele would have valuable information we could use, and I planned on exploiting that fact.

"Let's see what he knows," I whispered to Dorian. He nodded.

"No!" Zeele shrieked when he saw me pull out his bracelets from the pouch on my belt.

Ignoring him completely, I pressed the bracelets against the glass and waved for Dorian to follow me. Together we slipped through the yellow glass. The waiting vampires rushed to follow us, but I immediately snatched the bracelet away to reseal the barrier. They clawed angrily at the yellow glass.

Dorian smirked. "Sorry, guys. Not yet."

Zeele's face blanched in horror.

I faced him, letting my rage and the darkness he'd forced into my blood show through. "Are you afraid? You should be."

CHAPTER FORTY-FOUR

Dorian was quick. He yanked Zeele to the side and toppled him before the Immortal could react.

The ash wraith's head swung threateningly into the air, beak aiming for Dorian as Zeele went down with a pained cry, the reins pulling at the agitated wraith's head as he fell. I yanked the reins away from him, wincing as the leather scraped over my raw hand.

The wraith snapped at me but went right back to picking at the guard's body. I grimaced and glanced at Dorian, who held Zeele down.

"Lyra, can you help me with something?" Dorian asked dryly. "I'm trying to recall exactly how happy Zeele was when he tortured us together. Do you remember?"

I tapped my chin with a forefinger. "Hm, I'd say he was ecstatic."

How could I ever forget the excitement pulsing from Zeele as he performed his sick experiments? He looked far less confident without his team of guards to jump in and manhandle prisoners for him.

"We're on the same side of the wall now," I said icily, letting the cold anger wash over me for a moment. I wanted this awful excuse of a living being to feel truly afraid for what might be the first time in his life.

Zeele tried to jerk upward, but Dorian slammed him back down to the ground, prompting a pained moan.

"I should've harvested you both the moment you set foot in this place," he spat at us. "Your abomination of a romance wasn't worth investigating."

Red caught my eye. Zeele's wrist stump had been hastily wrapped in a cloth. While it was no longer bleeding, I could see his forearm swelling up, and the makeshift dressing was beginning to dampen with a viscous fluid.

I stepped closer to Zeele, yanking the reins for the ash wraith to follow me. It let out a sharp huff of scalding air in protest and tried to snap at me. Treating it like I would a stubborn horse, I turned and glared at its four glowing eyes. *Not today.* The force of my attitude seemed to do the trick, as it huffed again but followed me.

"You took my hand," Zeele snarled at me, writhing beneath Dorian's tight grip. "You took my spells! Where is he? Where is Prisoner One?"

"He went south," I replied, automatically noting which direction the itch in my head was pulling me.

Dorian and Zeele stared at me. Dorian, surprised—Zeele, hateful.

Wondering if the two elements were connected, I pulled the silver bracelet out from where I had separated it from the others earlier. As soon as I touched it with my bare skin, the pull inside my skull tripled in strength, and the metal glowed a silvery purple.

Zeele snarled and attempted to grab the bracelet, but Dorian pinned him down. The ruler let out a maniacal laugh.

"You'll never find him," he growled. "Even if you have that little trinket, you're nothing but a human. What do you know of magic? He'll be deep in the southern desert by now, lost to us. I hope you're happy."

My blood boiled as Zeele writhed around like a baby having a tantrum.

"If today has proven anything, it's that one human with even a basic knowledge of magic and some very angry vampires can defeat two arrogant Immortals. Now tell me what you know," I said, half snarling. "Unless you want to try to convince them you're worth saving." I pointed to the angry vampires that now surrounded all three sides of the cage.

There was only the stone wall for him to cower against. "How does the bracelet track the Gate Maker? I can feel it in my head, but is that all?"

The ruler gave me a genuinely confused look. "Who is the Gate Maker? I thought you were trying to trace Prisoner One."

Either he was lying, or he genuinely didn't know the ancient identity of the sanitarium's oldest prisoner. Or I was wrong.

"It doesn't matter what I call him," I said dismissively. "Tell me how it works."

Zeele scoffed. "You're the one who *cut off my hand* to steal my bracelets. If you can't figure it out, then I'm not telling you a thing." He jerked his head to the side but quickly looked back to us when he saw the hungry vampires that were clawing at the glass. There was fear in his eyes, but also an arrogance that suggested he didn't think we'd actually hand him over.

Dorian placed his foot on Zeele's stump and pressed down. The Immortal ruler screamed, the sound loud and piercing enough to startle the ash wraith. The creature took two steps back, its back feet trampling over the mangled guard.

"Stop," he begged weakly.

How could this pathetic ruler have done so much damage to so many others?

Dorian smiled coldly. "Tell us what we want to know." He pressed down harder.

Zeele screeched. "Fine! Fine."

Dorian relented. Zeele's forehead dripped with sweat. "There's a tracker embedded in the prisoner's body, and that bracelet is charmed to locate it, even over great distances." He grunted as he shifted his weeping stump. "Irrikus will find you and will dispose of all of you. You'll regret this."

His threats were useless. Not a cell in my body could find any pity for this man, nor did I want to. He'd shown nothing but cowardice and cruelty.

Dorian inhaled quickly, his face contorting as he furrowed his brow. His fangs extended slightly as he glanced at me, hunger beginning to overcome him. "I could feed on him, but... it would be nice to let the others have a meal."

I nodded. Zeele let out a terrified gasp.

"No! No! You promised."

"I did no such thing." I placed the bracelets against the wall, exiting the cell and pulling the ash wraith along with me. Dorian dropped Zeele and dived through the wall after me as a wave of starving vampires descended upon Zeele. His screams didn't last for long.

The wraith didn't spare a backward glance at Zeele as he was being drained dry but tried to snap its beak at me again. Thankfully it couldn't open its beak wide enough to do so due to the muzzle. *Annoying creature.*

As we walked away from the cell, a sense of detached coldness regarding the ruler's fate washed over me. Even as his death rattle echoed in the chamber, I was already focused on my next challenge. I needed to gather my team, and we needed to find a way to safely get everyone out of here. Find the Gate Maker, if that was indeed the real identity of Prisoner One, and return to the Mortal Plane in time to help our friends. Thankfully, I was pretty sure the ash wraiths could help us with some of that.

The smell of blood in the air made my empty stomach roll in a discomforting way, somewhere between disgust and a desire to feed. A head of red hair caught my eye, distracting me from my internal struggle. Roxy, who was waving us over, and a weary-looking Kane stood beside two wildlings at the base of a plant. The wildlings, both squat and covered with long wooly hair, watched with round eyes through their fringes as we approached. The visible parts of their faces were worn and gaunt from hunger, and as they lifted their hands in greeting, I saw scars running down their arms. The curled horns on top of their heads were chipped at the ends.

As soon as I reached them, I took out the still scorching stone and pressed it to their collars. They took deep sighs of relief, eyes shining with gratitude.

"What has this thing done to your hand?" Dorian asked, catching a glimpse of the raw flesh beneath my hasty bandage and taking hold of my wrist to inspect the wound on my palm.

"I'm fine," I assured him. "The stone just got very hot while I was undoing the chains. I probably won't need to touch it again. At least not for a while."

Roxy cleared her throat and jerked a thumb back behind her. "We've got some developments over here."

A few of the starving vampires had started feeding from the distended sacs at the bases of the carnivorous plants filled with vampire blood and distilled darkness. Dorian, still holding my hand, surveyed the plants from top to bottom with a disgusted grimace. The plants were full of vampire blood that had been obtained in the cruelest way possible.

"We need to get them off there," I muttered to Roxy. "And find a way out of here."

"I've taken control of the plants," one of the wildlings announced. Her voice was hoarse.

I raised an eyebrow. The wildlings' powers over the natural world never failed to amaze me.

"Can you destroy them?" Dorian asked tightly. His glare settled on the heads trapped in yellow cases. "We don't need the reminder of what went on here, and that much darkness is dangerous to leave behind, knowing what we do about Irrikus and his schemes."

The wildling nodded. "I can do better than that," she said in a fierce voice. "I can help get us out of this place."

The idea of escape was exhilarating. I desperately wanted to get out of here and head to our next mission.

She walked to the closest plant and placed her hand on the ribbed surface. For a moment, nothing happened. All I could hear was the desperate sound of the starved vampires as they tried to suck on the other dark plants.

Then, a small tremor vibrated through the ground. The plant began to pulse and shudder, and the captive heads began to writhe, the rows of grinding teeth whirring like a woodchipper. The glass cage containing its head was dislodged, and we jumped back as it tumbled to the ground before exploding into a million shards. The other wildling met his comrade's gaze and nodded, hopping over to the next plant and placing his hand on it.

The plants began to move. The heads fought against the cages, breaking open the walls and yanking themselves free from their confines. Vampires yelled and scurried out of the way as the containment boxes continued to fall. Roxy gasped. The plants' deep purple roots had begun to wrench themselves out of the ground, tearing through the stone like paper.

"What are you doing?" I asked the wildling closest to us.

She gave me something close to a smile. Her tiny teeth were sharp and shaped like jagged pebbles. "We can force the plants to grow and use up their dark energy. We'll break down the sanitarium as we leave." Her voice boomed with delighted pride.

I grinned and glanced at Roxy, who punched the air in victory.

The roots swirled with dark shadows, a stark reminder of how the plants had obtained their energy. My stomach turned.

"Let's destroy this forsaken place," I said. Dorian nodded.

The plants thrashed, and the ground shook. The shadows began to disappear in the roots as the plants started to grow bigger and bigger, stretching their leaves and heads toward the tear in the wall.

"What's happening?" someone cried from the crowd. The vampires began to jostle one another to get a better view. The vampires who had been trying to feed on the plants fled as their survival instincts took over.

"Calm down," Roxy said and hopped up onto a table that had once been covered in researchers' notes and records, making her tall enough to address the room. Her powerful voice was perfect for being heard over the crowd. "The wildlings are using the plants to help us escape. This is a *good* sign. Let's use that hole that got blown in this stupid prison to get out of here and go raise some hell!"

Prisoner One had left behind a gift, whether he meant to or not. We now had enough firepower—or *plant* power—to get through the thick walls of the sanitarium, and we didn't need to creep back up through the monochrome labyrinth that would only lead to the reinforcements that were no doubt on their way.

The plants began pulling their roots completely out of the ground. Rocks cracked and shook, scraping together and causing the entire chamber to shudder. Above us, the forcefully gathered souls trembled like gossamer butterflies. Pieces of the roof cracked, and chunks began falling dangerously close to our crowd.

Dorian glanced back to make sure Rhome was okay. He had scooped Kreya up in his arms and was running toward our group. Even with his limp, he appeared fast enough to dodge the falling chunks of ceiling.

I swore as a piece of stone nearly took out my left shoulder, and the ash wraith gave a pitiful squawk as a lump clipped its back leg. The vampires dodged easily while Roxy, whooping like a madwoman, kept close to the female wildling, riding on the actual plant at the base of its roots.

Dorian pulled me out of the way of another falling stone and kept holding onto my hand that was still in the gauntlet. Our eyes met. My rib, my hand, my head—the pain didn't matter anymore in that moment. A rush of relief and warmth replaced all the bad feelings, despite the building that was literally about to come falling down on our heads. He pulled us forward as the plants made their way to the crack. It was utterly wild to watch the plants march themselves to the wall.

The first plant with our wildling friend sent its massive roots into the crack, and the other plants soon joined it. They slithered inside the opening and began to break apart the stone slabs that made up the wall. The tear split open as vines began to cover the ceiling, holding it together as it threatened to completely collapse before we made it out. The first plants pushed through the wall, and the amber soul-light poured out in a wave of hope over our tired faces.

I hurried to the gap as the plants crawled out into the open air like massive eldritch horrors. We were below the main building of the sanitarium, and the gap took us directly out onto the narrow path on the side of the cliff—the one we had walked up only a few days before—that overlooked the dim, viscous ocean.

The distant amber sky had never seemed so beautiful.

We had done it. We were out.

CHAPTER FORTY-FIVE

W e followed the plants as they fought their way out of the lower
chamber. The vines continued to hold up the ceiling as we all
scrambled out behind the advancing plants.

Dorian squeezed my hand as we climbed to freedom, the ash wraith
following along behind us. The sound of the vines as they snapped
through the stone and earth of the walls was like the sweetest soundtrack
I'd ever heard. Our odd trio gathered in the growing breach in the wall,
watching as some of the vampires began to ride the vines of the leading
plant. Other vampires cheered and praised the wildlings as the plants
used their vicious teeth to tear out any stubborn areas of wall, creating a
gentle ramp of earth and stone that was easier to traverse than the
narrow stone steps that had been there previously.

I looked back, watching the wave of vampires continue to make their
way out through the crack in the wall. Wildlings and a few imprisoned
rulers dotted the crowd, pushing into the light. Several wept openly.

With a whoop, Roxy hopped off the vine she'd been clinging onto. She
wiped her forehead with the back of her hand, flicking away beads of
sweat. "I've never ridden a plant before, but I highly recommend it. So,"
she looked between Dorian and me, "how are we getting off this cliff,

team? I know we swam through the river that sourced this ocean, but I don't feel like high diving today."

I gestured with the reins I still held. Without its rider, my recently acquired ash wraith flapped its wings idly. Apparently, it was a fairly relaxed creature when not being tormented by the levers on its saddle. "We can use the wraith," I suggested, surveying its broad form.

Roxy pursed her lips and surveyed the length of the wraith's back. "Will we all fit?"

Someone behind us cleared his throat.

"We'll manage with two," Kane said. He shouldered his way through the crowd lingering outside the opening with the reins to Sempre's wraith held loosely in one hand. The wraith limped slightly from its fall but stretched its wings wide as if to banish any doubt in its capabilities.

"Kane," Roxy breathed. A slow, unconscious smile took over her face like dawn breaking over the horizon.

Relief flooded me. "I'm so glad you made it out."

"You can't get rid of me that easily," Kane said. He gave us a half-smile, one pointed canine catching on his crooked lips. His face twitched suddenly with exhaustion, and I realized he still wore a collar around his neck.

I pulled out the stone and pressed it against the collar. Beneath his torn shirt, the many cuts Roxy had been forced to make were still unhealed thanks to the suppression of the collar. "You've had this on the whole time?" My throat tightened as a wave of guilt struck me. The stone glowed in my hand, and his collar fell away. "I wish I'd gotten to you sooner."

Kane let out a hollow laugh, but the lines on his face were deep with exhaustion. "It's okay," he said, running fingers marked with cuts and scrapes along the angry red mark the collar left behind. "Once the guards were too preoccupied to turn up the heat on these things, it wasn't so bad."

Dorian clapped him on the shoulder. "I never doubted you'd make it out."

Kane's grin never faltered, but his eyes took on a haunted sheen as he hesitated. "I'm glad you showed up when you did," he said softly, eyes drifting to Roxy. He cleared his throat sharply. "Who else was going to get your dumb asses out of this plane?"

There's that same old tough guy swagger. It used to exhaust me, but now I found it comforting. "We're glad too," I told him.

Roxy pushed past me, and Kane let out a surprised grunt as she threw her arms around his neck.

"As if we'd have let you get wood-chippered by a damn plant," she said and squeezed him tight. After a moment she pulled back to land a light punch on his arm, carefully avoiding all the bruised areas.

Kane grinned and raised his reins. "Shall we?"

The wraiths' saddles and reins looked a little worse for wear, but it would have to work. Sempre's wraith had a broken muzzle dangling from its hooked beak, but the creature merely croaked weakly. Hopefully, it would keep its ear-shattering screeches to itself.

Just a few minutes before, our enemies had used these creatures against us. Now we would use them to gain our freedom. To think I'd been worried whether we'd ever get out of here. A small grin worked its way onto my face, hope briefly overcoming my dread-riddled anticipation of the dangers that lay ahead.

Roxy snorted, smiling back at me. "If we pull this off, we're going to have the most *epic* story to tell back at the barracks. A prison break that crosses two realms of existence? We'll get free drinks for years on this story."

"While I agree," I said dryly, "let's maybe survive the trans-planar prison break before we start dining out on the fame."

Dorian took a deep breath, and for a moment I imagined I could see all his charged thoughts, like a lightning storm in a glass vase. We would escape the sanitarium after tearing a literal hole in the power that the building represented. The Immortal rulers who'd kept their boots on the necks of vampires for far too long had weaknesses and flaws we could exploit just like anyone else. I flexed my wounded hand, feeling each ache and pain in my body, glad to be alive. My arm shook from the force of the adrenaline surging inside me. Alive, but still very much in danger.

Smash!

A rock narrowly missed Roxy's head as it plummeted from the rapidly collapsing gap in the wall of the sanitarium, tumbling past us to roll off the ledge and down the cliff before splashing into the ocean.

She glanced up, raising an arm to shield her face. "Looks like the plants can't keep the walls stable for much longer."

Dorian agreed. "Reunion was nice, but let's move."

Around us, a flood of vampires was scaling the cliffs in opposite directions. Some apparently intended to go up and clear out the rest of the sanitarium staff, while others retreated down toward the water below. I watched with mixed feelings, worrying for them, but knowing we had a greater responsibility right now. We'd done our part to release the prisoners—their journeys were their own now.

Kane helped Roxy climb onto the back of his wraith by steading it by the reins. I did the same with mine while Dorian pulled himself into the saddle. He settled his feet in the stirrups and took a moment to gather up the slack in the reins and examine the various levers and buttons on the saddle. A pebble fell on my shoulder, and I brushed it away. We didn't have much time.

"I think I understand," Dorian muttered. "Though, all we need to know is how to keep its mouth shut and how to make it move."

"That's good enough for me," I said.

Dorian pulled me up to join him, settling me behind him in the large saddle. The wraith grumbled and shifted to compensate for both of us but settled down after Dorian laid a hand on the bristling fur of its neck and made a few low murmurs. Wrapping an arm around his waist, I enjoyed the sensation of being pressed in close to Dorian's back without pain in my chest, feeling a hint of nostalgia for our first ride together on a redbill.

Roxy was right. Although the wildlings had directed the plants at the rear to stabilize the opening with their vines and leaves, as the last of their leaves pushed through the gap, the support inside lessened. A final few vampires slipped through at the last minute, swiftly followed by the thunderous crashing of falling masonry and dirt as the chamber inside began to collapse. Beneath us, the cliffside began to shake and crumble.

Vampires and wildlings scrambled aside as lumps of rock and clods of earth began to plummet into the ocean below.

The wraith batted its wings nervously, snorting yellow mist from its beak as it did so. Dorian tugged at a lever and murmured to the wraith again. As he pulled the switch, the muzzle clicked fully closed, causing the wraith to halfheartedly turn its head to snap at us. The shifting ground beneath its feet seemed to concern it more, however, and it danced anxiously on the spot, its huge body emitting heat that I could feel even through the saddle.

"We need to find Rhome and Kreya," Dorian yelled.

Kane nodded in response, guiding his wraith to the left with the controls. We went right, not quite flying but not completely running, as we searched the immediate area for our two friends.

The wraith growled as it dodged falling rocks. Above us, the souls embedded in the ground began to break free from the cliff as the stone collapsed. I kept an eye out for falling debris as Dorian used his superior vision to search for Rhome.

He inhaled sharply. "There."

Rhome was huddled on the stairs directly beside the collapsing exit, cradling Kreya. As we approached, I saw tears rolling down his face, cutting lines through the sweat and dirt as he lowered his head to press a gentle kiss to Kreya's bloody forehead. The bleeding appeared to have stopped, but she was unconscious. Rhome gently moved her head, tucking it against his chest.

"Rhome," Dorian shouted.

The older vampire looked up with tired eyes and watched us land nearby. Hearing Dorian's call, Kane and Roxy circled around to join us.

"You need to get on," I urged Rhome, reaching out a hand.

Rhome held Kreya to his chest, a tight muscle popping in his jaw. She looked like a broken doll. My heart twisted at the sight of his torn face. Even with his anger at Kreya, she was currently helpless after having her gem ripped out.

"She hasn't woken up," he said, voice cracking. "I can't leave her."

Dorian grunted impatiently, but his eyes were soft. "I'm not asking you to leave her." He slid off the wraith, leaving me to hold the reins. I grabbed them half-mindedly in a tight fist. Was he hoping to move things along faster? The wraith snorted beside me.

"I don't know if she'll survive," Rhome said, resting a hand over her injured forehead. "The kids... If she died, they would be devastated..." He trailed off, his tone draining like a dying battery.

"Nobody is dying here today," I said, holding the wraith steady.

"Let's put Kreya on the wraith with Roxy and Kane for balance," Dorian suggested. He extended a hand to his cousin. "Please, Rhome. I can't lose anyone else to these monsters."

Rhome blinked slowly, as if waking from a very long sleep. He looked up at Dorian for a long moment, not paying attention to the crumbling cliff. Finally, he nodded and released his grip on Kreya. As gently and as quickly as possible, Dorian scooped her up and hurried over to the other wraith. He handed her up to Kane, and Roxy wrapped her arms around the unconscious vampire as Kane gathered the reins back up.

Dorian offered Rhome a hand, pulling him to his feet and letting the older vampire lean on his shoulder. When Rhome took a step, I could see that his limp had been exacerbated by all the running and fighting. I helped him up onto the wraith, settling him before me so he was sandwiched between me and Dorian.

"Time to very politely ask for this creature to fly for us." Dorian dug his heels into the wraith's sides and made a little growl. The wraith tossed its head, unfolded its long, smoky gray wings, and launched itself into the air.

I squeezed Rhome's hand, holding onto him tightly as we all adjusted to the feeling of flight. "It's okay," I promised. "We'll figure something out. The kids are waiting to be rescued."

Rhome nodded, a new glimmer of hope sparking in his face. The corner of his lips quirked upward. "I'll find them." It was a promise.

I looked over my shoulder to see the other wraith take to the air at Kane's behest. Roxy shot me a thumbs-up as she held on to Kreya. My throat tightened, the joy of victory melting into concern about our next steps. Our thread of destiny splayed in three directions. Carwin and

Detra remained in the palace, meaning some of us would need to go and rescue them. The second fraying string led us back to the VAMPS camp, to hopefully prevent an attack or help them in the aftermath of one. We had to find a way back to the Mortal Plane, and fast. The third, final thread tugged at me. The persistent scratch called me to Prisoner One.

CHAPTER FORTY-SIX

The ocean sprawled before us, covered in its vaporous shroud. Near the base of the cliff, the female wildling clung to one of the vines, using it to rappel down to the water. She stretched her hand out toward something writhing beneath the mist.

On one of the switchbacks of the path, Kono ushered vampires down toward whatever the wildling was calling to the surface.

"Go closer," I told Dorian. "I think they're trying to get people out of here."

Dorian urged the wraith lower, and we watched a giant pink eel slither from the ocean. The aquatic creature raised its head, regarding the wildling with mild interest in its beady black eyes. It bobbed at the surface, and the wildling beckoned to the vampires that were scrambling down the cliff or jumping into the ocean. A few vampires hovered on the edge of the cliffside, stunned as they looked out onto the free world. One wept openly before leaping into the ocean, joining his comrades.

Our wraiths hovered beside it as the wildling climbed atop the creature's shiny, scaled head. The eel-like beast lifted its head from the water for a moment, eyeing the flying wraiths warily. It submerged itself again, but not before letting out something like a long sigh that made the strange vaporous water bubble up around its head. Kane shook his head in disbelief, watching the vampires crawl onto the creature's back. This had to be the oddest event in vampire history.

"We'll go to a safe place, where everyone can flee," the female wildling informed us and the vampires, wildlings, and rulers joining her.

I scanned their faces, seeing mixtures of relief and dread among furrowed brows that I knew would only relax when they were far away from the sanitarium. The prison's white form was slowly shaking and collapsing, the destruction of the lowest level bringing down the whole building.

"A true safe place?" Dorian asked, skeptical. Could there be such a thing in the Immortal Plane?

The wildling nodded and cast a fierce, broad smile at the crumbling sanitarium. "There are places wildlings know of that rulers do not. They have sent most of their troops to the central parts to obtain fearsome creatures, so there are vast areas to the west and south devoid of patrols. Where we go, they will not be likely to follow. Thank you for helping us."

"For any who are seeking family they lost in Vanim," Kono shouted, "follow me. We will follow the river to Lake Siron."

He waved his hand in the air, his dark body slicing through the chaos like a beacon of hope with its strong movements. Some of the vampires drifted toward him. After watching Kono get captured, it was a relief to see him healthy and whole, triumphantly leading a new charge to look for family. I hoped they would find that family. He caught my glance in his direction and gave a friendly wave.

A wiry vampire pulled himself from the ocean and climbed onto the creature's body. I glanced at the rest of the sea monster, which seemed to stretch on forever. But not everyone would leave on the back of this beast or with Kono. Vampires were scrambling like ants up the large roots of the carnivorous plants that dug into the side of the cliff. Their speed was impressive, especially after so much time in confinement. They clung on as the roots stretched, beginning to break up the ground as they headed to the island's edge. One of the plant heads dipped down to the short dock and swallowed up a small boat, crushing the vessel with its sharp teeth before gulping it down. Some vampires fell into the water, while others managed to hold on as the roots began to cross the strip of water between the sanitarium and the Immortal city. What would Zeele say now, if he could see how his botanical ambitions had played out?

Good luck with the killer plants, Irrikus.

These vampires were on a mission to feed and exact revenge. Watching them go was bittersweet; I knew that not all of them would leave the city alive. Irrikus had hunters and skimmers, and it was a huge city to battle through. The palace would already be expecting them. But the vampires had made their choice, and I respected their courage.

Dorian grunted abruptly as a buzzing sound filled the air. I glanced up to see skimmers dotting the sky above us, stark white metal against the amber sky. I stiffened at the sight. Rhome raised his head, sensing the change in mood.

"Skimmer patrol," one of the vampires shouted from the back of the sea creature. The wildling snapped something, and the aquatic beast began to swim. "Three of them!"

The skimmers dove toward us like a trio of wild birds. I aimed my gem gauntlet at them, and Roxy did the same, using Kane's back to keep Kreya balanced on the back of the wraith.

The wildling hauled one final vampire onto the aquatic creature's back, then shouted something. In response, a long pink tentacle struck out at the oncoming skimmers, which dodged out of reach.

The skimmers flew toward us, the bobbing lights on their sides making them easy targets. I fired a barrage of shots from the gauntlet, quickly joined by Roxy. Even with the automatic aiming, they were still too far away to hit.

Dorian gritted his teeth. "We've got to move."

He guided the wraith to the side, and I wrapped my other arm around Rhome's waist to keep us steady. I kept my gauntlet raised, waiting for the skimmers to get close enough. Two of them opened fire with mounted gem guns on their sides, and Dorian steered the wraith back underneath the cliff's overhang as we dodged the barrage. The third hung back, and I kept an eye on it, making sure it wasn't trying to get around or behind us.

Suddenly, the third skimmer released a volley of shots at its comrades. Taken by surprise, the two skimmers chasing us plummeted into the ocean. I squinted, trying to make out the two forms on the skimmer.

"What the hell?" I muttered, keeping my gauntlet at the ready as the remaining skimmer swooped down toward us. It never fired. An arm waved over the skimmer's side as it descended.

The machine drew level with us, and with a jolt of surprise, I recognized the pilots.

"Laini!" Rhome shouted, joy in his voice.

In front of her was none other than Juneau. He pulled up beside us and immediately lifted both sets of hands.

"I come in peace," he said with a touch of humor. I stiffened underneath his pleasant gaze.

Laini, her face alight with excitement, shouted, "I'm so glad you escaped!" She saw me tensely staring at Juneau. "He's okay. I'll explain."

"The bigger question is how *you* escaped," Dorian called. "Let's get closer to the cliff." His eyes darted upward. "I have a feeling more patrols are on their way."

The wraiths headed for the cliff's edge, close to the water, where we could hover safely beneath the cliff's overhang and look for approaching skimmers from a hiding place. They were slightly nervous around the skimmer, but Kane and Dorian quieted them enough for us to talk.

My mind immediately launched into everything we needed to catch her up on. There was Kreya, the dark vampires, the strange prisoner, the attack on the Mortal Plane. And she had just as much to tell us. Why was Juneau with her?

"We've got to get back to the Mortal Plane," I told Laini, immediately launching into strategy mode. "Sempre has sent corrupted, darkness-crazed vampires that he calls revenants to attack the VAMPS camp in Scotland."

"They turned Kreya into one," Rhome said.

Laini's gaze fell on Kreya, who sat in Roxy's lap. It was unsettling to see Kreya so passive and ghostly.

Between the four of us, we quickly relayed everything that happened.

My eyes slid to Juneau, who absorbed all this information with a neutral expression.

"What happened to you, Laini? How did you two escape from the house?" I asked.

Juneau bit his lip guiltily as Roxy snarled, "I'll punch your traitorous face if you sell us out again."

Laini shook her head. "He didn't betray us. When he returned from the ball with the guards, he trapped them in a back room." A feral glint came into her eyes as she relayed the tale. "He let me feed on them. I don't have time for the whole story now, but he had a backup plan. He came with me, and his entire household has gone on the run."

Juneau lifted a hand politely. "I chose to help Laini get out of the city and then back in again." For once, there were no outrageous tosses of his hair or grand gestures with his flowing sleeves. It was just Juneau and his honesty. My charged nerves began to ease.

Laini smiled. "I owe them all a lot, especially Charrek and Juneau. I'll tell you the longer story when we have time. What's most important is that you'll find Juneau's aura has changed a lot. It's noticeably lighter instead of neutral, so I'm taking that as a good sign."

"How did you make it through the city?" Dorian pressed. "We need information on what the city is like right now."

I eyed the broken skimmers floating in the ocean. How long until Irrikus and his patrol noticed that his first skimmer patrol was out of commission?

"I parted ways with Juneau, intent on leaving, and used my wildling disguise to get to the Gray Ravine," she explained. "I nearly went back to the Hive, but Juneau was able to catch up to me. He changed his mind about leaving with his household, deciding to help me instead. I almost requested he come to the Hive, but then he dropped the news about child vampires being kept by Sempre." She swallowed hard.

Rhome tensed at the mention of his children.

"That changed it for me. I felt like it had to be Carwin and Detra," Laini said. "I reasoned we could find a maker who worked at the palace, who might know where the kids are kept. I begged Juneau to help me hijack a skimmer. He's pretty good at tricking guards. We found a lone pilot out on patrol near the ravine and headed back to the palace. Charrek managed to send a messenger, a servant from the senate, to catch up to us. She gave us some news and indicated that Sempre had left for business at the sanitarium. I asked if she knew where the children were, and she told us the kids would be out with a member of the Immortal Council, but—" She pointed down to the skimmer's front. "There's a magical comm in all of these. We got word of a breakout at the sanitarium and came to find you."

"We were able to join up with a group of guards responding to the breakout," Juneau confirmed, wrapping up the tale.

I looked up, and my breath caught. Three new skimmers sliced through the sky with their sharp noses over the cliff high above us. "We need to get moving."

Juneau snatched a pair of purple crystals off the front of the skimmer, where they had been plugged into some kind of built-in charging station. He aimed and fired up at the skimmers.

The white constructs tumbled out of the sky and began spinning toward the ocean. The pilots were thrown from their crafts, yelling as they plummeted. Everyone scattered. Kane went left, Dorian drove our wraith closer to the cliff, and Juneau went low with his skimmer.

We narrowly dodged the closest empty skimmer, which was smoking as it hurtled toward the ocean. I grimaced as I heard bodies hit the water, and the cries turned to silence. Our group reconvened near the cliffside.

"We need to go," Kane yelled.

I locked eyes with Dorian. Kane was right, but there were so many things we needed to do. We needed to rescue Carwin and Detra, find Prisoner One, *and* prevent or help with an attack from mind-controlled vampires in the Mortal Plane. Three separate places, and one of them was in an entirely different plane of existence. It would be impossible to do them all together. Our group would need to separate in order to increase our chances of success.

Prisoner One's lavender eyes haunted me—the itch in my head still tugging but growing fainter. I needed to find him.

Dorian looked out at everyone, his jaw set with determination and eyes flashing with a new energy. "We need to split up."

CHAPTER FORTY-SEVEN

The controls of the skimmer were responsive under my hand—too responsive, actually. With one hand hastily bandaged and the other encased in an unfamiliar metal gauntlet, I struggled to determine how much pressure was needed to send us hurtling through the sky. Juneau only had time to give me the most basic instructions when we swapped transports, and we'd had a few hairy moments as I tried to get a sense of the skimmer's capabilities.

The skimmer plunged for a moment as I tried to steer it upward. It gave an angry shake as I pushed it fast and high into the sky, aiming for a higher altitude to avoid other skimmers. Dorian and I were about to find out how fast this thing could go. My heel slid back slightly to reassure me that the Hive pack Laini had stowed there, which contained a few precious rations and some of the remaining weapons, was still jammed between my seat and Dorian's. Laini, in her genius, had thought to grab it when she hid in the park near the Gray Ravine.

I wished we'd had more time to say goodbye. With everyone shifting into crisis mode, there were no precious moments to spare for emotions. Juneau and Laini had taken off for an unguarded stone circle that Juneau had found on one of his extensive maps. Laini would bring Kreya to the

Mortal Plane and alert the Bureau of their presence using the powerful distress beacons we'd brought with us. She would then find a way back to Scotland. Roxy, Kane, and Rhome were going to attempt to rescue Detra and Carwin. Their chances weren't terrible, given the current confusion in Itzarriol—the guards had their hands full with the vampire escapees.

The sight of the wraiths carrying all my friends away made my heart twist with pain, almost as bad as the curse that separated me from Dorian. I already regretted their absence, but I had to focus on our mission. Prisoner One was possibly the only creature who could end this entire fiasco with the rulers. The council had to have a reason for capturing him and keeping him around for nine hundred-odd years.

"No hunters," Dorian whispered behind me, leaning in to make sure I heard.

His lips brushed my ear for a moment, and it took all my self-control to keep the skimmer straight. My nerves were already jumpy. His sudden closeness still threw me off in the best way. Combined with the adrenaline, I felt harried and charged.

Guided by the glowing silver bracelet and the gravitational pull it created in my head, I steered us toward a section of the city that we hadn't seen yet. The growing inner compass swallowed up my attention and pushed me forward. I touched the bracelet in my pocket every minute or so, adjusting my steering to match where it and the itch sent me.

"Does it feel like an itch to you? When you sense someone's aura?" I asked Dorian over my shoulder. I stole a moment to admire his handsome profile glaring out over the Immortal city, searching for other skimmers.

"Not exactly," he said, but the magically powered communicator sparked to life before he could elaborate.

"It's tugging at me," I muttered as I fought the steering. "I can feel an itch every time I go in a direction away from him."

"Good, sounds like you're the perfect captain," Dorian said. The skimmer swerved to the left. He grimaced lightly. "Minus the piloting part, maybe."

"Senate Team A cannot secure the sanitarium," someone droned. The line crackled slightly, but otherwise the voice was clear. Another speaker chimed in, urging the others to try harder. From somewhere in the background, I heard Irrikus speaking icily at everyone.

"Those leeches—" His voice faded. It sounded like a guard was saying something, barking orders, beneath the Immortal overlord's complaints. "The sanitarium's collapse is unforgivable. We will maintain order no matter what. Find the prisoner and kill the rest."

The line went dead. My blood ran cold. Irrikus was furious but in control. Bad news for us. A man who'd risen to power over the course of hundreds of years would be a formidable enemy.

There was another crackle, and the comm sparked to life once more. "We've got activity near the bazaar. It's a riot over there. Wildlings are attacking hunter patrols and rulers. Makers are screaming about overdue wages. There are—" The voice ended in an abrupt snarl as someone else screamed, "Vampire!"

"Our colleagues are moving fast," Dorian noted. "Impressive, since most of them are still hungry. They'll be hard to stop after they've fed."

I hummed in vague apprehension, thinking of the powerful gauntlet on my hand. "As long as the hunters have gem-powered weapons, it's going to be an unbalanced fight." Part of me hoped the hunger would push the vampires to near madness, making them virtually unstoppable as they sank their fangs into darkness-filled hunters. It was definitely what they deserved.

"Attention all teams." The radio suddenly sizzled as the stomach-turning voice of Irrikus came onto the line. The rage had drained from his voice, leaving nothing but a tone as sharp as cut glass. "All city guards take care of the cretins and leeches. Hunters, pursue the prisoner. He has gone south to the Restless Desert. I will update as we learn more. And escapees, if you're listening, I would advise you to run faster if you hope to escape in one miserable piece."

A cold bead of sweat ran down my face as Irrikus took a steady, calm breath.

"Do not come back without him."

The line went silent again. I imagined the senate guards were pale and shaken right now.

Dorian snorted bitterly. "He's given up on containing the sanitarium."

I nodded. Even if he wasn't the Gate Maker, it seemed Prisoner One was even more important to Irrikus than we'd initially thought. We needed to get to him before anyone else did.

My hands shook as a sudden wave of pain and fatigue stole over me, pulsing hot and sharp in my damaged rib and hand. Deep down on a cellular level, I could feel the effects of the vampire blood slowly wearing off. It was like coming down from an impossible feeling of extended joy. I sucked in a breath of cold air, using the sensation to center myself.

Focus, Lyra.

The lower part of my body had begun to ache, but I had to keep moving. A new fire of determination arose inside me and spurred me on. I was the only one who could fly this thing. I tried to adjust my aching feet without Dorian noticing me wince. If he saw how tired my eyes were, he would worry. Worrying would waste precious energy, and we had too much to accomplish in the next few hours.

"Is your signal on him still strong?" Dorian asked.

I nodded as I touched the bracelet that had replaced the stone in my sports bra. I was careful to keep the two far apart. The force guided me to turn the skimmer a fraction of an inch to the left.

You got it, magical tracker.

The body Prisoner One had forced his frame into suggested he wanted to move quickly, so that he wouldn't be stopped. I leaned forward, urging the skimmer to go faster. It picked up a little speed but was clearly near its limit. The poor white vehicle began to putter unless I forced my entire weight into the steering.

My mind swarmed with thoughts as my body went on autopilot—touch the bracelet, adjust the steering, check ahead for obstacles and guards.

The bizarre and grotesque buildings of Itzarriol began to grow smaller and smaller beneath our skimmer. Soon, the city fell away completely. We flew over a narrow strip of lush vegetation on a hilly area surrounding Itzarriol, but it was short lived. Soon, following the command of the bracelet and my inner senses, there was nothing beneath us but the blue-gray sands of a bleak desert.

The desert below was filled with cracks in the ground, possible shadowy expanses that went on forever, for all I knew. I swallowed my nervous curiosity and swore we wouldn't find out.

This had to be where Prisoner One had fled with Sempre. The Restless Desert. Part of me expected to find Sempre's dead body strewn across the sand, torn apart and ravaged. I would've done it, if I had been kept in captivity for nearly a millennium.

My left eye twitched slightly from fatigue. How long had I been awake now? My head swam from dehydration and lack of food and sleep. Although the neon brightness of the sanitarium hallways had been annoying, it had at least kept me awake. Here, away from the painfully bright light, the landscape stretched out in an endless dusk that was at once calm and disturbing, like staring at a cursed watercolor painting. All I wanted to do was drop to the sand below and sleep, but Irrikus's furious threat kept me moving—we couldn't afford to lose our lead.

Hours passed, searching. I began to count the minutes, desperate for some sort of familiar, measurable timekeeping. Occasionally, Dorian reached over to squeeze my arm or shoulder, sensing that I was struggling to spur the skimmer on. We needed to keep a good pace if we wanted to outrun the guards.

"Isn't it odd that nobody is following us?" I asked, glancing back to look for pursuers in the hazy sky for what felt like the millionth time.

He also did a quick check, making use of his superior night vision. "Might be good news, if it means we're farther ahead than they are," he replied. His voice was nearly lost to the wind as it whipped around us. I nudged the skimmer forward and touched the bracelet. Ever onward.

The light above us grew dimmer. I cursed the souls as they drifted away, more and more disappearing to somewhere else in the Immortal Plane. The declining amber glow made it much harder to see, and I had to rely on the directions given by the bracelet to guide us, and Dorian's vision to protect us.

At one point I dug out one of the energy bars we'd brought with us from Moab. It was tough and slightly stale, but I gnawed on it anyway, hungry for any sort of energy as the power from the vampire blood continued to dwindle. A bitter taste entered my mouth in response to the food, and I shivered violently, stuffing the bar back into the bag.

Then, out of nowhere, the steady hum that had been prompting me onward for the last eternity burst into an insistent, powerful pull.

"It's getting stronger," I relayed to Dorian.

"Good," he breathed. "The creature must be nearby."

I eyed the dizzying cracks, the logistics of searching such a maze stripping away my hope. If Prisoner One could squeeze himself through the original, relatively small tear in the wall, he could easily slither into a crack to hide in the desert. Thankfully, we had the bracelet. It was nice to know that I had a built-in GPS system leading me to him.

I touched the bracelet. The itch now spread throughout my limbs, pricking at each one like a low-voltage electric current. Every single cell in my body buzzed.

One tiny course adjustment sent the itching sensation plummeting suddenly into the soles of my feet, obviously trying to draw us down.

Had we found him?

I eyed the high dunes on either side of the formidable valley beneath us. Here, the cracks ranged from small to large, some of them releasing rising steam that carried the faint smell of decay. "He must be down there somewhere."

"Let's comb the most immediate area," Dorian said. He scowled. "I keep getting hints of something like an aura, but it's unlike anything else in the Mortal or Immortal Planes. I can't make sense of it enough to follow it, and I don't *see* anything below us. No rulers either, even though Prisoner One took Sempre with him."

I licked my drying lips, wondering if Prisoner One had killed Sempre already. I tried to imagine being kept in a cage for so long, including what that would do to me and how much I'd grow to hate the person who put me there. Well, revenge of that caliber might be performed slowly. Maybe there was another reason Dorian couldn't sense Sempre's aura besides death.

My fingers fidgeted with the bracelet. Zeele might have set some sort of false alarm on the tracker, in case it was being used by someone who wasn't him. Was it a wild goose chase? I forced my tired eyes to look out into the dusk, searching for some sign of life or any indication that something had passed through here recently. I was hesitant to land without seeing some physical evidence. Magical navigation was new to me, after all. It might have a limited range, or Prisoner One could be running through tunnels beneath us, giving us a run for our money.

Yet the bracelet was all we had to go on—I had to keep trusting it for the moment.

Back and forth across the valley we flew, from one dune to the other and back again, the whole time keeping our senses on high alert for some sign of life. Dorian peered down, using his dark vision, and I clung to the bracelet, guiding the machine with minute twitches of my other hand.

Finally, Dorian let out a small exhale from his nose. "We're getting nowhere like this." He rubbed his eyes. "We should take a break, get down to ground level. We can regroup on land and check things out from there. Maybe there's something down there that we're not seeing. A new perspective could help."

A tiny scratch of frustration rose up alongside the itch. "Shouldn't we keep sweeping?" I asked forcefully, not wanting to break my focus. It was hard enough to stay awake with wind hitting my face. If we landed to search on foot, I was genuinely afraid that my legs would buckle, and I'd crash to sleep on the sand. "Our friends in Scotland and Moab are in imminent danger. The others are trying to rescue Carwin and Detra. Laini is heading back to the Mortal Plane alone with Kreya." I sighed. "I can't stop. There's too much at stake to stop, even for a minute. I can't fix everything, and I hate that, so I'm going to do the only thing I can until it's done."

My voice shook at the end, and I wiped my eyes roughly with my arm.

Dorian's fingers wrapped around my hand, and I turned to meet his eyes. They softened as he used his other hand to gently turn my face toward him. Behind the warmth and affection for me, I recognized a haunted look that my own gaze likely reflected.

How did we keep finding the strength to move forward?

I closed my eyes briefly, enjoying the warmth of his hand on my face. The skimmer glided to a stop and hovered above the desert landscape. Despite all our problems, I let go and lived fully in the beauty of this moment.

Look at us... as close as we want to be.

The hurt, anger, worry, and grief swirled through me, but I let Dorian's presence chase the chaos away for a blissful second.

"I wish I could numb my emotions until it's over and we're safe," I admitted. "But I also know that once I stop holding all the horror and trauma at arm's length, I'll have to face everything that's happened and process it. And that's healthy. We haven't had time to be healthy like that. We still don't have time."

Dorian's lips lifted into a bittersweet smile. "I know you don't want to stop, but there's no point in simply repeating the same actions over and over. It won't bring us different results. That way ends only in madness."

I sighed, absorbing the truth of his statement. I tried to nod along, but it was like my muscles gave up halfway through, and I ended up setting my head on his chest.

He held me tightly. I shivered against him, relishing his touch. I took a steady breath, enjoying his scent as it broke through the desert's fragrance.

"Thank you for being here for me," I whispered, my mind a tangled heap of a thousand thoughts about Dorian and our adventure up to this point. "Thank you for your unwavering support. You've cared for me so much."

Say love.

My heart began to thump wildly as the thought whispered through me. I wanted to tell him I loved him. No, I wanted to shout it as loud as I could for everyone to hear, then whisper it only for him. Tilting my head, I looked up at him. He was handsome, still rugged despite the bruises obtained during our fight in the sanitarium. He gazed down at me, brushing my cheek with the rough pad of his thumb.

"What is it, Lyra?"

I forced myself to straighten, not to lean on him. The feelings I had for Dorian reached depths I hadn't known I had, and I needed to see his face when I told him so.

"When I was in solitary confinement, I had no idea where you were," I whispered shakily. "Even if I had known, I couldn't have helped you. If they'd fed you to one of those plants, or if Zeele had tortured you until you…" I couldn't say *died*. I couldn't. "I would have lost you, Dorian."

"Lyra…"

He'd said my name twice, and I wanted him to say it over and over again until the end of time.

"I have something to tell you." I wrapped my arms around his neck. "I need to tell you that I love you, too."

For a brief moment, the desert disappeared. Only Dorian existed, as he brushed my hair back, running his fingers through it in a caress.

"I thought about telling you in the bath, but I chickened out," I admitted sheepishly. "I didn't know how to say the words to you. When you told me that you loved me while we were in the experiment chamber, it gave me the hope and determination I needed to take out Zeele."

He pressed his other hand to my face and pulled me toward him. "That's the kind of strength I want to be able to provide for life. I will love you as long as you let me."

I pressed my lips to his in a burning kiss. My wind-stung lips ached, but a warmth spread over me. I gasped as he pulled me flush against him. One of my hands dropped to his arm, the remains of his shirt tattered from the fighting. The urge to touch every part of him, to rip off every article of annoying clothing, hit me like a tidal wave. Unfortunately, we'd have to settle for this kiss right now. We truly didn't have time for more.

Our lips broke apart, and we wrapped our arms around each other. For a moment, we just breathed together. The rough intimacy melted into a soft, comforting embrace. I sighed with pure pleasure from it all. My muscles relaxed. Breaking through the fatigue, my body felt the tiniest spark of refreshed energy.

"Search party coming in." The magical radio suddenly sputtered to life. "We are officially in pursuit of the prisoner. There was some difficulty finding a tracking bracelet, and it had to be charged. The range to the Restless Desert came back when it reached full power."

Startled, I jerked my head in the direction of the radio. It had been silent for the last few hours.

A deep female voice came onto the line. "Don't worry. I will not fail you. We'll get that prisoner back."

Inkarri.

My gaze darted up to Dorian. "We need to move." Circumstances had changed. There was no time to reflect on the bracelet's trustworthiness. If it was good enough for the guards, it was good enough for me. I couldn't see Prisoner One out there, but this tracker could sense him.

Dorian squeezed my arms one last time. "Let's keep our lead."

I turned back to the steering as the radio chatter dropped back to dull check-ins between the patrols in the city. Below us, the desert looked less than inviting.

"I think we should go down in the central crack," I said. "That seems like it has the strongest pull."

He nodded. "I trust you completely."

That makes one of us.

I eased the controls down gently, but the skimmer lurched forward violently. Dorian grabbed me to steady me as we fell forward, and I jerked the steering back up. The skimmer leveled.

"Is there a land button?" he asked hopefully.

"Not a chance," I muttered. "Hold on." I went back to the controls with the most delicate touch possible, hardly more than an ounce of force on them. The skimmer didn't move at first. I applied a bit more pressure. The skimmer began to rotate and ease downward, wobbling the entire way. Dorian clutched the sides of the skimmer.

"I'll prepare myself for jumping and grabbing you along with me," he said. Such a gentleman, this vampire. The plane gave a shudder but held steady as it approached the desert floor.

I dropped the skimmer down closer to the sands, following the urge from the bracelet to settle in the middle of the valley. As our craft neared the ground, I saw the cracks more clearly for the first time. We needed to find one big enough to stash the skimmer inside.

"I'm going to try to hide the skimmer," I told Dorian. "If Inkarri makes it out here and sees it, she might destroy our only escape method."

He ran a hand over his chin. "Maybe, but how?"

"We'll figure it out." I managed to land the skimmer on a solid patch of desert edged by two shadowed cracks in the ground next to a large rock. I hadn't noticed the stones from up in the sky, but rocks—large and small —dotted the desert in a random pattern. Hopping off the skimmer, I glanced over the edge as Dorian pushed the skimmer over to lean against the rock.

"I don't know how far down these cracks go. Maybe we can hide it in —" I let out a startled gasp as my toe suddenly sank into a soft spot in the ground. I threw myself backward, the sand continuing to melt away at the edge of the crack, revealing it to be several inches wider than I'd assumed. "Watch your step," I said with a slightly hysterical laugh.

He jerked his thumb to the skimmer. "So what do we do with our escape craft?"

I ran over to the other side to look down the other crevice. To my delight, the bottom of the fissure was much closer. It was a shallow drop of only a few feet, but it was a bit too narrow for the skimmer to fit down, even if the wings were folded up. "We can park it in one of these fissures. Find one that'll let it go down with the wings folded in."

Dorian nodded and leapt over the fissure to glance down the next. After three attempts, he raised his hand. "This should work. It's broad but not too deep."

Hopefully, Inkarri wouldn't spot it. It was the best we could do. I hopped back into the skimmer and flew slowly over to where Dorian pointed.

Zeele's warning came back to me as I judged the sides of the shallow crevice. He'd said we would never find Prisoner One out here. I scowled as I steered the skimmer into the wider crack. Concentrating carefully, I folded the wings up and dropped with a sudden lurch to the bottom of the fissure. The soft sand broke the fall of the lightweight skimmer, and then the sand began to give way. I let out a startled gasp as I plummeted, but it was only a few feet before the skimmer sank against solid rock.

Dorian reached down to offer me his hand, and I pulled myself up, scrambling up the soft sides of the crack. I let out a sigh of relief and turned my attention to the fissures.

"Whether we can get it out again remains to be seen, but we'll deal with that issue later," I informed him. He nodded, and I kicked the sand off my boots.

I leaned over the deep main fissure. My voice had carried, echoing in some distant chamber beneath us. Somewhere, smooth rock sat beneath the sand to create such a sound. I squatted and peered down into the blackness, keeping a safer distance. My movement sent a few rocks down the fissure, and the sound echoed like my voice had.

"Deep caves," Dorian guessed and leaned toward the echo of the rock's fall. "I can hear the rock bounce, indicating a tunnel system."

I stared down into the darkness. "Has the creature been beneath the sand the whole time?" The long stripes and cracks across the desert that we had seen from the skimmer must hide a deep cave system. The blue-on-blue hues of the rock and the sand made it impossible to distinguish them in the dimming soul-light.

"There's a bottom," Dorian said as he squinted down the crack. "Maybe twelve feet down?"

"He would be expecting skimmers to follow, so what if he's been traveling underground?" I whispered with a beat of excitement. I kept my voice low, not wanting my words to echo farther into the caves and potentially startle our prisoner.

Dorian cocked his head. "Not sure how far they go. It looks like there's a lot of them, though." He surveyed the desert around us. It was filled with similar crevices.

The bracelet was warm against my hand as I felt it to be sure we were in the right place. It still tugged insistently downward. I pointed back to the fissure from before, the one Dorian had said was twelve feet deep. "Down we go, I guess."

Somewhere, deep beneath our very feet, Prisoner One was waiting.

CHAPTER FORTY-EIGHT

"**O**n my back," Dorian said.

There was rope in my pack, but it was quicker for me to use him like an express elevator down into the strange cave. I hopped up onto his back, wincing as my rib protested, and wrapped my arms around his upper chest, careful not to choke him.

He toed the edge of the crevice. "Hold on."

I checked the sky one last time. There was no sign of Inkarri or any other skimmers on the horizon yet. I hoped we had enough of a head start.

We plummeted through the darkness for a heart-stopping moment before his boots struck the ground with a jolt. My limbs protested lightly, sore muscles beginning to complain, and I grunted as I climbed off his back.

It was warmer down here, and I could feel heat rising from beneath my feet. My eyes slowly adjusted to the light inside the cave, a gorgeous dim dusk created by the glowing amber souls that flickered inside the jagged stone.

Entrances to small tunnels riddled the walls. I frowned and gingerly ran my hand along one, ready to yank it back if it fell into a hole. The texture of the tunnel was different than the smooth stone I had seen peeking through the sand—it felt more like thick cardboard than rock. Peeking into one showed me that the floor disappeared, becoming nothing but a plummeting chute into darkness. I spotted more holes in the floor and walls. While I suspected water could have once rushed through this land and formed a tunnel system like this, the sensation felt wrong. The stones weren't smooth but rough, like they had been formed by a burrowing animal of some sort.

"Careful," Dorian advised, catching my eye. "One wrong step, and you might fall to your death."

"What made the tunnels, do you think?" I asked. "It reminds me of the Hive built by the jaspeths."

Dorian dragged his eyes over the structures. "Not sure we want to know the answer to that."

I grimaced as a shiver ran through my skin. "Lovely." Hopefully, it was nothing as intense as the empty swarm.

Dorian smirked and squeezed my hand. "You tell me which direction with your magic bracelet and let me pick our way through the caves."

"Sounds like a plan." I pressed the bracelet firmly into my palm and frowned. The pulling sensation had stopped. The itch was nowhere to be found. Instead, all I could hear was the sound of my breath in the tight space as I tried to focus my attention on my body.

"What?" Dorian asked.

"I don't feel the itch prodding me much," I confessed. "It feels like he's not moving. Maybe forward, that way." I pointed toward the other side of the chamber.

"I can't sense any other aura." Dorian's lips curled into a sneer. "It looks like Sempre didn't make it this far."

Or we were chasing nothing. There was only one way to find out. I stared into the gloom. Dorian walked slowly in front of me, telling me when to avoid a hole as we made our way through the tunnels. Although my eyes had adjusted, I trusted his vision more than my own.

After a few moments, a distant sound reached my ears, like the slow march of something or someone marching with soft steps. As the buzz began to grow, I looked at Dorian. He looked more intrigued than alarmed.

The walls appeared to shift and move as hundreds of ants the size of medium dogs moved along them. *Whoa.* It was like someone shrank me and placed me inside a terrifyingly large ant farm. Their backs and legs glittered softly under the light of souls caught in the rocks and filtering through pockmarks in the ceiling. Suddenly the holes throughout the cave made sense.

"Is this going to be a problem?" I asked, yanking my foot back to avoid a smaller ant. It paused and felt my boot with long, spindly antennae. I tensed at the movement, uneasy and not wanting to startle the creature.

Dorian shook his head. "I don't think so," he said with a furrowed brow. "Creatures like this aren't usually hostile. Let's feel it out here. Give them a minute."

I quieted and hoped he was right. If the Immortal Plane had taught me anything, it was that I often had no control in this strange world. While I waited, I focused my breath and felt the warm metal of the bracelet. The itch faintly pulled me forward. At least it was there. It wanted us to keep walking. The ant near my boot crawled up my leg. Were Immortal ants carnivorous? I hoped not.

Finally, Dorian glanced over his shoulder and gave a nod. "They should be fine."

At first, the insects skittered away, then settled with our presence. One climbed halfway up Dorian, making him grimace and nearly giving him a kiss with a fierce set of pincers. The ants swarmed over us for another second before marching away, apparently uninterested in our presence.

Creepy. I stepped cautiously behind Dorian as the ants parted like twin currents of water around us.

"Still forward?" he asked as we came to a three-pronged split in the tunnel.

I touched the bracelet. "Yes."

Dorian tapped a sudden dead end. "Not quite, I'm afraid. This wall is definitely real." He rapped his knuckles hard against it. I frowned and tried to concentrate on the feeling of the bracelet.

"Left," I said as I felt a sudden tug. Dorian led the way, and I gradually corrected his path.

"Wait," he said suddenly. He stopped and pointed behind us. "This wall pulls away just like the last one."

Prisoner One was smart. Very smart. He deliberately hid in a series of animal-carved paths that made little logical sense to anyone with a humanoid form or brain. I pressed my fingers against my chin and stared at the wall in front of us, where it should have opened up to reveal another tunnel. If I tore down this wall, I might find his blank violet eyes on the other side.

"He's hidden himself inside a maze. Worse, he can change his size at will," I muttered. My mind tried to map the tunnels we had gone through. In my brain, I drew out a rough sketch of our recent movements… but it was hard. Prisoner One led us through dizzying paths for a reason. Dorian cleared his throat, and I sensed his meaning. We lacked the time to puzzle over Prisoner One's strategy, and the guards weren't far off.

I wondered if Inkarri had caught up to this area yet. Would she spot our skimmer in its hiding place and think to look down here? My stomach clenched as I recalled that Inkarri also had a tracking device for Prisoner One. There was no way to tell for sure whether anyone had landed up above.

The walls shifted around me again. The ants, or something else? I shook my head. I thought I had adjusted to the Immortal Plane, but it was difficult to tell whether the caves were actually moving or my mind was simply playing tricks on me. I rubbed my tired eyes, wishing we'd had time to rest. *Push through.*

As if sensing my discomfort, Dorian reached back and slipped his hand into mine. He squeezed, and I relaxed slightly.

The bracelet began to urge me in another direction.

"Left," I told Dorian as we came to an intersection.

We carried on like that for some time. Sometimes he stopped while I took several minutes to walk around the tunnel, holding up the bracelet, begging it for information that made sense. My borrowed sixth sense sometimes tingled stronger. I instructed Dorian to turn a few more times as the feeling grew.

The ants took to the walls. Their incessant marching next to my head make my skin crawl uneasily, but there was nothing I could do about it.

"I think we're getting closer," I whispered, not wanting to disturb our insect neighbors.

Huge boulders were wedged along the makeshift tunnel, making it difficult for us to pass. I strained to listen for any signs of life as we walked, but all I heard were my own feet and the gentle movements of ants.

Something flashed in the corner of my eye. I blinked and stared, but the passing light vanished. Instead, a swirl of shadows settled at the edges of the tunnel. It faded into near transparency. Some sort of illusion? The ants moved past it with zero issue, but I couldn't deny the feeling of dread the darkness inspired.

My lips felt numb. The itch grew even stronger.

Dorian stiffened abruptly. "I can feel something. I think it's the creature's aura." He paused for a moment like he was digesting the sensation. "It's… weird. I can't tell if it has lightness or darkness to it at all. It just *is*. Not balanced, just… nothing."

I pressed the bracelet into my burned palm, feeling the metal bite into the sensitive, blistered flesh. The itch felt like a hundred bugs on my skin.

"Just ahead," I whispered.

We only made it a few more yards before Dorian stopped.

"Cave-in," he said.

I peered around him to see a pile of jagged rocks that had effectively blocked off our path. He grabbed a stone from the top, and I did the same, pocketing the bracelet for a moment to move the fallen debris.

Prisoner One's resigned eyes flashed in my mind.

"He wants to be left alone," I guessed. "He certainly doesn't want Inkarri to find him. Maybe he needs to rest? He's been in prison for nearly a thousand years. That's got to leave you exhausted and damaged."

Dorian exhaled through his nose. In our current light, I could see that he was staring at the glamor behind me. "You're right. He's using the last of his strength to protect his hiding spot. Let's try to break through."

As soon as we moved the stones, sand and pebbles began to pitter-patter down from the roof of the tunnel. If we tried to clear this area, the ceiling threatened to collapse on us before we made it through to the other side. We backtracked, and he led us through another cavernous hallway devoid of ants. My tired eyes tried to make shapes out of the dim area. A small sliver of steam rose up between the rocks around us. I clung to the bracelet and instructed Dorian forward.

It was twice the length of the first route, but soon the itch grew to its previous strength again.

"Up ahead," I said. "And I don't see anything blocking us." My heart gave an excited squeeze. Had we finally found him?

Dorian put a hand on my shoulder in warning. "Dark presences." He stared up at the ceiling. "There's a group of them, and they're getting closer."

There was no way we could outpace them in such narrow tunnels. My eyes darted around the cavern. We would have to conceal ourselves, and quickly.

"We need to hide."

Dorian helped me through the dim area, then we sprinted the length of the tunnel until we came to the same three-way intersection. Without conscious thought, my hand flew toward the edge of the wall beside me. My arm fell into a deep crevice. It would barely be big enough for two people, but it was deep enough to work.

"Here," I whispered and yanked Dorian in beside me. There was no light from above or embedded in the stone. It was a perfect blind spot of darkness, tucked into the wall without looking like a hole at all. Dorian pulled his hands in to rest at his chest and turned his head toward me, leaning in until our foreheads touched.

Metal met stone as rushing footsteps echoed somewhere far down the passageway. I held my breath as something fuzzy touched my hand. I instinctually wanted to yank my hand back as a chill ran down my arm.

The furry leg of the ant passed, only to be replaced by another. I bit my tongue as the initial shock dissipated.

"The ants," I muttered, and pressed my ear against the wall to try to figure out their direction inside the walls. "One of them just walked on my hand."

Dorian looked up. "They're going somewhere."

With magnificent strength, he pulled himself up the wall and crawled onto an outcropping that I hadn't been able to see, then he reached down and yanked me up after him. The ants tried to step over us, but Dorian hissed at them, and they gradually changed their path. It was a better spot than the crack, with room enough for two bodies.

I pressed myself against the jagged surface of the wall as four pairs of footsteps came out of the passage.

"We'll never find anything in these forsaken tunnels," Inkarri snarled to her companions. "We need to be wary of his trickery. He's a master of false clues."

One of them coughed, uncomfortable in the face of her anger. Without her coaxing call, her icy tone merely sank into my body like a wintery chill. Dorian stroked his thumb over my hand. My lungs strained as I held my breath.

"Let's take the first right," Inkarri snapped. "Keep up, or I'll leave you here."

She stormed off down the side corridor. From my perspective, I could see the barest top of a gleaming helmet. I swallowed the grit in my throat as her companions rushed to follow her. I clenched my hand into a fist, waiting with anticipation for any sign of a return from her and her guards.

After a full minute, Dorian batted away an over-curious ant and jumped down. "It feels like they went lower. There might be layers even under this system." There was enough light for me to see him holding out his arms. I could make the jump myself, but it would be quieter if he caught me. And after so much pain, I would never pass up an opportunity to touch him. I jumped into his waiting arms, and he gently set me down.

"Bracelet says left, so she made a bad call," I said softly as I checked the jewelry. Indeed, Inkarri had gone another way, but perhaps she had information that I didn't. The Immortals knew the Restless Desert, meaning they might know the tunnels.

"Good for now."

We picked up our pace. Dorian pulled on my hand, and I did my best to follow with quiet footsteps. Occasionally, my boot struck a rock, sending it skittering, and I winced, hoping it wouldn't alert the hunters.

"If Prisoner One got down there, we should be able to," Dorian muttered.

All the walls looked the same—dark, blue, and unwelcoming even with the spattering of flickering souls. The bracelet felt cooler in my hand, but the itch grew stronger again. As we rushed, I tried to let my other hand reach out and note crevices. If we needed to hide, we would have to be ready to shove ourselves into a narrow hole again at a moment's notice. Luckily, the ants had created quite a few hiding places.

The bracelet surged against me with a little spark of static electricity, and my palms began to sweat. The feeling of *knowing* multiplied inside my entire body.

"I've got it," I told him excitedly. This was it. My pulse staggered, a renewed hope rushing through me.

Dorian pressed himself against the wall as he let me pass him. I led us through a chamber, then down a narrower passage to the left.

"He's down here. I can feel it." A pool of heat spread from the core of my body out to the tips of my fingers and toes.

My next step found nothing but open air when there should have been solid stone. I threw my weight backward, and Dorian grunted as I careened into his chest. He steadied me, and we peeked over the edge of the chasm. It opened up like the mouth of a hungry beast, nearly impossible to see in the low light. I blinked, and the chasm disappeared, transforming back into solid blueish ground.

Dorian wrapped his fingers around my arm. "What the hell?"

My head swarmed with a light feeling. I'd nearly fallen for a glamor, quite literally. It was more powerful than any of the ones I had seen before.

"He's doing illusion work now," Dorian confirmed grimly.

Prisoner One had to be close by. I turned the bracelet over in my hand and squeezed my fingers around it. Something stuck in my mind. What if this wasn't the first time he'd used glamor to protect himself?

"The cave-in," I breathed. "It could've been a glamor too."

Dorian dropped his eyes to meet my gaze. "We'll go back."

We carefully but quickly retraced our steps. It felt like Dorian and I kept backtracking, only to hit a certain point and be forced to repeat the same game trying it from another side. There was some central core that we hadn't been able to access yet, somewhere the prisoner had settled in and set up camp.

We carefully avoided crossing paths with Inkarri and her underlings, which they made easy for us by tromping through the tunnels and calling out to each other. I couldn't parse the words, but occasionally the noise cut off after an exasperated reprimand from Inkarri, only to start up again within minutes. It reminded me uncomfortably of Bryce scolding fresh recruits. Bryce would not have appreciated the comparison.

We were creeping through a tunnel parallel to theirs when it happened. I wasn't sure what, exactly; I only heard the shouts, which turned to screams, Inkarri's roar rising above the rest.

"Cling to the walls, you useless, spoiled idiots! Your gloves will do all the work. Vinke, grab that—*Yes*, Rotmar! Stay there!"

Incredibly, it seemed that one of her team had managed to stop his fall. He was hysterical, gasping for breath and emitting short screams on the exhale. I clutched Dorian's hand for support, feeling dizzy. It was hard listening to people die next to me, even my enemies. I couldn't help willing Rotmar to make it to safety.

"Don't look at them, look at me!" Inkarri snapped. "You're going to be fine. Calm down, then pull yourself up. All you have to do is dig in with your gloves, see? Like I'm doing. Use one foot to push yourself up, then grab. We'll make it to the shelf. Can you do it?"

The only response was whimpering.

"*Useless,*" she said with disgust. "All right, I'm coming to get you."

I heard a sharp crack, followed by two screams; one that faded into the distance, one that continued on and on right next to us, long after the other cut off. The hairs on the back of my neck rose with the realization that everyone in the neighboring tunnel was dead, except for Inkarri. Dorian and I exchanged a horrified look.

She swore at her team, berating them for being stupid, for not paying attention, for slowing her down. Even with magic, they hadn't been good enough. She finally trailed off, and after a long, fragile silence, she started sobbing. Dorian squeezed my hand, and we slipped away.

"It sounded like they fell through the floor," I whispered, once we'd reached a safe distance.

Dorian nodded. "Another illusion," he said solemnly. "We have to be more careful. Don't put your full weight down until you're sure the ground is solid."

I wasn't so sure about that. Dorian and I had been running around these tunnels for hours before Inkarri's team had even arrived, and the most lethal thing that had happened to us was when I tripped over a rock and bruised my shin. I'd flatter myself by saying that we'd been stealthier than Inkarri's lackeys, but realistically, Prisoner One probably knew where we were by now. I didn't think it was an accident that the lethal trap had ended up in their tunnel, and that told me something. Prisoner One might not have wanted us to find him, but he didn't want to kill us, either.

The sight of the cave-in came as a welcome relief, when we finally found it again. The pile of rocks rose up from the gloom, looking as solid and forbidding as it had previously. They had seemed solid when I grabbed onto them before, but as I looked for the telltale waver of a glamor, I saw that the left corner of the pile flickered.

"What would happen if I just... walked through?" I asked, taking a deep breath and reaching out my hands toward the cave-in.

Dorian, thinking quickly, dug the rope from my pack and tied it securely around my waist before bracing himself. "I'll pull you back, in case there's a giant hole waiting for you again." He pressed his fingers to me. "I'm always here for you." There was a brief moment of warmth between us. I grinned to myself and squeezed his hand.

"There's nobody I'd rather have with me."

I tried not to think too hard about the sickening sensation of falling as I stepped into the stones, choosing to focus on the sensation left behind by Dorian's touch. Despite looking jagged, the rocks felt smooth, like they had been polished by water and time. I frowned and pressed forward. At first, my arms bent as the wall tried to resist me, but then the sensation vanished.

I slid through the rubble like tearing through tissue paper, stumbling for a moment at the curious sensation. As soon as it became clear I wasn't plummeting to my death, Dorian followed me. A few yards ahead lay a cavern full of soft, periwinkle-colored light cast by glowing crystals that grew from the walls, ceiling, and patches of the floor.

The bracelet burned in my hand as I took a few steps forward. In a patch of shadow, banished to the corner of the room, I saw a pair of violet eyes devoid of pupils.

We'd finally found Prisoner One.

CHAPTER FORTY-NINE

"We're not here to hurt you." I slipped the gauntlet off and set it on the ground, holding up my hands to show that I was unarmed.

The creature gave no reaction. He had shifted back into the humanoid body he'd inhabited when he'd been imprisoned, but kept his reptilian skin. Surrounded by the blue crystals that sprouted from the stone like fungus, his sienna scales shimmered, giving the impression that he was not entirely corporeal. They glinted magnificently in the soft light. It was a more delicate beauty than I had seen anywhere in Itzarriol, and it was oddly calming, despite Prisoner One's powerful, unblinking stare.

He was sitting in a corner, beneath one of the jutting rock outcroppings covered in blue gems. To get to him, we would have to cross the room, a task made tricky by the fact that we stood on a ledge above him with a deep fissure in between us. I glanced down at the dizzying drop, not knowing whether it was real or fake. *Not taking a chance on that.*

The only thing resembling another exit was on the far end of the chamber, but it looked like the wall had collapsed and was blocked by crystals. Or was this blockage also an illusion? I glanced around the room, looking for any signs of flickering or wavering that might indicate glamor. Nothing caught my eye this time.

Prisoner One, shapeshifter and likely the long-lost Gate Maker, remained completely stationary, his legs crossed. The cave ants marched around him and across his knees. He did nothing to discourage them. In fact, it was as if he barely registered their existence at all. I could *see* their legs tapping across his scales, but he did nothing except stare at Dorian and me.

It was unnerving, to say the least. Although the Gate Maker was almost certainly the key to our mission, what would we do if he *had* gone mad during his awful captivity? I licked the corner of my mouth, wondering what I could do to help him. What did one say to a creature who'd had such a massive chunk of his life stolen from him?

"What would you like us to call you?" I asked him softly and took a tentative step forward.

Dorian advanced with me but kept his arm out to keep me from falling off the ledge. His doubtful stare told me that he wasn't sure whether the drop was real or not either.

The creature blinked once, extinguishing the glow of his purple eyes for a moment. "I knew you'd come," he said softly, the words tight, as if it pained him to speak after so long. "You just can't leave me alone, can you?"

I pushed down my rising anxiety. I'd faced fierce challenges before, but something was different about the Gate Maker. His intimidating presence radiated like vibrations through the air.

"We're not your enemies," I insisted, and spread my hands out, hoping he could see the peaceful gesture well enough in the light. "I freed you. I want to make sure you stay free."

He sighed, the sound like rustling paper. "No one performs good deeds without an ulterior motive. You may believe you did, but all you have done is place me in another cage. I owe you my freedom now, and such a debt is restrictive by its very nature."

His speech was slow going. Beneath the words, however, anger hummed inside him. The hairs on my arms stood to attention. I wanted to honor his feelings and make him feel heard, something that the rulers never provided for him. I needed to establish myself as his ally... but we also needed to obtain his help. He would sniff manipulation coming off me. How could I convince him I was genuine?

"I assure you," I said, taking another step toward him, "my only motivation to free you was my belief that no one should live in chains."

He straightened his back, and his eyes widened, an expression I wasn't sure how to interpret. I'd never met a creature like him before, and I couldn't read his mannerisms. His lack of pupils appeared oddly beautiful in the blue light.

"And your motivation for pursuing me was equally altruistic?" he asked, a knowing note to his voice that prompted a pang of guilt. He had a point, and I had guessed he would make this accusation. I had a motive, but to be fair it was a good motive. If he didn't help us, the tear could cause an explosion, and both our worlds would be gone. Boom. Just like that. It would kill everyone, including the Gate Maker. Helping him was actually in both our best interests, and I needed to make him see that.

"We want to help you," I said carefully, trying to walk the fine line between truth and keeping him on our side. "Help keep you free. Help find you somewhere safe to go. And then, yes, maybe you could help us in return."

Dorian took a step, flanking me, but the movement apparently startled the Gate Maker. Abruptly, he lumbered to his feet, his ancient body creaking as he pulled himself unsteadily to a standing position. My heart rate increased. How long did we have to convince him before he tried to run or the hunters caught up to us?

"Please," I said, but the creature snorted.

"I can make the earth crumble beneath you, human," the Gate Maker said, in a tone as powerful and all-consuming as a tidal wave. "I could rip open a portal and throw myself into the most savage places of the Immortal Plane, where you would be helpless to follow me."

The force of his voice made me tense. He spoke with an authority unlike the magical call of Irrikus or Inkarri. It was a tone that demanded obedience through the sheer display of his strength. His existence sparked wonder in me, unlike the fear and loathing that I felt for the Immortal council members.

The Gate Maker swept out a hand toward us. He splayed his long, gnarled fingers in a wide gesture. "I can show you the inner workings of madness so volatile your mind would break to witness such things. I can rend the sky into pieces, tear the magic from your souls—"

Dorian exhaled evenly. "No," he said, his tone firm but gentle. "You wouldn't be playing with grand illusions in a cave system that you're fighting to keep up, if you could actually do that right now. I saw some of your glamors flickering and fading. No doubt you are capable of such wonders when you're at full strength, but I think you're far from that."

The creature scoffed, puffing out his chest, but it was more evident than before that most of his words were driven by fear. I kept my face neutral but open, my body language as nonthreatening as possible. We needed to convince this very smart, scared, dangerous creature to trust us, and it might turn out to be the hardest thing we'd ever done.

"End it right here," Dorian urged. "If you're telling the truth, then do it. You could have escaped to anywhere on this plane in an instant, if that were the case. But being in prison drains your energy, doesn't it?" A melancholy, knowing note snuck into his voice as the question slipped past his lips.

Our own feelings of helplessness in the sanitarium were still fresh and raw, and they'd formed after only a few days of incarceration. How awful it must've been for a creature so powerful, yet bound by chains in a small box.

The Gate Maker hissed, anger bubbling in his throat like boiling water. The crystals close to him vibrated at the timbre of his voice. "You know nothing of my capabilities. You know nothing of what I have endured," he said with a growl. "Leave me be. I have no interest in receiving your help or granting you mine."

He sat again and folded his legs into a crossed position. Slowly, he dragged a long hand over his face and sighed. The sense of power drained from his entire body as he settled into the corner.

"I just want to be left alone," he muttered. His eyelids drooped for a moment, the skin of his lids shimmering gold, as he gazed out at nothing with a half-lidded stare. My heart squeezed as sympathy threatened to blur my strategic mind. *We wish we could leave you in peace.*

I eyed Dorian as covertly as possible. He'd hit on something when he challenged the creature to go ahead and perform his magical feats of wonder. The man in front of us was exhausted.

I sucked in a breath. "Please. This isn't just about us. It's about every single being in existence."

Dorian folded his arms across his chest. "She's right. We need to fix the tear or else everyone is going to suffer."

The Gate Maker offered no reaction.

I let my hands hang loosely by my sides. Some small bit of frustration died inside me as I drank in the tired silence from the Gate Maker. Even if he was finally in front of us, he felt more out of reach than ever. He truly wanted to be left alone after such a traumatic experience, but... I needed to find some way to reach him.

"We want to end the tyranny of the rulers, just as I'm sure you do." Hoping it would create a positive response, I ventured to add, "We want to remove all those like Sempre who are in power only because they crush others beneath them." I tried to think about what else would appeal to him. "We can restore balance to all the planes. There can be harmony."

The Gate Maker leaned his head back and stared at the crystals lining the ceiling. "You small creatures have no concept of what I want. You could never help me." His voice dropped into a hoarse whisper. "You are simply trying to use me. Little mouths claim that you are not like everybody else, but you are *exactly* like everybody else. Like Sempre."

As he spoke the Immortal lord's name, the creature broke into a grin that was too big and too happy, his teeth glinting in the dim light. His entire body shuddered under the force of his own bitter chuckles.

Dorian had said that there was no other aura besides the Gate Maker's. We'd seen no sign of Sempre since he'd been dragged, screaming, out of the sanitarium.

"Where is Sempre now?" I asked, forcing my voice to stay firm.

The Gate Maker met my gaze, his smile ice cold. "Oh, I dropped that one so deep in the ground, even the beasts who burrow there won't be able to find him. I ripped the pretty little gem from his head. He'll starve to death in darkness and despair, calling for help that will never come, alone in the bowels of this miserable plane."

Hairs rose on the back of my neck. *Remind me never to cross this guy.*

"Sempre was our enemy too," I pointed out, "and we're glad you got rid of him. He was instrumental in the slaughter of vampires in this plane and has set into motion plans to endanger people I care about." I paused, part of me blooming with a strange anger that Sempre was going to die without facing true justice. "But there are still others who want to capture you again. They won't stop until they are either removed from power or you escape this plane."

I nipped my tongue at the end. Part of me desperately wanted to know exactly why the Gate Maker was in custody and why the Immortal council members sought to keep him there. He was already suspicious of me, however, and poking at his traumatic experience to sate my curiosity seemed cruel.

"Sempre and the rest of the Immortal Council don't deserve to be the reason everyone dies," Dorian added, cutting into my thoughts. "If you give us a chance, we can figure out how to potentially stop the tear." His grave eyes settled on the prisoner, who merely shifted lightly as if his back bothered him.

"I don't want to hear it." The Gate Maker turned his face away from us. "What do I care? I can hide and sleep eternally after it's destroyed, knowing that darkness has been extinguished. The part I played in the council's plans was by force." He paused for a moment and opened his mouth, but decided against whatever he wanted to say.

"What part did they make you play?" I asked, keeping my tone gentle but not patronizing. There was no response, so I inhaled deeply and took a gamble. "Did it have something to do with you being the Gate Maker?"

Silence, tight as a drumskin, stretched across the cavern. A muscle twitched below my left eye as I tried to keep calm. The Gate Maker could be our only hope.

He narrowed his eyes at me, the purple slowly darkening to the color of thunderclouds. "So, you want me to help you fix that accursed tear, don't you? I have been exhausted and drained over the last several years unpicking the magical threads between our worlds, forced to perform a bastardized form of my work. Now you want me to turn around and stitch the fabric of reality back together. For what? Your half-baked promises of protection? *You* are going to protect *me?*"

For a moment, I couldn't breathe as I processed his admission. The Gate Maker was indeed the Gate Maker, and the Immortal rulers had been using him to deliberately weaken the tear between our two planes. This was proof for the Bureau, and if Dorian and I could convince the Gate Maker, then we might also have a solution.

"If you would just—" The sound of him clicking his fingers cut off whatever desperate argument I was about to attempt.

The Gate Maker began to shrink and darken before our eyes. His deep red skin turned two shades darker as his body melted into a crawling, pulsing piece of clay. I stared at him, equal parts horrified and fascinated, wondering what terrifying form he might take. Dorian *had* challenged him, after all.

But all the Gate Maker did was transform into an ant and scuttle off. Almost all the distant gap between us vanished as his illusions faded. Several patches of crystal also disappeared, revealing additional tunnels and crevices dotted across the chamber.

It was into one of these tunnels that the Gate Maker scurried, joining a group of ants walking down this central passage. He was immediately indistinguishable from them, taking a place in the steady march toward some unknown location.

I began to summon words to convince him to come back, but what could I say? He wanted nothing to do with us. Even if I had some brilliant logic, or even if we tried to forcibly capture him, the tunnel he'd taken was too small for us to follow unless we crawled. Gradually, the itch began to rise once more, telling me he was getting farther away. I snatched up my abandoned gauntlet and put it back on, a wave of frustration choking my body. Every minute we spent chasing him was a minute we weren't in the Mortal Plane helping our friends with the oncoming chaos.

What could we do to get him on our side?

Dorian hissed, "Someone's coming. Not him. Someone dark."

My gaze flew around the room. There was a deep crack in the wall that we might fit in, if we hurried. I gestured for him to follow me back the way we came, through the tunnel with the illusory rockfall.

The sand and stone shattered into shards of broken magic. They appeared like silver splinters of glass, then faded in less than a second, no longer stable now that the Gate Maker was absent. From down the passage beyond the broken glamor, the thunder of footsteps hurried straight toward us.

It sounded like Inkarri.

CHAPTER FIFTY

I nkarri charged into the room, her pale blue skin a deep cerulean in the dim light.

Her brief surprise at finding Dorian and me instead of the Gate Maker quickly turned to irritation. She tossed her braids of oceanic blue hair over her shoulder as her nostrils flared.

"You two have been remarkably annoying for such tiny, fragile creatures," Inkarri growled. "I'm almost impressed."

She ignored me, lunging at Dorian. I'd forgotten how lightning fast her movements were, even dressed in her standard chainmail armor. Dorian's stone still sat warm against me in the pouch, and we would need it now more than ever. She threw the entire weight of her seven-foot frame forward, crashing into him.

He had only a moment's warning before she hit, barely managing to turn and deflect the full force of her assault. Metal struck flesh as her shoulder connected with his sternum, and his breath audibly left his body. Inkarri gave a terrible smirk, her arm flying up with a morning star in her clutches. A round, spiked ball chained to the end of a staff, the iridescent spikes caught the light, making it a lethally beautiful weapon.

"You two won't stop me from doing my job," she promised ominously. Her eyes hardened. "I won't fail."

I pulled out Dorian's stone.

It was hot, and I yanked a scrap of fabric from my pocket to wrap around it. I skirted around the fight, looking for a good opening to dash in and press it to her magicked armor. Even though she was not using her gauntlet, possibly for fear of collapsing the cave, she still had boots, chainmail, and a variety of weapons.

"Don't move," Inkarri snapped, the cavern reverberating with the thrall she injected into her voice. Incredible, how she eased into it as easily as pulling on a glove. "I'll deal with the prisoner after I take you out. I'm sure I can find some way to make him pay for the trap that killed my comrades." Her tone was even, with no sign of her earlier tears, but her face contained a deep fury beneath her stony stare.

Dorian ignored her command, moving around to flank her, but my body froze, stock still. *Move,* I told my hands. My fingers retracted and opened again. I shook my head hard from side to side to dislodge her syrupy call and found that I could move once again.

I glanced at her boots, which I knew from experience would likely be the heaviest part for her to deal with. Still, Inkarri was different from those guards who relied entirely on their magicked weapons—she moved like a skilled fighter. If the stakes hadn't been so high, I would have stopped to admire her artistry. She used her armor as a tool, not a crutch, and Dorian could barely keep up. If I could level the playing field a little, that might make all the difference he needed. Even as I looked for a chance to use the stone, part of my mind was on the Gate Maker. How far had he gotten by now?

While she was distracted by Dorian, I raced forward and tapped the stone against the spikes of the morning star, which were made of jagged crystal set into the metal. A rich yellow glow lit the stone as it buzzed and sputtered, immediately losing its luster. Heat exploded from the stone, burning me even through the rag, but I gritted my teeth and clung onto it. I dropped my hand down to her left boot, feeling the stone singe my skin as it absorbed yet another powerful enchantment.

"What have you done?" Inkarri demanded as she glared down at me. She lashed out with her other foot, catching me in stomach, the force sending me into the cavern wall.

Bile sprang up in my throat, all that was left in my stomach, and for a long second my vision blurred with pain. I knew I was lucky even as I curled in on myself, gagging and gasping. It would leave a killer bruise, but I hoped it hadn't done any internal damage.

Inkarri glared at her dull weapon, a glimmer of the same fury and confusion washing over her face that she had shown when her gauntlet stopped working at Lake Siron.

Inkarri let out a long, rumbling laugh as she successfully brought the morning star down onto Dorian's arm. If it had been anyone else, the blow would have shattered the bone, but Dorian was protected by his vampire heritage. He still let out a yell of pain as he drew back, and a spray of his blood filled the cave with its scent. I threw myself back against the solid wall as she lashed out behind her with the weapon. She glanced over with a grin and changed directions. I scrambled into a shallow tunnel for cover just as her morning star struck the wall, sending up a shower of pebbles and narrowly missing my skull.

I ducked under her next blow, rolling back into the center of the cavern, yelping as my damaged rib hit the ground.

Using the opportunity, I launched myself toward her boots with the stone extended, hoping to slow her down enough to dispel her other magic items. Dorian caught her by the wrists with a strained exhale of effort, leaving the spiked ball of the morning star dangling down as they struggled against one another.

Dorian accidentally stepped on my leg as I crawled between the flurry of feet, but I stifled my yelp of pain.

Dorian pulled Inkarri forward by the wrists and released her, making her stumble. Without the morning star's magic, he grew braver and delivered a series of slashes with his dagger to gaps in Inkarri's armor. I grunted as I hauled myself up. My stomach and ribs felt like they might cave in from pain, but I would survive. I needed to get back in the action to hit her other boot.

She went to send a well-timed kick at Dorian with her left leg but was caught off guard by the change in weight. Unlike the other guards and hunters, she continued to be able to move when the magic came off her armor. Her well-developed muscles came from decades of training, and she knew how to fight. But her movement slowed just enough to give Dorian time to jump in and slash across the back of her right leg with his dagger. It pierced her armor, which crumpled more easily now without its magic. He nearly nicked her joint.

For the first time, her smugness wavered. Her eyebrows knitted together as a rage like I'd never seen before swallowed up her face. The Immortal rulers had marched on unchallenged for so long, they appeared to have forgotten what it was like to be bested in a fight.

Her magic wouldn't save her this time. I would make sure of it.

Dorian smirked, highlighting a jagged scrape along one side of his face. A long tear hung open on the side of his shirt where Inkarri had managed to slice him. Blood flowed in thin streams down his arm from the blow she'd landed with the morning star.

His chest heaved with strain even as he gave Inkarri a gloating look. It would piss her off, certainly, and that could make her wilder in her fight. Her gemstone shimmered in her forehead as she threw her braids out of her face. Her lip curled in disgust, but her gaze remained steady with focus.

She threw herself at Dorian, but her left boot betrayed her once more, and Dorian cracked her under the chin with a wicked uppercut. I darted for her legs again and managed to tap the stone against her other boot, rushing away just as Dorian kicked her into the wall, leaving a tiny, angry crack.

Still so strong. I ran my tongue over my teeth, tasting blood as I watched her closely.

"You may have tricks," she whispered hoarsely, hatred embedded within her gravelly tone. "But I'm no two-bit guard. I've been training my entire life."

"And yet you can never seem to best me. Interesting," Dorian said, with affected boredom. They clashed again, and he gripped the chain connecting the flail of her morning star to the handle, holding it close to the spiked ball without any worry of shock.

My hands went to my weapon belt, where I still had a dagger. I'd given the axe to Laini for her mission, knowing she might need it if she came across a patrol on the ground.

Dorian's eyes darted to my hand. "No," he said, shoving Inkarri back. He tripped her, using the weight of her new boots to throw her off balance. She fell back, but instead of launching himself at her, he focused on me. "I can still feel him. He's nearby. I'll handle her. You need to find him."

Inkarri sucked in a sharp breath between her bared teeth. Her hateful gaze landed on me. "The hell she will." She leapt to her feet and sprang toward me, but Dorian smashed into her from the side.

"Go, Lyra!"

I pocketed the stone and kept my blade drawn. There was a larger tunnel that looked like it might run parallel to the ant-sized passageway the Gate Maker had escaped through. I ran, the sounds of combat barely fading as I passed through the first section of the tunnel.

Inkarri's patrol, lying dead somewhere deep in a trap, flickered through my mind. Would the Gate Maker have enough energy to leave behind more traps? Without Dorian's eyesight to give me warning, I would have to be careful. I moved as swiftly as I dared and felt my way along in the dim light. Farther along the tunnel, I caught the glint of the edge of a small chasm just before I stepped into it. Somewhere far below rushed a stream of water.

Across the chasm, the steady movement of ants broke through the sounds of battle.

"Gate Maker," I called out. My voice sounded raspy and desperate even to my ears.

What could I say to persuade him to come with us? I had no idea what he really wanted, besides the eternal nap.

My hands groped the wall, feeling for fissures and cracks where he might have stashed himself. Shapeshifting took energy, which he must be running out of after his flight across the desert and all his illusions. He couldn't have traveled very far. I swallowed my worries.

"I want to learn your story," I called out. "There are things I think only you can help with. If the barrier doesn't get fixed, our two worlds will merge, and the rulers' actions will cause the destruction of both the planes. There will be no safe place for you to hide then. You'll be a pile of particles like the rest of us. There will be no peace. I don't want that for you."

There was a silence, but it felt tense. My heart raced.

"It's true that I'm being selfish in a way, and that I want something from you, but I only want to protect both our worlds. I want to restore the balance that existed before the Immortal Council was able to imprison you. We want to end this war."

The echoes of metal and hard punches floated above me. I looked back, praying that Dorian could hold her off a little longer.

"Please," I begged the dark. How could I reason with him? The back of my brain burned for a moment, remembering how Juneau had taught us the most important lesson about the Immortal Plane when he'd demanded a trade. Bargains were a currency in the Immortal Plane just as soul energy was.

It was worth a shot. "If you don't care about the world, that's okay. Fine. I want to bargain with you, then. If you do this for us, I'll do something for you. I don't know *what* you want, but I'll be in your debt. Both Dorian and I will help you if you figure out how we can take down the Immortal Council before the entire universe explodes." I paused for a moment to let the words sink in. "We want to take down the Immortal Council *for good* and heal the tear between the planes. Maybe we can try to give you justice in the process. Maybe we can even give you revenge."

I settled on the last word as I recalled the cold rush of victory I'd felt watching Zeele's last moments.

My fingers found a wide crack in the wall to my left. It was near the chasm, about a foot before it plummeted. I looked inside and realized it was another narrow passageway. Ants filed out of the shallow tunnel and onto the walls. My eyes adjusted better to see them marching all over. They appeared less than impressed by my desperate speech.

I tried to pick him out from the bunch, searching for a flash of sienna.

"Lyra!" Dorian cried from behind. "She's—"

His voice cut off in a grunt. I whirled around, drawing my knife. Inkarri appeared in the passageway, holding a struggling Dorian in her grasp. She grunted as she threw Dorian with all her strength toward me— no, past me.

He plummeted into the chasm with a shout that abruptly cut off.

No.

My vision flashed red for a moment as Inkarri came at me. Something awoke inside me, something shadowy that slithered into my mind and begged for violence and blood and broken bones.

"You've been a thorn in my side for too long," Inkarri growled.

She lunged at me, and I met her, fury coursing through me like I'd never known. I wanted to destroy her. I wanted to rip her face off with my teeth. I wanted to make sure she could never take someone away from another person again. Inkarri was growing weaker. I could feel it. I could hear it in her ragged breath.

The white-hot anger was so powerful, it cemented my jaw closed. A calculated fury came over me as I quickly surveyed her. Down on her leg, my eyes found a sliver of red where Dorian had managed to land a cut on her. A weak spot.

"I'll show you how painful a thorn can be," I said bitterly.

I stepped in close to duck under her swinging arm. Let her know I was hoping to rip out her heart. Let her see the fury of a human pushed too far.

"Just give up," Inkarri snarled as she pushed me. The back of my foot flirted with the chasm's edge. "You don't stand a chance against me."

I snapped my teeth together and found a new surge of strength. I sidestepped quickly away from the chasm. If she got close enough… I could throw her right inside, but she was fast. The blade in my hand reminded me to focus on her wounded leg.

Dorian had worn her down considerably, and I had stripped her of important magical elements.

You can do this. Think of Dorian.

And the deranged energy inside me pushed me onward.

"You're fighting the inevitable." Inkarri was breathing hard, despite her mocking tone. "You're a mere human."

She came at me, pressing all her weight on her uninjured left leg. It was a mistake. I dropped down, driving my blade into the flesh of her wounded leg, making it buckle and dropping her to her knees.

I snatched the chain of the morning star, wrenching the handle from her momentarily limp grip before stepping behind her and wrapping the chain around her throat. Rage drove me as I pulled it tight, enjoying the sound of her air suddenly cutting off.

Inkarri clawed desperately at my grip, but it was hard for her to reach me while in her armor. I pulled harder and tasted blood, biting into my own tongue as my anger soared. Everything was Inkarri's fault in that moment. I wanted to rip her head off. My arms trembled as I heard her struggle to breathe.

"You've hurt so many," I muttered in a voice so filled with loathing that I hardly recognized it to be mine. "I'll make sure you never do again."

Inkarri slashed her blue glass knife with the last bit of her strength. It struck my shoulder, but it felt like a child's dull scratch. I was numb to all feelings other than my rage.

Inkarri dropped the knife and stilled.

I kept squeezing.

Stop, something inside me said. *It won't bring him back.*

I loosened the morning star, my chest heaving. A tear slid down my cheek, hot and angry. As much as I hated her, Inkarri probably knew important information about how the Immortal rulers might plan to pursue us, and I needed to conserve my energy. If Dorian had survived, I would need all my strength to find him.

CHAPTER FIFTY-ONE

Inkarri slumped to the ground. Gradually my vision steadied, and I stared down at my shaking hands. Imprints from the morning star's chain, visible even in the dim light, marred my hands. It felt like someone had stabbed the side of my head with a needle, and it was now leaking scalding-hot blood. I threw the morning star into the chasm, making sure that if she did wake up, she wouldn't have immediate access to the weapon.

I leaned down to Inkarri for a second. A soft breath touched my cheek. She wasn't dead. I couldn't decide whether that was for the best, but I didn't have time to wrestle with that dilemma. She was out of commission for now. I needed the rope in my pack for the chasm, but I couldn't leave Inkarri unrestrained even if she was knocked out cold for the moment. I dug inside my backpack to find a scrap of rope just long enough to tie her hands behind her back.

I needed to find Dorian. The Gate Maker might be getting away, but Dorian was the priority.

I stared down into the chasm. Nothing. I couldn't see in the dim light. Only a few souls studded these walls.

"Dorian?" I called, my voice echoing down the drop.

Silence, unforgiving and tense.

Then his voice crawled up out of the darkness.

"Lyra," he croaked weakly.

My heart gave an excited leap. "Dorian!" I said, almost sobbing. "Are you hurt?"

He groaned, the sound ghostly as it rose up from the pit. "I'm wedged in a narrow part of the crevice. It's like I'm stuck in a chimney. I've tried to pull myself up, but I keep slipping. It's too wide and smooth near the top." He coughed, a terrible sound that violently wracked his entire body. "I have no idea how deep this crevice goes. I can't see the bottom."

My stomach churned nervously as I took in the information. Hurrying back to where I had flung off my pack, I dug out more rope, spooling it quickly in my hands. No need to think. My body just moved. I blinked away hot tears as I searched for a boulder or outcropping to use as an anchor point. I found a solid spire of stone just off to the side.

"I'm going to throw a rope down," I called, and eyed Inkarri, making sure she was still unconscious. "I'll fish it along the edge until it finds you."

A stray ant perched beside me on a boulder, waving its antennae, but I paid it no mind. We were probably causing a disturbance in this delicate ecosystem. I anchored the rope as securely as possible and let it drop into the shadows. I started walking the rope near the middle and worked my way left.

"Do you feel it?"

"Not yet." His voice had a slight wheeze to it. I hoped his lungs were okay.

I walked to the right, disturbing the ant, which disappeared down into the chasm.

Suddenly, the rope gave a tug.

"I've got it."

The rope pulled taut as new weight was added to it. I took as much of the pressure as I could on my burned hands, not wanting to rely solely on the anchor. Dorian grunted as he slowly pulled himself up, and I braced myself, waiting anxiously for that familiar head of dark hair to emerge.

Like a zombie escaping the grave, his hand burst out of the darkness, clinging to the edge. He hauled himself onto solid ground, and I rushed to help, grabbing him under the arms and pulling him to safety. He groaned as we collapsed onto the ground, me wrapped around him, a laugh of giddy relief rising up in my throat.

Inkarri's still form caught Dorian's eye. "Is she alive?"

"Barely." I checked for any sign of movement, but she still looked unconscious.

He rested his head against mine, both of us battered and weary. "I didn't think I was going to make it out." He looked toward the edge again. "An ant brought the rope to me."

I stared. "It did?"

The ant heaved itself over the edge as Dorian had done, then flopped to the ground. Like kinetic sand reforming, its body turned into a long, gangly build that I knew well by now.

The Gate Maker's humanoid form was significantly thinner and smaller now. His cheekbones jutted sharply from his face, and his eyes were deep hollows in his skull. The effort required to change his form was emaciating him.

"Thank you," Dorian said softly.

The shapeshifter looked up with flat violet eyes. He sighed, the movement visibly passing through his body. "I will help you if you help me."

I let out a sharp bark of laughter, unable to help it. "You were listening?"

"Yes," he admitted weakly and coughed. "Allow me to dictate the terms of my request, and I'll keep listening." He paused. "I want to escape this mess, and I can't do that if the wretched Immortal Council destroys everything."

Untangling myself from Dorian, I climbed slowly to my feet, untying the rope from around the outcropping. "Then we'll talk. Right after I take care of this."

I crossed to Inkarri and began removing her armor. Dorian helped me, despite his pained grimace. Pulling her out of her chainmail was a struggle when she was so limp, but it was aided by the fact that it was still magicked to weigh very little. The boots, without the spells, were incredibly heavy. I couldn't imagine being able to continue fighting in them. She remained entirely limp as I tied her up, ensuring her arms were tightly secured behind her back. She never stirred.

Sorry not sorry about the concussion.

Under her armor, Inkarri wore a simple blue sleeveless tunic and padded leggings. I had half a mind to roll her into the chasm and give her a fate like Sempre. But here she looked so ordinary, no longer a warrior, or Irrikus's daughter. No matter what she'd done, to be sent plummeting over the edge unconscious, bound, and stripped of her armor was not the death I wanted to give her. I turned away before any darker thoughts took hold. We would figure out what to do with her later.

"What do you want?" Dorian asked the weary former prisoner. "If we are to strike a bargain, then we need to know if we can fulfill our end."

"What do I want?" the shapeshifter asked, a note of wistfulness in his voice. "I cannot recall the last time someone asked me that question. I will work with you if you can help me get back to..." He trailed off for a moment as his eyes glazed over with a misty look. "Back to where I need to be."

I raised my eyebrow at his vagueness and sat beside them on the boulder. The deep sienna red had faded slightly from the prisoner's body. Everything about him was worn out.

Dorian cleared his throat, and the prisoner blinked slowly.

"I want to go back to where I'm from. You won't know the place. It's... far away." He inclined his head toward us. "I'll tell you more if you agree to help me. In return for your aid, I'll do whatever I can to fix the damage I was forced to inflict on the tear to widen it."

"Would you like us to call you the Gate Maker?" I asked. "Or do you have another name?"

He smiled, and his face crinkled. "You may call me Gate Maker if you wish, for I have been called Prisoner One for too long."

"And you're certain you can repair the breach?" Dorian asked. "If you have time to rest, of course."

"It's true that I can work with the tear. Unfortunately, I'm not strong enough to seal it entirely, not from here." He sighed wearily, then sneered.

"Sempre would take me out every few nights to fray it just a little. The source of my power remains in my home, however, and after years of being separated from it, I am a fading shadow of my true self. If I can't get back there, I won't have enough energy to fix the barrier. It's non-negotiable. I need to go home *before* I can help you."

Dorian caught my eye. It sounded plausible, but there was so much we didn't know. Our prickly Immortal ally hadn't been entirely friendly or trustworthy so far. But something in his voice twisted painfully at my core. Of all the creatures affected by the Immortal rulers' rampage against vampires, he'd been suffering the longest.

"My connection to the universe is weak here," the Gate Maker explained, as if sensing our skepticism. "The barrier between planes separates me from what sustains me."

I pressed my lips together as I considered everything. We were desperate. We needed somebody to help with the tear, or Irrikus would just replace Sempre and Zeele and continue his insidious invasion plan that would result in the explosion. There were already revenant vampires in the Mortal Plane causing damage, even though they weren't under perfect control with the new gem system. We had to get back immediately.

"Before we help you, we need to get back to the Mortal Plane and find out what's happened to our friends," I said. "Just as you need your home to get your strength back, we need ours. But we have to move quickly. We'll fly back to the tear from here, which will take some time. It's the only way I can cross between the planes."

The Gate Maker gave us a tired stare. He ran his long fingers down his face. "If you need to go to the Mortal Plane and require proof of my ability, I can create a portal. Unfortunately, I am weak, so we will need to find some magical energy to give me enough power to create it. I have to have a certain amount of strength to do it. If you have something, a powerful weapon off the ruler perhaps, then we can try." His violet eyes drilled into me. "I can make the portal to prove to you what I can do, but it will only work once. I'm not strong enough to stabilize it permanently."

"But can you bring us through to Scotland?" I pressed, doubtful. *"Both of us?"*

The Gate Maker gave me a crooked grin. "Oh yes. Unlike vampires, I can make portals that will allow any creature to pass from one plane to another. However," he rose unsteadily to his feet, "for the sake of us all, before we proceed, I insist that you enter into a pact with me." He displayed his scaly palm. "I demand no specific timeline, only that you will help me return home, and not abandon or betray me once we reach the Mortal Plane. Once I have returned home and regained my strength, I swear to close the tear between the planes once and for all. If you fail to help me, or if there is no time for me to regain my strength before the tear must be closed to prevent disaster, then the two of you will be responsible for providing the energy I need to close the tear."

"What kind of energy?" Dorian asked, wary. A hint of concern tingled along my skin as the Gate Maker shrugged his thin shoulders.

"Your souls, if necessary. Your living souls would provide sufficient energy, but it would also kill you. Is that a risk you're willing to take?"

A small pause stretched between us. Our souls. Were we willing to do that? I exchanged a look with Dorian, one of wonder and desperation. He frowned back. In some ways, we'd always been ready to give up our lives for the cause. If we didn't, and both our worlds were destroyed, what would be the point of holding onto our souls? Total world destruction would kill us anyway. I pressed a hand to my chest, imagining the feeling of my spirit being taken out and used like diesel fuel.

"If I have to give up my life to ensure the world's safety, and that vampires have a haven from Immortal persecution, I will," Dorian said firmly. "That's more important than me."

His glacial eyes gleamed in the shadows, and I could see the willingness deep within them. We were ready.

"I feel the same," I confessed. "I'll do whatever it takes, but I'll fight like hell to make sure that's our very last option."

The Gate Maker nodded. "Excellent." He drew himself up as tall as he could. The air around us grew tense, and we slowly rose to our feet. "Come forward."

Dorian and I both took tentative steps toward him, and it struck me again that we were strangers, not so long ago. Yet now we moved in perfect unison in this strange fight to protect our worlds.

The Gate Maker pressed a thumb to his forehead, the reddish skin shifting gradually into a glowing, swirling rainbow of colors. When he removed the thumb from his skin, the pad of the eerily long digit glowed in the same bright kaleidoscope of colors. He pressed his thumb to my forehead first. It was cool to the touch and strangely papery despite his scales, but it didn't feel particularly momentous or magically binding. He did the same to Dorian, then stepped back. His thumb stopped glowing.

"The pact is sealed."

I didn't feel any different. Was he bluffing? Dorian met my eye, and his lips quirked up slightly, as if to say, *What can we do?* We'd made our choice for the good of both our worlds, and we would have to trust the Gate Maker to keep his word unless he wanted to be destroyed along with us.

"If that's done with, let's get you some fuel so we can get out of here," I said, and headed back to the pile of Inkarri's armor. I was sure that between the chainmail, bracers, knife, scimitar, and various other scraps of armor, we'd be able to gather some magic... enough to satisfy the Gate Maker if we were incredibly lucky.

He picked through it, touching each item and making it glow momentarily as he drew latent magic from it. He grimaced as he did so. "Magic crafted from dark soul energy is not my preference, but it will have to do for now."

My eyes slid to the owner of the armor, then to meet Dorian's thoughtful gaze.

Killing her while she was unconscious was beyond me, but we couldn't just leave her here. Even if I was inclined to show mercy, she'd just report back to the Immortal Council and kick off a manhunt across both planes.

Dorian cocked his head, gears turning in his mind. "She'd make a good hostage, if Irrikus has any actual affection for her. She could also be a potential source of information." He glanced at the Gate Maker.

I narrowed my eyes at him. He knew why we couldn't do that; he'd been the one to tell me. "I thought Immortals wouldn't survive long in the Mortal Plane, without the ambient dark energy in the air." Was sentencing her to a slow death any better than rolling her off the cliff?

The Gate Maker let out a wicked laugh. "That will be the hunter's problem, not ours. If she survives the transit, she'll be a good prisoner for however long she survives. And I'm sure you mortals will find a way to make use of her before she weakens too much. If you'd rather not take her and don't want to leave her here as a witness, then…" He trailed off, and his gaze went to the chasm.

Reluctantly, we made our choice. Ensuring her bindings were tight, Dorian and I gathered our scattered weapons, and I shouldered my pack once more as we waited for the Gate Maker to prepare a secret trapdoor out of this miserable plane.

He poked anxiously through the pile of dulled weapons and armor again. "It's not enough. I need more."

I offered my gauntlet, watching with a hint of disappointment as its magical glow faded.

He shook his head again. "Do you have anything else? Anything at all?"

The stone was nearly burning a hole in my weapons belt. I fingered it gently, almost pulling away with a hiss as my finger made contact with the sudden heat. It was filled with residual magic, but I didn't know if the Gate Maker could use such an item. It was worth a try.

"I don't know if you can extract the magic from it, but this might work," I said, pulling out the stone, feeling its heat against my hand.

Dorian hauled Inkarri over his shoulder with a pained grimace. He'd taken a beating, today, and even a ruler would be a burden on his aching back.

The Gate Maker furrowed his brow as he gently plucked the stone from my hand. "Yes, this will do nicely." He closed his long fingers around the brightly glowing stone, and suddenly the light left it all at once. He sucked in a sharp breath and staggered back a step.

"That… there was a *lot* of power in there," he said shakily, giving me a slightly manic smile.

A white light began to emit from the Gate Maker, blindingly bright after so long in the blue-hued gloom with amber pinpricks of souls. Then the light began to change. It shifted, like a prism breaking open to spill out splendid shades of yellow, red, blue, and green. Violet wisps began to overtake the corners of my vision. They melded with the white light, swirling magnificently around me. I could no longer see Dorian or the Gate Maker. There was only beautiful light in the shape of a wide, perfect oval. I was unbearably hot and painfully cold at the same time, and my whole body began to shake.

From somewhere in the light, the Gate Maker reached out to pull me through. Dorian found my other hand, squeezing it tight.

There was a tugging sensation deep in my core, and the air felt like it was being sucked from my lungs. My ears popped, my vision exploded with purple light, and I felt the ground slip from under my feet.

And just like that, we went crashing back to the Mortal Plane.

READY FOR THE NEXT PART OF LYRA AND DORIAN'S JOURNEY?

Dear Reader,

Thank you for reading Darkblood.

Book 5: **Darktide**, releases **March 4th, 2020.**

Visit www.bellaforrest.net for details.

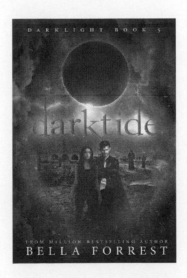

See you on the other side…

Love,

Bella x

P.S. Sign up to my VIP email list and I'll send you a heads up when my next book releases: **www.morebellaforrest.com**

(Your email will be kept 100% private and you can unsubscribe at any time.)

P.P.S. Follow me on:

Twitter @ashadeofvampire;

Facebook facebook.com/BellaForrestAuthor;

or **Instagram** @ashadeofvampire

READ MORE BY BELLA FORREST

DARKLIGHT

Darklight (Book 1)

Darkthirst (Book 2)

Darkworld (Book 3)

Darkblood (Book 4)

Darktide (Book 5)

HARLEY MERLIN

Harley Merlin and the Secret Coven (Book 1)

Harley Merlin and the Mystery Twins (Book 2)

Harley Merlin and the Stolen Magicals (Book 3)

Harley Merlin and the First Ritual (Book 4)

Harley Merlin and the Broken Spell (Book 5)

Harley Merlin and the Cult of Eris (Book 6)

Harley Merlin and the Detector Fix (Book 7)

Harley Merlin and the Challenge of Chaos (Book 8)

Harley Merlin and the Mortal Pact (Book 9)

Finch Merlin and the Fount of Youth (Book 10)

Finch Merlin and the Lost Map (Book 11)

Finch Merlin and the Djinn's Curse (Book 12)

Finch Merlin and the Locked Gateway (Book 13)

Finch Merlin and the Forgotten Kingdom (Book 14)

Finch Merlin and the Everlasting Vow (Book 15)

THE GENDER GAME

(Action-adventure/romance. Completed series.)

The Gender Game (Book 1)

The Gender Secret (Book 2)

The Gender Lie (Book 3)

The Gender War (Book 4)

The Gender Fall (Book 5)

The Gender Plan (Book 6)

The Gender End (Book 7)

THE GIRL WHO DARED TO THINK

(Action-adventure/romance. Completed series.)

The Girl Who Dared to Think (Book 1)

The Girl Who Dared to Stand (Book 2)

The Girl Who Dared to Descend (Book 3)

The Girl Who Dared to Rise (Book 4)

The Girl Who Dared to Lead (Book 5)

The Girl Who Dared to Endure (Book 6)

The Girl Who Dared to Fight (Book 7)

THE CHILD THIEF

(Action-adventure/romance. Completed series.)

The Child Thief (Book 1)

Deep Shadows (Book 2)

Thin Lines (Book 3)

Little Lies (Book 4)

Ghost Towns (Book 5)

Zero Hour (Book 6)

HOTBLOODS

(Supernatural adventure/romance. Completed series.)

Hotbloods (Book 1)

Coldbloods (Book 2)

Renegades (Book 3)

Venturers (Book 4)

Traitors (Book 5)

Allies (Book 6)

Invaders (Book 7)

Stargazers (Book 8)

A SHADE OF VAMPIRE SERIES

(Supernatural romance/adventure)

Series 1: Derek & Sofia's story

A Shade of Vampire (Book 1)

A Shade of Blood (Book 2)

A Castle of Sand (Book 3)

A Shadow of Light (Book 4)

A Blaze of Sun (Book 5)

A Gate of Night (Book 6)

A Break of Day (Book 7)

Series 2: Rose & Caleb's story

A Shade of Novak (Book 8)

A Bond of Blood (Book 9)

A Spell of Time (Book 10)

A Chase of Prey (Book 11)

A Shade of Doubt (Book 12)

A Turn of Tides (Book 13)

A Dawn of Strength (Book 14)

A Fall of Secrets (Book 15)

An End of Night (Book 16)

Series 3: The Shade continues with a new hero...

A Wind of Change (Book 17)

A Trail of Echoes (Book 18)

A Soldier of Shadows (Book 19)

A Hero of Realms (Book 20)

A Vial of Life (Book 21)

A Fork of Paths (Book 22)

A Flight of Souls (Book 23)

A Bridge of Stars (Book 24)

Series 4: A Clan of Novaks

A Clan of Novaks (Book 25)

A World of New (Book 26)

A Web of Lies (Book 27)

A Touch of Truth (Book 28)

An Hour of Need (Book 29)

A Game of Risk (Book 30)

A Twist of Fates (Book 31)

A Day of Glory (Book 32)

Series 5: A Dawn of Guardians

A Dawn of Guardians (Book 33)

A Sword of Chance (Book 34)

A Race of Trials (Book 35)

A King of Shadow (Book 36)

An Empire of Stones (Book 37)

A Power of Old (Book 38)

A Rip of Realms (Book 39)

A Throne of Fire (Book 40)

A Tide of War (Book 41)

Series 6: A Gift of Three

A Gift of Three (Book 42)

A House of Mysteries (Book 43)

A Tangle of Hearts (Book 44)

A Meet of Tribes (Book 45)

A Ride of Peril (Book 46)

A Passage of Threats (Book 47)

A Tip of Balance (Book 48)

A Shield of Glass (Book 49)

A Clash of Storms (Book 50)

Series 7: A Call of Vampires

A Call of Vampires (Book 51)

A Valley of Darkness (Book 52)

A Hunt of Fiends (Book 53)

A Den of Tricks (Book 54)

A City of Lies (Book 55)

A League of Exiles (Book 56)

A Charge of Allies (Book 57)

A Snare of Vengeance (Book 58)

A Battle of Souls (Book 59)

Series 8: A Voyage of Founders

A Voyage of Founders (Book 60)

A Land of Perfects (Book 61)

A Citadel of Captives (Book 62)

A Jungle of Rogues (Book 63)

A Camp of Savages (Book 64)

A Plague of Deceit (Book 65)

A Shade of Kiev 1

A Shade of Kiev 2

A Shade of Kiev 3

A LOVE THAT ENDURES TRILOGY

(Contemporary romance)

A Love that Endures

A Love that Endures 2

A Love that Endures 3

THE SECRET OF SPELLSHADOW MANOR

(Supernatural/Magic YA. Completed series)

The Secret of Spellshadow Manor (Book 1)

The Breaker (Book 2)

The Chain (Book 3)

The Keep (Book 4)

The Test (Book 5)

The Spell (Book 6)

BEAUTIFUL MONSTER DUOLOGY

(Supernatural romance)

Beautiful Monster 1

Beautiful Monster 2

DETECTIVE ERIN BOND

(Adult thriller/mystery)

Lights, Camera, GONE

Write, Edit, KILL

For an updated list of Bella's books, please visit her website: www.bellaforrest.net

Join Bella's VIP email list and you'll be the first to know when new books release.
Visit: www.morebellaforrest.com

Made in the USA
Middletown, DE
29 January 2020